Melanie Jackson

DIVINE NIGHT

D0003750

LOVE SPELL NEW YORK CITY

For my dear husband—
Thank you for being here

LOVE SPELL®

December 2007

Published by

Dorchester Publishing Co., Inc.
200 Madison Avenue
New York, NY 10016

ISBN 10: 0-505-52737-5
ISBN 13: 978-0-505-52737-0

The name "Love Spell" and its logo are trademarks of Dorchester
Publishing Co., Inc.

Printed in the United States of America.

10 9 8 7 6 5 4 3 2 1

Visit us on the web at www.dorchesterpub.com.

DIVINE NIGHT

How is it that little children are so intelligent and men so stupid? It must be education that does it.

—*Alexandre Dumas*

What would you say to an immense novel beginning with Jesus and ending with the last man of creation, divided into five episodes: one under Nero, one under Charlemagne, one under Charles IX, one under Napoleon, and one set in the future? . . . The principal characters are to be: The Wandering Jew, Jesus Christ, Cleopatra, the Fates, Prometheus, Nero, Poppaea, Narcissus, Octavia, Charlemagne, Rolland, Vittiking, Velleda, Pope Gregory VII, King Charles IX, Catherine de Medicis, the Cardinal of Lorraine, Napoleon, Marie-Louise, Tallyrand, the Messiah, and the Angel of the Cup. I suppose that sounds mad to you, but ask Alexandre (fils), who knows the work from end to end, what he thinks.

—*Letter from Alexandre Dumas to his publisher, Marchant,*
about a book that was never written

PROLOGUE

Christmas Eve, 2006

The man opened his black notebook and began writing by the light of the fire flickering contentedly on the hearth.

NIGHT TRAIN TO CASABLANCA
A Novel
By Alexandre Dumas

Alex smiled as he wrote because he had always loved his work. And because it paid well. Really well—especially his swashbucklers. This was his . . . what was this book? Six hundred and seventy-something. When he had first retired, his literary brood of novels, plays, travelogues, and memoirs had already numbered over five hundred.

It had delighted his current editor when Alex had first approached him with a manuscript for an historical thriller and the suggestion that the book be published under the name of his illustrious ancestor, the original Alexandre Dumas. Dear, ignorant Christopher thought it was a brilliant publicity stunt to have an author pretend to be the famous French novelist—especially since the two men were related.

Alex had allowed his editor to go on being delighted the last decade and more. He saw no need to complicate the beautiful arrangement by informing Christopher that he truly was Alexandre Dumas, and that his "novels" were actually installments of his autobiography—which were told almost without exaggeration. Almost. As a dramatist, he had never been able to resist the temptation to embellish a bit when history failed to supply the necessary touch of color or proper dialogue.

Of course, Christopher would be even happier if his best-selling author wrote faster, but some things could not be rushed. And though he had tried, Alex had yet to find a way to use a computer without causing catastrophic memory failure every time he powered up. He couldn't use cell phones either. Two minutes and the battery went dead, drained of all power and unable to be recharged. Nothing electrical had worked around him since his transformation. It was all part of paying the piper for his infernal gift, but it was annoying. He either had to wear rubber gauntlets when he used electronic machines or else had to have his secretary do everything for him—answer phones, send faxes, even use the photocopier.

Alex shook his head in irritation and then bent back over his notebook. The silence of the library was unbroken except by the scratching of the pen and the gentle snores of the neighbor's cat, which had attached herself to him three weeks ago. He called her Lady de Winter because she was white and because she had the hardest eyes he'd ever seen, excepting only those staring at him over a dueling pistol one misty dawn a century ago.

Casablanca. Perhaps he was romanticizing this chapter of his life a bit—but just a bit, and that was only for the sake of telling a better story, not some *Miles Gloriosis*. Perhaps he was editing himself a bit as well, but there was no need to upset readers by mentioning that he had taken up the career of a jewel thief because he was depressed and he'd become completely indifferent to society's laws once it engaged itself in a second world war. And because it had sounded like fun.

And also because back then he had still retained the natural prejudice of a Frenchman against the English, and hadn't minded stealing from the rich bastards of Britannia. At least he hadn't minded until the bombing of London started. He'd been in London when the first Luftwaffe bombers had flown up the estuary, following the Thames into the Old City. He wasn't an Englishman, and had reason to dislike his old enemy, but this sight offended him. London was beautiful and dignified. He'd had no love for the Germans after the First World War, but it was during this war that he had come to truly detest the nation that had invented the Nazis and all their various clones. After that, Frenchmen and Englishmen alike had been united in their anger against the Germans. Alex had even spied on the Germans for a time, helping the British when he could, even though they hunted him as a criminal.

There was another reason to write his novel as well.

Alex touched a hand to the earring he always wore. It looked like a thick gold hoop, but closer examination showed that it had been a lady's ring. The inside was inscribed with the words *je t'adore*. He told anyone who asked that he wore it for luck, but in reality it was more of a hair shirt. It had belonged to the only woman he had truly loved, a woman who had died for him. She was the real reason he had to tell this story. This was the time that Fate in the form of a woman had intervened in his life and helped him get off the road to ruin. The tragedy of her death had saved him from personal ruination, arrested his slide into depravity. He owed it to her—and himself—to remember this time.

There was the real possibility of pain in revisiting this time and place even after all these years, but Alex was not a coward. He thought that he was perhaps finally ready to write about what had happened on that fateful visit to Africa. It had been more than six decades—surely he was ready. He would tear the bandage off this lesion and see what his old wound looked like some sixty years on. Then perhaps he could finally put the incident behind him, stop dreaming of the woman who had died for him so many years ago. Stop feeling as if his own life had ended on the night she died.

But that came later in the story.

Alex began writing, his penmanship as florid as it had been a century ago.

Prologue
Adventure on a Train

January 4, 1943

He was traveling on one of the most luxurious trains in the world—all the guidebooks said so. Passengers were, the books insisted, held spellbound by the lavish blue and gold interiors decorated in the art deco style. The train contained no fewer than three dining cars presided over by master chefs, and every traveler's wants and comfort were seen to by a crew of attentive stewards uniformed almost as sumptuously as the upholstery and drapes where the pampered elite, those politically ambivalent individuals who liked to view the war through the charming lens provided by the bottom of a champagne flute, dined so long and lavishly.

However, in spite of his political ambivalence

and fondness for champagne, there was little evidence of this abundant comfort in his car. The luggage car. The section of the train where he rode had been decorated by someone of more minimalist tastes. Someone who might be thought to have had a mania about plain wood and exposed iron. Really, it had little to offer beyond tidiness, privacy, and cold—but those it had in abundance.

Of course, he wasn't paying for this trip. And when one wasn't charged even as much as was asked for shipping luggage, it could hardly be considered amazing that one was somewhat overlooked at the dinner hour.

Dinner. He sighed. It wasn't to be thought of. Not yet.

The man in the dirty brown burnous and fading walnut-stained skin shifted quietly. He would not be sorry to discard his garment. He had acquired it in Fez from a vendor's stall along one of the many labyrinthine streets that wove the crumbling medieval city together from fortified wall to fortified wall. At the time, it had seemed a good idea. Being among the somewhat pungent Fassis, he hadn't noticed right away that the hooded garment smelled quite heavily of goat. Shut up in the luggage car of the train, it was rather more noticeable.

However, the hood could not be dispensed with. Sweat—not caused by the warmth of his quarters, which were actually quite arctic, but rather from the too brisk jog he had taken just before boarding the train—had caused both his inferior hair dye and the stain on his face to sluice away in a tiny patter of salty brown rain

that was not yet apparent to his captor only because *his* garment was likewise dark and the
lighting so dim.

The man glanced up at his armed traveling
companion. Under other circumstances, they
might have passed for brothers—or at least
cousins. They both had black hair, tanned skin,
and piercing dark eyes, though the man suspected his captor's eyes were brown rather than
midnight black like his own. Both men were also
tall and what might be called lanky. But there the
resemblances ended. His gun-toting escort was
clean-shaven and wore a rather natty suit that
could only have come from Savile Row. It was
freshly pressed and lacked only a boutonniere to
place it and its wearer among the haute monde
of London. The suit had, most interestingly, replaced an equally well-pressed lieutenant's uniform, which was now folded neatly inside a small
portmanteau. Taken together, the garments made
this Englishman a very interesting specimen
indeed. However, the captive's enthusiasm for
deepening the acquaintance under the present
circumstances was rather less than unlimited.

The man had always enjoyed fine clothing, and
he felt the sartorial difference most keenly, and
was growing covetous as well as hungry. That was
understandable because he was a thief as well as a
chameleon—he was, in fact, *The* Chameleon, a
master jewel thief much sought by Scotland Yard
and most recently by the *aériennes de la Gendarmerie,*
though he supposed that the *gendarmes* were
rather more busy worrying about either the Germans or the *Comité D'Action Socialiste* these days.
Given his background, it was to be expected that

he would have certain larcenous impulses. However, though a master purloiner, he was also a man who avoided violence—particularly violence against his own person—whenever he could. His favorite weapons were disguise and fraud and the immoral use of thespian talent, and any other tool of wit that would not cause physical trauma to his victims. He delighted in jewels and precious metals, not bloodshed. His odd traveling companion had put his pistol aside while he dressed, but it was still quite close at hand, and The Chameleon was not certain that the modern-day Beau Brummel had completely bought his impersonation of a peasant of unusual bovine stupidity. It seemed wisest to continue to huddle on the floor and answer in monosyllabic grunts whenever he couldn't avoid making a reply altogether.

After all, this wasn't a civilized corner of the world, and handsome was as handsome did—not how one dressed. The local authorities still believed in chopping off the hands of thieves. And he didn't have enough hands—or other limbs— to go around. If his identity became known in the wrong quarter, the most he could hope for was to be killed on sight. Or to be turned over to the British authorities, though that didn't seem a particularly attractive option either. The Chameleon figured that he was already due for the doghouse, or jailhouse, for the rest of his life—plus six years for that little stunt with the mayor's wife in Shrewsbury—if he didn't receive a universal dispensation. Unfortunately, these were harder to come by than a well-paying career in crime.

Though he didn't speak, The Chameleon listened carefully to the crisp, incisive voice, and he had learned some interesting facts from his companion, who seemed to like the sound of his own words better than the clatter of the iron wheels, as he'd kept up a rather steady monologue as he changed clothes.

Churchill and the American president, Franklin Roosevelt, were headed for Casablanca for some sort of war meeting. Security in the part of Morocco under Vichy France was being tightened. Actually, it was tighter everywhere, what with either the Germans or the Allies suspecting everyone around them of being spies and traitors.

Clearly, it would behoove The Chameleon to leave the train as soon as possible and to find some other means of travel. Tangier was suddenly very appealing. It was a busy port of entry and egress, and from there he could easily escape to Spain or Gibraltar. It would be especially easy from the Spanish coastal towns of Ceuta and Molilla.

"But do you know the oddest part of this business?" the Englishman asked suddenly. He braced himself against the sway of the train as it rounded a bend and leaned over the packing case to have a better look at his dirty captive. The ride was not a violent one, but the pace was clearly less dilatory than usual. He spoke softly, and The Chameleon had to strain to hear him. "I do believe that I have been followed—and for the life of me, I can't say by whom or for what intention, since it is my first visit here. And my case has been resolved and all the guilty parties are in jail. Still, I sense a hostile presence, a pervasive evil. It is why it is necessary for me to alter my appearance and travel in such an unorthodox manner." He drew in a breath. "Now, I don't suppose that you would care to be a good chap and help a fellow Englishman out of a sticky situation? In turn, I may be able to help you."

Surprised, shocked even, The Chameleon looked up from his huddle on the floor, and stunned black eyes met knowing brown ones. In that instant, two things happened: The train straightened and returned to a smoother pace, and an arm in a red and white burnous appeared around the edge of a crate at the end of the car that opened to the passenger compartments. It held a gun—a Walther P-38—which was pointed at the Englishman.

The Chameleon opened his mouth to cry out a warning, but it was too late. Though the Englishman was warned by his expression and spun about quickly with his own pistol in hand, the other gun barked twice, bullets hitting him in the chest before he got off a single shot. The Englishman fell backward over the packing case. The arm disappeared immediately. The killer was apparently unaware—or uncaring—that there had been a witness to his crime.

For a long moment, The Chameleon did nothing and thought nothing. Normally, he was quite agile and able to think on his feet, but the twin shocks of encountering a stranger who apparently knew him—or at least knew what he wasn't—and then seeing the man murdered had given him pause. He counted to ten and listened and then counted to ten again. But no one returned.

The Chameleon finally rose to his feet. The first thing he did was retrieve the Englishman's pistol. It, too, was a 9mm. He next examined the En-

glishman's body, though he was quite certain that
the man was dead; two bullets delivered directly
to the heart would almost always do the trick.

"Bloody waste of a good shirt," The Chameleon
said, concentrating on that and not on the Englishman's open eyes.

Turning from the body, The Chameleon in-
spected instead the small valise that the Englishman owned. The contents were fascinating.
There was a Dutch edition of a French cartoon
called "Tintin in America." The Chameleon
smiled at this. He was also a fan of the Belgian,
Hergé.

There was a letter from a Colonel D'Aubert re-
questing the services of the great and reclusive
detective, Remus Maxwell, for a private difficulty
in Marrakesh. The financial rewards, the letter
promised, would be princely.

"Mon Dieu! Mon Dieu!" The Chameleon had
most recently posed as a French chauffeur, and
he was still thinking and swearing in French. He
glanced once at the man who, though almost
unknown to the public, was a mythic figure in
the world of crime. He was also the man who had
finally figured out The Chameleon's modus ope-
randi and reported it to Scotland Yard.

Galvanized, The Chameleon swiftly returned
to his search. There wasn't a lot. More letters re-
questing the detective's services, a collection of
currencies—lire, francs mainly—a silver flask of
brandy whose contents had been lowered to below half. Brandy . . . The Chameleon sighed. He
preferred whiskey, a single-malt when he could
get it. Still, France's finest would help to keep
the worsening cold out of his bones.

That left the lieutenant's uniform, a spare linen shirt, a hat, shaving gear, and a pair of shoes and socks, which the detective had not yet donned. There was a second concealed packet of money as well. A lot of it. And, at the bottom of the bag, the all-important documents that could save a man's life: a *lettre de transit* and an exit visa for Remus Maxwell.

He stared at these last two items for a long time.

"It's insane—not even to be thought of." The Chameleon spoke the denial aloud. But already, his voice had begun to take on the mellifluous inflection of the great detective. His posture changed, straightened. "This could put you in a sticky situation, old chap. Best give it some thought."

Good advice. Though this situation was hardly as sticky as the one he was fleeing. After all, though there was an assassin involved, the killer would have no reason to suspect that the great detective still lived. And the *lettre de transit* and the exit visa—these were worth more than gold.

Never an indecisive person, The Chameleon turned to the detective's body and began undressing it. Everything was set carefully aside. Watch, fob, cufflinks, and signet ring first. Then came the suit. There was only a little blood on the coat, and he preferred to wear it instead of the uniform.

Using a handkerchief and his burnous, he opened his own skin-bag and used the last of the brackish water for bathing and to have a shave. The job wasn't a complete one, but would have to do.

When his bath was done and the rapidly cooling body stripped of all outer garments, the new

Remus Maxwell took hold of the corpse's ankles and dragged it toward the side door where freight was loaded. He felt a twinge of regret for being so impolite to his benefactor's carcass, but it was necessary that the body not be found for a while. Hiding it in someone's luggage was not an option; a maid or valet was bound to notice it fairly quickly.

"Good-bye, old chap," he said softly as he tumbled the corpse out into the cold sunset that surrendered the desert to night's icy grip. "Thanks awfully for the help. And for the clothes."

A bitter wind answered him, and Remus slid the door quickly shut. The cold abraded his nearly naked body and kept him from further sentiments of parting.

Remus dressed swiftly. The clothes fit well, except for the shoes, which he regarded with disfavor. They were too narrow. However, beggars most definitely didn't get to be choosers, and in any event, he was alone, so he didn't bother complaining out loud.

It took only a moment more to repack the valise, minus some of the currency, which he slipped into his pockets, and he was carefully settling his hat on his head when the train began to slow for the next station.

"And let the games begin," he murmured.

Putting a polite smile in place, Remus opened the door that led to the last of the dining cars and away from the assassin. He entered the empty car casually, looking out for anyone else in a red and white burnous. No burnouses were present. In fact, there were no diners of any kind, just the lingering scent of lamb and mint jelly.

Two minutes later, he left the train, walking unhurriedly as he headed for the guarded exit from the train station.

Whatever the previous plan had been, Remus Maxwell was now going to Tangiers.

Alex paused long enough to pour himself what he chose to think of as a congratulatory cognac for beginning this book. His hands shook a little as he replaced the decanter, but he ignored their trembling.

"Ah, milady—those had been exciting days indeed! It was a pity that no one will ever know that it is all more or less true."

The blue-eyed feline tilted her head and sneered a little. She wasn't fooled by the hearty tone. She knew precisely how much effort he was expending on this attempted exorcism with paper and ink, and how frightened he was that he would fail to rid himself of his guilt.

General Dumas saw a priest, made his confession, and then died in his wife's arms on the stroke of midnight. Alexandre, who had been sent to stay with a neighbor and was fast asleep, was roused by a loud knocking on the door. Without the slightest sign of fear, the boy ran to the door and attempted to unbar it.

"Where are you going, Alexandre?" the neighbor asked.

"You can see plainly," Alexandre answered. "I am going to let in my Papa who has come to say good-bye."

But no one was seen at the door and the boy was sent back to bed. The next morning, the neighbor was told the bad news of the general's passing and left to break it to Alexandre that his father was dead.

"My poor child," the woman said. "Your father whom you love so well is dead."

"Papa dead? But what does that mean?" Alexandre asked.

"It means you shall never see him again because the good God has taken him to Himself."

"And where does the good God live?"

"In the sky."

Alexandre said no more, but as soon as he was dressed he went home to his father's study where a gun was hanging on the wall. He took it down and marched up the stairs. On the landing he met his mother, covered in tears.

"Where are you going, my poor boy?" she asked.

"I am going to kill the good God who has killed Papa and taken him to heaven."

His mother dropped to her knees and took him in her arms. "You must not say things like that, my pet. We are already wretched enough as it is."

—*An account of the death of General Dumas*

Happiness is like those palaces in fairy tales whose gates are guarded by dragons: we must fight in order to conquer it.

—*Alexandre Dumas* père

CHAPTER ONE

New Year's Day, 2007

He had seen a dead man walking.

Which shouldn't have surprised Alex much since he, too, was a dead man and quite able to move about as he willed. Yet Alex was very surprised because he had killed this man himself in Tangier in 1943. He'd ripped the heart out of his chest and then tossed the body off of a seawall where it rolled down a rocky cliff and into a roiling ocean whipped to frenzy by a sudden storm. The retelling of this event was to be the exciting climax of his new "novel"—though he might substitute a knife for his bare fist because it was more plausible.

Yet it now seemed that the impossible had happened and the sea had prematurely rendered up its dead. At least one of them. Maybe she couldn't stomach Saint Germain any more than Alex could. Perhaps this was what happened when even hell wouldn't take in heaven's rejects.

The timing was unusual, though. Why would Saint Germain appear on the day after Alex began to tell the story of how they met? All answers he considered made him shiver.

Their eyes met as the lean man sauntered by Alex on the opposite side of a busy street. He continued down Rue Royale, passing Maxim's and then disappearing down another street, leaving a trail in the air behind him that had other passersby wrinkling their noses as they passed through. Alex didn't smell him above the car exhaust, but he could see the psychic trail of smog-colored miasma that boiled behind him.

Perhaps this man was a very good actor, but Alex was ready to swear that there was no recognition of his nemesis in the man's blank black gaze. Yet it had to be Saint Germain. For one thing, only the Dark Man's get had those hell-black eyes. Alex should know, because behind his own tinted lenses, he had the same shark eyes. But more distinct than that was the creature's aura. It was the same boiling gray and red aura that had always surrounded the late Saint Germain. It was a signature, a fingerprint. No two people ever had the same exact aura. Yes, this was the Dark Man's evil legacy.

"Alex, *cher*?" His companion touched his hand. Her fingers were an almost ethereal white and her hair golden blond. Her aura was a sunny yellow—just what he preferred in a woman. "What is wrong?"

"Wrong?" Alex forced himself to relax his posture and smile at the woman—Collette? Claudette?—he had chosen to spend his evening with. He felt a pang of sadness that passed nostalgia and neared actual pain. She was young—heartbreakingly so. They all were, though. No one was as old as he was. No one living. "Why, nothing, *chérie*."

"Who was that man?" she asked, her green eyes slightly curious, but only slightly.

"No one really. Just one of my harsher critics. We came to blows once." That was an understatement. He didn't think it quite covered smashing through a man's sternum and ripping his still-beating heart out of his chest, but he wasn't about to say anything that would upset the evening.

Alex stroked a hand over the young woman's wrist, testing her pulse, willing her to forget about Saint Germain. It was a challenge, because Saint Germain exuded immense sex appeal. Even Alex was aware of it.

"Is he French?" Her profile was lovely as she looked down the street where Saint Germain's doppelganger had disappeared. Alex stroked her again, and her aura shifted to a soft golden yellow of candlelight with hints of burnt orange.

"Partly. Probably. No one knows for sure. The man is . . . an enigma. And a bore. So let us not waste time on him."

"Oh. I thought he was an actor. He's very pretty." She didn't know what the word *enigma* meant and Alex didn't bother to explain; he hadn't selected her because he was in the mood to play Pygmalion. Why expend the effort to educate her about anything? He would never see her again. She was to be a moment's joy and nothing more. He didn't allow any woman to be anything more to him.

"Come, *chérie*," he said, making another gentle push against her thoughts. "We shall be late for the theater."

The smile she turned on him was blank but lovely. She was exactly what he had set out to find. He tried not to feel disappointed that he had succeeded in finding her.

I prefer rogues to imbeciles, because they sometimes take a rest.

—*Alexandre Dumas*

He is blamed for being entertaining and prolific and prodigal. Would he have been greater had he been boring, sterile and miserly?

—*Henri Clouard on Dumas* père

Once the guests had gone, Dumas would take over my father's desk and set to writing. The words flowed from his pen with incredible ease. He never reread or corrected anything. He had in front of him a packet of large sheets of white paper, wrote on one side of them only and tossed the sheets, once they were covered with writing, to the ground without giving any further thought to them. His secretaries would collect them later and put them in order. This work went on most of the night. He slept only a few hours in the morning.

—*Henri Lhote,* Souvenirs sur Alexandre Dumas père

CHAPTER TWO

Spring, 2007

Alex shoved aside his collection of yellowing scandal sheets
that obscured his desk, a decorative affair from the old Per-
sian room at Monte Cristo. The top was made of tortoise-
shell and bronze marquetry and came from the palace of
some potentate. Alex had repurchased the desk and a few
other things from his estate after his "death."

Though it annoyed his secretary, he read the American
and British tabloids at least weekly. When Millie asked why,
he told her that he loved the absurd. That wasn't the entire
truth. The rags were where mention of certain types of
strange events often first appeared. For instance, it was in the
scandal sheets that he first learned about the timely death of
the Dark Man in New York. An investigation had satisfied
him that the man who had killed the Dark Man was none
other than his literary hero, Lord Byron.

Alex's favorite tabloid was *The Weekly World News.* He

told his secretary that he liked to keep up with Bat Boy sightings, but that, too, was a lie. The last edition had some very interesting stories about a burned-out ghost town in Mexico where some sort of werewolf creature had appeared. There had been few specifics, but something about the headline set his nerves to tingling. Alex checked the date. The paper was two weeks old. Probably it was too late to do any useful follow-up. Probably. Still, the itch at the base of his psyche was not settling itself. And though the timing was dreadful, he felt compelled to try.

Alex glanced at the notes for his new book that sat in a reproachful huddle at the edge of the desk. His attention had been only half given to what he had written, and he knew the notes were a mess and his secretary, Millicent Pierce, would complain bitterly when she began trying to transcribe them. Two centuries of practice had allowed him to write even when distracted, but he greatly preferred to focus his concentration on one task at a time. He sighed. It was annoying that the reappearance of Saint Germain and these stories about ghosts and monsters in Mexico should happen now when he had a book due.

Well, one crisis at a time. The first thing he had to do was write a second, coherent draft of the first chapter of *Night Train to Casablanca*. He had delayed writing on it for several weeks, feeling a strange reluctance to tell this story now that the process had begun. He had had some trouble concentrating last night when the shadows of old ghosts had seemed endless. But now it was morning, and the sun was shining as it should in the spring. He could write now. Alex exhaled slowly and allowed his mind to let go of mysteries in modern Mexico and turn back to 1943. He picked up a pen.

Chapter One
The Chameleon Makes a Friend

Crowds! How he loved them. There was nothing like a port town for getting lost in. It assimilated foreigners with joy, delighted to accept their money, their goods, their many plans and dreams. There was a flourishing trade in treason too—and despair as well—but that, like all black-market activities, was at least partially hidden. And Tangier, the White City, was so beautiful that it made it easy to forget both the danger within and the unfriendly, arid lands without. One might also forget that there was a prison.

Remus Maxwell—for The Chameleon had decided to remain the detective for the time being—sat in the cold sunshine of an outdoor bistro, the Café de Paris, enjoying his coffee and fresh croissant and watching the people stroll and scurry and march by. There were dark-skinned Africans, tall men with hawk-nosed faces and hard eyes. There were Arabs too, of course, and Indians, but also Greeks, Britons, and many Europeans. Laborers, refugees, fishermen, traders, and omnipresent Spanish police and soldiers—for Tangier was occupied these days. It must be so to keep the Germans out, *sí*? But even so, there were so many faces, so many styles of clothes, so many voices, all doing business in the supposedly neutral territory that was second in popularity only to Switzerland. Spanish and French, both familiar to The Chameleon, were the loudest of all dialects, but there was some German and English too. The babble of tongues was delightfully cacophonous.

He had been there for a week already, having come in on the Cape Malabata Road from Cape Spartel where a fishing vessel had dropped him—a town so lovely and untouched that even in winter it wore masses of vibrant rock roses and cork oaks. It was hard to believe that there was a war raging nearby. And the happy fact was that he could easily remain submerged in the foreign rabble while he found suitable transport to healthier climes.

Remus paid for his meal with some of the great detective's purloined currency and then strolled for the quays. He enjoyed ambling the palm-lined promenade that bordered the golden shore where Atlantic and Mediterranean met, though this was not solely what attracted him there every morning. There were always newly arrived ships tied up at the piers and docks, unloading cargo— salt, lamp oil, fish, and humans, always more humans—and replenishing their stocks of fuel and water from the dockside reservoirs and tanks that held the precious liquids that fueled travel.

He stood in the shadow of a water tank and evaluated his transportation options. A Sudanese fishing vessel carrying tuna, an Algerian oil tanker, other smaller boats that could get him to Gibraltar but no further. Sadly, there was nothing that interested him today. He would have to wait, spend another night looking at the twinkling lights of Spain and planning what next to do.

Remus next turned his eyes to the shallow pools where the seabirds congregated. There were a few herons picking delicately at the water. Farther out were pelicans, less fastidious with their table manners, and above them both were the ubiquitous seagulls. They, too, contributed to the babble.

There was a flicker of movement at the corner of his eye, a flash of color that caused a ripple of unpleasant awareness. He turned his head slowly, making no other betraying movement as he scanned the crowd. It was difficult to see into the milling throng, but he was almost certain that he caught a glimpse of a familiar red and white burnous. There was no sign of the Walther P-38 that had killed the great detective, but that didn't mean the man was unarmed. One could carry an entire arsenal in the folds of those robes. The red and white burnous seemed to be traveling with a second cloaked figure, this one in white.

"Well, how bloody annoying," Remus said softly. "Why didn't you stay in Casablanca?"

If he recognized the burnous, the converse could be true of that man and Remus's suit. It might be time for a change of wardrobe.

And identity?

No, not yet, The Chameleon decided. There were too many benefits to being the great detective. And it was very unlikely that anyone had actually met the real Remus Maxwell; not around here.

The man in the red and white burnous was annoying, though. This was a problem that had to be dealt with or it would spoil everything. Perhaps it was time to make its owner see reason. One way or another.

Remus turned and followed in the general direction the red burnous had gone. At a guess, the two men were headed for the Grand Socco,

the giant market at the entrance to the old medina. Remus hadn't spent a lot of time in the old
Arab quarter; he felt more at home among the
villas and mansions of the Montagne where the
wealthy congregated than among the attractive
but less affluent sugar-cube houses where the
merchants and workers lived.

He heard the Grand Socco before he saw it.
The cobbled squares echoed with voices, laugh-
ing children, shrilling mothers, merchants calling out their slates of goods, and the unhappy
bleatings of the goats and sheep that would end
the day on someone's dinner table. The smell of
spice and produce was everywhere, masking the
less pleasant odors of dead fish, slaughtered
chickens, and other butchered wares that hung
in the open with a complete lack of concern for
the flies and other insects that congregated on
the meat.

A flash of red and white, heading south. Remus followed swiftly. As the smells of the market
faded, he began to scent something else—
something sickeningly sweet. They traded in
drugs in Tangier, too, and hashish was popular.

Once inside the old city, it was harder to navi-
gate. The streets were labyrinthine, and it was
only when he found an open courtyard and could
sometimes see the mosaic minaret of the Sidi
Bou Abid mosque that he got his bearings. He
went for some while without catching another
glimpse of the red and white burnous, but he finally did see the man slipping down one of the
many narrow, twisting streets that led toward the
Petit Socco, the other market at the south entrance of the old city.

"Beautiful silks!" a voice called in French as he hurried by. And when Remus did not respond, the merchant added in Spanish: "I make you a very good price."

Remus ignored him. He had been in this part of the world before, and he knew from experience that a polite refusal only invited further cajolery. He tried not to deal with local merchants too often. By and large, the sun had baked their bodies and their brains. Their narrow thoughts and bigotries had hardened into uneducated bricks that could not be reshaped, only worn down by the imbecility of old age, which would turn their minds back into sludge, assuming they weren't first smashed open by a sledgehammer—sometimes literally.

The crowds gradually thinned. The market was left behind and the street grew twisted and ever more dark. The place became so silent and so deserted that one might think a plague had struck and carried off every living soul.

Or that everyone had been warned away because something bad was about to happen.

Remus turned a corner cautiously, and at the end of the street he caught a glimpse of a white robe disappearing down an alley. The man had some sort of heavy bundle flung over his shoulder that looked suspiciously like a body. There was no sign of the red burnous, though.

Remus walked cautiously and quietly, sticking to the middle of the cobbled alley, his eyes scanning the scene quickly. The blank plaster walls on either side were broken only occasionally by barred windows and narrow doors that guarded the occupants' privacy. The alley was grim. The houses wouldn't be dark inside, though. As was the custom in Arab homes, there would be a large courtyard that the houses looked out onto. Courtyards where no one would see or hear anything distressing, like an English detective being murdered.

The acoustics in that part of the medina were odd. In some places, like near the giant mosque or the marble columns of the Kasbah, one might hear the whisper of some other person speaking one hundred yards off. In other places, the sound was dead. An assassin might steal right up behind his victim and never be heard. Remus was walking in just such a street, and it occurred to him that it might not be entirely by accident.

Second thoughts were irritating. Remus tried not to have them. On the other hand, you didn't survive long as a cat burglar unless you paid attention to your surroundings.

As dead as the acoustics were, smell traveled just fine, and it was this that alerted him to the other's presence a moment before the red-burnoused figure sprang from one of the narrow doorways with a knife upraised.

The Chameleon's reflexes had not abandoned him when he left the name and career. He twisted around with the speed of a hunting cat, dodging the knife that cut downward, and caught at the man's thick wrist. Unfortunately, he didn't see the second slim blade in the man's other hand until it was flashing upward. Remus slashed downward with his other hand, blocking the blow that would have landed in his side, but a quick splash of hot fire told him that his arm had been cut.

Fighting a man who used a knife was bad. Fighting a man who used two was suicidal. Especially if one was unarmed.

Remus and his attacker were of similar weight, though the Arab was shorter by half a head. Remus, however, had two advantages. He could see the superstitious fear in the man's eyes. Had he not tried to kill the detective once already? And yet somehow the Englishman had survived two bullets to the heart. Also, the Arab had likely been hired as an assassin by someone who didn't dare approach the great detective directly. Remus's attacker was fighting for a wage. Remus was fighting for his life.

With that fact clear in his mind, Remus slammed the Arab up against a door, carved and ornamented with sharp bits of wrought iron that would stab like dull knives. The Arab grunted as his skull bounced off the wood, and he nearly fell. In fact, the bludgeoning worked so well that Remus did it again. The knife in the Arab's left hand dropped as he gasped in pain.

At that moment, it occurred to Remus that this time *he* was the victim of a crime—a person out on legitimate business with no need to fear the law—and so he did something he had never done before. He gave a loud shout, hoping to summon the police so he wouldn't have to commit murder.

Surprisingly, a yell answered him immediately.

Remus glanced in the direction of the shout and saw a gentleman of portly stature and mature years tottering toward him. He was brandishing a cane in a reckless and ineffectual manner. So much for aid from the outside. Remus turned back to his attacker.

"Who sent you?" Remus asked in French, again slamming the Arab against the cruel door. He was grateful to the elderly man who was rushing so recklessly in their direction, but he wanted some answers before there were any witnesses. "Who dares to think that they can kill the great detective?"

The Arab's eyes were beginning to lose focus.

"El Grande," he slurred. A little more pressure on the wrist, and the second knife fell to the ground. "But he did not say that you were immortal."

Remus hesitated. Though he abhorred violence, he knew that he should kill this man. The creature had murdered, and breaking his neck would doubtless be a service to the entire world. However, Remus doubted that it was what the great detective would have done. Particularly not when there was a witness.

Remus slammed the man against the door a last time and then let the unconscious body fall to the ground.

His would-be rescuer arrived at that instant, face the shade of boiled ham and wheezing alarmingly. His white linen suit was dark with perspiration.

"Steady on, old chap," Remus said, his voice and inflection absolutely perfect. He would have taken the old man's cane away since it was still occasionally flailing about, but the poor creature obviously needed it to lean on between gesticulations.

"Thought you were a goner," the man puffed, leaning against the wall. "These market thieves are getting bolder every day."

"Bloody street rats," Remus agreed, in the great detective's voice. He pulled out a handkerchief and pressed it against the cut in his arm. Half of his mind was on what the would-be assassin had said before collapsing. Someone called El Grande wanted the great detective dead.

"Good God, sir!" exclaimed the elderly man. "You are bleeding. Here. Best let me have a look at that. I'm a physician. Dr. Watson Travers, at your service." He didn't offer to look at the man in the red burnous.

"Remus Maxwell. It isn't a deep cut," he said reassuringly. He didn't offer to shake hands, though; the bleeding wasn't profuse, but it was steady enough to be of concern.

"But there is always the danger of infection," Dr. Travers answered, straightening. His color was still alarming. "Come with me to my hotel. It isn't far from here, and I shall have you patched up in no time."

"You are too kind." Remus didn't hesitate. The doctor was probably going to need help to get back anyway. His breathing had barely settled, and he seemed in danger of collapsing. Remus said tactfully: "It is fortunate for me that you were out and about this morning."

"Not at all. You had the matter well in hand. It's just this way," the doctor said, pointing toward the south entrance to the medina. They began walking slowly in that direction. "I fear that this is the end of your coat, though. What a damned shame."

"Yes, I fear it is beyond saving." It had been a damned unlucky suit anyway. "This climate is hard on one's clothing."

"I know a good tailor, if you need one. The fellow is quick and not too outrageous in his charges. He could probably do something for you right away."

"Thank you. I shall have to do something." Remus could well believe that Dr. Travers had a quick tailor. He was betting that the doctor was a heavy perspirer even when he wasn't rushing down dark allies brandishing his cane, and white linen was entirely impractical for him. It would get a single day's wearing but no more.

Remus paused at an intersection and inhaled. He could smell the faint scent of hashish. That brought to mind the man in the red burnous's companion. Should he let it go? He was tempted—the cut in his arm was a painful reminder of what could happen if one got too close to these rats. On the other hand, it might do to make a clean sweep of things so he didn't have to spend his time watching his back.

There was also the matter of that bundle. Criminals' bundles were usually worth investigating.

"Travers, wait here a moment. I think I hear someone calling for help."

"But, old chap!" Travers protested. Remus didn't wait. He followed his nose down the small side alley where the smell of hashish was strongest.

The atmosphere of this dank little crevice was oppressive, as though evil deeds and ill will had been accumulating for a very long time. Remus moved quickly, but he could hear the doctor stumbling along behind him, puffing and wheezing like an overheated engine.

Remus was about to turn back and spare the doctor a heart attack when he rounded a curve and saw his quarry up ahead. Once again Remus shouted, quite enjoying the fact that he could make as much noise as he liked. There were definite benefits to being on the right side of the law.

The man with the bundle twisted around and, seeing who was bearing down on him—a man they had thought dead, probably twice since red burnous had had a second go at it—as well as a second large European in a white linen suit, he gave a small squawk and dropped his burden. Much lighter, he fled on unhappy but swift feet.

A part of Remus felt that he should chase the man down, but his arm was bleeding again, and the bundle had begun to moan and thrash. It was a soft, female moaning.

Remus knelt down by the carpet bag—a tapestry, actually—and using his good arm, set about unrolling its prisoner.

The woman who spilled out the other end was a surprise, as golden as any treasure he had ever stolen, and reeking of perfume. Dark eyes the color of blueberries blinked up at him.

"Thank you," she gasped in English. "I thought I should suffocate."

Remus nodded and tried not to recoil from the floral scent that rose up in an invisible cloud.

"They kidnapped me in the perfume market," she explained, though Remus had gathered as much from the smell and the two empty vials she had clutched in her hands. Following his line of sight, she looked down at her clenched fists and then dropped the two perfume bottles. "My name is Thomasina. Thomasina Marsh. I'm Senor Diego-Vega's personal secretary."

"Remus Maxwell," The Chameleon answered, offering his good hand to her and noticing how her eyes widened at the name. "And this is Dr. Travers," he added as Travers arrived, looking more than ever like a boiled ham basted in cherry sauce. His white suit was now a dirty gray and very damp under the arms.

The hand that grasped Remus's was delicate. He also liked the way concern darkened her eyes when she saw his wound.

"Did they do that to you?" she asked, appalled, as she regained her feet. She obviously meant the kidnapper. "I am so sorry that you should have been hurt rescuing me."

"Think nothing of it. It's just a scratch," Remus answered, resisting the urge to help Thomasina Marsh smooth the dust off her frock as she pulled the skirt back into a modest position, hiding the white lace garters that held her stockings in place. He didn't correct her incomplete understanding of what had happened. And since Dr. Travers could still barely breathe, the older man didn't correct her misapprehension either.

"Are you hurt, too, Dr. Travers?" Thomasina asked, looking more concerned than ever as she saw his face.

"Not. A. Bit." He gasped gallantly. "We've just had a smidgen . . . of a run . . . trying to catch up with you. Brutal stuff, this heat."

"Yes, indeed!" Thomasina agreed readily. "You must both rest immediately and have some tea."

"My sentiments exactly," Remus agreed, preparing to leave the dismal alley, though truthfully he was more in the mood for a gin and tonic.

"Wait," Thomasina said. She knelt down and started to gather the tapestry.

"That's very heavy," Remus pointed out, eyeing her actions with misgiving. "And it will only add to the heat exhaustion we all feel." He said *we* because he had a sinking feeling that Thomasina wasn't going to be able to carry the heavy wall hanging alone. It was also clear that Dr. Travers, between his fractured breathing and his cane, wasn't going to be of much assistance. Tactfully, Remus didn't say anything about the tapestry choking them with the reek of rose and patchouli perfume.

"It's also fifteenth century. And stolen. The thieves took it from Senor Diego-Vega's villa. That's why I confronted them in the market," Thomasina added. She turned her large blue eyes upon him. "I know that you'll want to do what is right."

Remus kept his left brow, the one that tended to shoot up when he was skeptical, firmly in place. If she knew who Remus Maxwell was, then her conclusion was probably a correct one. How fortunate that she was there to tell him what was acceptable behavior.

He looked again at the tangle of threads with an appraiser's eye. That bit of fabric probably cost about five hundred times what those men had been paid to kill him. He wondered which failure they would regret more.

"That's one of El Grande's tapestries?" Travers asked, shock stopping his ragged breath long enough to ask a question. "Well, of all the bloody cheek!"

The name registered—it was one he had heard before, and not in church.

"Yes!" Thomasina affirmed. "I couldn't believe my eyes. They must have stolen it right out of the grand salon while the painters were working, though I don't know how they managed it. There are guards at the estate."

"El Grande's, is it? Then it must be returned to him," Remus agreed, finally kneeling down to assist Thomasina. He made his voice light. "I shall take it to him personally. As soon as I've had my arm stitched up, of course."

"Of course," Thomasina agreed, smiling at him with approval. "Senor Diego-Vega will be very surprised and grateful."

Surprised? Remus was inclined to agree. Grateful? That seemed rather doubtful. If the would-be assassin was in his pay, then the arrangements for the tapestry and Thomasina's abduction would hardly come as a shock.

Alex put aside his pen. It wasn't perfect, but it would have to do. Millie was far too spoiled anyway. A little suffering in the line of duty wouldn't hurt her.

As though guessing that he was taking her name in vain, his gray-haired secretary appeared in his office doorway, arms full. Her posture was stiff as an ironing board as she crossed to his desk. Around her the air danced with little orange spikes. Ever since his *change,* he'd been able to see auras around people when they were experiencing strong emotion. He knew now that it had something to do with an alteration in his magnetic resonance, but back when he had first noticed it, all he had been able to understand was that his body wrought a strong effect on compasses, and he sometimes saw bright colors around people when he was drinking. Had he been a sailor, the trouble with a compass would have been inconvenient. However, that wasn't exactly a problem he faced daily back then, so he had viewed it as a sort of parlor trick. However, as the world of electronics came into being, his capacity for wreaking havoc on equipment had grown. So had his ability to "see" into people. And it had gotten stronger each time he had gone back into the fire to renew himself. It was a gift that most days he would rather not have.

It wasn't until after his second electrocution that he had acquired the ability to "hear" people's thoughts. Not all thoughts, and not in all people. But enough to be sometimes entertained, embarrassed, and even disconcerted by his companions. Unlike seeing an aura, "hearing" took effort and only worked when a person had formed his various chaotic impulses and desires and mental images into an organized flow of thought that resembled an inner monologue. The ability to tune out people's prattle made the gift bearable. If he could hear every thought in everyone he passed, he would surely go mad.

Experimentation had taught him that people with untrained psychic abilities were usually the easiest to "listen" to. They seemed to broadcast their feelings like a radio, and he could tune in with little effort. Many times their thoughts sounded about as clear as if someone was actually speaking. Their auras were also easy to read. They were a sort of color code of moods—at least in the living—that told about the state of a person's well-being. Though he had never stopped testing his abilities, exercising his talents, it was only in the last decade that he had found a way to influence others' thoughts and to suggest things to the people he sometimes eavesdropped on. It wasn't true mind control—not even close. But if their auras were a certain color, and a person was inclined in a certain direction anyway, he could sometimes nudge them into action. Especially with physical contact. The simple radio in his brain had become a walkie-talkie.

A pity he hadn't had the ability back when he met the great detective. It would have been useful then, and also when he was spying on the Germans later in the war.

Millie shook her head sadly as she unloaded her postal burden onto his writing table and began the routine nagging. Alex would listen for about five minutes and then send her away. He liked Millie, but her voice could cause brain damage with prolonged exposure.

"I don't know why you read this tabloid garbage." She sniffed. Millie had what looked like a chronic case of pinkeye but which she claimed was allergies. She slapped the latest *Weekly World News* down in front of him. "Look—just look! This stupid magazine has a story about monsters in a ghost town called Lara Vieja."

"Does it now?" Alex reached for the paper and glanced at the photo. Story on page three. He quickly opened the newspaper and began reading.

Millie continued to unpack her tote and complain, though she knew it would do no good. Once a week she made the trip to the grocers and picked up pâté and champagne—Dom Perignon, of course. Not precisely the meal recommended by health-conscious doctors, but he didn't worry about such things anymore. Cholesterol and cirrhosis of the liver weren't what would kill him. Millie didn't agree, though. She was a vegetarian, a lifestyle she treated as a religion that required endless proselytizing. She believed that Alex's chronic pallor was due to a lack of vitamins.

Alex was equally convinced that her diet was to blame for her sallow skin, which was the same color and texture as the tofu she ate for lunch every day.

A low-protein diet couldn't explain her oddly shaped head, though. That had to be due to some freak of genetics.

Her skull was pinched in at the temples, as though someone had applied a tight rubber band to her head when she was an infant. She had to buy children's frames when she got eyeglasses because that part of her head was so small.

Alex preferred to surround himself with beauty and usually only employed the young and attractive. However, he had learned the hard way that in a personal secretary discretion and efficiency were paramount—especially these days. Millie was both, and loyal besides. That she looked like a freak was unimportant.

"*Merde!*" he muttered when he reached the end of the article. Then, when Millie glared, he added: "Apologies for the language, *chérie.*"

"What's wrong?" she asked, looking at the newspaper with another sniff of disgust. The picture in the middle of the page was fairly grotesque. The victim had been blown up by a grenade and then burned in some kind of building fire. But in spite of the extensive damage, it was very clear to Alex that what he was seeing was not a human—at least not completely human—but was in fact a designer ghoul. He knew of only two people who made such creatures, and both of them were supposed to be dead.

Millie picked up the paper. "Disgusting! You know they doctor those photos, don't you?"

"*Oui,* I am aware. And nothing is wrong. I have just recalled that I need to phone my editor and he shall be leaving the office soon." He also needed to call some other people that Millie didn't need to know about. That meant using the landline in his office and wearing those repulsive rubber gloves.

"Oh." She blinked, and in an instant had transformed into his secretary. She knew his dislike of phones, even the landlines. "Shall I do it for you?"

"No. I must speak to him myself. But you may cancel my trip to New York this week and see about getting me on a flight to Mexico, somewhere near the border. Or perhaps

San Diego would be best. I can drive down from there. I shall want a jeep—an older model."

"San Diego?" Her eyes went from his face to the newspaper. "You aren't really leaving now—"

"Research, my dear. This ghost town is very interesting. You know how important historical details are to me."

This time Millie snorted, but her aura had settled down to the gentlest of orange glows. She was a very efficient secretary and she knew that he always made his deadlines, even when the book was refusing to come along willingly.

"Uh-huh. I know *exactly* how much you care about historical details."

"Nevertheless, be a pearl beyond price and make the arrangement for me. I shall call Christopher at once and break the news to him."

"He'll give birth to kittens," Millie warned. "The book is due next month."

"*Oui.*" Alex allowed himself a small smile. "But birth shall be a novel experience for him."

Millie shook her head. "You're a cruel, selfish man, Alex Dumas."

"That has always been my reputation," he agreed, but softly. It wasn't something he was proud of.

I understood my life was threatened. A few days later a prison doctor appeared and prescribed for me a diet of biscuits soaked in wine. . . . About ten minutes after he left I was seized by fierce intestinal pain. . . . As a result of repeated poisonings I found myself afflicted with deafness. One of my eyes had completely lost its sight and I was in an advanced stage of paralysis. The symptoms of senile decay came upon me at the age of thirty-nine years and nine months.

—*General Dumas on his time in a Brindisi prison, arranged by Gustav of Sweden probably at Napoleon's request*

Macaroni à la Napolitaine
4 pounds silverside (lean beef from hind leg of cow)
1 pound raw smoked ham
4 pounds tomatoes
4 big white onions
1 sprig of thyme
1 bay leaf
1 small sheaf of parsley
garlic to taste (at least one bulb)

Chop meat and vegetables and moisten with water. Reduce at a simmer for three hours. Prepare pasta, boiling in lightly salted water until it is *che cresca in corpo* (swollen in body), then remove from heat and add iced water to halt cooking. In a soup tureen (warmed) place a layer of finely grated parmesan cheese. To the bed of cheese, add a layer of macaroni, then one of sauce. Repeat until tureen is full. Cover tureen and let stand ten minutes, then serve.

CHAPTER THREE

"Christopher, *cher ami*, I am afraid that I have to put off our visit for just a while." Alex spoke with a pronounced French accent. He could lose it when needed, but it was expected by his publisher, being that he was Alexandre Dumas and had supposedly lived all his life in France. "I am very afraid that I shall have to go to Mexico this week to do some research."

There was a pause, and when his editor spoke it was with a bit of tightness in his voice that always preceded a panic attack. He had them regularly, so Alex knew the signs.

"But I thought the new book was set in Tangier—that's what I told marketing and the art department. Tangier. And it's due in three weeks, Alex. You can't be doing research still."

"It is set in Tangier." Alex made his voice soothing. "I just need to interview someone who is now living in Mexico about a small but important detail. I shan't be gone long."

Another long silence. Alex reached out and examined the

cover of his latest release: *An Affair in Algeria*. It amused him to see that his publisher had taken his suggestion and used as the cover quote a review Victor Hugo had given him for *The Three Musketeers*: "Gripping drama, warm passion, true dialogue and sparkling style!" So what if the cover quote was a century and a half old? The book had made the *New York Times* best sellers list.

Chris cleared his throat and managed to speak. "I see, well . . . Did you want me to try and approach Claude about a further advance? Because you know how Claude feels about expenses related to research—"

Alex laughed. He knew exactly how Claude felt about spending money. It was easier to get blood from a stone. This was probably a good thing in a company president, if it wasn't carried to extremes.

Lady de Winter hopped up onto Alex's desk and regarded him with unblinking eyes. Alex frowned back. She was beautiful but not exactly inviting, and certainly not affectionate in any usual sense of the word. In fact, he was glad that he did not suffer from sleep apnea, because he had a feeling that if his chest ever stopped the steady rise and fall that affirmed life, she'd move straight in for a late dinner. He really couldn't understand why he kept the cat around. He couldn't be that lonely, could he?

But perhaps he was. To this day he missed his aviary at Monte Cristo. He'd had two parrots, a golden pheasant, a cock—what had he called that cock and pheasant? Caesar and Lucullus!—and there had been a vulture from his tour of Tunisia that he had ended up calling Diogenes. There had also been three monkeys, five dogs, and his cat, Mysouf, an animal of a very different stripe than Lady de Winter. Things had often been loud at the château, but he had found the animal clamor comforting. It drowned out all the greedy voices of the avaricious humans who always wanted something from him back then. And it helped him forget that he had been forsaken by his creator.

"Alex? Alex, are you there? Damn it! You haven't wandered off again, have you?"

"*Oui.* I am here. Be at ease. I think we need not mention this trip to our parsimonious friend—or anyone else." Calling Claude a friend was stretching the truth, but it made Christopher feel more comfortable to believe that Alex regarded his publisher as one of his circle of intimates. "Adieu for now, *cher ami.* I shall see you in a few weeks."

"*Three* weeks. *Three.* You promised." Chris's voice was tight again. "And you don't have to come—just get me the manuscript! I'll take it with me on vacation. Though why they call it vacation, I don't know, since I have to work the whole time."

"Did I say three weeks? Then three weeks it shall be," Alex promised again, wondering if this time he would keep his word. He had never had writer's block before, but something about this book was causing him trouble. Just as in real life, he could not move forward and he could not go back.

Alex hung up the phone and peeled off his kitchen work gloves. He reached for a handkerchief. He had dozens of them tucked in his pockets and desk drawers, all monogrammed, of course. He took a moment to scrub the rubber smell from his hands. He had to keep the phone insulated from his skin or he got static on the line, but he had yet to find a suitable sheath that didn't leave a vague trace of sour rubber smell on his hands. It was probably because of the constant electrical currents passing over his skin.

Fingers sufficiently clean, Alex reached for his notebook. The mood to write was not upon him as often as he would like these days, and he wondered if it would help to go to his old apartment. He had kept the residence under a series of names since the days before the Dark Man. He called it an apartment, but that was a rather grand term for the small single room that held a small cot and an enormous Louis XIV writing desk. The only decorations were two paintings that had come from his son's collection, bought at auction some years after Alexandre *fils* died. One was a study of cats by Eugene Lambert, the other an *Interieur d'Atelier* by Meissonier showing the charms of the bold Louise Pradier posing naked for her husband. Alex supposed it was careless to leave such valuable paintings in a place he rarely visited and that had no security beyond a locked door, but he didn't want them in his current home, which felt entirely too modern for these artifacts that were also a kind of *memento mori*. He'd kept little else. The rest were relics of a dead life and it didn't do to burden oneself that way. One ghost haunting him was quite enough.

"And you, m'lady? Would you like to visit my ancient *pied-à-terre?*"

The cat considered his offer.

The apartment had been built in the seventeenth century as barracks for the king's musketeers, and it felt old. The building still had no elevator, and the only access was up a narrow winding stair that was badly worn, or down the sheer exterior stone wall below the room's lone window. It had neither heat nor air-conditioning, but then, he didn't need either of those things. And sometimes being in an old place helped him to focus and remember the past more clearly.

Alex looked over at the enormous clock standing against the wall. There wasn't time to go to his apartment now. He would force himself to work here and then perhaps on the plane. It would be good to have something to keep his mind occupied. Flying still felt like the most unnatural thing a man could do, and he had to remain calm so that his own magnetic field did not reach out and disturb the plane's electrical systems.

Chapter Two
A Polite Exchange

El Grande had not been home—which was perhaps just as well since both Dr. Travers and Detective Maxwell had been staggering with exhaustion and blood loss by the time they reached the Montagne and El Grande's very grand villa. Thomasina Marsh assured them that Senor Diego-Vega would be devastated to have missed them, and Remus agreed; if it turned out that the man had actually sicced assassins on him, he would probably be very sorry to have missed them.

The two men declined a drink, citing their disheveled clothing, but agreed to come around for a visit in a few days.

Remus had seriously considered paying a call on the villa that same evening after everyone was abed, but El Grande kept dogs, and he had still felt dizzy, even after being stitched up and having a short nap followed by an excellent dinner with his now nearly unshakable friend, Dr. Travers.

Remus was up early the next morning, though—early enough to notice that the dawn was delayed by the weather. It was an unusual event that time of year. There was an eerie lightning—St. Elmo's Fire—accompanying the sudden squall, but no wind to speak of. The storm just stalled suddenly as it came up on land, and the black clouds dropped their load of rain all at once, as if they were too exhausted to carry it any further.

Ten minutes later, the deluge was done and the clouds scattered, letting in the delicate light of the delayed dawn. He had seen such a storm only twice in his life and never in Africa. He wondered if it was some sort of omen.

Remus pried open the shutter to his room and looked out into the street. A small scorpion sat on the windowsill, taking shelter from the wet. Remus was not fond of the stinging creatures, but he had to agree that it was still a bit wet to be out and about, especially with the torrent not yet subsiding in the street.

"Just stay out of my shoes," he said to the scorpion. "If I find you in there or in my clothes, you're going for a long swim."

He did have new clothes for scorpions to hide in. Dr. Travers's tailor had done well by him, which was fortunate, because the detective's splendid suit was beyond repair; shooting, stabbing, and hauling heavy tapestries—and the resultant spilled blood from these activities—had ruined the fine wool.

Remus pulled up a chair near the window and, giving the scorpion plenty of room, allowed himself to have his first deep thought of the day.

Who was Remus Maxwell? And how much of him could The Chameleon use while getting into the role? Understanding motivation was important in playing a part well, and he was going to play it. There was no longer any doubt. This affair with El Grande quite intrigued him, and he was prepared to embrace the role of a lifetime.

The first important question might be why Remus was a private detective. There were a num-

ber of reasons why a detective might like to remain private rather than join a formal police
force. Money could be one of them. Certainly, if
his letters were anything to go by, the detective's
fees per case were roughly five times the yearly
salary of the average British policeman.

That was probably not the overriding consideration, though, The Chameleon was fairly sure.
The detective had been bright, ambitious, and
didn't like losing. Official police were con-
strained by things like rules and regulations, also
interdepartmental rivalries, politics, and public
opinion. Remus would have had little tolerance
for these things.

In other words, he was intelligent, impatient,
and arrogant. This posed no problem for The
Chameleon, because he was all these things, too.

Would he have been a total loner, though?
The Chameleon was less sure.

Personally, there was little that he allowed himself to be attached to. He traveled light and put
his trust in gold and gemstones, which, while
they did not offer love or praise, were always
solid and held their worth in every country. It
wasn't that he abhorred property or other, less
portable possessions, but he had learned early
on that such things could be taken away—a sudden hike in taxes, a capricious landlord, even
eminent domain or courts bribed by so-called
creditors who wanted the widow and kids out on
their ears because they looked like a losing
proposition for paying off a debt and they
wanted their pound of flesh immediately.

And there were the unofficial crooks, too, professional gamblers who lured men into play, con-

fidence men of many stripes who could lure a man into terrible debt—and to do even more terrible things when he could not pay.

The detective seemed a loner. Probably he had rooms somewhere, but The Chameleon had never heard of Remus Maxwell having property—certainly he had no country estate. If there had been one, The Chameleon would have gone to call. The new Remus Maxwell smiled briefly at that thought.

Well, then, probably he should play this as a lone wolf. After all, part of this mobile lifestyle meant that one probably had few if any friends. Important lesson number one: Two people could successfully keep a secret—if one of them was dead. Remus Maxwell was a man with many secrets. It seemed unlikely that he had a confidant. Or a wife. This would simplify things for The Chameleon. He wouldn't worry about some intimate friend appearing out of the blue and spoiling his game.

There came a small scrape on the door. Recognizing the noise, Remus called out to the houseboy who brought his morning tea. Later the boy would be back to look through Remus's belongings. He didn't take this personally. It was cultural tradition. And they could search his rooms to their hearts' content; they wouldn't find anything. All of the detective's papers were well hidden. That was important criminal lesson number two: Leave no clues to one's real identity or plans—present or future. The detective would have understood this. It is possible that he would have chosen the same hiding place for his papers.

The tea was very strong and sweet. Remus would have preferred coffee, but the stuff at the hotel was nearly undrinkable. He would wait until he visited the Café de Paris to collect his coffee and the day's gossip. It would be interesting to see what the masses had to say about the odd theft of El Grande's tapestry and Remus's role in its recovery. If there was too much talk about Remus Maxwell, he might have to move on before dealing with El Grande. Important lesson number three: Be flexible. People who fell in love with a certain plan of action tended to be rigid. The rigid got broken when the winds of change blew though.

He would also have to keep an ear out for news of any bodies found near the railroad tracks. Eventually someone would probably find the detective's remains. Unless it was thoroughly scavenged, his identity would ultimately be discovered.

And that led to important lesson number four: Disappearing after using an identity for criminal activity was always a good idea. Dying was even better. And death was easy enough to arrange in certain foreign countries—so many exotic diseases, so many wild animals and dangerous jungles. All it took was an official whose greed matched or surpassed your immediate need. A funeral, death certificate, and obituary could be had relatively cheaply from the wild outposts of the world, and it nearly always discouraged any law-enforcement figure or insurance investigator determined enough to follow you to a foreign shore. And if he had to pay more—well, then he did. Remus smiled again. He had once joked with a friend: Do you know why funerals are so expensive? Because they're worth it. His friend hadn't understood.

Of course, all this couldn't help if one's true identity was suspected—which led to important lesson number five: Don't repeat your crimes. If you had an identifiable pattern, you could be anticipated. In his time, he'd been a footman, a chauffeur, an ambassador's secretary, and a courier for a museum. All successful jobs that had led him to even more successful robberies. And he had gotten the jobs because of a combination of good timing, good documents, and an uncanny ability to blend in with his surroundings. That was important lesson number six: Don't stand out. You had to be believable. When he was a footman he was an exemplary footman. No secretary had ever been more secretarial. No one had ever suspected he was anything other than what he appeared. The victims might think that the footman had stolen their jewels, but they never thought the footman was an actual jewel thief. Indeed, if a brilliant outside detective—Remus Maxwell, hired by one of The Chameleon's victim's—hadn't gone to Scotland Yard and compared notes on unsolved crimes, they would still be in ignorance of him.

The detective owed him for that inconvenience. Or he had. Lending The Chameleon his identity and letter of transit had rather repaid the debt. After all, the Bible even said that greater love hath no man than that he should lay down his life for another. And there was also something about carrying rancor to the grave but no further.

Remus finished his tea and then went to gather his hat and linen jacket. It was going to be an entertaining day.

Millie tapped on the door and then poked her head inside. Relieved to have actually written something, Alex looked up and smiled.

"Alexandre? The car is here."

"*Oui*. I am prepared. Here is the latest chapter." And good riddance—he really was not enjoying this book at all. The man he had been then was quite unlikable.

"I'll enter it into the computer first thing tomorrow," she promised. "Safe travels. Please don't bring any animals back from Mexico. That cat is quite nuisance enough. She behaves like she's the mistress and I'm her servant."

Alex looked at Lady de Winter and realized for the first time that her eyes were the same color as Thomasina's. It was like seeing a ghost. Shaken, he looked away from the cat's intent gaze.

"I am not planning on collecting souvenirs in Mexico," Alex assured Millie. "I shall return alone."

Millie snorted, suggesting she didn't believe him. Alex wasn't sure he believed himself either. He was going to Mexico to find something or someone.

And perhaps to die. The notion was an odd one, for if God had forsaken him years ago, Alex had in the meantime become one of Death's favored few, one whom Death spared even when circumstances were against survival and all around him died. Perhaps this was because he'd reaped enough souls through the centuries to be useful to Old Grim. Perhaps it was because when he killed it was done with a pleasing ferocity and high style. Whatever the reason, The Reaper hadn't made an earnest attempt to kill him in decades. Alex had to wonder why he felt as if this had now changed, that Death was on Saint Germain's payroll and coming for him with an extra-sharp scythe.

To expect human nature not to be ungrateful is to expect the wolf to be a vegetarian.

—*Alexandre Dumas*

Nobody who has not traveled in Prussia can have any idea of the hatred felt for us by the Prussians. It amounts to a monomania which clouds calm and untroubled minds. No minister in Berlin can be popular unless he makes it pretty plain that, sooner or later, war with France is inevitable.

—*Letter warning about the rise of German aggression from Dumas in* La Terreur Prussiene

If God were suddenly condemned to live the life which He has inflicted upon men, He would kill Himself.

—*Alexandre Dumas*

CHAPTER FOUR

Alex spent a lot of the trip thinking—but not about what awaited in Mexico. Perhaps it was because he was probably going to confront an old and dangerous foe that his mind turned back to other times of pain and danger that had had to be lived through. Like the moment when his son died.

Alex had found the letter from Alexandre *fils* on his own tomb while visiting the General's grave, something he did annually as a sort of pilgrimage to his patriotic father. The note from Alexandre to his supposedly dead father was short, but it had moved Alex, changed him in a fundamental way. Of course, regret came too late. The Paris newspapers had reported it that morning—Dumas *fils* was dead. And for the first time since his own "death" Alex had wept.

He still had the note, though he no longer needed the paper to recall what it said. His prodigious memory had grasped the contents at once and written it on his brain in bitter iron-gall.

Father, does one still remember, in the world where you now are, the things of this world of ours, or does eternal life live only in the human imagination made childlike by its fear of no longer existing? That is something we never discussed in the days we lived together, nor do I think that you ever worried your head with metaphysical speculation. . . . For close on a quarter of a century you have been sleeping peacefully under the great trees of Villers-Cotterets between your mother, who served as your model for all the good women you portrayed, and your father, who inspired all those heroes to whom you gave the gift of life. . . . The world moves fast. Soon we shall meet again, and then I will know.

But they would not meet again. At least not for a long time, and only if God could forgive and open His gates to such a terrible sinner as Alex had become.

Kneeling beside the tomb, Alex had folded the paper carefully, his tears having disturbed his son's writing, which was already as thin as cobwebs and obviously written by an ailing hand. His son had grown old while he remained young. And he hadn't even been there at the end.

Why had he left it so long? Why had he not found some way to see his child, to save him from mortal death?

Not sure why, since there was nothing to be done, Alex had gone to his son's home at once, presenting himself to the widow as a distant cousin. He had been allowed to sit awhile with his son's body, to hold the frail, cold hand of the vessel that had once contained his son. Alexandre *fils* was lying in a carved bed, the pretty lemonwood adorned with bronze swans. The boy—no longer a boy, but an old man now—had been laid out in his working clothes, his feet left bare just as he had instructed in his will. Alex had stared at those pale toes and the narrow, arched instep that shoes had pained all through his life and felt the urge to weep again.

He was too late. His son was dead and beyond reach. He

would never again have the chance to give in to temptation and reveal that he was alive—after a fashion. He would never have to decide if it was right to offer this strange and often painful form of life to his moralistic son. He would never have to risk being reviled by his child as an evil, damned thing. He had been a coward, letting his son die rather than risk being hated.

Shaken by his thoughts, Alex had left the house, bitter tears coursing down his cheeks and even more bitter thought and memory bringing on a kind of insanity. The next morning Alex left Paris, and nearly twenty years passed before he returned. He'd run hard and he'd run far, but that didn't mean memory and regret didn't follow him like his own shadow everywhere he went. Some things could not be outrun.

Death wasn't so bad for Alex in the beginning. He'd had to give many things up, of course, but at first, he hadn't been entirely sorry to escape the burden of being Alexandre Dumas. The last years of his mortal life had been wearying and unhappy. And he had enjoyed being restored to full physical health and vigor. His children were established, he had argued when the moments of temptation came, economically secure, married with families of their own. He was free to do as he pleased, and so were they.

But there was a dark side that came with Dippel's gift, and Alex was made aware of it every time he closed his eyes. Night after night when the moon was on the wane, he was attacked by a murder of phantom crows. They were brutal creatures, tearing not just his body but trying to rip out his soul. And he wasn't young and strong when he fought them either. His body had returned to the natural state of decay it had reached when the Dark Man intervened in his life, insisting he knew a way to save France's greatest writer from slow heart failure and blindness. The dream implied that someday, Death would have to be repaid—if not with Alex's life, then with the lives of others.

The terrible dreams felt like premonitions, and so they proved to be—and on a scale so massive that Alex couldn't comprehend it at first. It was right before Bismarck's rise that he had felt old age come upon him almost in a night. And it was not just the aging of the body, the dimming of his sight that plagued him, but also the enfeeblement of the mind, the draining away of his creative powers.

Being unwilling to face this horror, he had done what the Dark Man had told him he would need to do. He had killed himself during a winter storm, dying so that he might rise up renewed once more. And when he was reborn with a clear mind and strong body, he'd left America and also his old regrets about his dead son, and returned to Europe to see what ravages the new war had wrought on his old home. He was ready for adventure and optimistically certain that he could once again influence events in Europe.

But Death got there before him.

Of course, Alex knew that the world had changed. War had changed, but he had thought he was prepared. He had ended up at the Battle of Liège in August of 1914, and then at the Battle of Verdun in the winter of 1916. Not before or since had he ever seen so many dead. There was no place to step on the battlefield without treading on corpses—French, German, their lifeless bodies littered the ground. Like many of the soldiers around him, he had gone into a state of shock. He had no memories of the battle itself, no sense of how long it lasted, just killing and killing and more killing. He had been awarded a medal for his valor, but he never felt as though he deserved it. He had been Death's pawn.

After the war, he had left the shattered remains of his country and returned to the States. But times were hard there, too, and then the influenza pandemic had swept over the land, killing even more people than the Great War. Nursing was not his vocation, being so tame and boring for a creative mind, but he had found himself working in a hospital at Camp Funston because there was almost no one else who could. There were only a handful of nurses or doctors left. The flu had spared no one.

His body never sickened from the virus, but his soul did. He might not ail in carcass, but he did in spirit. There was no escaping death in those years. He had had to grapple with it daily. It was divine punishment for wasting his own life.

This wasn't his first plague, of course. Cholera had come to Paris in 1832. He recalled the streets being filled with black hearses that rolled to the cemeteries from sunup to sundown. They were soon replaced by moving vans that carried up to twenty bodies at a time. There were no funerals then, just mass burials in common graves. He had contracted the disease, but was nursed by friends with treatments of ether and constant bed warmers, and by the grace or God—or something—he had survived.

1832 was not the end of the dying. Cholera came and went and came again. But Alex was brash and thumbed his nose at Fate, and a year later he gave a grand ball. Republican Paris— those who had survived the uprising and the epidemic—came in droves to see what Alexandre Dumas would do to celebrate.

He did not disappoint them. Alex decided to serve venison, which he hunted himself, trading away one of his six deer for a giant salmon that he personally prepared. He ordered five hundred bottles of champagne iced, three hundred bottles of Bourgogne properly chilled, and three hundred bottles of Bordeaux properly warmed. Ciceri, set designer of the Théâtre-François, was brought in to paint battlefield murals on the walls, and there were two orchestras hired so that Paris could dance in defiance of death and an unjust government.

He'd thrown no balls after the Great War. He was no longer so impetuous. Modern war and death on a scale he had never imagined had beaten it out of him. Alexandre Dumas was humbled.

Alex hadn't written of that time, and probably never

would. His bravery on the battlefield was something of which his father would be proud, and his mother would have applauded his humanitarian efforts in the hospital, but he had no intention of ever revisiting those memories in a book. Not ever. Especially not when a part of him wondered if the Dark Man and his son hadn't had something to do with unleashing this horror on the world. He had no proof of this belief—none—and logic argued against it. But he had seen the Dark Man in 1919, far from sane, ranting about owning the world and acquiring it through his puppet, Bismarck. And the son? Well, from what Alex had learned through research, Saint Germain had been born evil. He should have found some way to kill both. Forever.

Was such wickedness contagious? Had that same evil tainted him as well when he accepted the Dark Man's gift? Alex always wondered. Would he know if he were wicked? Could evil recognize itself? He feared that perhaps it would not. And like him, it would live on indefinitely, perhaps spreading poison, all while unaware.

Alex had lived in many places since the Great War, most recently in France, but he always came back to America eventually. He loved the people of that land. They were innovative and optimistic and young at heart. Innocent really, naïve and childlike. They reminded him of his younger self. This was both a good and bad thing. Because of their unaging culture, the people of the United States lived in a quick-fix, instant-gratification society that did not do well with concepts or projects that required long-term attention. He understood this. He had not been a patient man. His own son had called him a giant baby. But an extra century of life had taught him many things, among them the need to look ahead, to plan carefully for the future that would surely come. It did not do to live in the past; but one had to glance at the past from time to time, see the patterns and then relate them to the future so that mistakes were not repeated.

Most Americans did not plan. They were good at applying technology to problems, and they tended to think that they could always find a solution to their troubles in the laboratory when troubles came along. Sadly, that wasn't always true, and they were always so surprised and indignant when they encountered loss, privation, or pain. In their indignation, the men tended to lash out and lash hard. They didn't do well when put on diets, be they fiscal or caloric. Again, he sympathized. He had never been able to live on a budget. But he now understood that this could be fatiguing for those in power who had to grapple with long-term problems. It made them cranky and ruthless. Sometimes they acted impulsively.

Which was all the long way of saying that there would be no help from his American friends with the conundrum of Saint Germain—even assuming that they believed his wild tale of a man who would not die. Without volunteering for a DNA test to prove his own strangeness, Alex doubted he could convince any of his contacts in the government that something terrible was afoot in Mexico. After all, what did he know? He was just a famous novelist.

He wouldn't be in the United States long enough to find help anyway. Better this affair be dealt with over the border. The people of Mexico—though geographically American— were a different group altogether. Their thinking was more European, at times more fatalistic. They might be more willing to believe in the impossible, and Alex had some friends there as well. He wondered if that was why Saint Germain had chosen it for a base. It wouldn't be the first time that he had opted for the desert over the city or more verdant and gentle countrysides, not the first time that Alex had followed him into the wilderness either.

Feeling resolved and at last ready to write, Alex accepted another glass of champagne from the lovely blond creature with the soft blue aura working first-class, and then opened his notebook. It was jumping ahead a bit, but he felt it was time to write about the first occasion when he'd seen Saint Germain face to face. Like many momentous occasions, he hadn't realized how important the moment was.

Chapter Three
Enter the Femme Fatale

Thomasina Marsh came slinking into the music room in a silk dress the color of dawn that clung to her like sunlight on bare skin. Remus knew his clothes, and that dress had not been designed in England where everyone was sporting stiff winter wool that could have been used to scour pots.

He watched her move toward him, smiling slightly, and thought that the frock was so smart it probably had independent thought.

"Norell?" he asked, recognizing the designer.

She blinked and then smiled widely.

"Why, yes. One must look to Hollywood now that Germany has ruined French haute couture. And I feel so patriotic when I do my part for conservation. Why, there is barely a yard and a half of fabric in the whole thing."

Remus let his eyes compliment her for a moment longer and then forced them away.

How was it possible, he wondered, to have a body like that and not use it for immoral purposes? He knew that he couldn't have resisted using it for self-advancement had it been his.

Remus felt a frown pull at his mouth. At that moment, he would have welcomed the conviction that she was one of those women who misused their beauty, but in his heart he was convinced otherwise. Thomasina might occasionally flirt with evil in the form of men, but she didn't routinely embrace them.

So why was she working for El Grande?

Though he willed it otherwise, his eyes flicked back to her once more. Remus admitted that he liked her hair, too. The color was rich and vibrant. It had the same power that had invested Samson's hair—only her hair affected other men's strength and not her own. And she was merciful in her power; otherwise, she would probably never have put it up.

Annoyed at himself for being distracted, he looked away. His eyes searched the room, quickly finding the man they called El Grande. The gentleman was strange. Physically he was tall, very lean, very pale. And he had eyes like midnight in the tropics. His accent was also odd—European, but not Spanish, not French, not Italian.

"Senorita Marsh." As though sensing the scrutiny, El Grande turned and called to his secretary. "Be pleased to join me and meet La Senora Tarantella."

Thomasina stiffened slightly, her smile freezing. Remus understood. That black gaze was unnerving even if you didn't know that this man worked hand in glove with the Nazis who were smuggling treasure out of Europe.

Though not called for, Remus offered his arm to Thomasina and joined the large group around the talkative soprano who was going to perform that afternoon, and waited to be introduced. He did it to help her, and to annoy El Grande, who doubtless felt territorial simply because Thomasina was female and in his employ.

Though Remus had half expected to feel a supernatural chill in the evil man's presence, there wasn't a single shiver of apprehension. No sense of threat or danger. All emotions were cloaked.

Remus turned his gaze on the others. He watched with fascination as the diva repeatedly wrung the neck of the peacock whose taxidermied and bejeweled head and neck served as the handle for her enormous ostrich-and-peacock-plumed fan. It had small rubies for eyes that flashed brightly with each of the fan's sweeps.

With the best of intentions, Remus couldn't prevent his own eyes glazing over as the diva's inane and ceaseless chatter continued, and he began to think fondly of the mute foreign women who lived in repressed circumstance that encouraged quiet when their menfolk were near.

Then he noticed Thomasina watching him with a barely repressed smile. He instantly smoothed out his contracted brow and made his face agreeable.

"Miss Marsh," he said, stepping firmly into the flow of babble and letting it eddy around him. He didn't raise his voice, but he didn't bother to whisper either. "You look pale. I think you need to come over to the window at once and find some fresh air."

In point of fact, she was in the bloom of high health, but she did her best to look suddenly wan. He offered his arm again, and she took it immediately. They did a neat about-face and strolled for the French doors. The weight of El Grande's stare followed them the whole way, and it seemed they could smell faint whiffs of sulfur in the air. It was a relief to slip behind the screen of a potted windmill palm.

"Thank you, Mr. Maxwell. I do feel a bit closed in," she said for the benefit of the few people who might be listening. "I am not yet accustomed to the heat of this region."

"Really, it's the least I could do," Remus assured her with a charming smile that helped hide the fact that the least was almost always what he did for other people.

"I think the burning question is whether we stop at the window or just keep going," Thomasina answered, her voice carefully lowered now that they were alone. "The concert is about to start. Finally."

"I'd rather be drenched in cheap whiskey and set afire than sit through it," he said sincerely, but with a small grin that didn't belong to the original Remus Maxwell. "And please don't bother telling me that you want to hear her either."

"As it happens, I have some whiskey—good whiskey—back at the villa. I mention this just in case you are bent on self-immolation."

He looked at her carefully. Her eyes were clear, innocent even, at least of any intent to lure him into danger. The offer was tempting, but it was not one that Remus Maxwell would have accepted.

"I'd never waste good whiskey that way. As it happens, they have an excellent whiskey at my hotel—which is closer. There are also some very comfortable chaise lounges near the pool that seem to be calling to me." His eyes were also clear, though very dark.

"Calling all the way from the hotel? It's the heat. You're hallucinating." Thomasina looked around and then added more seriously: "Do you think we'll be missed if we slip out this door?"

They looked back at the crowd taking seats around the piano. The diva was fanning herself vigorously and still chattering. El Grande seemed to have disappeared.

"I'd say it's doubtful. They seem mesmerized by the remains of that dead bird she's carrying. Anyway, it doesn't matter. Her voice could strip paint. There are limits to what I will endure without pay." He added truthfully: "Or even with."

Thomasina gave a small laugh that she turned into a cough and looked at him reproachfully.

"No more of that until we've escaped," she scolded.

Remus found himself smiling again. There was something about this woman that fascinated him.

"Agreed, no more until we've escaped."

Alex closed his notebook. He found that his hands were shaking.

Thomasina, I'm so sorry, my love. I didn't know what that small act of defiance would cost you.

It had cost Dr. Travers too. That kindly old man had also ended up dead, murdered by Saint Germain's cruel hands.

"More champagne, Mr. Dumas?" the flight attendant asked. Her pale blue glow identified her more than her face or hair.

Alex smiled at her without really seeing her face. He held out his glass as he nodded, and prayed to the God he had so long shunned that he really was prepared to meet his enemy again. Perhaps if he triumphed this time, all would be made right. He didn't know what he would do if he was confronted by Thomasina's ghost on the battlefield and found no forgiveness there.

June 9: I read in a legitimist newspaper that I had been caught, weapons in hand in the Saint-Merri cloisters court-martialed in the night, and shot at three o'clock in the morning. The news had such an official tone, the narrative of my execution—which, it was reported, I accepted with great courage—was so detailed; the information came from such a good source, that I had a moment of doubt. I threw off my blanket, jumped out of bed, and ran to my mirror to prove to myself my own existence.

—*Dumas's diary (from* Impressions de Voyage)

Thank God no acts of cannibalism have been reported, but, in future, when dramas of fifteen scenes, preceded by a prologue and finished with an epilogue, it should state clearly on the handbill that *a succession of meals will be provided.*

—*Theophile Gautier (in a review of Dumas* père's La Reine Margot *that ran over nine hours)*

CHAPTER FIVE

It hadn't been his intention, but on the last leg of the journey, Alex found himself trying to get a grasp on the ever more elusive narrative by actually telling part of the Casablanca story from Thomasina's point of view. It was pure fiction, of course, because he had never in point of fact read her mind, but he thought he knew her well enough that it was not too great an impertinence to write for her. Besides, though painful, there was no one else now who knew the tale, and it deserved to be heard.

"Wish me well, *chérie*," he said softly to the gentle ghost who still haunted his memory all these years on, and then began to write.

She was attracted to Remus Maxwell, and it felt a bit like Christmas Eve whenever he was near. Of course, that was the problem.

As a child, she had loved Christmas, but as she had gotten older, the feeling had changed. She still felt the anticipation—the heated curiosity about what gifts she might receive from her scholarly parent. Or which foreign visitors would come to call with unusual treats in their pockets, and whether Mrs. Barkley's traditional plum pudding would be a culinary triumph. But along with that exhilaration came a sort of melancholy, a realization that the pudding—great or terrible— would soon be devoured, that the visitors from faraway places would soon go back to their far- away home, the gifts would be opened and their secrets—usually so mundane and practical— would be known.

The anticipation only rarely proved worth the letdown that followed. It seemed wisest, both then and now, to reserve her feelings. This was especially true where men were concerned.

But she was so moody these days and disin- clined to take her own sensible advice. It seemed as if she was pulled this way and that by the sun and the moon and the orbit of things closer and less celestial—like Remus Maxwell.

Thomasina raised her wrist to her face and in- haled. She liked the perfume he had given her. It was very different, a custom blend that he had ordered for her birthday. She hadn't worn scent for a few years. The modern perfume aesthetic was so confusing. The Americans—what few there were in her own country—were making scents that were overpowering.

She giggled suddenly. Remus had said that they were like Niagara Falls or the Grand Canyon, scents that seemed to belong on giant, hairy- chested men and Valkyrié-like women. The En- glish were better, but still doing the same old pale toilette waters, diluted lilacs and roses, the castoffs from a flooded garden. Perfumes for men and women alike that smelled as if they belonged on fops and blue-blooded hemophiliacs. And then there were the French. Their scents were—what had Remus called it? An indigestion of smells. Spice and flowers together until you could not separate out any one note and say this is frankincense or this is jasmine. The message they sent was confused. They did not say "I am pretty" or "I am sexy" or "I am independent." They just said: "I like to smell like something other than myself." Everywhere it was the same; there was a uniformity to scent, an appeal to the new middle-class masses that had no elegance or individuality whatsoever. An average woman's taste in every uniform bottle. Scent had become like shoes or a hat, everyone had to have at least one. To fill the need, the perfumeries were producing scent in vats.

There were a few commercial perfumes she liked—Chanel No.5, of course—but in general, it was all very boring. She found the safety of good taste in high doses to be very dull. Remus understood this about her and had made her a perfume that was warm, slightly wicked, and stayed close to her skin.

This was dangerous. This man saw her too clearly. She wasn't sure she wanted to be with someone who read her thoughts and knew her wishes even before she did. Such a relationship could be dangerous.

Alex closed his notebook softly and resumed breathing. It was difficult to force air past the pain in his chest. He had thought he was strong enough to face this chapter of his life, but now he wasn't so certain his heart could endure it. Wound it enough and the heart became scar tissue: hard, ugly, unfeeling. He had stopped loving before that happened—around the time of his marriage really—telling himself that in his circumstances it was better to have a lonely heart than an unfeeling one. But Thomasina had been his one exception in the centuries after. He didn't regret loving her, but he had paid for it every day, every year since. She was the beautiful mistake he had promised himself he would never make again, and he had taken a kind of comfort in the idea that with her death his heart was finally too scarred to ever again feel pain.

But he had been wrong. His heart felt—or at least remembered vividly—what loss was.

"Ah, what was I thinking to start this book?" he asked himself. "The one thing I have learned: Don't look back. There's no point. Something from the past is always gaining on you, and you lose time every instant you take your eyes off of the goal to look back at it."

He really didn't know if he could go on with the book, even if he altered the characters and moved the setting someplace else. Of course, this did raise the question of what he was going to do about this story that was due in three weeks. Could he write another story in that time?

He supposed that it would all depend on what he found in Mexico.

The plane set down in San Diego. It took some arranging on Millie's part, but the car rental agency had an older-model jeep waiting for him. This pleased Alex. He had no trouble with things mechanical, only items that were electronic.

There was no difficulty passing over the border into Mexico. He stopped on the other side only to pick up weapons before heading to Lara Vieja. It wasn't the usual stop for a tourist, but what was the American witticism? He had high friends in low places who wouldn't ask questions as long as the money was right. For a generous donation to their off-shore accounts—or the shoebox under the bed; he wasn't certain which—they would not question why a visiting French writer might want to exert some influence of an explosive nature on whatever he was researching. Alex felt at once paranoid to be carrying a shotgun and two pistols, and yet also uncertain that he shouldn't have asked for larger armaments. If he truly were going to find Saint Germain, could he be certain that a shotgun would do the job?

Alex drove, guns on the seat beside him, keeping his mind blank and quiet so that he wouldn't miss any whispers from the subconscious.

There were maps in the glove compartment of the jeep; finding the once-drowned town of Lara Vieja that had been mentioned in the newspaper was not difficult. Night was falling when he arrived, mercifully cloaking the brutal countryside in shadow. Already the spring flowers had shriveled in the sun. Living in a city, it was easy to forget that in rural areas the residents still lived as slaves to the seasons. Summer here was dry and hot, and if it rained it flooded. In the distance there was one tiny stream that wriggled like a large black worm caught out by the hostile sun. It would be dead soon unless fed by a summer storm.

To the human eye, there wasn't much to see. Nothing lived there—nothing. What hadn't drowned had burned. The reemerged ruins had the smell of Saint Germain about them, though, a kind of rot and brimstone. Saint Germain and something else. Most people would never notice it, but there was a lingering smell of ozone, as though the magic that had opened up the graves of the newly dead for the wizard still lingered in the soil and the air. Alex had been in other places like that. Places where evil had congealed and all living things shunned them. There had been just such a place in Tangier.

Though it was what he had half expected, the confirmation of supernatural forces in the area still alarmed him. The timing of Saint Germain's reappearance was bad and probably not coincidental. Alex was nearing the time of renewal and not at his strongest. Finding someplace to accomplish a renewal down here might be tricky at this time of year. St. Elmo's fire didn't happen just anywhere, and it was the only thing he had found that could help him when age came upon him. Saint Germain probably knew this.

"*Merde.*"

As the results of his dealings with the Dark Man had begun to fully present themselves, Alex had begun looking for other answers, other solutions to his succession of deaths and fiery rebirths that held pain and old age at bay. Alex's son had questioned his late-life dealings with somnambulists and magnetic séances, and there had been little that Alex could say to defend his interest except that they were fashionable. Certainly, revealing the truth wasn't an option, not after his son's openly expressed horror of Mary Shelley's book. Alex could never admit to being Frankenstein's real monster.

Finally, at the start of World War I he thought that he was ready to face his end rather than submit himself to the fire again, but every time he went to end it, there was some sound reason—some worthy cause or person—that held him back from suicide.

Or maybe it was cowardice. It would have been easier to face his end had he matured as a normal man, but when age returned it came swiftly, first to his eyes, then pain quickly accumulated in his joints and chest. Within weeks his shoulders rounded until he had the posture of an old man carrying the weight of the world. Worst of all was the heaviness around the heart. He should die within days of the return of these ailments . . . but he didn't. And the longer he lingered, the more he doubted that he could die. Perhaps this was what hell was: physical damnation without relief.

A return of blindness and mental feebleness was not his desire, but neither was this cycle of death and renewal that had forever changed him and set him apart from the rest of mankind, a change that made him hide his unnatural eyes in daylight and dye his skin, first with a tincture of walnut and now with self-tanners so that it remained dark enough to pass for human. Also, his psychic powers grew stronger each time he died, making him feel ever less a part of humanity. Sadly, though he had searched the world over, he had found no answers for his ills in the modern fads and new sciences that spoke of prolonging life. His deal with the devil was left to stand, even though the Dark Man was himself now dead.

Alex sniffed at a handful of dust and then threw it away. He spat, trying to clear the bad taste from his mouth and sinuses.

Of course, Saint Germain had to have the same problem as the rest of the Dark Man's get. He too had age rushing upon him, which he was obviously trying to deal with in some sick and dangerous—and as yet unidentified—way.

Against his better judgment, Alex stepped into the ruins of the Lara Vieju church where the feeling of evil was strongest. Around him on all sides and arching overhead were the burned ribs of the cathedral. A strong, vile smell inhabited the air, and got worse as he neared the opening to the underground vaults. The vapor that hung there had gorged on fiery death, and recently. It tried to hide underground, but the odor dribbled out, and the sickening smell made him think of Jonah in the belly of the whale.

Only, this whale was dead and barbecued.

He thought then of the passage from the Bible he had seen on Millie's desk just before he left for the airport. She had left a blue satin bookmark just under the verse, "Be sure your sins will find you out." It was Numbers 32:23. Had that been Millie's chiding, or actual canonical admonition? Had his sins finally been found out and was he going to pay for them now?

Alex discovered a carcass burned to charcoal on the stairs leading down to the vaults beneath the church. Beyond the first body he could make out the charred head and entrails of a jackass. There was also a pair of blackened human legs tossed to one side. There was no proof that this vile work belonged to Saint Germain, but Alex was absolutely certain that it did. Apparently, in the years since he had seen his foe, the man's evil and insanity had grown exponentially. And the fact that he was demonstrating his powers so blatantly likely meant that he finally felt strong enough to take on anyone who objected to his work. For everyone's sake, Alex hoped this wasn't true.

Alex turned abruptly, feeling sick and more than a bit touched by supernatural dread. There was nothing to learn from these artifacts, he told himself, and the odor was making him ill. He left the ruins of the burned-out church and climbed back in his jeep without a backward glance.

Shadows gathered in the folds of the red land he traveled, earth wracked into canyons long ago by earthquakes and glaciers. He chose a dirt path at random, having no definite plan but wanting merely to get away from the reek of evil that filled his head. Still, he wasn't surprised when he shook off his reverie a short time later and found himself on the road to Cuatros Cienegas. The name on the sign made him shiver—part with anticipation and part with dread. This was his goal. A part of him had known it all along.

He liked to believe in free will but had the feeling that in this case his destination was preordained. Whether he was ready to face his past or not, Fate had finally caught up with him and arranged a rematch. First had come the insane impulse to write about his encounter with Saint Germain, then the pieces in the newspaper about monsters raised by storms, and now this psychic temblor that insisted he head for Cuatros Cienegas. He was being led.

But by what or by whom?

Feeling a strange tingling in his skin, Alex headed for what he was certain was his date with destiny. He stopped at the first town and made a reservation at the best hotel in the area. He remembered the name from when he'd read the second story about monsters in Mexico. It was a small hostelry called Hotel Ybarra. This town had also been mentioned in the papers a few months back as being a place where ancient vampires had dwelled, but this related phenomenon hadn't been anything more than a curiosity until he visited Lara Vieja and smelled a new kind of evil. Vampires and Saint Germain—a marriage made in hell.

But if this meeting was meant to be, then . . . Alex shrugged. One could not argue against Fate. And he wasn't afraid of dying anymore. Or, to be more precise, he was more afraid of living as he had been than facing whatever the Reaper had arranged for him.

He did not turn on his headlights as he drove, preferring to enjoy the night. The roads were mostly deserted, so he made good time. This was excellent, because he was aware of a growing sense of urgency that he be in Cuatros Cienegas the next day in order to avert some calamity.

Alex arrived well before dawn and was somewhat surprised to find the hotel alive with activity. Most small towns outside the tourist areas were not nocturnal, though it made a kind of sense for people to be out at night given the heat of the day.

There were a few foreigners at the hotel when he checked in, but also some local toughs drinking in the cantina. They were scar-carrying members of some deadly serious knife and gun club, or else every one of them had had a nearly fatal encounter with a thresher at some time in his life. There was no sign of drug use in them, though, not even marijuana, which was unusual and probably unfortunate. If it wasn't the drug trade keeping them here, Alex wondered, then what were they doing in this sleepy town? Were they drawn to some subliminal evil? Alex had tried looking in their minds but could hear nothing but white noise. Their auras were an unhealthy shade of gray he associated with ghosts and people near death. This made him wonder if they were Saint Germain's creatures.

Alex stayed awake in his room until sunrise and then closed his eyes on the world. He slept the day through, dreaming of a giant eagle that fought off a flock of screaming crows when they attacked him. The crows might perhaps have won, but a second eagle surrounded by green light appeared, and together they drove the scavengers away. Alex rose at sunset, feeling calmed by this omen, refreshed from the deep sleep and prepared to face anything.

Not sure who was coming, but having a strong presentiment that someone important was indeed drawing near, he took a seat at the back of the cantina and waited for Fate to unfold her plan: He just hoped that she was in a pleasant mood and ready to fight on the side of the angels. Otherwise, given the general hints of vampires and ghouls and who knew what other kinds of living dead that had been heaved up from the bowels of this damned earth, there could be literal hell to pay. For both Alex and whoever was coming to help him.

Every one of us is responsible for our faults and infirmities . . . but none have the right to shirk onto the back of a third person the burden of their personal faults, or the consequences of their misfortune. . . . Before ever the child was conceived, I was aware of these objections. They were carefully weighed, and my conclusion may be stated thusly: for the sake of my child I shall have the strength to acknowledge everything and see that it turns out for the best. It was a result of an action of mine that this being who does not yet exist, who has been condemned in advance, was set in train. This child who is on his way, though not yet born, is already in the sad position of being refused social recognition. Children of adultery can be acknowledged by neither father nor mother. This one, therefore, is doubly branded by adultery. What will be his position with the mother's state of health—she may die at any time—and a father, already old who, by asking another fifteen years of life, might seem to be making an excessive request? By the time the child is fourteen, he may find himself stranded in a hostile world. If she is a girl, she will be on the streets, selling herself for ten francs at a time. If a boy, he will play the part of Antony or Larcenaire. In that case, better to destroy a life, better to never create it. But it would anger me to make such a decision because of social pressure. It would do violence to all my feelings of justice. . . . Monsieur is impotent—too bad for him. Madame has been weak—too bad for her. But let no one dare say "So much the worse for the being who owes his life to that impotence and weakness." . . . Madame risked divorce by her husband. I risked being shot or run through with a sword, and that is a risk I am perfectly prepared to take for this child.

—*Letter from Dumas* père *to his daughter Marie*

Oh! This is Théâtre-Francais. It is certainly one of the circles of Hell which Dante overlooked, where God has seen fit to confine dramatic authors who have the curious idea of making a deal less money in the theatre than they could have done in other employment.

—*Letter from Alexandre Dumas*

CHAPTER SIX

"So, details please. What's he really like? Is he a perv or something?" Ashley asked, her gray eyes squinted against the smoke in the tavern.

The hotel might have been nice at one time, but the cantina's decor was a step beyond disheveled. It hadn't actually passed into being disreputable, though; it was still barely clean enough to take advantage of the area's new cash crop, *touristas*. Harmony Nix had known better than to expect luxury, but the hotel's decorating motif could be best summed up as Aztecan Sparse—which was extremely practical in this case. There was no point in putting the maids through the trouble of chasing the giant cockroaches around a lot of plush furniture.

"No, he wasn't a perv." Harmony was tired of thinking about what had led her down to Mexico, but Ashley wasn't going to let the dead relationship go without one more autopsy.

"He must have been," Ashley objected. "I can't picture anything else making you split like this. I mean, he was so cute. And everyone was saying that he wanted to marry you. That had to be better than exile in Mexico." Ashley looked around with a small sneer.

Harmony was thinking much the same thing, but had to flinch at her friend saying it aloud. There was a reason that their fellow countrymen were called ugly Americans.

Ashley and Harmony had booked themselves into the Hotel Ybarra because it was near Cuatros Cienegas, a nature reserve that had sounded charming in the brochure put out by Ashley's new environmental tour-guide friend, but which was proving to be rather less than the five-star— or even three-star—experience she'd been hoping for. Harmony saw this as a salutary lesson on the evils of letting others plan her . . . vacations. Yeah, *vacation*. That sounded better than *retreat*. Ashley seemed to believe that Harmony was here to write a story for the newsletter. Harmony didn't correct this impression. Misdirection had become a way of life for her. The organization she worked for was full of ardent, dedicated environmentalists, but the front office that put out the newsletter and engaged in other innocuous public activities was a petri dish for gossip. Gossip could get her in a lot of legal trouble.

"He's not a pervert. Far from it. He's actually a corporate-climber complete with hammer, ax, and pitons— and a pile of colleagues' metaphorical bodies he's scrambled over to reach the top. Beau knows exactly how to keep his steel-toed designer boots on the neck of the common man," Harmony answered, surrendering to Ashley's pestering and feeling free to speak her mind since she was now hundreds of miles away from Beaumont Davidson and the miasma he had cast over her psyche. The tequila shooters were helping her sense of well-being, too. However, far from being therapeutic and restoring her tranquillity, the more she talked about Beau, the more indignant she became.

"You know the type, bursting with the conviction that

they are always right and therefore the ends can justify any means—and a brain shrink-wrapped in macho claptrap that prevents any new ideas from getting in. Bad enough to know he's like that on the job, but it didn't end there. For him, the women's movement never happened. He was expecting me to retire to a little cottage with a picket fence where he planned on keeping me impregnated until I had produced enough Beau Juniors to field a hockey team." And she had almost fallen for it.

Even as she spoke, half of her mind was on the dark man in the corner. Harmony hadn't noticed him at first because he was just one more shadow in a room full of murky places that she didn't want to peer into. But as she had started speaking, he had leaned forward as though to better hear her conversation, and the candlelight had painted his fascinating face with wavering light.

Of course, he couldn't hear her from where he was sitting. The room was too loud. But she liked looking at him anyway and pretending that he was listening to her. This man was different. He almost had bedroom eyes—those sleepy lids that promised that any woman who went to bed with him would end up likewise exhausted. Harmony didn't buy it, though. No, the more she looked at him, nursing a Dos Equis with a bit of lime, the more certain she became that this wasn't a man looking for a quickie vacation fling with the first available blonde. Those dark, dark irises—or perhaps they were his pupils, dilated by shadows or drugs of some sort—were far too intent on his surroundings. This man might wear a slight, seductive smile as he looked over the bar, but he had more than sexual fun and games on his mind. She was a bit psychic that way.

That only made him more intriguing.

And maybe dangerous. Stupid, stupid—to be interested in someone like this, but that had always been her favorite flavor of man.

"Beau said that? About the kids? That's so . . . so retro."

"Yes." Well, he hadn't *exactly* said it, but she had known what he wanted. She had these moments when she absolutely knew what some people were thinking, and this had been one of them. "I don't even know if I want kids. For sure I don't want half a dozen. Sheesh—that's a lot of emotional mouths to feed."

She was half speaking to the dark stranger, though he couldn't hear her. As a rule, she no longer confided in anyone, hardly even herself. The only place she felt free anymore to tell even a veiled version of the truth was in her novel. And now to this shadowy man in the corner of the cantina.

"Wow. That would totally wreck your body. Think of the stretch marks! I'd have split too. That's too bad about Beau, though. The man is going places and he was good-looking for a rich guy." Ashley sighed. *Too bad,* she said, but Ashley didn't look particularly compassionate. Harmony knew her friend would in all likelihood try to arrange to meet with Beau when they got back.

But what had she expected? Ashley was very self-centered and not someone that Harmony actually liked. They'd ended up traveling companions because everyone else she knew in *the movement* had a regular job and couldn't run off with only two hours' notice. And because Harmony had been too afraid to run off to Mexico alone in a fifteen-year-old Honda Accord with almost two hundred thousand miles on it. The Honda was loyal, but it had an aging engine that was fussy. There was only one mechanic who could work on it—thanks to the many experimental "green" devices that had been grafted onto the original engine—and that was a six-foot, seven-inch schizo named George, who periodically went off his meds and then left town to follow his voices that said it was his destiny to destroy the Great Satan who was residing most recently at the Alameda Naval

Station. He'd gone from shipyard to jail to mental hospital in quick order. Just like all the other times. He'd always come back to work eventually, but not on any predictable schedule, and this time he'd been gone for weeks. Harmony couldn't wait any longer. So, though she got great gas mileage and emitted few toxins while doing it, she couldn't drive over forty miles per hour, and broke down at least once a month while waiting for the medication to clear George's brain of demons. It wasn't the way she wanted to travel in a foreign country.

She could have rented a car, but if she used her real name that would leave the kind of trail that Beau—or actually Beau's security chief—could follow. She had a fake I.D. and passport, and could have used them to rent a car, but she was holding these papers in reserve for the day when she might really and truly have to disappear. Though she didn't like to think about it, she knew that it could happen in her line of work. So she had chosen Ashley and her new Jeep Cherokee as the lesser of evils.

"Yes. It disappointed me too. We weren't compatible, though—in any way. He was in missionary position on Wednesday nights at eight o'clock, in bed, with the lights off." That wasn't one hundred percent true—but maybe ninety-eight percent, which was close enough for this kind of conversation, which dealt more in emotional truth than actual statistics. Harmony didn't add that the sex with Beaumont in any position had become awful once she had fought through his psychic barriers and made a clear mental connection with him. The man had turned out to be an emotional vampire, able to suck the fun out of anything by making what she did—or what he thought she did, writing for an environmental magazine—sound trivial. His every act was deliberate, calculated, and competitive, and sex turned out to be no different. So intent on his own pleasure was he once he slipped between the sheets that she would have suspected him of thinking of female nude mud-wrestling to hurry things along. But that would be far too vulgar a sport for him. More likely it was golf, and he was thinking that every thrust needed to be a hole in one. In any event, golf or mud-wrestling bimbos, it hadn't had anything to do with her or what she thought, felt, or did. To him, she was a pretty accessory that could breed, little more.

"Bo-o-oring. And I thought he was so romantic, always sending you flowers and stuff. The guys in the office would laugh about how clever you were to seduce him. Not everyone will put out for the cause like we do, you know." Ashley was serious.

Harmony didn't flinch, but she made a note to be sure and punch the noses of the gossips at headquarters who were telling people she was an environmental whore, though that was more or less what they were supposed to think. Few people in her organization knew who she really was and how vigorous her participation in illegal activities was. To keep too many questions from being asked about her, she had been assigned the role of bimbo spy, a honey-pot who checked things out for a small environmental newspaper by hanging out in bars that catered to developers and other land-rapers, and then called in the big guns if anything was actually going on. No one knew that she actually *was* the heavy gun.

Her involvement with Beau wasn't job-related, though—at least not officially. That was hard to explain, however, because most of her work friends would be contemptuous of any confession that she had found this man in the enemy camp appealing because of his self-confidence, and that the exercise of his power was a kind of aphrodisiac. She had, though. Beau was a bad boy in a nice suit. Like many strong women, Harmony was looking for a man that shared and maybe even surpassed her strength and focus. Too bad that when she found one, he turned out to be a predictable jerk.

"I'd rather have good sex than good flowers." Though the flowers and other presents had been nice. And Beau had really liked her. At least as much as he liked his car and house, though perhaps not quite as much as his stock portfolio. As wealthy workaholics went, that made him almost romantic, even if seeing him in full work mode had eventually felt more like she was tagging along on a drive-by shooting than a date. Ruthless was one thing; heartless was another. Beau, she could now admit, was both.

"Tell me about it." Ashley threw back another shot. "You can't marry a guy who's a bad lay. Unless he's really, really rich. Beau isn't really, really rich, is he? Not like Bill Gates."

"No. Not really, really." But close. And Beau would get there someday. He had that kind of drive.

Harmony felt a slight pang as she further maligned her ex in order to justify her panicked flight. The sex *had* been pretty bad at the end. And mostly the bad sex was his fault for being a Neanderthal about women. Mostly, but not entirely. Partly the problem came from her actually seeing into his head and knowing what was really there. Women always said they wanted to know what men really thought about, but in her experience, knowing wasn't any comfort. The male psyche was murky, with base impulses that women were better off not knowing about. However, confronted with the reality of Beau's belief system, she had eventually given up trying to improve things between them. The mountain wouldn't move. He couldn't help most of what he was, at least not physically. Retrograde attitudes aside, he was a colossal perspirer who insisted on always being on top, where he dripped on her right through the silk pajamas he persisted in wearing even when they were being intimate—possibly because he was self-conscious about sweating, though that seemed like giving him a great deal of credit for sensitivity he probably lacked. Whatever the reason, at the end it had been like having sex with a smelly comforter with sharp knees and elbows.

He also always seemed to be trying to set some land-speed record at foreplay, only to interrupt things so he could make a last call to check on the Asian markets before closing. And that was on a good night. On a bad night, sex with Beau had been like having a plastic bag tied over her head while being jackhammered from below. She had tried to clue him in, but nothing worked. He just refused to listen. About anything. He nodded and said yes to everything she asked for, but she could tell that at his core he was as unchanging as concrete.

It was crazy, but as the weeks had passed and he had become more insistent about seeing her daily, she had found herself developing full-blown claustrophobia every time she passed the bedroom. And then there finally came a similar sort of phobia every time Beau got near her. It was his growing attitude of possessiveness. He felt that he owned her. And after that, sex had become something overwhelming, like being ravaged by a Viking horde. Except worse, because the horde just wanted your body and Beau wanted what he sensed she was holding back.

He'd begun with a campaign to meet her friends. She'd managed to duck that by claiming they were all in Indiana, and saying they would go back for one of her high school reunions. A month into the relationship, Beau had begun questioning her specifically about old boyfriends. He'd told her about his first failed marriage, encouraging her to greater intimacy by sharing his supposedly shameful secret. Only, she knew that he wasn't ashamed, because he didn't believe the failure was his; it was just a ploy to gain her trust. He'd waited patiently for days for her to reciprocate with tales of her past relationships, but she couldn't. Something told her that the patience wasn't there from love. It was the vigilance of the cat outside the gopher hole. She had laughed when he pressed her again for the name of her last lover, and said she had never been married, had no alimony payments and no kids and nothing else mattered.

He'd changed tactics then, asking to see photo albums or school yearbooks—hard to produce since she had never lived in Indiana. He continued to push her for details of her past, and she continued to evade. It was a sort of game, but it was growing less playful. She'd begun to worry that he'd call in a private investigator to follow her.

In the beginning she was reticent because she had been spying on him and didn't want to leave him any clues that he might follow up on later if she had to out him for being an environmental foe. And after she had found out he wasn't just another sentient slime-ball in a good suit, but actually very smart and ambitious and his company had surprisingly good ecological policies, and after they had become lovers . . . well, then it was too late. Whatever had held her back from being truthful after they were intimate, the natural time for her to confess her unusual hobby-job came and went without confession. She never found the way to tell the ultimate corporate warrior that she didn't just write little articles for the local newspaper about recycling, that she was actually what some people called an eco-terrorist. Or that she was wanted by the police in several cities and probably by some of the federal authorities as well. That he had probably even read about her in the papers.

It wasn't that she feared Beau would turn her in. No, Beau would protect what he felt he owned, however flawed it might be. But he would put an end to her career, and she couldn't endure the feeling that he was spinning a web around her, making it tighter every day so that he could eventually consume her mind and soul and remake her in some new image.

That a part of her wanted to be made over was frightening, a flaw she wasn't pleased to discover.

Hope began to die. She had started drinking then to dull the pain of his visits and the knowledge that she was probably going to have to end their relationship. First it was just a cocktail before dinner . . . and then wine with dinner. And then more wine after dinner. She never got drunk, but she drank just enough to mute the inner voice that was telling her that no matter how much Beau said he loved her and how exciting he was, the relationship was doomed to fail. He could endow her with all his worldly goods, but it would never be sufficient compensation for living a lie. She would become nothing but a shadow.

Yet even knowing this was true, she still hadn't left him. This part baffled her still. All she could imagine was that she had grown so lonely since her parents died that she had lost her reason.

Finally, in desperation to relieve the pressure, she had confessed to Beau that she was trying to write a book—a novel. That had surprised him, but it seemed a satisfactory explanation for her mental distance. Beau laughed at the idea of doing anything that frivolous but said it was perfect for her—was it one of those romance things? She had been annoyed by his patronizing tone, and had had to work to keep the thumbtacks and barbed wire out of her answers that night. Not that it would have mattered if she had yelled at him. Beau had a really thick hide when it came to her. He tolerated her foibles with what he thought was remarkable forbearance. In anyone else, it would have set her teeth to grinding—in fact, it *did* set her teeth grinding. Still, she found that she couldn't bring herself to write him off completely. People sometimes changed, she told herself. Things might still work, if Beau eased off a bit.

Harmony could see now that it was mainly guilt over toying with Beau's affections as she tried on the role of domestic partner that had kept her there, but it was also partly because Beau's attention *was* flattering. This powerful man could have had anyone, and he had chosen her. Never before had she been wanted this way. The men in her life had always been committed to larger causes, had other priorities and assumed that she did too. Marriage was out of the question for them. The difference between the life Beau offered and the one she had chosen had led her to question what she really wanted, kept her sitting on the fence long after she should have moved on.

Then one day she had discovered a jewelry box with a big fat engagement ring in it sitting on her nightstand. When she had touched it, she had had a flash of Beau's plans for her—the house and the kids and everything—and she had panicked. She had actually had a hallucination that a pack of murderous crows had come swooping down on her and tried to carry her away.

Harmony wasn't proud of herself, but she'd bolted. No longer unclear about what she did or did not want, she'd scribbled a Dear John note saying she needed to go to New York to be a writer, dropped off her ailing ficus with a neighbor, and alerted Anthony that The Spider was ready to work again and she would need a new job when she got back from Mexico. The Beau episode was over. There would be no marriage for her.

Anthony was elated. He had been terribly worried that he'd lose his greatest asset to another man.

Her clothes and portable computer that held her novel she took with her. There weren't all that many outfits in her closet anyway. Sometimes the lack of possessions and the roots they implied made her feel lost and a bit sad, but that day she was grateful for traveling light; she was able to close that chapter of her life in a matter of hours.

And that was how she had ended up in Mexico with Ashley, waiting to join a group of her conservationist friends of friends who were giving tours of the ecologically challenged lakes. Field work for the office girl. She would finally get to see the thing she had been fighting for—mosquitoes, leeches, and all. It was amazing what bad relationships could drive a fastidious young woman to do. Men!

And now she faced going back to work, a prospect about as alluring as a form letter from a credit-card company. Working undercover had been exciting at first, but eventually all the jobs and offices began to blur. Corporations are designed to be impersonal, and since she had to keep a low profile, making friends who might notice her activities was out of the question. And even if it hadn't been obliged to be distant, she didn't want to make friends only to move on a couple weeks or months later. So she had played the role of a corporate veal, staying in her six-by-six cubicle and growing anemic with the rest of the fodder. Not even the satisfaction of catching the bad guys was enough for her anymore.

Writing her novel was the first thing that had excited her in months. She hoped it wasn't a complete waste of time.

Looking around the tavern, Harmony now thought that perhaps she had overreacted to the situation with Beau. She stared at the smoky air and tables kept at something less than the highest standards of hygiene, and thought now that maybe it hadn't been necessary to leave the country to escape an engagement. Surely Beau would be so insulted by her leaving that he wouldn't follow. He was possessive but not obsessive. Wasn't he?

But the fact that there was any question in her mind was the best argument for playing it safe. Not just for herself, but for The Spider and what she and all the others in the movement were working for.

The man with the dark eyes and hair tilted his head, as though hearing her thoughts and weighing them for truth. Long fingers slowly turned the beer bottle he wasn't drinking from. When he tilted his head she caught a flash of gold at one earlobe. He looked like a pirate.

Harmony shivered.

He had beautiful hands—strong. Hands she suddenly thought that she might like on her body. He swept his long black hair to the side, showing more of his face. The candlelight was deceptive, but his skin seemed white, almost radiant, though his features were not Anglo. His hair was also thick and luxuriant, something that came from a mink. She found him superhumanly attractive.

Which was a strong clue that she should stop doing tequila shots before enough of them were able to unite and overthrow her brain's few remaining moral barriers. Or worse, demand their freedom from her weakening stomach. The booze was cheap down here, but throwing it up would be a waste and she was on a limited budget. She hadn't taken the time to fully invest in her emergency escape fund, and this trip was proving to be rather more costly than imagined, even with the price break she got for being in the trade, so to speak.

Besides, stopping now might mitigate the hangover that was surely coming her way. There would be enough to regret about the day ahead without that. Hiking through nature, staring at rare fish and endangered patches of grass in a crowd of earnest people—what had she been thinking? She could have just gone to visit her uncle in Iowa and saved six hundred bucks.

"I've lost my mind," Harmony muttered, still staring at tall, dark, and handsome.

"It's allowed after a breakup," Ashley assured her, but she was finally getting bored with the topic and her eyes had begun to wander over the men at the bar. There was a nice selection of new arrivals if you weren't fussy.

The shadow man smiled at Harmony. At least she thought he did, but it might have been a trick of the candlelight. There was something about him that grabbed her fancy—his face especially, though the body she could see under the table was long, strong, and lean. He obviously wasn't local, standing—or sitting—a good foot taller than the other men in the room. It was hard to identify where the exoticism came from. Not his chin; that was just a chin. His nose was just a nose. His mouth . . . well, the mouth was unusual. Full lips but slightly curled at the corners, as if everything amused him.

Yes, the mouth. And those eyes. She'd never seen anything like them. They were so dark that they seemed to have no pupils. Under their unblinking gaze, she felt her mind emptying of all wariness and common sense. With shock, Harmony realized that she was squirming in her chair, squeezing and releasing her legs in a subtle form of self-pleasure. She was completely turned on for the first time in almost a year.

"Oh no. No. No. No. I just escaped a man. And I'm a wanted woman. I can't. I can't. I can't."

"What?" Ashley turned to stare at the stranger. "Oh, he's *yummy*—like Johnny Depp. I could just eat him up."

"Not me. I'm on a diet." Shaken, Harmony reached out and poured herself another shot of tequila, keeping her eyes averted from other temptations. *Better the devil you know*, she told herself.

She was the one. The psychic tickle said so. Here was his reason for being in Mexico. Her body was small, but her power was great.

Alex cocked his head, tuning out the babble of voices around him so he could hear what was being said at the table by the room's one narrow window. His hearing was acute, but he was also listening with his mind. It was hard to tune out the other mental babble of the crowd, but he could if he concentrated hard enough. A few things about her he knew already. She was seeking succor in alcohol from a relationship gone wrong, but any balm she found there would be short-lived. This wasn't a woman who harmonized with an imperfect world. And she found the world imperfect, though she was far less discontented with it than her nymphomaniac traveling companion.

"I'm just the opposite of you. I had to give up celibacy, I really did," the one called Ashley insisted. Her voice and thoughts were easier to make out. Her aura was a topaz color that he associated with sexual irresponsibility. "Without sex, all I did was eat ice cream until I was the size of the mother ship from Mars. The only thing that keeps me on a diet is vanity and wanting to impress a new boyfriend. Or two. I do better with at least two, especially on these nature jaunts. There's just something about camping in the outdoors that turns me on. At least, I think it does. I haven't actually tried this Mexico thing before. . . . They'll have bathrooms out there, won't they? I mean someplace where I can shower. Maybe I better try for three. I hear that they have some really cute guys on these trips, and we won't have pay-per-view, I'm pretty sure."

Alex allowed himself to grin. Forestalling weight gain was the most ingenious reason he had ever heard for being promiscuous, but he wasn't going to quarrel with it. In his own youth, he had been romantically impetuous, not just involved in love triangles but love pentagrams. He and this female had this much in common. However, it wasn't this bleached blonde of easy virtue that intrigued him. It was her companion—less blond, less bold, worlds smarter. Her aura was a beautiful aurora crystal shot through with streaks of green. He could smell her too. She had an understated musk with a hint of fresh vanilla bean.

Her name was Harmony, and her nearly feline gaze was confident and shrewd—amused without being actively scornful of those she observed. Or it had been, before she and the blonde started making inroads on the bottle of tequila. Even after that, she had no trouble holding his own stare on the occasion their lines of sight collided, a rare feat because his unveiled eyes usually disturbed people. Not her, though. The mental connection between them was already strong and growing more so by the minute. He had had the feeling a moment before that she had mentally unzipped him and given him the once-over with psychic fingers. He thought that he liked this, but was also inclined to be a bit wary of instant attraction. Something told him that this meeting wasn't going to end as some casual sexual pickup. Fate wouldn't have dragged him to Mexico just to get laid. Fate was a bitch who always had big plans.

Harmony carried herself well, too, her posture belonging more to the nineteenth century than the twenty-first, though she was neither rigid nor corseted. She looked somewhat expensive, but not fat from pampering. She was lean, muscled, capable, and educated. This wasn't a sweet kitten who but a full-grown huntress could care for herself if push came to shove. He wondered about her pedigree and how many generations of strong women it had taken to breed a female this sure of herself. They were rare creatures. He'd only known two before her—Thomasina and George Sand.

Alex leaned closer, observing openly. She used silence well. From his years in the theater, he understood that silence is its own language, and few spoke it well because they could not endure the quiet. But she was fluent in the long pause filled only with a half smile or an ironical gaze. This was wasted on her companion.

Given her nature, he couldn't help but wonder what on earth she was doing with this blond bimbo in the wilds of Mexico. It couldn't actually be because of a boyfriend—not entirely. Not in this day and age. And why did she refer to herself as a wanted woman? Did she mean she was a criminal? How intriguing that would be. This kind of woman would only be involved in complicated, possibly political crime. He wanted to know more.

The waiter came by, bringing a plate of pulled pork marinated in tequila. The fork and knife were dirty, but Alex didn't complain. The old waiter, surrounded by a cloud of roiling gray, was like an apple-head doll that was rotting, caving in, and slumping forward on its stick body as bacteria did its work. It looked a bit as if the ancient creature had started to exhale and forgotten to stop. In another day, he would have been completely curled in upon himself. This place had a way of sucking the air out of your lungs and moisture out of your skin. One could drink fluids all day long, but over time, the inner tissues went dry. If you stayed in the desert long enough, you became a desiccated shell, a living mummy. But that wasn't what ailed this man. The smell of death was certainly on him, a scent Alex vaguely recognized, at least in its broadest outlines. It wasn't the desert that was draining him, though. It was something else. A parasite. Probably a vampire, though Alex didn't recognize this particular tang of evil.

Once, he would have wept for this man whose body and soul were in peril. But the sensitive youth had eventually grown up and learned that weeping changed nothing. It didn't alter Fate, or soften evil men's hearts. It couldn't raise the dead or cure the sick. . . . It was just that not weeping had once denied something inside of him, and it killed a little bit of his humanity when he denied it, so Alex had cried—cried for his dead son, and his lost friends, and lost ideals.

Then one day he had woken up in a waterlogged trench somewhere in France with shells falling around him and his companions dead or dying, and there were no more tears. The losses had become too many; any more grief and he would perish.

Instead of allowing himself to express any sadness for this doomed soul, Alex smiled at the old man and thanked him gently for his service as the tired body trudged back toward the kitchen. *Vaya con Dios*, he thought. *Go with God*. That was an odd prayer to say before a meal, but it would suffice.

The pork smelled good, but he had a sudden craving for shashlik, a dish he had learned to make in Russia. It was too bad that it took so long to prepare. Lamb had to marinate for twenty-four hours in vinegar and chopped onions and was then cooked on skewers over a coal fire. He liked it best with a side of crude bread with rose jam made with cinnamon and honey. When had he last fixed this? Was it at one of his dinners with Hugo, Balzac, and George Sand? Could it truly have been that long ago? The thought shook him. It was why he so rarely allowed himself to think of the past in any context except as material for his highly embellished novels.

And there wasn't time to be thinking about these things now. If there were a vampire nearby, he really couldn't allow these two women—or at least the one called Harmony— to wander into its path. Mexican vampires were not his specialty, but he knew that they were especially drawn to young, fertile women, particularly ones with psychic abilities.

Saint Germain might well be drawn to her, too. The thought was sobering, though it would make his old nemesis easier to find, if he came out of hiding in order to capture this female.

Alex wondered if she was at all aware of her abilities. It would be easier if she were. She might sense the evil floating in the air and believe the rather incredible story he had to tell her when he finally got her alone. If she didn't understand what she was, getting her to accept the danger she was in would be very difficult. That would be unfortunate, because he couldn't use her as a lure unless she was aware of the danger. That would be unconscionable, and he wasn't that big a bastard.

Alex ate with more patience than enthusiasm, watching

both Harmony and the bartender, who was flicking glances at the table where Harmony and her friend sat. The barkeep was a brown Chihuahua of a man with many of the stereotypical short-male idiosyncrasies. He also had an aura streaked with violet-red. Ten to one he beat his wife. If he caught the creature at it, he would hurt him, Alex decided. And if he went after Harmony, he would kill him. Alex abhorred men who were violent with women, children, or animals.

Alex mustered his patience, calmly and repeatedly making the mental suggestion that Harmony join him and that her companion go away. Finally Ashley got up from the table to go to the bar and began flirting with a sunburned Australian who was going on some sort of nature hike, leaving Alex's quarry alone and undistracted. When he turned his attention back to Harmony, he was pleased to see her get up and come walking toward his table. He wouldn't have to go to her after all. It was a small point—a bit of a power play—but he was glad to have it. This woman would be a challenge. It wouldn't be a bad thing if they began their relationship by establishing which of them would be on top—metaphorically speaking.

Alex allowed himself to look at her slowly from head to toe as she walked toward him. He couldn't help but smile at her shoes. They consisted mainly of a few extremely impractical straps of pumpkin-colored leather on heels high enough that it made walking a kind of performance art. And she managed it with grace even while inebriated.

Her skirt swayed as she walked. It and her blouse were made of an extremely fine woven cotton called Liberty Lawn. It wasn't something you bought in a department store. The style was old-fashioned, and she could have gotten it at some vintage shop in the U.K., but he was willing to bet that she had made it herself.

He regretted his own clothing. For this trip he was wear-

ing a dark linen shirt and practical black jeans with cowboy
boots—upscale but off-the-rack. Glib and pretentious. He
was not fond of clothing that required it be identified by a
brand. It was tactless, the announcement of the insecure that
they did so have taste but were also uncomfortable with
individuality—and he didn't see any benefit to having an
uncomfortable bas-relief of some designer label embedded
in his butt. Usually he preferred to wear the linen or lightweight wool suits that were made for him at a small firm on
the Rue du Faubourg-St. Honore where, it was rumored,
they used handmade Italian loafers to beat the couture-
challenged tourists who wandered in off the streets with
their rude T-shirts, rubber sandals, and melting pink ice
cream and then threw them back out with their dripping
gelatos. Though a loyal French Republican and a believer in
equality for all people, Alex still approved of this ruthlessness when it came to rude tourists. They were locusts,
spreading slovenly thought around the globe.

Unfortunately, he was playing the role of tourist this trip,
and like the chameleon, took on the protective but hated
coloring of his role. He hoped Harmony wouldn't hold this
against him.

"It's a good thing that looking at girls is free down here,
because you would have run up quite a tab by now. And
why that is, I cannot imagine," she said, pulling out the
chair across from him and sitting down. Her voice was
calm, but he could see the color in her cheeks and the pulsing red at the base of her aura. Before he could reply, she
added: "But then, I've been looking at you too. I've got to
tell you, I've never seen anyone like you before."

"No, you haven't," he agreed, and felt himself beginning
to smile. His mission might be grim, but this woman was
utterly delightful. And he'd barely had to push her at all to
get her to his table.

"You're French?" she asked, clearly surprised. Her

slightly elongated vowels and the rhythm of her speech said that she was either from or had spent a lot of time in the regions of the U.S. that bordered Mexico. The slight accent was music to him.

"Sometimes. I am also a writer."

"So am I." She smiled back. "A writer. Sometimes."

A writer—that would explain in part why her mind felt so familiar and was so easy to read. She was used to thinking with words rather than images. Word thoughts were easier for him to *hear*.

"I am Alexandre Dumas. But please call me Alex." He extended his hand. Alex didn't like this modern custom of shaking ladies' hands, but he wanted to touch her, to confirm by feel what he suspected.

"*Pére* or *fils*?" she asked without blinking.

"*Pére*, of course."

"Of course. He was the sexy one. You're a little paler these days, though, aren't you?"

"And thinner. It's this low-carb diet I'm on."

She smiled and finally took his offered hand and frowned slightly as a small shock traveled through her flesh, a bit of psychic sonar he used to know women. He watched her shiver and saw the red of growing desire flare around her. She said with a hint of breathlessness: "I think that I may be a bit drunk. The trouble is, now that we've met, I'm not sure if I should stop drinking or just keep going. It isn't every day that you meet a famous novelist. In Mexico. In a dive."

"So true. But don't underestimate yourself. You're already quite drunk. More would be pointless and probably even counterproductive." Reluctantly he released her. She felt good—very good—but he needed to move slowly and carefully and keep his mind clear. That was difficult when they touched. The echoes of her personality reverberated through him in disturbing ways.

The tiny frown disappeared as she stared at her freed hand. When she looked up her gaze was quizzical but still approving. He thought—not for the first time—that the eyes of a woman were the best of all mirrors in which to check one's appearance. Alex didn't care what was in the pages of *GQ*; he cared what would please his readers and lovers, who were mostly female and over forty. They wanted romance in their idol, and he gave it to them—watered down from the days of his youth, but still recognizable to anyone who read. For this reason, he wore his hair long. Older women especially loved this. He was glad that the younger Harmony responded, too.

"I'm Harmony Nix. The nix is a supernatural creature," she added helpfully.

"So is Alexandre Dumas."

"Apparently, though you seem more of a pirate to me. It's the . . ." She stood suddenly, looking about quickly as though searching for someone who had called her name.

"Would you come away with me, Harmony Nix, if I invited you?" he asked, looking about the room to see what had disturbed her but seeing no one new. He willed her to return her focus to him.

"I don't know. I suppose it would depend on how far away the invitation was for." Her eyes slowly returned to his face. Her words were distracted, though, and her head was cocked as though she were still listening for a voice.

"Ah—so it is a matter of meters and kilometers?" he asked, also listening intently but hearing nothing.

"Perhaps."

"I understand. I am a test of your judgment. Please take all the time you need to calculate a safe travel distance." He listened harder, using all his senses, but still sensed nothing. This didn't reassure him as much as it should have.

"Are you waiting for someone?" Alex finally asked. Harmony shook her head, then looked full into his eyes, probing

his secrets with her other senses. Fortunately, none of his secrets lay near the surface and she seemed reassured by his
calm demeanor.

"Let's go for a walk. I need some air that doesn't require
chewing." She managed to say *require*, but he saw it was an
effort. She really was quite inebriated. "Now. Please."

He raised a brow at the suddenly preemptory tone but
rose obligingly. If she were sensitive she would feel that the
room's shadows truly were growing fretful and suffocating.
And even without any psychic ability, the level of smoke
and noise was oppressive, as though the occupants sensed
that something hostile was closing in around them, and they
sought by force of will to drive the darkness back with
chatter and cigarette smoke.

Harmony looked to the bar. Alex saw Ashley give her
concerned friend a thumbs-up, encouraging her to leave
with a stranger so that she might do the same. Alex smiled
reassuringly at the equally concerned Australian who
thought he might be abandoned by his lucky find if the
girlfriend left the bar first. Alex waited for the man's face to
relax into bland acceptance, then opened the bullet-ridden
door that let out into an eerily dark night.

A trickle of music followed them into the breathless
darkness. There was only a ghost of a moon to light their
way, but this didn't bother Alex, whose eyes were as keen as
a cat's. Harmony seemed comfortable as well. Perhaps because she was using her mind's eye to find her way.

He inhaled slowly, checking the air for danger, but everything was calm. And if it became less calm, he had a Sig-
Sauer 220 tucked into the back of his jeans. The .45 was
very reliable, especially when loaded with silver bullets. He
had a second, smaller .22 pistol in his boot. It had only minimal stopping power and no range to speak of, but it was a
backup.

"So what do you do, Harmony Nix, when you aren't be-

ing a writer?" he asked, tucking her hand into the curve of
his arm. It was an old-fashioned gesture, one that he knew
wouldn't alarm her but allowed him to touch. They began
to stroll down the paved path lined with palm trees that led
toward the Iglesia de San Jose. The church was the tallest
structure in town and a natural destination. He allowed
himself to slip more deeply into her mind. He had used to
think of this trick as brain-visiting, but he had run into a
term in a science-fiction book that he liked better—a
mind-jack. He was plugging himself into her thoughts,
jacking into her feelings.

"You wouldn't believe me. Even the people who know
me don't believe me."

Her answer surprised him. Was she about to confess being psychic?

"You would be astonished at the things I can believe."
This wasn't a lie. He had never told anyone about his gift—
not after the night his father died. His mother had been terrified by his story of seeing his father's ghost, and had
worried that he would be called a witch. Later, there had
been other reasons for hiding his abilities. He was doubtful
that the seat of his mental powers could be discovered with
a scalpel, but he wouldn't put it past some eager-beaver Nazi
scientist with government funding to try finding it anyway.
Nothing much had changed since Hitler's day. Governments were not inherently evil, but they often gave refuge
to evil men. Some of those were scientists. He had no intention of ending up as someone's guinea pig.

Harmony hesitated, her aura spiking green as she tried to
clear her head. She was groping her way toward sobriety,
but the tequila still had the upper hand. Alex pushed her to
answer, and was glad when the emerald barbs paled back
into complacency.

"Is this heat normal this time of year? Do you think it
would be cooler on the roof of the church? We could go

there. Maybe there would be a breeze," she suggested, plucking at the thin cotton of her blouse as she turned toward the church. It wasn't physical discomfort that annoyed her, though. It was their conversation, which she had to sense he was guiding. And perhaps their proximity. He felt her like static electricity on his skin and was sure she felt something too.

"Only if you jumped off and enjoyed the wind of free fall as you plummeted toward the ground. It hardly seems worth the broken bones for only seconds of relief."

She smiled at this playful answer and began to relax. He did too. Something about her made him feel light, like a helium balloon that evaded gravity both physically and emotionally. Surely his earlier premonition of danger had been wrong. There couldn't be any real peril here.

"You want to know about me?" she asked.

"Definitely."

She seemed to think hard about this and then gave a mental shrug.

"Okay. What if I said that I'm a sort of cat burglar? A criminal? Though I am considered a folk hero in environmental circles. They sometimes call me The Spider. Maybe you've read about me. Certain papers absolutely adore writing about my exploits." She didn't sound defiant, but he sensed her sudden indignation as she recalled her press coverage. "Go ahead. Tell me that I'm mental, that The Spider can't be a woman. After all, all the newspapers have me pegged as a male because of the computer angle. Like you have to be able to bench press a truck in order to be smart enough to break into a computer network."

Alex laughed softly and quoted from memory the latest piece he had read on her: "'*The forces of law and order have proved no match for the master criminal who, with preeminent artistry and dexterous hands, has left behind a wake of dismantled alarm systems, empty safes and—most distressing for the victims—*

missing computer hard drives whose contents have shown up in the hands of "sensation-seeking reporters" and "the environmental lunatic fringe that make up the political arm of the radical new environmental movement." An enormous reward is being offered for any information about the identity of The Spider, but so far, law enforcement and the heads of corporate security remain baffled by this criminal who seems to have escaped from the covers of a comic book.' "

"Stopping global warming and preserving our forests—yeah, that's lunatic fringe all right." She added: "Was that the piece in the *Weekly World News?* They exaggerate a little."

"Perhaps, but the world needs heroes, and we have so few of them these days. You can't blame the press for trying to find one."

She blushed a lovely rosy color that only he and perhaps a few night creatures could see. The smell of sweet musk and vanilla grew. The scent was heady.

"Thank you. But it's not heroic," she said modestly, and with surprising truthfulness. "Usually, all I really do is get a job as a secretary or a cleaning lady in whatever business we've targeted. Then, when I know my way around and have learned some passwords, I copy files to my own machine, or else take their hard drives to a friend who can crack the security codes and open the files. Then we go public with the truth about who is taking bribes or getting kickbacks for evading governmental regulations and poisoning the world with illegal toxic dumps and stuff. It's really all about being patient and not losing your nerve."

Alex felt himself blink with surprise.

"But this is brilliant. You have no idea how delighted I am to hear this." And he was. The Spider had come to The Chameleon. This woman sounded as if she might be a female version of his younger self—brave, idealistic, and willing to take risks. Could it be an accident that she had come into his life just now? No, it had to be planned. She was the other eagle in his dream. She was the sign that things were about to change.

Out of nowhere, a shiver took him and he felt his heart begin to pound. It beat hard enough to shake his body. He was flooded with sudden hope and intense physical desire, a giddy combination that was new to him.

Harmony looked up at him, smiling slightly at his response. Her inner senses were probably telling her that he was sincere in his admiration. He just hoped it didn't also tell her how very much he wanted her. His eavesdropping had led him to think that this sort of naked desire in men seemed to be an issue with her.

"Either you don't really believe me, or you're nuts. I just said I was a criminal. That isn't delightful. At best it's titillating."

"Insanity is always a possibility," Alex admitted. "But in this case I don't believe it is a problem. You see, I am actually in Mexico on a similar type of mission. I too work undercover for the betterment of the world."

She blinked. "Really? I didn't know that you were an activist. You work for the French environmental movement?"

"In a way."

"Wow. That's some coincidence."

"Yes, I suppose it is. But true nonetheless. What do you Americans say—cross my heart and hope to die? I just keep my profile very low so that I do not disturb my American publisher. It is not entirely true that all publicity is good, you see."

"No, I know that. I don't suppose you can tell me what it is you're working on?" she asked. Her expression was earnest. "Is it more of those factory pollutants up by the border? Someone has to stop the dumping. I hadn't realized that it was so bad. The land is all but dead, and the people will be too if something isn't done immediately."

Alex chose his truths carefully.

"It's more of an outbreak of suspicious disease that I am investigating, and not in a factory. Perhaps I can tell you about it a bit later. Like you, I worry about being disbelieved when I as yet have no proof to offer in support of my rather wild supposition. I have not the standing of The Spider. I must collect more evidence before I can act."

"I understand. That's what I do—collect evidence. But usually from a safe distance. I'm not a foot soldier. I don't chain myself to trees or bulldozers. I don't go looking for diseases. That sounds a bit frightening." She leaned her head against his shoulder, clearly feeling comfortable. The red-orange glow of returning desire began to tint her aura. "Actually, I'm writing a novel about being The Spider—all heavily disguised, of course. I've made myself into a man and set it in England. It's taking me forever, though, because I never have enough time to write, and sometimes I get nervous about talking about . . . well, things. I'm not used to admitting what I do. It's too dangerous. I think I'm up to about fifty years of jail time now. I hardly even tell *myself* the truth anymore."

"Ah! But this is interesting. And I understand completely. Of course, you would have to change some facts to protect yourself." He didn't add that he did this all the time.

"And to make the story more out of the ordinary," she confessed. Her eyes positively glowed with enthusiasm, and Alex felt himself being drawn in by her excitement. "It's really rather boring, what I do, if you don't understand computers. Almost no close calls at all. I've never been shot at, or even threatened with a gun—not on the job at least. The worst I've ever done is play hide-and-seek with a security guard to move some things past airport security."

"I understand entirely. And it is not just sensible caution; it is a kindness to our readers that we take literary license to move the plot along. But tell me more about being The Spider. This fascinates me professionally. How came you to this line of work? Has the added security of the post-9/11 world made it a more difficult place to function?" he asked. Perhaps if they talked long enough, his desire would diminish and they could be in close proximity without endangering themselves. As it was, Alex was feeling that it might be wisest to stop touching her, at least for the time being.

"It actually started in college. My folks were elderly when they had me, and I lost my dad my senior year of high school. Mom went to live with her sister in Florida and I found myself at loose ends. I was asked by an old boyfriend if I could help with a project he was interested in. We had heard that this local mining company had gotten ahold of some old-growth forest and was planning on strip mining the land. Not just cutting down the trees but destroying the land utterly and completely. I was on spring break and not heading down to any of the parties in Daytona and thought—why not? I could use my vacation to do a good deed." She shook her head. "I did okay, but was careless and not as efficient as I could have been. Back then we were unorganized and testing methods of collection. We believed that simple civil disobedience and handing out a few flyers telling the facts would lead to consciousness-raising." She snorted. "I know, that sounds so naive. But our intentions were good. And we did learn from our mistakes."

"No, I don't think it naive. The pen is a mighty weapon when wielded correctly. And we need to have a bit of idealism to keep the cynics of the world from ruining our lives," Alex answered, thinking of his own efforts to bring about change in the French Republic. He'd done far wilder things than she had to further the causes he believed in, like supplying arms and even manning the barricades that Victor Hugo had written about in *Les Misérables*. He'd also ended up in jail for refusing to do military service for King Louis Phillipp. Had he not been so famous, his head would have rolled with the other patriots who were arrested during the uprising.

"I guess. I just got so frustrated when nothing changed, and I knew I had to take it a step further. That doesn't mean that I like everything I have to do. I hate lying to people all the time about who I am and what I do. And these fights aren't personal, like some of the papers have said. I don't do this to ruin anyone's reputation, you know. And I'm not a Communist trying to bring down all capitalists. Making money is fine if you're not killing the planet to do it."

"But many capitalists are?"

"Yes, too many of them. Some out of ignorance, but some because they are sociopaths. And, I admit, sometimes ruining these especially rotten jerks is an added bonus of the job. Many of these guys are utter bastards—complete psychopaths. Odds are ten to one that if they're raping the land they are also raiding their employees' retirement funds. Sociopaths rarely confine themselves to just one selfish activity."

"Like Beau?" he asked, testing the water.

"No, not like Beau. He's actually fairly honest." She didn't notice that he had brought up a name she had never mentioned. That was probably because of the tequila blunting her wits. "It started that way, though. I thought maybe Beau was doing something illegal. But he wasn't. And he seemed to really like me and he was nice. And exciting. That's rare in a man. Sometimes . . ." Harmony sighed. "But as we've agreed, nice doesn't get it done, does it? And to stay where there isn't love or at least honesty and a bit of respect would be to live a lie."

"Yes. And you are wise to know this. There is no substitute for genuine passion. Or the truth."

"There certainly is not. Or for freedom. I hate being closed in. He laughed about my book, too," she added in injured tones.

"The cad!"

"I thought so." She asked almost casually: "So, are you *really* Alexandre Dumas, the novelist? I mean, the modern one? I read one of the new stories and liked it a lot. You got the Dumas voice just right."

"I really am."

"But you're not really Alexandre *père*—like your publisher says?" She blushed as she asked this. Probably because what she was asking was if he was insane enough to believe something impossible. "Sorry, that was a dumb question. It's just that you have the right manner."

"That would be hard to believe, wouldn't it?" he answered without answering. "It does sell books to reincarnation enthusiasts, though, so let's pretend that I am. And perhaps I was him in another life."

"Okay. That's one lie I can live with."

She stopped walking when they reached the gazebo stairs and craned her neck upward. The structure had a Moorish feel that reminded him poignantly of Tangier. Abandoning her architectural study, she faced him, chin still lifted so she could look full into his eyes. Alex felt his breath catch. In the moonlight, she looked so much like Thomasina that he found himself thinking: *Come close. This time I know we'll get it right. I know how to keep you safe.*

No sooner had the thought formed than red desire flared around her and then reached out for him. Startled, he reeled some of his own emotion back in. This was not Thomasina. Persuading a stranger was one thing; overwhelming an inebriated innocent was something else altogether. A mindjack was acceptable; mind-rape was not.

"I don't think you're a liar. I sort of know things about people," she confessed. "I've always had a kind of gift that way. You seem very . . . shiny to me."

"I haven't lied to you," he said. Which was true, as far as

it went. But that was also still a long way from telling the truth, the whole truth, and nothing but the truth.

"Would you be upset if I said that I wanted to . . . kiss you?" she asked.

"No." He found himself smiling again. This woman made him giddy. "I've been hoping that you might return some of the . . . feeling I have for you. However—"

"Feeling," she murmured, leaning into him. "Yes, lots of feeling. We might almost call it lust at first sight. You may think this amazing, but I really didn't know that such a thing existed. I thought it was just a literary device, an excuse for characters to be promiscuous in the first chapter of a novel."

Lips pressed to lips. The almost forgotten jolt of pure desire and even harsher longing hit him, a memory of his last love repressed because the remembrance was more bitter than sweet. Thomasina—and yet so clearly not Thomasina.

He shut his eyes against the thought and braced himself against the waves of onrushing desire that would surely batter his heart. Sweet—so sweet! But only a fool would seek this out again. And what of her? Just because love's wounds left no visible marks on the body, it didn't mean that one did not suffer lasting pain inside once the anesthetic of first attraction wore off.

Or once someone died.

It was wonderful to enjoy women. To have sex—yes. He had to have that much contact or his soul would shrivel and die. But anything more? No, and then again a thousand times no.

Yet, he didn't break away from the kiss. The temptation was to taste just a bit more of what desire truly could be with someone who was tuned in to him mentally and could be his equal. It was elation he hadn't known in decades. It was panic too. And a crazy tingling in every nerve as electricity ran over his skin and tried its best to find a way inside her body and mind so that she would give herself to him without reservation, in spite of her fears of possession.

Harmony gasped as he thought this and arched into him. Beneath his shirt, he felt the net of golden scars that roped his chest stirring into life and spreading over his body. His flesh said it knew her as an old love, the other half of his wounded heart, and it wanted her immediately.

Insanity—sheer madness!

"*Mon Dieu!*" Alex leaned back onto the latticed wall of the gazebo. Harmony pressed against him. He raised his head to gain some distance, to assure himself once again that this was not his old, dead love, but rather a lovely stranger he had met only this evening.

Inches away and she was still beautiful. Still more desirable than any woman he could imagine. And yet achingly familiar because of the emotion she aroused.

Her hair was tangled in his fingers, a tumble of red-gold, feather soft. Gorgeous, the stuff of a thousand passionate dreams. He touched the strands, marveling at the silken texture of the mane around her shoulders. It was soft, like her mouth, and again he felt flooded with a surge of desire that was close to insanity—the kind that inspired artists and musicians to create great works, saints to renounce vows, and made even the sanest of men do foolish things.

He hadn't felt this way in seventy years. The knowledge was an almost physical blow. This was what he had been hungering for all this time. It was the balm of Gilead—a drug of blessed if temporary amnesia. It was forgetting, a divine intervention by a kindly Fate that made the pain of living an empty life for the last seven decades suddenly seem worthwhile. It was what he had believed he had to deny himself if he was to win the struggle to live after Thomasina's death.

Ever reckless, for a moment he let this desire blot out old

misgivings. He kissed her again. He would indulge, just this once.

Alex didn't need to do more than kiss Harmony to resurrect the recognizable feeling of the lust that preceded wild, life-altering love. And, on some level, he was grateful for the passionate memories she gifted him with, and aware of the rarity of this perhaps never-to-be-repeated insanity. The thought of further, deeper touching added to the pleasure of the moment of anticipation.

He forgot that he wasn't human anymore, that there was danger around them.

Alex picked her up with an ease that revealed his unnatural strength and went quickly up the stairs into the gazebo. Moonlight cut the darkness with bright bars of silver light that crisscrossed their bodies.

"Are you certain about this? I don't think this is something you usually do," he said softly, thinking she was perfect. All that was missing was music—something soft and probably heavy with a bass beat, an erotic soundtrack to score this most-longed-for of events. All he could hear was his heart.

"No, it isn't. But, yes, please. And be as wicked as you like." She sighed as he set her on her feet, as though now able to read his mind and see all the things he wanted to do to her. "I have been in a prison for so long and just want to feel without fear. To have without guilt."

To feel without fear. To have without guilt. He understood—*bien Dieu!* Yes, he understood.

"The pleasure is all mine."

He undressed her, enjoying the resistance of the buttons on her skirt-waist that only reluctantly came off to reveal the velvety skin of her abdomen inch by tempting inch until the strips of cotton could be pulled down her hips and pushed away altogether. Her blouse went next. She wore a camisole beneath it, a confection of coffee and raspberry lace that reminded him of a Viennese Sacher torte. It was more tempting than functional, though it extended down her torso and had a series of small pearl buttons that had to be undone. He kissed around the edges and then pulled the tiny loops free one by one, pushing the bit of silken non-sense away, revealing the perfection of her lightly tanned body, darker than his own.

He knelt before her, letting his eyes feast. As he had sus-pected, she was lean like a cat. Her breasts were gorgeous, her stomach a stretch of perfect skin interrupted only by a small tattoo of fleurs-de-lis at her hipbone and a fading scar from a long-ago appendectomy. For some reason the tattoo disturbed him, reminded him of someone in his past, but its association with his long-ago history eluded him.

She was thin, so he could plainly see the delicate articula-tion of the muscles beneath the velvety skin. He reveled in the perfection of her body! No knots of hard muscle to dis-turb her sleek expanses, no coarse hair bristled up to mar her flesh, just the smooth, almost liquid flow of erotic progress when she knelt and wrapped herself around him.

Finished with the first round of tactile exploration, he laid her on the floor. He took her right breast in his mouth, and bit softly with the edge of his teeth. Her skin was both sweet and salt, perfume and drug, a balance of the human and the divine. Alex shivered. He knelt again, reaching for his shirt. He wanted to rid himself of his clothes as quickly as possible.

"What's this?" Harmony asked, running a hand down his back and encountering his .45.

"A gun," he said. Then, realizing that this might be dis-turbing, he added: "Don't be alarmed. This is a wild place. I never go unarmed when I'm working."

"Oh. But you'll take it off now? I don't like the feel of cold metal." What she meant was that she didn't like the feeling of cold intent the weapon carried. He also sensed that it had been used to kill before, and death lingered on the gun like an invisible fingerprint.

Alex paused. He was almost mindless with desire, but what he had said was true. He didn't go anywhere without being armed. Especially not when his senses told him that danger was nearby. Still, Alex hesitated for only an instant. What harm could befall them in the middle of town? And it would just be for a while—minutes, perhaps an hour. Nothing more. And the gun would be close by. It wasn't necessary to hold the cruel thing in his hand.

"Of course. . . . Do you have any weapons with you— beyond being female?" he asked.

"Brass knuckles," she confessed. Her voice was a bit breathless and he could see her heart beating beneath her pale skin. "In my purse. I got them years ago in an antique store. They belonged to one Madame Belle who ran a brothel in New Orleans. I thought they might be useful down here."

Alex found himself smiling again. He put his gun aside, at a distance so she wouldn't feel it but still within reach.

"But how perfect! Still, I promise you'll have no need of them with me."

"I know. You're not dangerous . . . in that way."

Harmony was dazed. The usual self-consciousness of first-time sex was gone; like a cat on the prowl, it had slipped into the night at the first touch of Alex's lips. It never oc-curred to her that nudity in a public place was probably in-appropriate. And if it had occurred to her, she wouldn't have cared as long as he touched her.

A part of Harmony realized that this stranger—this Alexandre Dumas who carried a gun—was somehow inside her head, perhaps guiding her to this moment, perhaps against her will or at least her better sense. Odder still, she had this feeling that if she shifted her thoughts just a bit she

might be able to see into his mind too. As it was, it seemed
as if she knew what he would say and do a split second before he said or did anything. This should have alarmed her,
but her senses seemed entirely taken up by the weird but
overwhelming erotic sensation that was making her skin
dance and her muscles go weak.

Perhaps she was more drunk than she realized. But drunk
or not, she didn't care. She had thought about an encounter
like this—dreamed about it—for a long time: a sexual attraction to a strong man who wanted her, admired her—her
and only her—but didn't need to possess her for more than
the moment. She looked and looked at this Alexandre Dumas but couldn't see—couldn't *feel*—anything that frightened her. He wasn't insecure, or anxious, or domineering.
All she felt in him was intense desire tinged with a sort of
amusement, and a kind of expectation that reminded her of
a child waiting in the dark on Christmas Eve for Santa
Claus to arrive.

And he understood about her work, was involved in the
same area, so she didn't have to explain or shade the truth or
even flat-out lie about what she was doing. She could be
The Spider and not worry that he would be angry, frightened, condescending, or jealous. She could also admit to
trying to write a fictional book and not be ridiculed for her
goal because it was shallow.

Harmony sighed with pleasure and for the first time gave
herself over completely to the experience of brain-fogging
passion, letting Alex enter her thoughts fully and willing
him to share her elation and arousal.

She knew that this was a night she'd never forget.

Alas! In every man's life there are but two genuine loves—the first, which dies; and the last, of which he dies. That, unfortunately, is the love I feel for you.

—*Letter from Alexandre Dumas to Isabelle Constant*

I find my subjects in my dreams. My son takes his from life. I work with my eyes shut, he with his open. I draw, he photographs.

—*Dumas* père *on Dumas* fils

CHAPTER SEVEN

1801, near Brindisi, Italy

A turbulent darkness had fallen over the Cistercian monastery, lit-erally and spiritually. Saint Germain, though distracted by an over-whelming sense of accomplishment at his unearthing of La Cuore del Strega Sicilian, *still found time to appreciate the thunderous setting that lighted the austere beauty of the twelfth-century archi-tecture with flashes of heavenly fire. It was a fitting setting for his hour of triumph.*

Around him, oil torches burned, filling the air with noxious smoke that was damaging the beautiful frescoes on the chapel's ceil-ing. It was probable that the four monks in the room would have liked to protest the vandalism, but they had taken a vow of silence, and anyway, they were already dead, dispatched one by one with a bayonet to the heart.

Four men wearing various uniforms of Napoleon's army were busy packing up oaken crates with the many treasures that had been secreted in the monastery over the years. There was some low-voiced commentary about the smell coming from the corpses, an odd whistle of appreciation for certain relics made of gold and set with precious stones, and covetous glances as the men loaded the crates with spoils of which they would receive only a fraction, since they would need to bribe a lot of people to get the treasure home. The raid had already been an expensive one and required much planning and effort, not the least of which was convincing Napoleon Bonaparte that his Minister of Humanity needed to be imprisoned.

Once the boxes were loaded, the men began dragging them out to the cart that waited in the courtyard. It was hard work, but no one disturbed Saint Germain or suggested that he should participate in the physical labor that occupied the other men.

This might have been a sign of respect for the man who had masterminded the raid. It might equally have been due to the fact that Saint Germain's right-hand man was watching over them. The Russian, known only as Ivan, was a cold creature who had no passions for the things men were supposed to enjoy, like booze, whores, and looting. Ivan's two passions seemed to be serving Saint Germain and hurting people that his master was angry with. Rumor had it that Ivan sometimes went into a kind of blood frenzy and had been known to kill prisoners with his teeth and bare hands. That night, he also had an English blunderbuss, which he kept fingering suggestively.

Finally Saint Germain seemed to awaken from his fugue and he reluctantly closed the lid on the small casket that held the withered heart he had been searching for. The relic was misnamed; it hadn't come from a witch. It was something far rarer and more useful. His men thought that he had arranged this raid on the monastery for the gold and treasure inside the ancient building, but that wasn't the case. Of course, he loved gold as much as the next man, but there were other, wealthier targets he could have looted had that been his sole aim. No, the men were in this monastery because of this not-quite-dead heart. They were after a prize that he had desired most of his already long, long life.

Saint Germain's father had told him many fantastic tales when he was growing up, but the one that had most grabbed his imagination was the one about the Vesper massacre of Palermo.

It had happened on a gray Easter, in March of 1282. Through the collusion of Pope Urban IV and King Charles of Anjou, the French had been in occupation of Sicily for several years. As was the case in so many towns, the soldiers had rendered themselves abhorrent to the population by looting, raping, and generally carrying on as an army of occupation. The Sicilians had learned that they were not just Charles's new subjects, but were in fact being subjugated and with a fair degree of brutality.

The official story went something like: As the sullen crowd gathered under an equally sullen sky outside the Palermo Cathedral, a band of French officials joined the crowds, insisting on participating in the local worship. One of the soldiers in their retinue, drunk on the newly discovered stores of raisin wine stolen from a merchant from Malvasia, assaulted a woman at the edge of the crowd, attempting to drag her into an alley where it was assumed he was not planning to discuss theological issues. Most versions of the story said he intended rape, but Saint Germain knew better. The soldier had been one of his father's first inventions: a ghoul. He had not been able to get his regular meal of raw meat the night before and had gone crazy.

Unfortunately for this newly made ghoul, and indeed for France, the woman had an equally drunken and violent husband, one Galizia Caruana, who objected to the soldier's treatment of his wife. Caruana had come up behind the soldier and stabbed him. Repeatedly. Some would say excessively, since a bungled pig slaughter would not have been as messy.

Of course, such a mess had to be expected when you were cutting out someone's heart.

Naturally, when the murder was discovered, the officials ordered the soldiers to retaliate against Caruana by dragging him into the square for execution. And, naturally—but quite unexpectedly, at least for the French officials who had thought their positions secure—the crowd also responded in violent kind. Numerical superiority assured victory for the Sicilians. French blood ran down the steps and into the street outside the cathedral in a satisfying torrent.

Caruana was said to have bathed in it. Saint Germain knew what he had been doing. He wasn't bathing; he was drinking. And eating. Those early ghouls had been highly contagious, their condition passed on through blood contact. It was why his father had had to find another way to make them. Like smallpox or plague, their disease spread quickly and efficiently.

Father Charles Issert, a priest from Anjou visiting Palermo in the company of another French cleric, Father Jean Miroy, saw the violence erupting from inside the church and attempted to stop the bloodshed by rushing into the crowd with a cross upraised. But he was also slaughtered—by Caruana. History recorded it as a tragic, pointless death. Issert's dying did serve a useful purpose, though. Seeing a man of the cloth crumpled on the very steps of the house of God was a profanity profound enough to interrupt the escalating violence and allowed time for the Dark Man to clean up his experiment. Nevertheless, when the bells tolled later that morning, they did not call the faithful to church; they called the people to arms.

However, this was not the part of the story that fascinated Saint Germain. Slaughters in Sicily were commonplace. It was a side drama conducted between the dead ghoul soldier and the husband of the woman he had assaulted that interested him. Drunken Caruana, not content with killing the soldier and priest and escaping execution, had rounded up an ax and returned to the soldier's corpse. They said that he was setting about taking a trophy that could be displayed in the town square as a warning to others. He did not get far in this bloody task. His first blow severed the Frenchman's head, but rather than lying about as a dead head should do, the bloodied thing was said to have started cursing the drunken Caruana. Beside the body, the heart he had torn out earlier began to beat. Hearing fresh screams from the alley beside the cathedral, the shocked mob rushed into the narrow side street and discovered Caruana with a still-beating heart clutched in his hands.

Too horrified to intervene with anything more than prayers, the crowd allowed Caruana to be killed by the remaining soldiers, who, fortunately for them, used their pikes and therefore were not covered *in corrupted blood. Only the second French priest was brave enough to approach the body. Enraged by what he had witnessed and perhaps a little mad, Father Miroy had held aloft the beating heart and pronounced it to have been a judgment from God against the Sicilian people for defiling their cathedral and murdering innocent men on a holy day.*

After the verbal excoriation was complete, the chastened crowd had parted for him—and for his grizzly trophy, now wrapped in a cassock—and the Frenchman had returned to the cathedral unmolested.

The heart had disappeared after that, but it was rumored that it was kept by the other terrified priests after Miroy died that night— driven mad by what he had seen, they thought, but really by the contagion in the bloody heart he had handled. A good man, and by his own standards a damned one, he had gone ahead and hung himself rather than give in to the impulse to eat his brothers in Christ. It had saved the Dark Man a lot of trouble.

Now, finally, Saint Germain had the heart back—and he would put it to good use. Perhaps not at once, but someday he would have a use for this heart that wouldn't die. His father was wrong to have wanted it destroyed. . . .

No longer burdened with outgoing chests, two soldiers entered the looted chapel rolling a large barrel of wine between them. They laid it on its side near the altar and then set about punching a hole in its staves. It was unnecessary, since the barrel had been tapped and set with a spigot, but Saint Germain let them have their fun. A third soldier arrived, this one carrying a small drum of gunpowder and a flaring torch. Saint Germain was careful to remain a safe distance back, though this soldier was more prudent than the others and seemed content to merely remove the cork, rather than beat the gunpowder-filled drum into submission.

The remaining soldiers soon returned with several more kegs of gunpowder, which they stacked up near the leaking wine. The men had conveniently left their rifles out in the hall.

"The cart is loaded?" Saint Germain asked, his voice almost jovial.

"To the rails and she's ready to roll," one of the soldiers answered, flashing a small grin as he opened the last of the gunpowder.

"Good." Saint Germain nodded to Ivan and then, transferring his treasure to his left arm, picked up his dueling pistol. Taking careful aim, he shot the nearest soldier dead center in the back. Ivan, being careful of the drums, shot the other three unarmed men with the blunderbuss. They weren't killed, but they were too injured to do more than crawl.

"Ivan, I do believe we are ready to depart." A loud clap of thunder echoing up the passage underscored Saint Germain's words. The storm was worsening and so were the conditions of the road. It was time to go. He took down a torch, preparing to throw it into one of the many connected puddles of wine on the floor.

The Russian cleared his throat. Saint Germain turned and was met with a hopeful look.

"My apologies, Ivan. By all means, you may have the honor." Saint Germain handed the torch to his henchman and then walked quickly away. He heard a whoosh and then the heavy slam of the door. The explosion that followed was loud, but not sufficient to bring the building down. That didn't trouble Saint Germain. He wanted to get rid of the bodies of his comrades so that they could never be identified and traced back to him, not burn down the monastery. He was a godless thief and murderer, not a vandal.

Ivan rushed ahead of Saint Germain, shaking out his cloak and holding it aloft so that his master wouldn't get wet on the short walk to the heavily laden cart.

"Chi vuol esser lieto, sia; di doman non c'e certezza," Saint Germain whispered softly, staring sightlessly out into the night as Ivan settled the second cloak around him.

"What's that, sir?" Ivan asked, starting carefully down the mountainous road. The storm continued to rage about them, keeping close to Saint Germain, and Ivan began to shiver with cold.

"Whoever desires to be merry, let him; for tomorrow is never certain," Saint Germain translated, raising his voice slightly. *"I do believe that this calls for some champagne. Why stint ourselves? Almost all the scattered pieces have been gathered up. And isn't one of life's pleasures savoring the job that is well done? Is not the laborer worthy of his hire?"*

"Yes. Certainly, sir." Uncomprehending and unconcerned as long as Saint Germain looked happy, Ivan turned his attention back to the rain-slicked road. He never sensed the bullet that killed him a moment later.

Saint Germain laid the second of his dueling pistols aside and took up the reins. Ivan's body was pushed out into the mud. If he had more time, he would remake the man, but traveling with a corpse was inconvenient.

It was a pity that he couldn't tell his father about what he'd done. But the Dark Man was busy destroying an old rival, General Dumas, so that he could consolidate his power and influence over the emperor. He'd left it a bit too late, though. Word was that the general had already married, and the Dark Man's dream that he would produce a son, a child with certain gifts, might well come true.

Something—some ghostly finger—touched Alex lightly on the earlobe, the one in which he wore Thomasina's ring. It wasn't Harmony; her hands were busy elsewhere.

Disturbed, Alex raised his head and looked out through the gazebo's latticework and forced his eyes to focus. It was difficult at first because the night seemed ablaze with lights, an aurora borealis of color. But he forced himself to concentrate and finally saw something disturbing enough to engage his brain. Sly movement on the horizon. Were those clouds at the edge of town—a sudden summer storm? Or something else? As he watched, the stray wisps seemed to gather themselves. Then, in defiance of normal weather patterns, they began moving due east. A moment later, as though sensing they were observed and abandoning all pretense of stealth, they veered slightly north. They came rolling toward the gazebo and church, seeming eager to reach the only buildings of any size. Ahead of it came a hot wind that smelled of things unworldly.

Al Azif, he thought, remembering this Arabic word that referred both to the chirping of nocturnal insects and to the eerie, dry sound made by the chattering of demons who brought great storms at the behest of the wizard Abdul Alhazred, also called the Dark Man.

Alex gave himself a mental shake.

A storm . . . that wasn't the best news. He and storms had a love-hate relationship. On the one hand, they made him feel very high and potent and were the source of power from which he drew life. But they also sometimes made him lose control, his brain and body seized by a divine madness that made him do crazy things. They also interfered with his ability to mind-jack safely. And fight as he might against sexual arousal, the storm called up his erectile tissues, some delightful, but some old and vibrant-colored wounds that spoke of encounters that should have killed a normal man. In moments his body could be laced with a cobweb of golden scars that would actually begin to glow. If the storm was strong enough, he could sometimes be completely overcome, glowing unnaturally and shorting out anything electrical that was near him. Once, he had blown out a transformer that left several blocks near his Paris apartment dark for almost two days.

Alex glanced down. Harmony was lost in the moment of arousal, reveling in the strange new feelings. She wasn't paying attention to their surroundings, but surely even the most besotted of women would be bound to notice if he lit up like a sunrise and lightning began hitting the ground around them.

That cold touch came again, doing its best to regain his attention, and he knew even without the second warning that they had to leave this open space at once. As much as he desired to complete the act of sex—and he did, more than he desired his next breath—he couldn't spend any more time with Harmony Nix until they were away from the influence of this storm. As much as he hated to admit it, there was real danger of exposing his oddity to her before she had time to know and trust him. He was sometimes adventurous, but not foolhardy. Already the channel from his mind to hers was filling up with white noise and what looked and felt like black dust.

This thought had no sooner formed than a cloud of bats rose up from the church tower and momentarily blocked out what there was of the moonlight. For a moment he thought they were a murder of crows and he had another instant of dread. The bats did not fly as if on a hunt, but rather as if they were fleeing the approaching bank of clouds. They circled the gazebo twice, leaving him and Harmony at the center of a black tornado. Their shrill screaming pierced his ears, making him wince with pain.

Danger! Danger. Flee!

Yes, they should flee. But . . .

Alex frowned and shook his head, trying to clear away the sensual haze that, rather than diminishing before his resolve, was growing stronger by the second. If he didn't know better, he would think that someone was attempting to mind-jack his own brain.

Not knowing what else to do, he broke away from Harmony completely, realizing that their shared arousal was distracting him far more than he had appreciated. Her arousal was feeding his, which in turn fed hers and so forth, making it exponentially greater than anything he had before experienced.

This was bad—very bad. It was like some nuclear accident about to reach critical mass. Any more and he would be lost, out of control.

Shaken by his close call, he realized that for the first time the mind-jack truly was working two ways. Gooseflesh spread over his skin. Who or what was this Harmony Nix? This two-way mind-jack had never happened before—ever—and the recognition that it could made him wary.

"Alex?" Harmony's voice was groggy.

"I'm here."

Once apart from her, Alex tried again to think logically, to order the strange information that was pouring in via his standard five senses and his extra senses as well. Hadn't the article in the paper mentioned some freak meteorological events in the area where the ghouls were seen? Could this storm have been created by Saint Germain? Did the wizard have his father's powers to control the weather? And was that why it was affecting him so strongly?

Tezcatlipoca—Lord of the Smoking Mirror.

Alex blinked, wondering where the thought had come from. This *was* the land of the Aztecan death god, the storm-bringer, Smoking Mirror.

"*Merde.*" Saint Germain. Tezcatlipoca. Neither name was on his Christmas-card list. "Harmony," he said urgently. "We must leave—now. Get dressed."

"What?" Her voice was slow, drugged, her eyes glazed. She had been deeply affected, too, and was slower to recover.

The air around them began to vibrate and then shimmer. Unwilling to touch her, Alex sent her a sharp mental jolt, commanding her to awareness. He hated doing it, knowing it must feel like being slapped. Her glazed eyes opened and then focused as mental and physical responsiveness returned to her power. Like him, she seemed to have a difficult time reeling back her sensations, identifying which parts of arousal were hers and which belonged to him, but she was definitely trying. He attempted to put up a barrier in his mind, ending the strange mental translocation that was confusing her. The withdrawal from her thoughts, though only partial, left him feeling cold and lonely and very, very frustrated.

"What is this?" she asked, alarm finally focusing her eyes and lending her better muscle coordination as Alex pulled her to her feet. They both snatched at their clothes. A quick shimmy had her skirt back in place. She didn't bother with the camisole but pulled on her blouse and knotted it at the waist.

"A storm," he answered, pulling his shirt over his throbbing scars. But that wasn't all it was. This was nothing natural. It was coming fast now, and it trapped the rays of moonlight that dared to shine on it and bounced them back and forth between the watery mirrors caught in the flickering clouds. Finally, as if deciding that all was bright enough, the storm parted and sent out a beam ahead, questing over the ground like a giant's flashlight.

"What the hell is that?" she demanded again as she hunted for her shoes. "It isn't lightning, is it? Is it a plane? A helicopter?"

"It's trouble," Alex said grimly as he zipped up his pants and picked up his pistol. It was trouble that might follow him wherever they went, as storms so often did if they got a lock on him.

"This can't be natural, can it?" Harmony asked, concern growing in her voice as her wits sharpened. "Is it a weapon of some kind? Maybe something experimental that the military is testing?"

"Yes. I think it may be." But this wasn't from the military. Too late, he understood that they had wandered into some kind of trap.

A finger of light strobed in their direction, stabbing the ground near the gazebo. The smell of electrical burning filled the air.

Alex pulled Harmony down the steps, half carrying her because she hadn't had time to put on her sandals and the rocks in the street would cut her delicate feet. He carried her body with ease like—

—*like a pirate carrying booty.*

Harmony looked quickly from side to side.

"Was that voice real?" she asked in a whisper. Her eyes had grown wide. "I thought I heard it earlier—in the bar."

He hadn't heard any alien voices in the bar, but he had definitely felt the alien presence of something not human when he had begun making love to Harmony, and something had put the thought of Smoking Mirror in his mind. Perhaps it was some kind of ghost trying to warn them. That had happened to him before, once in New Orleans and once in Madrid, and it was the most benevolent of the explanations that occurred to him.

"It was real, but not a voice," he answered. He moved quickly, keeping to the deepest shadows, trying to get a sense of who or what was invading their thoughts. He also wanted to know if it was targeting him and she was accidentally intercepting its messages, or if it was after Harmony. Was she the prize it sought?

Or was she bait? For him? If so, she had to be unknowing.

The night was stubborn, reluctant to give over its darkness to the growing light, but even it could not hold back this strange beam and the lightning that began striking the ground. The claps of thunder that followed shook the air with enough force to make Alex think of earthquakes and volcanoes.

Alex put her down once they reached smooth pavement. Harmony finished putting on her sandals and then gasped and clutched her ears as a prolonged rumble of thunder rolled over them. It was so strong that it made his heart stutter as its own rhythm was replaced by that of the storm.

"I feel sick—dizzy."

"It's a fluctuation in the electromagnetic field. Into the church," he ordered, breaking off from his run toward the inn and dragging her back toward the old brick church. It was the tallest of the town's buildings, but also the sturdiest and had the thickest walls. There was also bound to be a basement area where they could shelter from the worst of the tempest.

Lightning struck about ten feet behind them, a deadly warning, but Harmony's steps still slowed as they neared the church.

"Oh, God!" Her head whipped to the right and she began to sway. "I can hear them! It's getting stronger."

Alex didn't ask what had upset her. He could clearly see the onrush of rats, snakes, and scorpions coming up one of the side streets, scurrying toward them in a panicked, stinging, and biting horde.

"They're running from the storm's floodwater. They'll ignore us," he said, but knew that what they were fleeing was being charbroiled by something unnatural, the same something that had driven off the bats. He heaved Harmony onto the steps of the church. A thick expanse of old planks blocked their way inside. "Stand to the side while I open the door."

Harmony pressed herself against the wall, eyes focused on the approaching multitude of scorpions and rats that had spilled into the main street. The rats' screeching hurt his ears.

"Hurry. They're close."

The church was locked and the door heavy, but a portal was only as strong as its hinges and latch, and these had aged. Knowing he'd need his right hand for shooting, Alex leaned into the door with his left shoulder. He broke his clavicle forcing the door, but he got them inside before either the lightning or the terrified animals found them.

Alex shoved the door shut as soon as they were inside, then leaned against it, breathing hard and fighting off the waves of pain that radiated down his arm and into his neck as he shoved the bones back into place. It was bad at first, but he knew from experience that he could heal very quickly when there was a storm in the air.

"Thank God the church was open," Harmony whispered. In the dark, she had not seen him force the door, though she must have heard the scream of the hinges tearing loose even over the thunder. Or maybe she hadn't. The rats' squealing had been very loud.

"Yes. Thank God." His voice echoed, too loud, too eerie. "Come sit down."

"Gladly. I've never felt anything like that. My God! I've got a headache too big for Excedrin."

"I hurt as well," he admitted.

"Thank God you thought of the church. I don't think I could have made it to the inn. My muscles just seemed to give out all of a sudden. Could it have been the storm?"

It had partially been the storm, but mostly it had been him. His arousal had almost killed them both.

"Just rest. We'll leave when the storm passes."

At his words a silence fell, but they had only a few moments of relief from the deafening noise and then all around them the darkness began to rustle.

"I hear something. We're not alone." Harmony's voice was softer than a whisper and her body had stiffened. Her eyes were wide.

"No, we're not." He swore in French. A thought about the church—a really nasty one—occurred suddenly, and he cursed his earlier inattention. This town wasn't just a trap. They were being herded someplace. And where had the worst of the lingering magic been in Lara Vieja? The old church. "It's the crypt, of course. I should have thought of that. That's where they'd be."

"More rats?" she asked, doing her best not to sound alarmed. "We can get up on the pews. Maybe they won't notice us if we're still."

A horrid but familiar odor touched Alex's nose.

"No, it's something worse." Alex forced himself to move toward the small table where a few votive candles flickered in pools of spreading wax. This wasn't the way he had planned on explaining why he was in Mexico, but he was going to have to say something. He was going to have to trust that his eagle was ready to fly. "Come here. We don't have a lot of time."

Harmony's body moved jerkily, but it moved. Panic hadn't paralyzed her. Yet, it was hard to know how much more she could take. She was, after all, only human.

"Light the other candles," he ordered. Light would reassure her, and this would give her something to do while he tried to explain what was about to happen. An occupied brain was less likely to panic. She would need help, he was sure, because the mental tie between them was failing in the growing storm, and he wouldn't be able to aid her much with what lay ahead if it failed. Already his head was filling with white noise, masking her thoughts and even muting her aura until it was only a dull glow. He hoped it wouldn't actually storm inside the church.

To her credit, Harmony didn't argue or ask questions. Perhaps she was still sufficiently mentally attuned to him and sensed that they were in real, if as yet unidentified, danger.

"Here. Take this gun." When she was done with the candles, Alex handed her the small pistol he kept in his boot and then drew his .45. He regretted not bringing a spare clip with him, but who would have thought that he'd want more ammunition than could be carried in the full loads of two pistols?

"You have two guns?" she asked.

"There is something very, very bad coming up those stairs," he said. Alex kept his voice calm, doing his best to dislocate the alarm that he sensed gathering in her reptile brain and threatening to invade her thinking mind. A bit of caution was good in a tense situation, but floods and riptides of adrenaline could paralyze a person, and he needed her able to respond quickly, to defend herself. To run if all else failed. "I need you to stay calm. Panic would be unwise."

"How bad?" she asked.

Alex stopped talking and inhaled through his mouth, tasting the air, trying to tell how many of the enemy they might be facing. He smelled the scorching stone where the lightning danced, but something else as well. To the nose of an uninitiated, it might seem like rancid grease on the top of a cold stew. But this lard didn't come from mutton or beef. It was almost human. That was a strong hint that Saint Germain—or someone else just as evil—had been there.

"The worst thing you've ever seen or imagined," he said truthfully.

"Great. Lucky me. I guess this is destined to be a night of firsts."

Harmony's words were unhappy. The gun felt fine, though—much better than being without one in this situation. That was rather odd, because she'd been raised as a dyed-in-the-wool pacifist.

Harmony's parents married late and she came from a family of mostly elderly, squeamish people. Added to that, she had worked all of her adult life for a nonviolent ecological group, so she couldn't explain why she had taken so readily to guns and shooting. Forbidden fruit maybe. Or perhaps it was the cool factor of being a female and carrying a gun. Miguel Santos, her first boyfriend, had certainly made shooting seem fun. It had become part of their regular Saturday routine back in high school. They would hike into a deep wood whose only path was along a deep stony creek. She would bring a picnic lunch and he would bring the rifles and a box of ammunition.

In any event, though badly frightened by what was happening, the small handgun Alex handed her didn't feel as alien as it might have, and she had no problem opening it up to check that it was loaded. She looked up from the pistol and found Alex actually smiling at her. His eyes were as black as midnight and danced wildly in the candle's flickering light. She found that her desire for him had been driven back by the storm and danger but was not entirely gone. Something about this man appealed to her at a fundamental level, the same place that said she needed air and water to survive.

"I'm so glad I found you in time. God knows what might have happened if I had lingered another day on the road," he said, turning toward a dark opening that presumably led down to the crypt. "Now, *chérie*, the matter is fairly simple really. You must kill the things that are coming for us. Kill, not wound. It's one to the head, one to the heart—and don't hesitate because they seem vaguely human, for they will try to kill you. Or worse."

"Worse?" These were hardly the words of a guardian angel.

"Yes. I don't know precisely what is coming, but none of these creatures is a vegetarian, and they carry a . . . disease. One you don't want."

"But—" The first of the things—the monsters—came boiling out of the dark before she could say more. It arrived in a flurry of limbs that passed over their heads and landed spread-eagled against the wall where it clung like a spider. Alex spared it only a glance, but Harmony spun around, able only to stare in disbelief. The creature's hairless head pivoted around until it was facing backwards. To turn like that required the dislocation of every vertebra in the neck. The eyes glowed as they looked in their general direction, and its jaws full of needlelike teeth snapped open and shut with an audible click. Something that looked like a giant stinger jutted in and out of its mouth.

Impossible. It was impossible. Yet the thing hung on the wall in front of her.

Harmony raised her small pistol and sighted on the thing's head. It quickly repositioned itself so it faced downward. The flesh of its neck surrendered to gravity and gathered in folds at the chin. Had the bony protuberance not been there, the skin would have slid over its head like a cowl. Its mouth opened and it made a noise that she had never heard outside of a nightmare, a vibration of dead and decaying vocal cords. Its skeletal arms flexed twice. It was getting ready to spring.

"Marymotherof God," she whispered, her aim wavering for a moment.

"*Non.* This one plays for the other team. Shoot it. Now."

Harmony didn't ask for clarification of Alex's instructions. There was no need, because it was suddenly as though he were still with her—not just in her mind now but actually in her body—guiding and steadying her hands. She put a round into the creature flying at her at an unbelievable speed, and watched with unnatural emotional detachment as the bullet entered and then vacated the thing's head. It rocked backward in the air and then hit the floor with a squishing sound. It raised its shattered face and looked her way. One eye was gone. It didn't bleed, but a bit of what looked like beef jerky and clotted jam dribbled down its cheek. Something in its ruined expression finally was reanimated and it seemed to again recognize her. Then it did something awfully human. It raised its clawed hand to its head and touched it. It mewled as if hurt.

Ha-a-armony, it seemed to wail.

The thing knew her name.

Kill it, something whispered.

Horror and panic tried again to touch her, but she pushed it back. Or Alex did. Coldly, methodically, she lowered her pistol and put a second bullet in the monster's heart.

Beside her, Alex, who was facing the opposite direction, did the same. Repeatedly. Belatedly understanding that the attack wasn't over, she shifted her aim back toward the crypt and repeated the horrible process of killing these . . . these things. This time, she did so without aid. Alex was gone from her mind. He'd left, somehow taking her fear with him.

In less than a minute, four monsters were dead. If there were others, they had retreated back into the vaults.

Silence fell like an avalanche. Outside, the lightning had stopped, ending as abruptly as it began. Almost immediately, Harmony felt herself mentally reconnecting with Alex. For a moment she resisted the joining, and then relaxed and let it happen. He didn't push in rudely, just hovered near the surface, waiting for an invitation.

"That better be the last of them. I am out of ammunition." He sounded matter-of-fact when he finally spoke. This definitely was not an angelic being.

"Were those things infected with the disease you are trying to stop?" she asked shakily. The candles wavered madly and reached for the door as though wishing they could flee the scene. She didn't blame them. It wasn't the first time killing had been done in a church, but that didn't make it any less blasphemous or shocking. Her first impulse— second and third as well—was to run out into the night and not stop until she found the sunrise.

Alex blinked once and shook his head as though clearing it. Harmony realized that her ears were ringing from the gunfire.

"Yes. They are part of the plague. Though I did not know that things had . . . taken this form. Not in an actual city. I'd heard talk of this happening long ago in Sicily, but . . ." He trailed off. "Surely even he is not that mad. He wouldn't bring them into populated areas. He'd be found out."

"I don't know what *he'd* do, because I don't know who *he* is. And I think all I want to know right now is what we do next," Harmony said, taking a step in the first monster's direction. She was unable to look away from the thing she'd killed. Its mouth was open, unhinged like a snake's jaw. Beyond the teeth it had filed into points, it had some sort of scorpionlike stinger attached to its tongue. "Is this . . . it looks like some kind of . . ." She couldn't think what it looked like. "Are they escaped lab animals? Mutated chimps from a genetic experiment maybe, or . . ."

But surely chimps couldn't talk—couldn't cry her name.

"Don't touch it! It isn't just an animal," Alex warned. He added: "And I don't know if they're contagious."

She halted mid-step.

"But, surely they aren't . . ." She stopped. She had been going to say *human* and then found she couldn't. But of course that was what they had to be. She didn't believe in aliens or monsters, and these were not any kind of animal she had ever heard of. They were diseased, mutated perhaps, but surely human. The dark and storm had just confused her senses. Her eyes and ears were lying. She just needed to look again and she would see the truth.

Of course, if they were human—no matter how diseased and mutated—did that mean she had just committed murder?

Harmony began to feel a bit ill, but before emotion ran away with her, Alex intervened. His mental touch was gentle, reassuring, as though he had laid a steadying hand on her arm.

"Human? Maybe once upon a time. They are what the locals call vampires, but I think that they are also some kind of ghoul. Designer ghouls are his breed of choice, though he traffics in zombies if he hasn't time to make a ghoul. We'd be better off with zombies." Alex exhaled, letting some of the rigidity leave his body.

"Zombies? Like flesh-eating monsters? Or do you mean those poor drugged souls that voodoo priests bury alive and then dig up once their brains are gone?" She knew what the word usually meant, but for some reason couldn't quite accept what Alex was saying. It was beyond what her rational brain could accept. "But this is a disease. Isn't it?"

He took a moment to answer.

"Yes. I don't mean zombie like in the movies. None of these creatures is like anything dreamed up in Hollywood. I use the words ghoul and vampire because that's what the locals call them and I don't have better words to describe what they are."

That was better. Still terrible, of course, but within the realm of reason. Disease was awful, but she could deal with it.

"So these are . . . what? Genetic experiments? Illegal ones? Maybe something dreamed up by terrorists?"

"Some are genetic experiments," Alex said carefully. "But some are surgical creations—involuntary ones. Look at the legs on this creature. Those aren't human."

Reluctantly she did. It was dark, but she could see enough to be horrified. The only image she could come up with was an ostrich. The scars showed every stitch plainly.

"Emu," he suggested.

"But that's not possible," she said, horrified. "It's against the laws of nature. The human body would reject—"

"And yet it is here."

She shook her head slowly. She was thinking that she had put armor over her emotions years ago as a way to deal with the stress of her work, and usually it offered enough protection. But this horror had gotten inside her, and she could feel its corrosive visions eating at her resolve and at her reason. It was as though someone had taken away the underpinnings of her universe, that she had suddenly discovered that the sun was gone forever, or that gravity had disappeared.

"And no one knows about this? I mean, I'm in touch with a lot of people down here and I haven't heard anything about a disease or surgery that could cause this . . . this kind of mutation." The creature in front of her had had its lower jaw blown off, and its black tongue hung down like a necktie. The tongue also seemed to have some kind of stinger or needle on the tip. Could it be some kind of ritual piercing? She knew that there were sick people who were into body mutilation, but she had never suspected that anyone could carry things this far.

"You have to go back to the Aztecs to get a clear account of things. They knew about these creatures." Alex spoke calmly.

"Vampires and ghouls?" She was skeptical.

"If you don't like the term vampire or ghoul, try Jabberwocky or Bandersnatch. Lewis Carroll's names for monsters were as well suited as 'vampire.'" Alex went on quickly, returning to the medical explanation she seemed ready to accept. "As for no one knowing about this, you're right. It isn't common knowledge. I don't think there was an IPO on this venture, given how very illegal this kind of experimentation is. Our evil genius isn't exactly a practitioner of mainstream medicine anyway." Alex added softly: "I wonder if the Dark Man knew about any of this."

"The Dark Man?"

Alex shook his head. "We haven't time for more explanations just now. Do you still have ammunition?" He waited as she checked the gun.

"Two rounds."

"Good. Wait here. If anything moves, shoot it. I have petrol and flares in the jeep. And a mask and gloves for you and some sanitary wipes. We'll take some samples, then I'll roll the bodies into the crypt and burn them; then we can go."

Harmony let the words *vampires* and *ghouls* and his plans for illegal cremation slip by without further comment, being much more concerned with the thought of being left alone in a place where monsters lived that could survive being shot in the head and heart.

"I'm not waiting here alone! And don't you need a mask and gloves, too—if this is a disease?"

"I don't know. I shouldn't. I am supposed to be immune

to such conditions, unless . . ." He shrugged his right shoulder and looked down at his gore-spattered shirt and grimaced. "But, you're right. Best not to take chances. Everything has changed. I need more information before I do anything. And we need to get you out of here before they find you again."

"They?"

"The rats, the ghouls, the storm—take your pick." He swiped at the clots on his shirt.

"Oh. Right. . . . But you're really safe? If so, thank God for small miracles. But how is it that you're immune? Is it—oh, geez!" She looked at her blouse, now freckled with gore, and backed up a step. "The contagion isn't airborne, is it? You can't get it from casual contact?"

"No, this disease isn't casual. You have to exchange body fluids to get it."

Harmony forced herself to breathe.

"Then how are you immune?" she asked.

"This is the hair of a dog that already bit me. In Greece." He rolled his shoulder carefully. "And as I said, I don't think it can be spread except through blood-to-blood contact. If it were airborne, everyone in town would be infected. We're safe." He glanced toward the vault. "Relatively."

"Right." Harmony exhaled. "So, you mean you've actually been inoculated? There's a vaccine for this? Can I get it?" Wild thoughts about secret government experiments on third-world populations raced through her head. It was crazy, paranoid to think that way, but she liked that idea better than the thought of supernatural vampires that had begun to sprout in her brain.

"Not inoculated, but exposed long ago—and I lived through it. At least, it was a form of this disease. A less lethal one, I think."

"Did it change your eyes? I've been meaning to ask you

about them. They're beautiful, but I've never seen eyes so dark."

Again the pause as he weighed what to say. She wondered if he would believe her if she told him she wasn't given to panic and that he could trust her with the truth, however disturbing.

"Yes. All of us who had Dippel's treatments have eyes like mine. It is a sign of our exposure and change." Alex moved toward the door.

"Dippel?" Realizing her feet were cold, Harmony looked about for her shoes. She had dropped them when Alex handed her the gun.

"The Dark Man. I'll tell you about him later." Alex opened the church door carefully and the main brace fell to the floor. He was favoring his left shoulder. It was only then that she realized he had actually smashed open the church gate, dislodging the heavy iron latch with his body. It was one more shock on top of many.

"Alex, how did you . . . ?" She gestured at the door as words failed her. It was three inches thick, made of solid wood planks. Not even the king of Hollywood kung fu movies could have broken through it.

"Another side effect of my condition is that I am very strong. Just as they are. That is why you must shoot them from a distance. You are not strong enough to best them in a hand-to-hand fight." He looked at her, clearly willing her not to take fright now that she knew some of the truth about him.

"They're like you?" she asked.

"Not hardly. I haven't been surgically mutilated. But we were exposed to this condition through the same person. We have some of the same . . . side effects."

"I see. You're psychic, aren't you? That was you in my head, helping me shoot." She didn't mention that he had been in her head when they were making out, a conduit for the sexual attraction that flowed between them. Eventually she would want to know about that—but not now.

He waited patiently, a long-fingered hand resting against the ruined door. The smell of the corpses was beginning to pollute the air. A quick glance told Harmony that they were already rotting. Just like in the vampire movies. Only, way less attractively. They weren't turning to dust but rather to goo.

"Yes—after a fashion. But the psychic abilities are not from the . . . disease. Or the other changes that have happened to me over time. Not entirely. I have always been . . . gifted." He paused a beat and then added: "Like you. And that's why we are in particular danger. I believe we were deliberately targeted by the man who reinvented—or reengineered—this ancient plague. Those creatures wanted to capture you and to kill me. At least, that's what I believe. They wouldn't have been so careful with you had they wanted you dead." He seemed to add this bit to himself.

His words chilled her, but she didn't doubt them. Now that she had time to look inside, this was what her gut was telling her as well. How else had that creature known her name? And how had they found her? She had only just arrived in Mexico. Had she been followed? And if so, why? And then there was the strange voice, the unanswered questions that were causing a logjam in her mind.

"Why not capture you too? You're psychic and . . . different."

"Because they knew they'd never take me alive." He was calm when he said this, but the words were still horrible. "As you may have gathered, I know—intimately—the man who is responsible for this. I . . . I encountered his father many years ago when I was looking for a treatment for blindness . . . and got something else altogether."

She gazed into the blackness of his eyes.

"Is it an accident that you found me here?" she asked finally, putting a hand over her nose and mouth, trying to shut out the odor. It didn't work, though. The vile scent was sly and had a certain filthy robustness that she knew would cling to her clothes even after she washed them.

"I did not know of you before tonight, though I think I sensed you earlier," he said. Then choosing his words carefully, he added: "But as to whether it is blind luck that we should meet now . . . well, I have never thought that luck is particularly blind. Good or bad, I believe our fortunes are guided. But enough of this. We have to move now. Danger still stalks us. Our enemy will send others after you the moment he knows that something went wrong here."

"Okay. I don't want to wait around for a face-to-face with whoever dreamed this disease up. So I'm going to take you at your word about all this." She definitely needed more answers, but Alex was right; this wasn't the time or place to indulge in long conversations.

"That's best. You really don't want to meet the man responsible for this."

Harmony took a last shallow breath and then stepped out of the church. She looked about quickly, but the streets were empty.

This time she managed the walk toward the inn on her own. The last side effects from the tequila had been burned from her body by the fires of panic. Though she peered cautiously in every shadow and listened with all her might, there was no sign of the rats and scorpions that had been rioting in the street. All was peaceful, washed clean by the violent rain.

If only that were true of her mind.

They moved swiftly through the drying streets, in spite of Harmony's high heels. Alex was thinking hard about what had just happened and what it might mean. *There are more things in heaven and earth, Horatio*—as the world's second-greatest dramatist had said—and perhaps vampires really were almost routine down here, so no one was upset about them living in the church crypt. But he couldn't accept that these hybrid ghouls were part of the local ecosystem. Unlike the stories of vampire priestesses who lured strangers to the lake by night, there were no legends about ghouls—no folktales, no Aztec art, no ancient artifacts. No, these creatures might have been the local death god's priestesses once upon a time, but they were Saint Germain's creatures now.

Of course, that rather begged the question of what had happened to the local godling who had made these vampires: Tezcatlipoca—Lord of the Smoking Mirror, god of sorcery, nighttime, and storms, the shape-shifting trickster, the Great Tempter, the vampire-maker. Surely he wouldn't have surrendered his priestesses willingly. Was Saint Germain strong enough to kill a god and take his worshipers? The thought was chilling.

"What's that building across the street?" Harmony whispered, her words a welcome interruption. She stared hard at the small square that had only one small window and a narrow door.

"A jail—let's hope we don't end up in it." His tone was absentminded as Alex scanned the stone facade. His senses said it was empty. "Even if they know about the monsters, I can't imagine that the locals will be happy about a spot of arson in their church. We'd best do what we must and then be away this very night."

"Have you ever been arrested?" The question was tentative, but not fearful.

"Many times and in many countries."

"Oh, are you with Amnesty International or Greenpeace?" she asked optimistically, obviously still hoping for a logical explanation that fit in with her understanding of the world. He didn't blame her, though it would be easier for him if she could accept what was really happening.

"Something like that," he answered with a sudden grin as he glanced back. "If it makes you feel better, I've almost always ended up in jail for refusing to do things than for anything that I've done."

"You're a conscientious objector." She eyed the pistol dangling casually from his hand for a moment and then looked up at his face. "But not a pacifist."

"Sometimes I am both." He decided that this wasn't the moment to bring up the fact that he had fought several duels and even wars and had probably executed more men than most serial killers. "Let's say that I am not ruled by dogma, and have learned to be flexible. I have one firm belief, though: war is usually wasteful. It's a wholesale squandering of lives usually for the benefit of a few powerful men and their corporations. And yet, sometimes, it is the only option. This may be one of those times. This creature I am hunting—the one who re-created this *disease* and turned it loose on the world—he hates me. He hates all people. And he would kill us—or anyone else, indeed, *everyone* else—if there was some profit to be had in it. He might even do it just for sport. He is completely insane and amoral."

"And that's why you want me away from here. Do you think he will eventually kill me if I stay here?" She clearly found this difficult to ask, though he had told her his opinion before. "And he'll kill you, too, if you don't leave here."

"I know he'll eventually kill you if you stay, especially if he thinks you are important to me. He hungers after spiritual power—after psychics and other *gifted* people—and he believes that he gets his power by ritual murder of people like us. And if he can also inflict psychological torture and pain, he likes it even better. In this, he is also like a vampire, but one who feeds on psychic anguish. He may have wanted you just for fun before, but now? Killing you to hurt me would be the absolute apex for him." Alex looked her in the eyes, thought of what had happened to Thomasina and also to Remus Maxwell, and said firmly: "I also know that I will kill him first if I get the chance. One of us will certainly die when we meet again. Maybe both. Either way, it isn't something you need to see. Our quarrel is an old one. This isn't really your fight. And I need you to be safe and far away so I can do what must be done."

He began walking again. Alex didn't sense any immediate threat, but haste seemed wise since they had no idea when Saint Germain might return.

She said slowly, "But I think it *is* my fight now, whether he intended it or not. He's come after me tonight, and I take that very personally. And if it's true that he's after psychics, then you know he'll never let me just walk away now that he knows I'm here and know about him. I'm not *you*, of course—not so mentally strong—but obviously he's making a sincere effort to grab me."

"Harmony—"

"Anyway, you need me to watch your back. You'll have to sleep sometime and so will I. I think our chances of survival go up if we stay together. At least for now, until we know what's going on."

She had a point. That she was willing to make it—and so swiftly and decisively—amazed him. Most women would have been packing their bags and screaming for a travel agent ten minutes ago.

It shouldn't surprise him. In spite of downplaying her role as The Spider, Harmony wasn't one of the ineffectual theoretical types grown pale and squint-eyed from long weeks spent indoors, staring at columns of numbers from charitable donations and reading ecological books with footnotes in small typeface. Her figure was lean and exercised, her reflexes quick and sure. And she looked ready to wrestle what she saw as an environmental danger to the floor and grapple with it until it surrendered. With or without his help.

She was also good with a pistol. Someone had trained her.

It was difficult to accept and sometimes he forgot, but he was living in a new era where women were sometimes warriors.

"Can you use a rifle as well?" he asked.

"Yes." The answer wasn't hesitant. She asked calmly, "You say he's insane, but how smart is this man? And what the hell is his name? Who are we dealing with?"

"His name is—sometimes—Saint Germain. Down here, they call him Ramon Latigazo, The Whiplash. He's some kind of local *politico*. And I don't know how smart he is. That is an interesting question. He's cunning, but as you probably know, you don't have to be diabolically astute to be a villain." He smiled ironically. "Of course, one's career will last longer if you are. He's been around a long time, so we must conclude that he isn't rock stupid, even if he's madder than the proverbial March hare."

"Saint Germain? Like the alchemist Comte Saint Germain?"

"Yes." That was exactly who he meant. "And the Saint Germain who has the free clinics all over Africa and South America—and the CEO of the Johann Dippel Corporation."

"Dippel? Like the Dark Man Dippel you mentioned?" She blinked. Alex didn't blame her. Most people thought of Saint Germain as a philanthropist, a savior of the poor. Harmony had probably even donated money to his foundation and written it off on her taxes.

"So you would say that this Saint Germain is actually diabolical?" This wasn't really a question, merely the logical mind's desire to have a hard fact reiterated before it accepted a bitter truth. He understood. He hadn't been able to accept things all at once either.

"Without a doubt. He is a villain dyed the deepest shade of black. But far worse than that, he is an accomplished seducer. I don't mean that in the sexual sense—though he is certainly the most beautiful creature I have seen." Alex said this coolly, but wasn't surprised when Harmony raised a brow at this admission. "No, *ma chérie*, I mean that he is a seducer of the mind—like Hitler, or Rasputin. And he has political ties in many countries that keep him supplied with blood money. Those clinics didn't build themselves in the war zones of the world. He had the blessing of many corrupt leaders."

Harmony exhaled and then nodded twice, looking more troubled than ever. He decided not to bring up Saint Germain's connection with the Nazis. She had managed to accept genetic monsters caused by a designer disease and the political corruption of a renowned philanthropist; he wouldn't strain her credulity by bringing up the matter of Saint Germain's—and his own—quasi immortality. They'd tackle one impossibility at a time.

She said: "Don't take this the wrong way, and after what I've seen I'm not doubting you at all. But this story is a bit hard to believe. I mean, it's the twenty-first century. We have CNN and cell phones and the Internet. I believe in monsters—no one can watch TV and not know they are real. But they're *human* monsters. Every one of them. And everyone knows that there's no such things as vampires and ghouls. We don't have the kind of technology that can graft an ostrich's legs onto a human. We can barely manage pig valves in the human heart. We can't . . ." She trailed off. "Well, maybe the military can, but the rest of us don't know how. Anyone we tell about mutant vampires and ghouls will think we're crazy. And I can't go back to my people and tell them that Saint Germain, savior of the third world, is making genetic monsters—not without solid proof. As far as everyone else knows, he's so clean he squeaks. They'll just tell me to see a shrink."

Alex spoke carefully. He didn't want to lose her now.

"Yes, it's the wise and wonderful twenty-first century, but that doesn't mean the same thing here—or in the rest of the third world—that it does in a place like the United States." He stopped in a clump of oleander outside the hotel and scanned the parking lot. He wondered how to explain that they wouldn't be contacting any authorities. "Not a decade ago I was in places in Africa where they still believed in magic. The locals wore T-shirts and had phones on their belts. But cell phones or not, I was in one village where a man forgot to pay homage at his dead chieftain's grave on his way home from a hunt. He died ten days later without saying a word. I asked what was wrong, why this healthy man just lay down and died, and they told me that he died because it was holy law. He died because of his true belief, which was so strong that it caused his healthy body to die."

"But that's something he did to himself."

"True, but it was an outside influence—a powerful one—that planted this belief in his mind. If faith can do that, what else might it do? Some ideas are plagues, highly contagious. Especially if the carrier is religion. Think what the Church did to the Jews."

"The Nazis—"

"Yes. And people here have believed in vampires for centuries." He saw her lips part and went on before she could object. "Who knows why? Probably there was an ancient sub-population of humans with strange characteristics that lived off the villagers in some way."

"There are conditions that cause people to drink blood," Harmony agreed slowly. "And eat human flesh. Many cultures have practiced cannibalism. That could be what happened here."

And these humans ate flesh and drank blood—but not spinal fluid and brains. He didn't add this thought out loud, though.

"This is true. Now, show a superstitious population something like these creatures of Saint Germain's. Tell them they are the old gods returned, and the ancient faith or old beliefs can reignite." He shook his head and moved toward the empty parking lot. The sight of the lighted but now silent cantina should have been cheering, but succeeded only in seeming sinister. "In light of this, I don't think it would be wise to tell anyone that we killed off the local demigod's handmaidens. They would have only our word that it was self-defense."

"I know."

"Your State Department wouldn't like it, nor would the local authorities who might see this as a religious murder. And then there's the media. We don't want to be exposed in the press."

"Wait. Did you say handmaidens? Those things were women?" He didn't think it was possible, but she sounded more appalled at this news than anything else he had told her.

"Yes, once upon a time. Before Saint Germain got to them and altered them." Alex took a risk. "You won't believe me, but I accept as true that there is a surviving cult of priestesses worshiping an Aztecan god called Smoking Mirror. He was a shape-shifter, magician, storm-bringer, general scourge of the sinning masses." Alex paused. "Legend says they live by the local watering holes and lure men to their lairs on nights of the full moon. The rest of the time they spend underground worshiping their god. Such a phenomenon would attract Saint Germain. He would have wanted them for his experiments."

And how the hell had Saint Germain managed that feat, anyway? Alex wondered for the second time. In his experience, vampires were fast and strong, if not very bright. In a group, they should have been able to resist him. And why would he do it anyway? Was he in a struggle for power with Smoking Mirror? Maybe trying to steal his power as well?

Or had they formed an alliance? It wasn't something Alex wanted to think about, not when he was still somewhat connected to Harmony and the direction of his thoughts might alarm her.

"A cult for an underground death god?" she asked weakly. "That sounds crazy. They were very pale, though—almost albinos. Living underground would explain it."

"Yes, worshipers of a death god. A creature—an ancient one—that locals have worshiped for centuries, in spite of the Catholic missionaries doing their best to stamp out the old religions. There are statues of him in the museum in Mexico City. They even have the stinger on his tongue."

"But you think it's more than that. You think he's still actually alive?" she guessed unhappily.

"Yes. Or some facsimile of him—a clone maybe. I don't *know*, though. Perhaps not. People don't need living gods to inspire worship." Discussing religion always made him uncomfortable, especially with people born in the twentieth century. They were too rational to concede the existence of anything they couldn't see with a telescope or microscope. God—any god—was a conceptual matter for them.

Alex pulled open the jeep's rear door and reached for the gasoline and flares he had on the floor. He'd brought only one can. He wanted the bodies burned, all trace of them gone and the church decontaminated, but he didn't want to burn the town to the ground. Not just yet.

"Was that voice a ghost?" Harmony asked.

"I think it was. Maybe one of Saint Germain's victims. Or maybe it was one of those creatures trying to warn us. They could be psychic."

Or it could be someone else. It could be someone Alex knew. Perhaps he was being haunted by more than guilt.

Harmony looked down, clearly doing some hard thinking. Alex took it as a good sign that she wasn't arguing about the possible existence of either ghosts or psychics. Apparently, these things didn't raise the same mental objections that ghouls and vampires did.

"We need an escape plan, and quick. Will your friend believe you if you write a note and say you've gone off with me for a romantic vacation in Acapulco?" Alex asked. He set down the gas can and began reloading his pistol.

Harmony eyed him, trying to make out his expression in the dark.

"Probably. She isn't . . ." Harmony paused.

"Diabolically astute?" he suggested. He handed her the rifle. As he had anticipated, she handled it confidently, immediately checking to see if it was loaded.

"Let's say she won't be that surprised, because it's something she might do." Harmony was a reasonably loyal friend, and Alex sensed her reluctance to add that Ashley didn't want men to be rocket scientists. In fact, all brain functions beyond those needed to create a hard-on were actually more bother than they were worth. Alex understood this. Stupid women were often easier to deal with as well.

Harmony cleared her throat. "But am I going with you? You don't look ready to start a vacation. And if you're not . . . I thought you wanted me away from you and the battle zone. And given what happens to women around here, I think I'm inclined to agree that leaving Mexico would be wise. And there are other ways to track this man down—ways I'm good at. What we need to do is follow the money trail." Her voice warmed a bit.

"I'm not doing anything about Saint Germain until I have more information—not unless I'm cornered. And I really think it would be best if you left with me tonight. Stay close, at least until we find somewhere for you to wait in safety. We can split up then if we need to." But only if they needed to. He didn't know why Fate had brought her to him, and until he did, he wasn't letting her out of his sight. She might actually have the nerve to try to investigate Saint Germain on her own.

She nodded once, acknowledging that she had heard him but not that she necessarily agreed. Then she asked again, "Are you really Alexandre Dumas?"

So, she had guessed at some of what he'd left unsaid. Or perhaps she just meant, was he really the author pretending to be Alexandre Dumas. He couldn't ask just then. Either way, the answer was the same.

"I really am. Check my author photo."

She nodded again.

"Are we really going to Acapulco?"

"No, we're not. We need to be a whole lot further away than that while I try to find some people who may know how to help me."

"And Ashley will be okay? She's with that nice Australian tonight, and tomorrow they'll leave for their tour." Harmony was clearly trying to reassure herself that she was doing the right thing.

"Saint Germain has no reason to want her." That was as much as he could promise. There was no knowing what Saint Germain was planning. They might all be in a great deal of danger.

"And she wouldn't believe us if we tried to tell her about what happened and attempted to get her to leave."

"No, she wouldn't. But others at the hotel might if she mentioned this. Even if they weren't actually in on the creature's creation, the locals have to have had some suspicion about what was going on in that church. They have probably taken bribes." But not monetary ones. Saint Germain would be offering—forcing—something else.

"And that would be bad for us."

"Very bad. I don't think they would let us leave. I'd fight, of course. But . . ."

"Then I guess I'd better write a convincing note."

"Thank you." He wasn't thanking her for an epistolary effort, but for trusting him.

She nodded.

"I just hope that you really do know someone who can help us start the search for this monster, because right now, unless you can get me into his computer system, I am all out of ideas."

Does one still remember, in the world where you now are, the things of this world of ours, or does eternal life live only in the human imagination made childlike by its fear of no longer existing? That is something we never discussed in the days we lived together, nor do I think that you ever worried your head with metaphysical speculation. . . . For close on a quarter of a century you have been sleeping peacefully under the great trees of Villers-Cotterets between your mother, who served as your model for all the good women you portrayed, and your father, who inspired all those heroes to whom you gave the gift of life. . . . The world moves fast. Soon we shall meet again.

—*Letter from Dumas* fils *to his deceased father, Dumas* père

CHAPTER EIGHT

They drove through the night, much of which she missed. It surprised Harmony that she actually slept. Her unconscious must have decided that it trusted Alex to keep her safe from the monsters, because she curled up in her seat almost at once and went to sleep. She had a vague sense that Alex was standing guard over her dreams. Whether that was true or just a wish, no nightmares wriggled into or out of her subconscious to trouble her.

The touch of sunrise through the glass finally roused her and she sat up, feeling stiff but surprisingly fit otherwise. The horror of the previous evening seemed very far away. Perhaps she was in shock.

"Where are we?" she asked, rubbing a smudge from her window. The glass was warm, though the air-conditioning made the temperature in the jeep bearable. With temperatures like these, she wondered how anyone could deny the phenomenon of global warming. The scenery that stuttered by in sharp, bone-jarring jolts looked an awful lot like what she had seen before giving in to sleep. Only a whole lot brighter.

"We're headed for San Pedro. I know someone who knows someone who might be able to help us." Alex smiled at her. He didn't look at all weary. "We'll get breakfast there."

"Good. I can hardly believe it, but I'm starved." She reached for the radio. "Any news about Curatos Cienegas?" Like, if their church fire had burned up something other than monsters. They hadn't stayed around to toast weenies and marshmallows at the monster roast and so didn't know if their act of arson had spread beyond the vault.

"I don't know." He hesitated, then added: "The radio isn't working."

"Maybe it's just poor reception."

"Maybe." Harmony got the impression that Alex thought it was something else. She tried to tune in a station—any station—but could only get a high-pitched squeal that hurt her ears.

"That sounds like a fax machine."

Alex nodded.

They passed a few villages, really hardly more than wide spots in the road where a few lonely houses huddled together. Though there was little to see, Alex watched carefully as they passed through each one, searching for some sign that things weren't normal. There was nothing obviously wrong, but Harmony found herself feeling increasingly ill at ease, and also watching the road and buildings for signs of . . . something.

They reached the small town of San Pedro about twenty minutes later. Admittedly, Harmony had only been in tourist areas of the country, and she had heard that mornings down here tended to be drowsy affairs where one slowly recovered from the festivities dictated by a nocturnal lifestyle. The day that followed would move even slower. This was simple self-defense in a climate where a body's passage would seem to push the air before it and leave a roiling, shimmering wake behind. Still, even by these standards, the towns they were driving through felt unusually lifeless. Dead, even.

Harmony felt a frown pull itself together on her forehead. These weren't abandoned ghost towns; there were some vehicles about, and the buildings were in repair. But there should have been children, animals—an old lady out sweeping the veranda of the hotel, chasing off the ghosts of debauchery and any evidence of the previous night's accumulations of wind-borne dust before the sun became unbearable. Instead the inhabitants seemed to be hiding indoors behind shuttered windows that stared out on the empty streets with glassy eyes blinded by their wooden cataracts.

Alex pulled up just beyond a cantina where a small table and two aged chairs sat in the dirt street to the right of an open door and the first unshuttered window that Harmony had seen. They got down from the jeep and walked slowly, even warily, toward the blank opening of the door that felt vaguely like a bully's taunt at the rest of the sleeping village. Though there was no overt threat, Harmony found herself reaching for the small pistol she had in her purse. She didn't draw it, but she felt better with her hand curled around the butt of the gun.

The dark doorway grew larger and more ominous, but before they could cross the threshold into the gloom, the expected old woman finally appeared, bearing not a broom but instead an old-fashioned, dusty slate that proclaimed in smudged chalk letters that they had soup and tortillas for lunch. She was thin to the point of emaciation, and her skin hung in pale folds around her neck that reminded Harmony a little too much of the creatures they had confronted the night before. The old lady walked with jerky movements, as though being pulled by the strings of an impatient puppet master. She didn't say anything or even smile as they seated themselves at a small table the unpleasant color of an old smoker's teeth, merely nodding when Alex said in what sounded like the local dialect that soup would be fine and did she have beer in a bottle? Her eyes remained completely blank and unfocused as she nodded again and then retreated inside.

Harmony ran a finger over the table. It was dusty. It had been her experience that the people of Mexico, however poor, were scrupulously clean. This sort of slovenliness was rare, and suggested that something had disrupted the normal routine. Perhaps there had been a windstorm last night that shorted out the power? Certainly there had been weird weather events in Cuatros Cienegas.

"Alex?" she finally whispered.

"Just wait. We can't be certain."

Certain of what? she wanted to ask.

The food came right away and smelled good enough, but Harmony found she suddenly had little appetite. She stared at the soup and imagined there were foul things floating in it. Alex hadn't said anything, but she knew he was unhappy with something too.

Harmony looked about discreetly, peering in the open door. Besides the bleached-out old woman, there was a bony old man inside the cantina, mending what looked like a fishing net by the light of an oil lamp that smoked obnoxiously. Harmony would have thought the task would go more easily if he came out into the daylight, but the old man seemed to prefer the shadows. It wasn't until later that the fact that they weren't anywhere near the ocean or even a lake crossed her mind, along with the question of why a net might be wanted. Also, there were power lines in town. Why weren't they using electric lights? Perhaps the storm *had* caused a power outage. Of course, if that were the case, wouldn't more people have their windows open to let in light?

Yes, Harmony shared Alex's unhappiness with their surroundings, though she couldn't explain why. Perhaps it was these unsmiling people who looked as if the hard earth had worn them down, abrading their minds and bodies, taking their . . . what? Humanity? Alex hadn't said anything, but she wondered if he sensed something else. Had Saint Germain been here as well? Was it his taint she sensed?

She looked to her right, down the small alley that ran between two buildings—homes, she assumed, since they bore no business signs. Though it was late morning, the alley still clung to unfriendly shadows.

Harmony shivered in spite of the heat. Not all darkness was sinister; she knew that. She had in fact always loved the night, had felt that it protected her in her work. But something about this darkness was sullen, even predatory, and it was watchful.

"Is this town . . . ?" She stopped, unwilling to voice her question since it sounded so paranoid. "Is that old woman on drugs?" Harmony whispered her query, hoping it was something so simple.

"No. I asked myself that the first time I saw . . . a place like this. It was in Greece during a local power squabble—a town that had been overrun with . . . a disease." *Disease*. After the previous night, the word would always mean something different to Harmony. "I know drugs are a natural assumption given our era, the region, and these people's seeming state of ill health. And there are so many drugs to abuse down here, and most users tend to be multipharmic, so it can be difficult to know what combinations of hellbroth someone might be taking. There could be some very strange symptoms. But I haven't seen a hint of marijuana or mushrooms or any injectibles since I crossed the border. So, no, I believe this is a *disease* and not drugs."

"Saint Ger—"

"Don't use his name. Not here," Alex interrupted, and then smiled ruefully. "Walls have ears. And I'm feeling superstitious this morning. Let's not risk summoning him if he should be nearby."

Harmony shivered at these words, but didn't argue that Alex was being superstitious. The town made her feel less than rational.

"But is it *the* disease? Are there . . . ?" She looked about again, feeling her skin pull tight as she thought about what might be lurking in the shadows. "Is there a clinic here—someplace where the disease might be . . . festering?"

"No. And I don't smell any *things*. But this town is located along the same river as Cuatros Cienegas. I think that perhaps some of the . . ." Again, he paused to select a word. "Some of the older contagion may have reached here."

"You mean . . . ?" She stuck out her tongue and flipped the end up and down.

"Yes, I think Smoking Mirror's priestesses have been feeding here. Heavily—perhaps because their other feeding grounds have been taken over. I wouldn't be surprised if these two are the last ones alive. That suggests either unusual desperation or boldness on the creatures' part."

"Why don't they leave?" Harmony asked, feeling distressed and flabbergasted. She pulled her blouse away from her chest and flapped it ineffectually. It was now buttoned up high enough to be considered demure, but Alex's appreciative eyes still flicked over her.

"They can't. The vampires' grip on their minds is too strong." His bleak words were at odds with his warm look.

Frowning at him, Harmony dropped her blouse. This was no time to be having lascivious thoughts.

"You know, I think maybe you should consider taking up some safer hobbies—like bullfighting or cliff diving. Maybe Russian roulette," she suggested.

"It's just the heat bothering you," he answered. But she

knew, as certainly as if he had warned her, that he was speaking for ears other than hers. A moment later the old woman stuck her head out the door and looked at them for a moment. "California has spoiled you. You'll feel better in a few days."

They both turned their heads sharply when they heard an odd clicking sound coming from between the buildings. A moment later, a painfully thin dog appeared in the alley Harmony had been watching. She stole up to their table on uncertain feet, her body trembling. She looked at them with eyes that pleaded. She was clearly starving. Just as she had been yesterday. As she would be tomorrow if no one helped her, and if she did not actually die before the day was over.

Alex looked down and made a sound that was a mixture of pain and anger and frustration. He set his dish on the floor, moving slowly so he didn't frighten her. He needn't have bothered. The dog wanted—needed—food so much that she would have accepted a beating to get it.

"Poor bitch," he said softly to the mutt as he tore up his tortillas and added them to the broth. "But don't worry. You're coming with us. I will not leave you in this damned town to die with the rest." He said *damned* like he meant it.

This announcement should have surprised Harmony but didn't. Had he not picked her up in much the same manner when he saw that she was in trouble? Anyway, hadn't the original Alexandre Dumas always been a soft touch when it came to animals?

Hearing that thought, Harmony blinked. Where had that idea come from? Surely she wasn't thinking that Alex was really *Alexandre*? He couldn't be. Really, they looked nothing alike. And she didn't believe in reincarnation. It wasn't amazing that this Alex liked animals. Many people did.

"Will we have trouble at the border if we bring her?" she asked distractedly, putting her own dish down for the dog. She reached out slowly to give a gentle touch to the bitch's silken ears. Troubled brown eyes shifted her way, but just for a moment. Food was all-important.

"No. I have chartered a private plane for my return trip. It will meet us in Guaymas where I can leave this poor creature with a friend. The plane will take us to Mexico City. From there a private jet will take us back to . . ." He trailed off.

"To?" she prompted.

"Cornwall."

"Why Cornwall?" she asked, curious but unalarmed. Cornwall, Mexico—it didn't matter anymore, as long as it was far away from ghouls and vampires and whatever diseases made them.

"It puts an ocean between us and whatever is going on here. And it's very private. I have a home there. It's actually an island."

"You own an island?"

"Yes."

"And a jet?"

"No. That belongs to a friend of my publisher. I do not actually care for airplanes—nor they for me. Particularly the smaller ones. I use them only when I have no other choice."

"Hopefully it's not the friend who knew someone here." She reached down and caressed the trembling dog again. Its ribs were easy to count because much of the hair had fallen out. This degree of starvation hadn't happened overnight. Harmony wasn't an expert, but it would have been days, maybe even weeks if she had scavenged for scraps, for a dog to get that thin.

"As a matter of fact, it is. And it wasn't just anyone who lived here. It was his grandmother and an elderly uncle."

"Not—?" She jerked her head at the inn door.

"No, not them."

Harmony shook her head.

"This isn't good. I don't think your friend is going to like anything you have to say about what's going on here."

"No. And I am aware of a certain irony in this situation. It makes me wary. Still, I think this is a better option than using a commercial airline."

"I'm not arguing, but why are you wary?"

"I have just recalled that my friend Esteban Rodriguez, among other things, sits on the board of the Dippel Corporation." Harmony started to speak, but Alex shook his head in warning. "I don't think he's involved. But I will say nothing to him. For now." Alex shook himself. "Are you done with breakfast?"

Harmony looked at the empty bowls and the dog's grateful expression and said: "Yes, I think we are."

Alex rose, laid some money on the table, and then bent down to pick up the dog. She was still trembling, but bestowed a small lick on his chin as he tucked her against his chest.

"Let's be off, then. The sooner we are shut of this place, the better. I'm seeing shadows where shadows shouldn't be."

Harmony didn't need any further encouragement. They walked unhurriedly to the jeep, covered now in powdery earth, and opened the back door. To anyone else they might look like two tourists taking their time after a meal, but she knew that Alex was as tense as she was, muscles coiled, prepared for attack.

The dog seemed happy in the back of the jeep. She sniffed a few times at the upholstery and then curled up, prepared to sleep off her first meal in days. Harmony wished that she herself could do the same, but knew that her body and mind were fully awake, flooded with low-grade fear.

"Alex?"

"Yes?"

"Your accent is gone. It seems to have disappeared in the night along with your linen shirt. You really look and sound like an American."

"I know. It seems best not to attract too much attention.

A Frenchman would be too memorable here. Especially one so pale. I'll have to apply the chemical tanner as soon as we can buy more. You may have noticed the smell last night when it burned away. It's a bit like soggy cereal."

"Ah. I did smell something odd." *Besides rotting monsters.* Harmony took a deep breath and watched as the town disappeared behind them in the side-view mirror. "Alex, I have a question. It's a crazy question . . . I guess . . . but this whole situation is rather crazy. And I would feel better—at least I think I would—if I asked about this."

"Then ask. What is your crazy question?"

"Well, it's about the disease." Harmony took another breath and looked down at her hands. They were bare. She did not wear a watch or rings because whenever you took them off, they left betraying marks. "You said that one of the side effects was unnatural strength."

"It is."

"And it gave you dark eyes."

"Yes—well, something did. My eyes were not always this color."

"Are there are other side effects as well?"

There was a pause as Alex chose how to answer.

"Yes, there are. Increased sensory abilities are one side effect—better hearing, better sense of smell and taste. Keen eyesight—most of the time. When it fails, it fails fast. And, as I explained, it has increased my psychic gifts as well. I . . . see auras around people. It helps me guess their mood and sometimes their intentions."

"I see. Those all sound like good things."

"They certainly do. But that isn't all of it," he admitted.

"Would one of the other side effects of this disease be unusually long life?" She cleared her throat, and when he didn't answer, she went on: "I mean, you talked about this god, Smoking Whatsit?"

"Smoking Mirror." She felt Alex look her way, but kept

her gaze locked on her hands. She felt both vaguely afraid and ridiculous as she sneaked up on her real question.

"You think that maybe he could still be alive, right? So the disease would have to have a side effect of long life."

"Perhaps. But not in everyone. Remember that he is the source of the local contagion. I think that long life is . . . selective in its victims. It depends on other things." It was Alex's turn to take a deep breath or two. "For instance, those ghouls we killed. It's hearsay, since I've never kept one for myself, but as I understand it they can only live about five years—and that in a dry, cool climate. The process of disintegration—or rotting—of the grafted parts is slowed but not stopped. I don't think Saint Germain has yet discovered a foolproof immunosuppressant that allows transplanted limbs—or other things—to survive indefinitely. The bodies eventually reject his add-ons and they return to death unless constantly reanimated. And that causes brain damage, since it is basically done with electrocution and we have a finite number of brain cells."

"But that's because of what Saint Germain is doing with the virus or bacteria or whatever it is?"

"Yes. No. Perhaps." Alex's hands tightened. "I just don't know."

"Why does he do these things? Is it . . ." She wanted him to say that there was a logical reason, that Saint Germain wasn't merely evil or insane. She didn't know how to fight insanity, and it frightened her.

"He does it because he has an affinity for the dead. They are the only ones who can tolerate him. Ultimately, I believe he is looking for a way to prolong his own life indefinitely. And perhaps a way to prolong the use of his dead army. Ghouls take time and effort to make. Zombies are easier, but they're stupid and have no initiative. And the Dark Man's treatment is not enough—alone—to sustain any of the . . . patients. Eventually the effects wear off and

one must undergo the process of renewal again. He is looking for a way of avoiding this trial."

"I see." She didn't. "But Smoking Mirror and his
priestesses—the untouched, pure ones—might live a long
time."

"Yes, they might."

"And you, Alex? Will you live a long time?" He didn't
answer, so she asked quietly: "Have you already lived a long
time because of this disease? Or because of the treatment
you got?"

Harmony finally turned to look at Alex. She studied his
profile carefully. He glanced her way briefly, but she
couldn't read anything in his expression.

"I know that the real—I mean, the first . . . Hell! I know
the pictures of Alexandre Dumas always showed him to be a
black man, heavyset, with light brown eyes. Your eyes are
obviously different. Your skin too. But the skin and weight
loss could be side effects of this disease, couldn't they?
Those—those priestesses were very pale and skinny."

"Yes. It could be a side effect." Alex looked her way
again. "But I don't think my pallor is a side effect of that
disease. It's a side effect of the medical treatment I received
from Saint Germain's father. The two things are separate.
Or they were until recently. Now I don't know where one
ends and the other begins. And the mix could be a genuine
hellbroth in Saint Germain's hands. Ghouls gifted with
longevity. It doesn't bear thinking about."

"What exactly was that treatment?" Harmony asked. She
was finding it increasingly difficult to force the questions
out. "And why did you go to him if you knew he was . . .
not ethical?"

"I didn't go to him. He came to me." Alex raised a hand
and then let it fall back on the wheel. "It doesn't excuse
anything, but it was during a time when I was in great financial difficulty. I was writing fifteen hours a day and my

health was failing. I was going blind and I had ulcers. This Dark Man came to Italy where I was . . . exiled. And he made me an offer I couldn't refuse."

"*Couldn't* refuse?"

"I was vomiting blood hourly by then, confined to my bed. And I had just found out that my ex-mistress—a suicidal Russian princess married to an old and dying prince—was having my child. Since I am the grandson of a slave woman from Barbados, and I was clearly a mulatto, there was a good chance that child would be obviously black as well. Something completely unacceptable in Russia at that time."

"Oh."

"Yes. Oh, indeed. My other children and ex-wife were furious with me for going to the courts and having it put on record that I was this child's father and not the prince. But if the prince disowned the child, or died—and if the babe's mother succeeded in killing herself—there would be no one to see to the child's interests." He exhaled. "Harmony, it is hard to believe, living as you do in this place and time, but the fate of an unwanted child—even one born to a good family—was grim beyond telling. There were no child protective services, no welfare to intervene. If the unwanted bastards and orphans didn't starve in the streets, they would be prostituted or else have to turn to thievery or selling drugs to survive. And people let it happen because they believed it was a moral judgment upon the bastards of the world."

"Alex." She reached out and touched his hand fleetingly. His pain was palpable. She didn't quite know how to assure him that she understood why he had done what he did, that this was why she went on being The Spider. It was to make the world safe for the children who were coming after them.

"Don't think about it, *chérie*. I don't anymore. But I needed to be well—for this child. I needed to write so I would have money to go to Russia to retrieve him, and at that moment, I had none. I had been bankrupted—everything taken by the courts and my ex-wife during the divorce." He looked at her and gave a wry smile. "And that was when the devil came calling. Maybe it was weakness—certainly it was unwise—but I was willing to listen to what he offered. He talked about a cure for blindness and my ulcers, not something that would . . . completely change me."

"And the treatments actually cured you?"

"Oh, yes. My sight returned within a day. I was healthy again. Suddenly as pale as a noblewoman and black-eyed—and it turns out, sterile—but healthy otherwise." He looked over at her again. His black eyes were calm. "So ask your real question, Harmony. Ask it so that I can put your mind at ease."

Harmony took a bracing breath.

"When you say Russian princess—you don't mean Mafia princess. You mean, like the czar's daughter?"

"Niece. Yes, that's what I mean."

"So, you're really, really Alexandre Dumas, author of *The Count of Monte Cristo* and *The Three Musketeers*, born in France on the twenty-fourth of July in eighteen-oh-two?"

"I really, really am."

There was a long silence that neither rushed to fill.

"Wow, I guess there's some more story not covered in the standard bios," Harmony said at last. This made Alex laugh once.

"A great deal of it. The next installment of which is due at my publisher's in three weeks. This little jaunt to Mexico has messed up my writing schedule. My editor is having fits at the delay, and I can hardly blame him. As it is, I'll have to refuse a book tour. They wanted me on *Larry King* this time, too."

"Refuse Larry King? I can imagine that would cause some unhappiness. I know writers who would kill for a spot on national television." Harmony let herself smile and relax a bit. Alex's announcement was difficult to believe, but no more than anything else she had faced in the last twenty-four hours, and it all rang true to her. Her intuition said he wasn't lying. "Is it too much to ask what the Dark Man actually did to you?"

"Probably, but I'll tell you because you need to be aware of the danger in being near me when it storms." Alex, as ever, sounded matter-of-fact, but his hands were a bit tighter on the steering wheel. "Dippel cured his patients by feeding them a concoction of drugs—mainly cocaine and hartshorn—and then electrocuting them with St. Elmo's fire. I think that there was also some sort of psychic power used as well."

"Like in *Frankenstein*."

"Almost exactly. Mary Shelley had her inspiration from what happened to Lord Byron. He sought out Dippel because of his epilepsy. The Shelleys witnessed the process—and were horrified."

"I didn't know Byron had epilepsy."

"He didn't—not after the doctor cured him." Alex added: "And it was a variation on this process that the Dark Man used to create the first zombies and ghouls."

"And which the Dark Man's son is now using to make monsters of these vampire priestesses? So we are actually looking at both Frankenstein monsters and some kind of native vampirism down here?"

"Yes. And I know it sounds ridiculous. Impossible. Also, I don't like thinking of myself as Dippel's monster, so I prefer to believe that what happened to me was an experimental medical treatment and not the research of a mad scientist bent on taking over the world." Alex rolled his shoulders, trying to get comfortable. "And, as you may have guessed, yet another side effect to this dark healing is my reaction to storms. You noticed some slightly odd things last night?"

"With you? Like the scars on your chest? I didn't see

YES! ☐

Sign me up for the **Historical Romance Book Club** and send my TWO FREE BOOKS! If I choose to stay in the club, I will pay only $8.50* each month, a savings of $5.48!

YES! ☐

Sign me up for the **Love Spell Book Club** and send my TWO FREE BOOKS! If I choose to stay in the club, I will pay only $8.50* each month, a savings of $5.48!

NAME: _____

ADDRESS: _____

_____

TELEPHONE: _____

E-MAIL: _____

☐ **I WANT TO PAY BY CREDIT CARD.**

☐ VISA   ☐ MasterCard   ☐ DISCOVER

ACCOUNT #: _____

EXPIRATION DATE: _____

SIGNATURE: _____

Send this card along with $2.00 shipping & handling for each club you wish to join, to:

**Romance Book Clubs
1 Mechanic Street
Norwalk, CT 06850-3431**

Or fax (must include credit card information!) to: 610.995.9274.
You can also sign up online at www.dorchesterpub.com.

*Plus $2.00 for shipping. Offer open to residents of the U.S. and Canada only.
Canadian residents please call 1.800.481.9191 for pricing information.

If under 18, a parent or guardian must sign. Terms, prices and conditions subject to change. Subscription subject
to acceptance. Dorchester Publishing reserves the right to reject any order or cancel any subscription.

JOIN NOW!

them at first. It was only when we were in the church that I noticed them. Later they were gone." She didn't add that some of them had looked like knife wounds.

"They weren't there before the storm. They only come up when lightning is near. I also get higher than a kite, blinded by lust or rage sometimes. And I burn off my chemical tan. It just disappears. I hate that—I smell like burning toast. It's even worse if I'm wearing scent. That smells as if someone is burning potpourri."

Harmony tried to think of what to say.

"That sounds potentially embarrassing—being high and out of control, I mean. If you were in public." Harmony wasn't anxious to talk about what had almost happened between them last night out in the gazebo. She wasn't embarrassed by her sexuality, but if Alex had been blinded by lust because of the storm, she didn't have his excuse. She had been like a lemming. There had been no hesitation at all last evening, no thought of consequences. She would have screwed this stranger in a public park and enjoyed every minute of it. If Alex hadn't noticed what was happening with the storm, she would probably have still been screwing him when the rats and scorpions arrived.

The thought had her shivering. They could have both died because of Alex's storm-induced sexual obsession and her inability to tell him no.

There was also a part of her that didn't want to think about this happening with some other woman. Bad enough if this response was specific to her. But it would make what happened downright sordid if he would have reacted that same way to any woman.

"You don't have children? Or any family?" Alex asked her suddenly. Once again she noticed his earring. This time she could see there were words on it, though she couldn't make them out. This was something new. None of the old photographs of Alexandre Dumas showed him wearing an earring. "No one who will worry if you are gone for a while?"

"Just an uncle, and we're not close. The Spider moves around a lot, so no one is going to get too anxious if I'm gone a week or two. As for having a husband and kids—not yet. Maybe not ever. Frankly, I'm not sure I want children," Harmony babbled, saying anything to get away from her memories of last night. She met Alex's sidelong glance and shrugged. "I feel like I should, though. My mother used to say that children are our best shot at immortality. I feel like I owe it to her and Dad."

Alex grimaced. "Immortality? That's not entirely true—about children, I mean. I managed to make my mark against the darkness, against oblivion, but it was my books that endured, not my offspring. At the time, I never would have guessed that this would be the case."

"That might be because you're a literary giant, a rare talent that comes along once a century," Harmony said dryly. "The rest of us aren't that lucky. We need to do it the old-fashioned way."

His lips twitched. "True—and the thought of this immense talent has sustained me at times when I had nothing else to hang on to."

His suddenly smug tone earned him a punch in the arm. The touch was stupid, fleeting and unloving, but she enjoyed it anyway. Her hand tingled briefly after she pulled it away.

Alex glanced at his arm as though also feeling the tingle, and sobered quickly.

"I have to tell you, quite seriously, that the absence of my children—my son especially—is a hollow place in my heart. I keep a likeness there that is as perfect as memory can make it, but I know it's not alive. It doesn't change or grow. And many days the memory is not enough, probably because the memories are of pain and failure. Of course, at the time I didn't realize what would happen with my children. They were always a distant third behind my writing and my love affairs. I barely knew them." Alex rolled his neck from side to side. His expression was hard. "Parents aren't supposed to outlive their offspring, to have time to understand their personal shortfalls and see how their sins are visited on future generations. Eventually, though I did my best to remain oblivious, I came to understand that I was a bad father. Want some good advice? Never read your own biography. Even the best, most sympathetic portrait won't match the image you have of yourself. Society, in my day and age, did not condemn me for how I treated my children, since it was the norm for that era—at least among the upper classes—but karma has certainly made its conviction clear. I didn't deserve to be gifted with their lives. And my punishment is sorrowful memories. On many days I wish I had not had them." He paused. "Maybe it would be different for you. If you gave up your career and did something safer . . ."

Alex's openness on this subject surprised her. The historical Alexandre Dumas would never have talked this way. Harmony made a sound of sympathy and encouragement but didn't try to offer any words of consolation. There really weren't any. She did tack up a mental sticky note to ask for details later. For Alex, this was just a memory of the son he missed. For her, this son was—if she truly believed Alex's claim—Dumas *fils*, a famous writer in his own right.

"People change," Harmony suggested.

"Do they? It is my experience that they rarely do. They prefer not to evolve—and why should they? Especially if they are talented or beautiful. It is only when such gifts are paired with something else—something that makes them a misfit—that you get . . ." He looked over at her.

"The Spider?" she suggested.

"Yes. Or The Chameleon. I'll tell you that story one day." Alex went on, his calm voice at odd with his painful words. "I was not so wise or adept at change as you are. For a time after my son died and I realized I was truly alone, I found myself squandering my life, as if my added years were pocket change to be flung at whatever passing fancy caught my eye. Sometimes it was women; often it was worse. I no longer cared for anything or anyone. Anger tucked me into bed each night and awakened me with its bitter kiss each morning. It was with me when I made breakfast, went riding, made love. It held my hands whenever they were idle. I didn't write during that time, didn't create. I was too bitter and too regretful. Because I was also stupid, I tried drink and drugs of every kind, but they no longer helped— another side effect of my 'treatment.' One glass of wine was too much for my heightened senses and left my nerves raw and exposed to memory, and a hundred drinks weren't enough to make me forget all I'd lost. Finally I left France, trying to escape the memories.

"That didn't work, though. It never does." He took a deep breath. "But eventually time did its work and I healed after a fashion. The pain became blunted and life grew more normal again. As a stranger in an even stranger land, I set about creating a new Alexandre. I traveled west until I hit the Barbary Coast. I decided to stay and to build a new life, publishing a small newspaper in San Francisco. The gold rush had died, but the city by the bay thrived. I established myself there, made friends—not close ones, but I had company and adventures. I wrote about this in *The Ghost of the Barbary Coast*. It's still in print."

"I've seen it. Nice cover."

Alex grunted.

"And then?"

"Then came the first of the world wars—a war I had predicted half a century before but prayed would never come. Then a pandemic, which I had not expected. There was nowhere to run, to hide from the horror." Alex shook his head. "So many died, Harmony! You can have no idea of what such mass death is like. It rode over all of us, with us, like our shadow, inescapable even if we ourselves did not succumb to the disease. Hope alone sustained me, because I truly thought then that we would come through the experience wiser, more compassionate, that we would rebuild a better, more equal society. . . . But then the world went to war again. Many more died. Hope finally died too. Life again seemed hopeless, and I fell back on old habits. I began living recklessly again—selfishly. I'm ashamed of it now, but I became a thief and what you would call an adrenaline junkie. It was the one drug that was not barred from me. It was the one drug that kept me from painful memory. I lived always in the present." Alex shrugged again, as though trying to loosen the muscles of his neck.

"Would you like me to drive for a while?" Harmony asked.

"No. I'm fine."

"Okay. Just tell me when you need a rest." She couldn't help but prompt: "What happened next? Were you caught? Did you go to jail for being a thief?"

"I was almost caught. There was a great detective in England at that time called Remus Maxwell, and he finally figured out what I was doing. Somewhere in Scotland Yard there is probably a case file on The Chameleon. After I was discovered, I fled to the continent, but it was difficult to travel because of the war. Everywhere I saw destruction and death. By then my hatred of the German war machine had reached a kind of mania. Though I was wanted by the British, I began passing information about the Germans along to them. My efforts, because of my psychic gifts, were fairly effective but short-lived. I was discovered by a psychic the Germans had on staff—I think it was Saint Germain, though I can't prove it—and had to flee the German-occupied territories. The hounds of hell were after me. Night and day I ran, barely a step ahead of them. Then circumstances put me on a train bound for Casablanca. Fate finally intervened in my life. She threw down a gauntlet and I picked it up—why, even to this day I do not know." Alex again raised a hand and let it fall, a favorite gesture when words failed him. "That fickle bitch saw me as far as Tangier and then she abandoned me to the unfortunate woman who was to become my greatest love. And to the man who is still my deadliest enemy."

Harmony swallowed and then asked reluctantly: "Saint Germain—and he killed her, didn't he? That's why you have such a bitter hatred for him. It's why you came halfway around the world on little more than a hunch. You think it's him, and you want revenge." Harmony wanted to ask the woman's name, but couldn't.

"Oh, yes." Alex stared into the distance. His face was cold and a bit frightening. "Though she was a powerful psychic and he was grooming her for greater things—perhaps to be his consort—the moment he discovered my identity and that I was in love with her, Thomasina was doomed. And I blame myself for it—believe me, I still do, though logic says I had no way of knowing what would happen. You see, here's the tragic irony of the situation I was in. Saint Germain didn't hate me for being the person I was then—a supposed detective who was investigating him for the British government. For a long time, I thought that this was why Thomasina died. You see, the real Remus Maxwell was dead by then—murdered by Saint Germain's assassins, probably because he too was a powerful psychic and would be able to track Saint Germain for the British—and I had taken his place. But Thomasina didn't die because she was helping a British agent bring a Nazi criminal to justice. He didn't care about that at all. He simply cared that the son of his father's greatest enemy had dared to touch his possession. She was soiled goods."

Harmony made a sound of disgust.

"Yes, the notion of humans believing that they can own

other humans is offensive to me, too." There was irony in his voice that reminded Harmony that he was the grandson of a slave and would know better than anyone how loathsome slavery was. "But remember that this was a man who killed at will, who had no limits set upon him except perhaps those imposed by his father. A failure to see Thomasina as a human with rights, though that hurts me the most, is the least of his crimes. Perhaps I should have sensed that something was wrong with him—I mean, that he was inhuman—but I never did. His aura was terrible, but many horrible people were about in those terrible days. I didn't guess that this man, called El Grande, was actually Le Comte de St. Germain. I didn't know that he was in reality the son of the man who had my father tortured in prison because he feared that the General would topple Napoleon, the puppet emperor that Dippel controlled."

"General Dumas, you mean? Saint Germain's father was responsible for his arrest in Brindisi?" Harmony couldn't help her reaction. The story was legend. Alexandre's father had been a very popular general and governor, so popular that Emperor Napoleon had come to fear that the general was more admired by the people than the little emperor himself. The people of Italy had started calling General Dumas the Minister of Humanity. Enraged, the previously supportive emperor had arranged for his rival's arrest and imprisonment.

"Yes, and the Dark Man was the one who whispered in Napoleon's ear, inciting his jealousies against my father. And it was the same man—then called Johann Dippel—who came to me later and offered a seemingly miraculous cure for my failing eyes and stomach. Not out of regret or penance for what he had done to my father, but because he hadn't succeeded in punishing my father enough and this was his twisted way of carrying out revenge. You see, the General should have died from the repeated poisoning and torture, but he was too strong, and he survived prison long enough to father a son to carry on the family line—a son with certain gifts. Gifts perhaps greater than those of Dippel's own son. Watching me live with his curse was more appealing than letting me die. It made Dippel feel like God." Alex shook his head. "His hubris was punished, though. As it turns out, the Dark Man was right to fear my father and me, because in the end I was the one who killed his son, Saint Germain. A very dramatic story, isn't it?" Alex pulled down his visor. The sun was higher in the sky, but its rays were getting stronger.

"But Saint Germain isn't dead," she pointed out.

"Apparently not. It's more than a bit perturbing."

"I don't know what to say. You might have scripted this thriller yourself." Alex shot her a look, asking if she was joking. She wasn't. Nor was she suggesting that he was making everything up. "Why did Dippel hate your father? How did he know you would be psychic?"

"I think he first hated my father because the General was a patriot, and he saw the little emperor being manipulated by his new adviser, a man that many thought was a wizard, a creature who talked to ghosts and bragged that he lived among the dead. The emperor had betrayed the Republic, and my father wanted him gone. Dippel had other plans for Napoleon. He was to be the front man for a new dynasty."

Harmony exhaled and nodded.

"You mean plans for Saint Germain, of course," she guessed. "This is out of my area, but I recall that he—or someone claiming to be him—was everywhere back then, sticking fingers in every European political pie. He is supposed to have predicted the beheading of Louis the Sixteenth and Marie Antoinette."

"Exactly. In fact, it wouldn't surprise me if he arranged for their capture that time they tried to escape. But I didn't know any of this back in Tangier. My father died before he could

tell me all this, and my mother never knew. No, all I understood on the night that El Grande strangled Thomasina and
then threw her body into the ocean, was that he was a Nazi
collaborator who trafficked in stolen art and we had found
him out. It was only much later that I discovered the truth—
that she had died because he learned that I was a Dumas and
one of his father's creations. And he feared that I might have
a child with Thomasina that would be even stronger than its
parents, an *über*-psychic. A useless fear, since I am sterile, but
that's a fact he either wasn't aware of or couldn't chance having proved false."

"But if this process of his father's makes people sterile,
surely he would know this."

"Yes. But he also knew I had been bitten by a vampire in
Greece, before they were all wiped out in the war. The creatures had amazing regenerative qualities, and he couldn't
know how my body would react to the vampiric contami-
nation. A normal person would die, but those get of Dippel
never sicken. He couldn't risk that perhaps I would be able
to procreate after all."

"I see." Harmony opened her purse and started looking
for aspirin. Suddenly it was all too much. Her head had begun to pound.

"He thought that maybe I'd father a vampiric child that
would be likewise changed—as I am—and therefore be
strong enough to kill him."

"It's all wilder than Shakespeare's dramas."

"Yes, and that isn't a bad way of looking at it. Thomasina
died because the Dark Man's family and my own were the
Montagues and Capulets, and we did not know how to
make peace. . . . That was not because either my father or I
ever wanted that much power, but they looked at us and saw
their own ambition and reacted violently." He sighed. "For
all my talk of peace, I wouldn't have done anything differ-
ently had I known he was the son of my father's old enemy

and their quarrel was not ours—at least not after he killed Thomasina. Peace be damned. I wanted him punished— *dead*—because of what he had done to her." He shook his head. "Ignorance on a mission can be deadly, though. Because I didn't understand who he was, I didn't do everything that was needed to ensure that his line ended there. All evidence to the contrary, I am not an expert monster-killer, and didn't always routinely burn bodies in churches after dispatching them. He looked normal, and I thought him merely an evil man. It therefore didn't occur to me to burn Saint Germain's body—and to kill everyone around this monster because someone might find a way to carry on his evil, to retrieve his body, put in a new heart, and reanimate him. I thought he was just a wicked man. Evil, but still human. Look at me. I should have known better." Alex's voice was hard with self-loathing, and it hurt her to hear it.

"Don't," Harmony said. "Just don't go there. You are nothing like this horrible man. And maybe—maybe you didn't actually kill him. Perhaps he survived somehow. A bullet or knife wound might not have been fatal. . . ."

Alex shook his head as she trailed off.

"I may or may not be like Saint Germain. But I killed him that night—I am as sure of that as I am of anything. It was revenge for Thomasina, and I was thorough, blinded with fury. Do you know what's odd, though? Even when lost to a killing rage, with my hands around his throat and wanting nothing but his death, a part of me began to wonder why we had the same eyes, the same unnatural strength. It was like grappling with my twin. Again, I didn't know then that the Dark Man had made more creatures like me. That he had 'cured' others like Lord Byron and Ninon de Lenclos—that it had amused him to create a sort of not-so-dead-poets society beholden to him, and he had traveled Europe looking specifically for artists and writers to seduce. To damn us even as he studied us. I thought I was a freak, a onetime experiment gone awry. But I should have known. I should have trusted my senses. If I had finished him then, none of this would be happening now."

Harmony made another small sound of distress but didn't interrupt with reassurances. This was not something she felt able to speak to. Alex would have to live with his guilt until he found a way to forgive himself.

"Le Comte said something that night that I didn't understand. 'It doesn't matter if you kill me,' he whispered the moment before I tore his heart from his chest. 'For worlds without number has my father made.' Then he said something else. It was Italian—'*La Cuore del Strega Sicilian* lives for me.' "

"*La Cuore del Strega Sicilian?*" she repeated.

"The heart of the witch. It's an obscure Sicilian legend about a wizard or a priest that wouldn't die—and anyone who was exposed to this evil relic became a flesh-eating ghoul. He didn't say anything more about it, because I didn't let him."

Alex cleared his throat and then looked at Harmony. His eyes were intent as he willed her to understand why he had committed such an act of violence. Why he would do it again.

"You think this *heart* is the original . . . contagion?"

"Possibly. Again, I don't know. A part of me has been waiting ever since that night, waiting and watching for a sign," he said. "You see, on some level I believed him. As much as I wanted to think otherwise, I somehow knew that his evil wouldn't die with him. I'm not so lucky. 'Worlds without number' had he—or his father—made. We know what that means now. His father did it out of scientific curiosity and to protect his son. Saint Germain—for him it's all about power. Though I never admitted it to myself, I've been watching for signs of their resurrection ever since that night. A part of me isn't certain that the Dark Man will remain dead either. Byron killed him and burned the body, but all

that Saint Germain needs is a bit of skin or hair—something
with DNA—and I know he could grow another."

Harmony felt the small hairs on her arms lift themselves
at these words.

"Human cloning? Shit." She exhaled. "And that is how
you ended up in Mexico?"

"Yes. I was reading some amazing stories in the tabloids,
the significance of which would elude all but a handful of
people. You see, I found out from another 'patient' who
contacted me once Dippel's pogrom against us started, that
though he had disappeared, the Dark Man had never actually died—and that he actually had many other clients who
lived on as I did. This could have been a help had I known
of them earlier and been able to organize them, but the
Dark Man killed most of us before I was aware of the others. As far as I know, only Lord Byron and Ninon de Lenclos have also survived."

Harmony shook her head. It was hard to take in no matter
how often Alex said it—Byron and Ninon de Lenclos? Alive?

"Do you know where they are now?" she asked hopefully.

"No. Once we were hunted, I believed that we were safer
not knowing where the others were, that we should remain
scattered, holed up in hidden fortresses. Saint Germain is
said to have the ability to eavesdrop on one's dreams, and ignorance seemed best. But now I must find them. I think I
can. I have a bit of a gift that way sometimes." Alex exhaled
and shook his head once. When he spoke, his voice was
again light and pleasant. "And that's enough of that. Lately
the past has been very much present for me, and that isn't a
pleasant circumstance. The thing with long life is that once
one has learned from one's mistakes, one must let go. The
guilt is too heavy otherwise."

"But was it really all a mistake?" Harmony asked, feeling
wistful without knowing why. She didn't tell him that it

looked to her as if guilt had him by the throat and was slowly tightening its jaws.

"All? No. I do not entirely regret loving either Thomasina or my children. But I have no wish to ever live any part of that life again. Some losses should never be faced more than once in a lifetime. Think about that before The Spider chooses to marry, and especially before she has children. Even if you evade Saint Germain, there will always be another danger looking for captives. In our line of work, it doesn't do to give hostages to Fate."

It is rare that one can see in a little boy the promise of a man, but one can almost always see in a little girl the threat of a woman.

—*Alexandre Dumas*

For seven years, not an hour has passed without my thinking of you. . . . Why did not God put himself out to the extent of whispering in my ear: "One day you will be loved by this child. Keep yourself for her." Some angel also might have said to you: "One day you will be eternally adored by this man. Keep yourself for him." God did not do what he should have done; the angels passed by without uttering a word.

—*Dumas* fils *to Henriette Regnier (September 22, 1893)*

A person who doubts himself is like a man who would enlist in the ranks of his enemies and bear arms against himself. He makes his failure certain by himself being the first person to be convinced of it.

—*Alexandre Dumas*

CHAPTER NINE

Santorini, Greece
June 10, 1912

Loneliness made men do strange things. Alex had ended up in Greece looking for others like himself who were resurrected by fire and lived beyond their allotted years, but he had found only stories of a kind of vampire that lived deep in the island caves. It was bitterly disappointing.

His traveling companions, a pair of professors from Oxford collecting local fairy tales, thought the plethora of vampire stories were because the natives of Santorini were a superstitious, half-heathen people who loved their legends more than their everyday lives. Really, it was just because Greece had a lot of these vampires—and not the romantic revenant so dear to English literature, as it turned out. The local vampires weren't humans who had died and returned from the grave in physical form to slake their lust for blood with beautiful women. No, the Greek vampires were wholly inhuman, small but strong supernatural beings that preyed mostly upon infants and pregnant women, though the sick and elderly were often victims too. They came in a variety of styles—there were lamias, mormos, empusas—Broucolokas, Byron had called them. Child-eating demons. Thoroughly nasty creatures whose filthy bites got so infected that the victims died from being envenomed even if they managed to survive the blood loss.

Alex now knew that they also would occasionally attack a healthy man if he was walking alone on a night when the moon was full.

Alex sighed with disgust as he looked down at the tear in his arm. The thing's grimy teeth had ripped away both flesh and muscle and ruined his best shirt. He'd broken its neck before it could do anything more, but this was probably bad enough. He had to pray that the Dark Man had been right when he told him that his own resurrected condition would protect Alex from all disease. If the Dark Man were wrong, then legend had it that Alex would fall into a coma before the full moon and then rise at the next dark of the moon in a zombielike thrall and showing symptoms of hydrophobia. After which, either the vampire would finish feeding on him or the villagers would try to kill him—a difficult and unpleasant proposition because the Dark Man's creations didn't die easily and it would take a great many painful wounds to accomplish the task.

Alex snorted as he bound up the gash. As if he hadn't enough problems already. This was what happened when you played the quixotic fool and chased after legends. He just had to accept that he was the only one of his kind.

As the jeep bumped along the country roads, there were many things that Harmony could—should—think about before she climbed on a plane bound for Cornwall, but her brain chose the one that was most seemingly irrelevant to her present situation.

It was no great surprise, given the tale he had related, that Alex felt he had fulfilled his quota of romantic relationships and didn't plan on having another. Not even with her—another psychic and now a comrade in arms. In fact, her being a psychic was probably a bad thing. He hadn't been that blunt, but she was a veteran of the dating wars and quite capable of reading between the lines. She couldn't blame him for feeling this way, either. Not really. She understood the appeal of "not having a lot of emotional mouths to feed." Her internal resources were needed for her job, which was sometimes exciting but often filled with corrosive tension. Besides, hadn't her brush with Beau frightened her enough to send her fleeing to Mexico? And she hadn't been blindly in love with him, just very hopeful. Poor Alex. The record of his disastrous love affairs was public knowledge. Cupid didn't use little gold-tipped arrows for some people; he seemed to favor hollow-point bullets. And Alex's last affair had been a trifecta of disaster, composed of residual guilt over past love affairs, a superhuman enemy engaged in a vendetta, and a dead girl. All of which he seemed in danger of repeating now—except the dead girl part, or so she hoped.

But given that neither of them wanted to be involved long-term with someone, and that Harmony was not what her mother would have called a woman of easy virtue, what the hell had happened between them back in Cuatros Cienegas? She had imagined the intensity of their encounter in the gazebo, had she? Or imagined Alex asking her if she was certain that this was what she wanted, because he could tell that screwing a total stranger wasn't something she would normally do?

Maybe the storm had overcome him later, but he had first led her outside with the purpose of . . . influencing her in another way. This wasn't the happiest thought, but the idea that Alex, knowing that a relationship with her wasn't anywhere in the cards, had still almost seduced her within minutes of their acquaintance was more maddening. That part had to have been an accident.

Alex—damn it! What was it about him? Why did she still

feel attracted to this stranger? She should be furious and wary, and instead she was . . . horny. And thinking in circles, but she couldn't let it go. He was an itch under the skin.

Understanding why the emotional deck was already stacked against even a short-term relationship didn't help, either. It had been hours, but Harmony was still feeling cross and even a bit bereft that they hadn't had their night together.

He hadn't just been using her, had he? Manipulating her sexually to gain her trust and help? Could he really have been so carried away with hunger that he had simply forgotten everything else? But then, where had the lust gone? Did it truly come and go with the lightning? And what if it happened again?

What if it *didn't* happen again?

Not that she wanted to get involved with him romantically! Her life didn't allow for that. But it just seemed sad that he had ruled out the idea completely and forever. Wasn't there someplace for tender feelings? Or plain old wholesome sex? And shouldn't she have some say in this, anyway? Wasn't refusing supposed to be the woman's prerogative?

"Damn," she muttered. "I'm ruminating. Stop me, please, before I brood again. Running emotional laps is stupid, stupid, stupid."

"I was an atheist," Alex announced, apropos of nothing, but definitely grabbing her attention. He looked sideways, eyes twinkling, and she wondered if he had somehow guessed her spiraling thoughts and was trying to intervene before she had a hissy fit over being rejected. She hadn't felt him in her mind since waking up, but that didn't mean he wasn't able to eavesdrop from a distance. She was probably going to have to find some way of jamming his radar if they stayed together for any length of time.

"Was?" she asked.

"Was—and a firm one. After my change—my resurrection—I felt that religious rules no longer applied. It was easy to turn my back on other moral fixtures too, especially when the societal landmarks were changing so rapidly. Law—civil and canonical—was not immutable after all. It changed with whoever had political power. It even altered with fashion.

"Then one day I heard God. After that, everything I believed changed."

"God? Like . . . *God*?" Harmony hadn't thought that anything could shake her out of her distraction, but she had been wrong. Once again, Alex had surprised her.

"Yes. It was during the War to End All Wars, on what would eventually come to be called Armistice Day, the eleventh of November. We were in the field, slaughtering one another as usual, when suddenly all the soldiers just stopped. As one, as if by drill, they lowered their weapons. Some even dropped them in the mud, and we all stood, staring up at the sky. Silence fell—there wasn't any sound, not a bird or bee or even the wind. Nothing the ear could hear. And it was in this unexpected, even miraculous quiet that hadn't existed for years that I finally recognized God's voice. Oddly enough, He doesn't use words to get our attention, no angelic trumpets, no burning bushes with voices of thunder—he uses perfect and, on that day, impossible silence, stilling our minds so we could look about and really see what we were doing to ourselves and to others. You're thinking I had a hallucination?" He shook his head. "I would think that, too, but I wasn't alone in this. Others heard him as well—unfortunately, not enough. And not for long. Moments later the silence broke. We picked up our guns and we were killing each other again only moments later." He added briskly but with a trace of bitterness: "And then, because we weren't done being destructive and thought we could do better a second time, we went on to have another world war a couple decades later. It is the way of mankind."

"Not all of mankind," Harmony protested.

"No, but the way of far too many." He shrugged. "I could have enlisted again for the Second World War, but I'd already done my time in the trenches and then some. I remembered that silence and decided they could have that war without me. I was done killing for governments. I changed my identity and moved on. Again. And then again. I never went back to church, though, never prayed. Still, now I know the truth. There is a God. And that makes everything that happens so much harder to accept. It was easier when I didn't believe. Now I have to take this fact into consideration and acknowledge that there may be a time when I will have to pay—even more than I have—for the life I have led. I want to be able to make an unashamed answer. There will be no innocent blood on my hands. Especially not yours."

"Jesus, Alex." But if this was his excuse for not having an affair, it was a good one. Who could argue with religious conviction?

He laughed. "No. Just God."

"I . . . I don't know what to say. Which happens a lot around you," she complained.

"Should I apologize?"

Should he? Was any of this really his fault?

The countryside was growing wilder, and the jeep bounced gaily over the ruts with no concern for the anatomy of the humans riding in it. If that weren't torture enough, the sun beat in on them mercilessly. It felt pernicious, life-threatening, and she began to have the feeling that they were not driving toward their destiny, but rather being driven by it.

Harmony didn't want to talk about God. She wasn't sure if she believed—or wanted to believe—in an omniscient being that guided the universe. As Alex had pointed out, if you believed there was someone in charge, then it was difficult not to be angry at him when things went wrong. Also, it seemed the height of foolishness to surrender any attention or will to some perhaps nonexistent Divine Plan; one could get killed waiting for God to fix things or reveal your purpose. And that didn't even begin to address the question of guilt for every petty—and not so petty—transgression that one might have made.

She didn't want to talk about their close encounter in the gazebo either—not with God maybe listening in. However, Alex's vast experience with creating new identities was something Harmony felt fine talking about.

"How do you do it?" she asked, ignoring God and sexual attraction.

"Disappear?" Alex said, still apparently able to follow her thoughts even when she didn't voice them aloud. He didn't pursue his explanations of the Almighty. "Various ways. You get good at faking records, faking deaths and births, and all kinds of financial sleight-of-hand so you can move your assets around. It's getting harder, though. About the only place you can safely 'die' these days is in war-torn Africa."

"Computers?" She nodded to herself. "They're everywhere. And databases are usually cross-referenced. Handy for me—at least sometimes."

"I admire you for dealing with them. I still think of them as the spawn of Satan. Certainly, in the wrong hands they *are* the tools of Satan. Yet, there are ways around them. The machines are only as smart as the people who program them."

"I know." She smiled a little.

"I figured you would. You might have to give me a crash course on defeating them. It's a technology I've been avoiding because of my effect on electronic things—and also because I have an aversion to anything that tyrannizes us as computers do . . . but I may not be able to ignore them much longer. Though I refuse to have a cell phone. I cannot understand why anyone would put themselves on an electronic leash." Harmony couldn't help but stare at the man next to her. The transformation of Alex was complete.

The sophisticated Frenchman was gone. Now he looked, at least superficially, like any one of her wholesome activist friends who liked camping and hiking in the wilds.

Still, she wasn't fooled by the new facade. She had already seen what he really was. Alex moved silently, elegantly, not like a dancer but with every bit as much grace; and a whole lot more threat. Those long hands that gripped the wheel could deal death efficiently. It was amazing that the other people they encountered didn't seem to see it.

But his ruthlessness might be something only she noticed, because she was aware now of how lethally capable he was. Until he had put a gun in her hand and told her to shoot whatever came out of the crypt, she hadn't been alert to anything about him except that he was the sexiest man she'd ever seen.

"How do you not lose your sense of self?" she asked him. "I mean, changing identities all the time. It's something I have tried to prepare for, in case I need to disappear one day, but I can't quite imagine what it would be like."

"Who says I don't lose my sense of self?"

"You seem very much like your old self—confident and . . ."

"Arrogant?" He grinned at her. His moods were mercurial. "I was originally born a Leo, you know. But my second birth happened in June. Now I am a Gemini. That seems fitting, since I have had two very different lives. I can live either with ease. And leaving behind my old life has always been easy. There was little of it that I wanted to keep."

"You've had more than two lives, it sounds like."

"Indeed. You should read more of my books—the new ones. The current one, supposing I can ever finish it, is a great romp." But he didn't sound as enthused as he should be. The idea that the great Alexandre Dumas could have writer's block was a strange one.

"Believe me, I have every intention of doing so the

minute we find a decent bookstore or library." Harmony took hold of the armrest and steadied herself. The road was worsening. "Do you really think you won't make your deadline?"

"I've never missed one before, but this situation is unusual."

"And then some," she agreed. "I don't suppose there is anything I can do to help with this."

"Probably not. But the thought is a kind one."

A cloud moved over the sun, and no longer trusting the sky to be benevolent, Harmony looked quickly about. But it wasn't the harmless clouds forming overhead that she found disturbing, it was the sudden shift in light that made the gullies around her appear fleshlike, wounds carved in a giant beast. Beneath the flaking dirt there seemed to be not normal stone but gristle and bone. The earth was sick. Something had infected it. Harmony couldn't repress a shiver.

"It's getting to you?" Alex asked. "I'm not surprised. Even before this recent evil, the land here was haunted. It isn't an easy place to visit if you see ghosts. Sunrise and sunset, they gather here—humans and animals—looking for the old river that drowned them. I can see their shadow auras."

Harmony shivered again. She didn't want to think about the unseen world that might be brushing up against her as they moved through it.

"Please . . . talk about something else. Tell me more about when you were—"

"Alive?" he asked.

"Stop that! I mean still living in Paris," she answered. Then: "Don't be morbid, Alex. I already have the creeps."

"My apologies. Well, let's see. . . . Understand, Paris in those days was very different—emotionally—from the post-World-War city that you know. I was born at a time when the rationalism of the eighteenth century was being wooed by the new romanticism of the nineteenth. My father died when I was four, so much of what I know of him is from others. He was almost all reason and logic, at least to those he served with in the army, though not with my mother. He loved her passionately—even blindly. And I was, because of my profession but also by inclination, always an open romantic, even when it wasn't fashionable. It was probably the company I kept. Think of the writers and composers who shared their creations in the coffeehouses every day. We were an inspiration and a goad to creativity. I still miss them."

"And Dumas *fils*? Was he also romantic?" she asked without thinking.

"I like to believe that he was a romantic too—though he did his best to appear otherwise. I think that much of what he wrote about women was his version of rebellion."

"Really?"

"If you consider it, you'll see that it's hard to mutiny against parental teachings when your parent is openly licentious and sets no limits on his own or his children's behavior. There's really no way to do it except by being tiresomely moral."

Harmony nodded slowly. She had read Dumas *fils'* thoughts on women. He had supported the idea of education for females, but he had also been harsh with those who gave in to their sensual natures. His letters to his lovers were a mix of tenderness and criticism.

He had also been in favor of a homeland for Jews—another romantic idea rather ahead of the political thoughts of the rest of Europe. Even without Alex's personal reminiscences, Harmony had thought that his son must have been a very unhappy person.

"You think it's in the blood, then? There's a gene for romanticism that can pass from parent to child?"

"Perhaps. I think it can be a mistake to try and explain

anyone simply by their heredity, but I have to admit that in my case—and that of my son—certain traits must be labeled as familial, not least among them a gift with words and a bloody-minded stubbornness when it comes to writing and doing what we wanted. And it must be nature, not nurture, that caused this, because my father died when I was only four and I saw little of my son until he was grown. We all grew up as wildflowers; untended if not unwanted. Our only guidance was what came within the parental seed."

"From what I've read, it seemed like a lot of wine, women, and song was going on after Dumas *fils* moved in with you." Harmony regretted speaking these words almost immediately. She really didn't want to hear anything more about Alex's past loves. She had read some of his love letters back in college when she had taken a class in French literature, and they had been frankly erotic. She'd developed the worst crush on him and had been teased mercilessly for it. Given what she was now thinking—and what she had so recently been feeling—she didn't want to chance Alex picking up on any stray embarrassing thoughts.

"Certainly women." Alex smiled a little. "But more poetry than music—though Donizetti and Rossini were good friends of mine, and Donizetti gave me my favorite pasta recipe. And there was always politics, of course. We argued often. My family had an absolute genius for getting on the wrong side of political movements. My father and son were especially affected, because they tried so hard to shape social morality with these means and took each failure to heart. That they persisted in these endeavors even in the face of authorities' open disdain did not endear them to those in power, especially not with Saint Germain and the Dark Man always in the background making sure that we were kept from office or any other form of mass influence."

"Except, they failed with you and your writing."

"To a degree. Much of my work was actually suppressed."

"Really?" This was startling. Alexandre Dumas had been one of the most prolific writers to ever live. That he could have written even more stories and plays that were censored was amazing.

"Yes. It sadly is true."

"You were made Minister of Antiquities, though," Harmony pointed out, then winced as she was thrown against the jeep's door. The road was little better than a goat path now, and just as narrow. "You led the first dig on Pompeii."

"They appointed me only to get me out of the country during the elections. Hmm. No one knows about this except tiresome scholars. You've been studying me a bit too much, I think. You need a new hobby." Alex couldn't let go of the wheel on this rough road to wag his finger at her, but she knew he wanted to.

"Literature major in college. I wrote a paper on you," she confessed as she was again tossed against the jeep's door. Her right arm was beginning to feel bruised. "Damn! Where the hell are we?"

"I'm not sure," Alex admitted. "But we are headed in the right direction."

"How can you tell?" Harmony asked. "Everything looks the same and I haven't seen a sign in hours."

"Intuition. Or maybe Fate. In any event," Alex said blithely, "you will find that I am always exactly where I need to be."

"And here I was thinking we were in the wrong place at the wrong time," Harmony muttered.

Victor Hugo: Would you believe it, there's a wretched scribbler who claims Vigny invented historical drama!
Alexandre Dumas: The fool! As though everyone didn't know that it was I!

At present I am living by my penmanship, but someday I shall be living by my pen.

—*Dumas* père *when hired as a copyist by the Duc d'Orleans*

CHAPTER TEN

Normally Alex didn't like flying, but he was actually quite pleasantly distracted from his usual nervousness by watching Harmony alternately scowl and bite her lip as she read and reread the file on her portable computer. Watching her hand hover and then retreat from the delete button, he recognized her difficulty at once. It was first-book-itis, a condition that rendered a new author incapable of deciding when it was time to call a chapter finished and move on to the next. In his experience, it was best to let a writer work his way through decision-making processes alone whenever possible, but beyond a certain point there were no more lessons to be learned from editing and reediting.

Finally, when he could endure it no longer, he decided to take pity on her.

"Would you like me to read that? I promise I can be honest and yet humane with my comments."

Harmony hesitated for only a moment.

"Yes, please—if you truly don't mind. I'm afraid that I'm so close to this that I can't tell if what I've written is actually passable or if it's just crap." She tried to hand him the portable computer, but he shook his head.

"Best if you hold it. I'm hard on electronics. You'll notice that I don't wear a watch or have a cell phone. That isn't solely because I loathe them."

"Oh. Okay."

Alex began to read, hoping that Harmony had some talent. He could fix anything, of course, but it would be better if she was actually gifted.

Her first sentence made him laugh.

THE SPIDER
By Anonymous

Prologue

"I want that sodding son of a bitch's head on a platter!" Captain Jack roared, upsetting the stack of unread reports gathering dust on the edge of his desk.

"Was that with or without an apple?" inquired the lately retired Detective Inspector Dan Tracy, sotto voce from the back of the room. He had been called in by Captain Jack to assist in the town's crisis in the vain hope that Tracy could solve the case without recoursing to his former and unwanted (at least by Captain Jack) employers at the Yard.

No one so much as cracked a smile at the quip. The quiet town of Dunnstone was having a bout of upper-class hysterics, and the constabulary were all too tired—too bloody pissed—from chasing this phantom spectre over slate rooftops of the picturesque village and down blind, cobblestone alleys to find anything humorous in Tracy baiting the chief.

"What were you lot doing last night that you managed to miss him?" The chief's question was purely rhetorical, which was just as well, as the shaken bobbies were understandably reticent about answering this unfair accusation; they'd done all they could to defend against the foe's incursion. It just wasn't enough to stop the seemingly supernatural force that was attacking Dunnstone.

There were few lasting stars in England's firmament of famous crime—Jack the Ripper, Deacon Brodie, perhaps Robin Hood. But a new sun was racing toward ascendancy in Albion's night sky. A nouvelle folk hero of the environmental movement was blazing criminal trails, and, according to the chief—and most unfortunately for the men in the briefing room—the Dunnstone police constabulary had been cast in the role of bumbling foe.

Added to their woes, Captain Harry Jack was very unhappy about heading up the local chapter of the Keystone Kops, and said so frequently and with increasing bitterness to anyone who would listen. As his wife and friends were avoiding him these days, that left the luckless men in his employ to hear the ever more acrid tirades. Consequently, every last man who worked under the irate chief was also very, very unhappy, and growing more bitter by the day.

The point had been driven home over the past weeks that Dunnstone's forces of law and order were no match for the master criminal who, with preeminent artistry and dextrous hands, left behind a wake of dismantled alarm systems, empty safes and—most distressing to the victims—missing computer hard drives and captured diskettes whose contents showed up in the hands of "sensation-seeking reporters" and the "lunatic fringe" that made up the political arm of the environmental movement.

And the private detectives hired in London by the hysterical victims, the police's paid snitches, the story-hungry tabloids, none of them had a reasonable guess as to who The Spider might be. Even a gigantic reward for "information leading to the arrest of . . ." had failed to elicit a favorable response from the underworld. It was frustrating for the men on the side of law and order.

The weary constables filed out of the captain's small office a short while later, looking and feeling thoroughly mauled.

"Harry." Dan Tracy paused in the chief's door.

"What?" Harry had calmed down some, but he was still growling.

"You're going to have to call in the Yard." Tracy's tone was apologetic as he stated the distasteful fact. "The press is going to get wind that The Spider's moved north, and you'll have hostile press and the Yard shoved up your arse if you haven't made an effort to coordinate with London."

"I know," the chief surprised him by answering. "But I still want to be the one who catches the cocky bastard. He has some nerve waltzing up north to have a flutter on my home turf."

"Well, yes. I see your point, but you shouldn't take it so personally—"

"Well, I bloody well do!"

"—because he's after Carter! And only Carter. No one else lives up here."

That wasn't strictly true; Dunnstone boasted a population of nearly a thousand souls, some of them well-heeled enough to attract regular burglars. But none of them mattered in terms of the current crime wave.

Harry Jack glared at his friend but didn't argue. They both knew that The Spider was after anyone and everyone who had stuck a thumb in Terry Carter's latest mining venture. Harry could even sympathize with The Spider's feelings about what Carter did to the lands he bought, because "rape" was too mild a word to describe his methods of mineral extraction.

But that didn't alter the fact that a third high-profile robbery had been carried out at the Carter estate, the sixth theft from Carter's many properties. Those were the seventh, eighth, and ninth in a string of burglaries directed against both Carter and Tewson, Tewson being the man who'd arranged for the probably illegal sale of undeveloped land to Carter.

"I'll authorize double shifts. Double pay. But I must find that bloody thief before he strikes again," the chief said emphatically, marking each syllable with a flat-handed blow to his desk that shook his overfilled

tray and brought his magazine pile ever
closer to the edge of the desk.

    Dan Tracy rolled his eyes, but left the
room without further argument. They could
quadruple the hours and the pay and it
wouldn't make any difference. The Spider
was a criminal like a character of wildest fic-
tion, and Dunnstone's meager police force
wasn't going to catch him.

"Wow," Alex said at last. He added enthusiastically, "I'm
impressed. This is excellent for a first draft. Do you have
more?"

"A few chapters—actually quite a few chapters—but
none of them is very polished. I keep thinking I may be
writing for the wrong reasons."

"There are no wrong reasons to write. Don't worry," Alex
said absently, scanning the final page again. "I polish faster
than anyone. We'll have you ready to submit in no time."

"*I know*"—Harmony blinked—"I mean, I know that you
were a quick writer. History has it that you were the terror
of your secretarial staff. They could barely keep up with
your output. In fact, they called you . . ."

She trailed off. His nickname had been a racial slur. He
had in fact called out the man who had printed the article
saying he was a "nigger slavé-driver lording it over the
other blacks he employed." It had been only one of many
duels he fought with the men of the press.

Alex chuckled, the memory apparently no longer cause
for anger. Perhaps that was because he'd won those duels,
and history had awarded him a moral victory as well.

" 'The slave-driver.' Almost no one knows about that
anymore. I've been whitewashed by the literary world. It's a
bit strange after all these years to have someone around who
knows who I am. Or was. I'd like to think that I've changed

some—and for the better. These days I hardly ever call out critics who pan my books." Alex lifted his eyes from the computer screen. Though she should have been accustomed to his ebony gaze, she apparently still found it riveting.

"Well, I think you'd be okay as an editor, if a bit bossy in other parts of life," Harmony answered, holding his stare for an instant and then looking away. Something was doing funny things to her breathing. "How much longer do we have before landing? Were you able to fax off your next chapter to your secretary before we left? I feel guilty letting you help me when you still have so much left to write."

"We are about four hours from Gatwick. And then a long car ride that may be excruciating because of tourist traffic."

"There's nothing closer?"

"There's actually a small airport at Newquay, but I prefer not to announce our arrival in Cornwall. It may be paranoia, but I am not certain anymore about who might be in Saint Germain's pay. But don't worry, Millie will have had the caretaker go around to the cottage, so everything will be in order for us, with no one—at least, no one who is too interested in our whereabouts—being the wiser. That gives us plenty of time to concentrate on the matter at hand and get this book whipped into shape." Alex said ruthlessly: "Show me the next chapter—and stop worrying about *my* manuscript, if that's what's making you frown. It's all under control."

The plane hit a small pocket of turbulence, reminding them that they were no longer safely on the ground. Alex glanced out the window and grimaced. Harmony did the same.

"I'm not sure I'm in the right frame of mind to write just now. It feels frivolous when I know that there's so much . . ." She trailed off, still having trouble articulating her reaction to all that they had seen in Mexico.

"But of course you must write—that is what we do." Alex was definite.

"But what about Saint Germain?" she protested weakly. "We can't just forget about him."

"Would you suggest to a cherry tree that it not grow cherries just because there is a man with an ax somewhere in the woods? Or that fish stop swimming because there are fishermen in his stream? My dear, our character is our destiny. You are what you are, Harmony. Embrace it. It is not enough just to survive—not in the long run. Take this lesson from me. One must thrive, not just endure. What is life without bliss? You know your joy, now . . . pursue it. A very wise American once said that a house divided against itself will not stand. This I know to be true. And you can write even now. I have written in exile, in prison, with a bounty on my head—as did Victor Hugo and Descartes and Molière. And many others before and since. Writers write. Let me worry about Saint Germain while you finish your book. We can't act effectively until we have more information anyway. Take the gift of this enforced air travel and stay on my island and put the time to good use."

Harmony felt herself being persuaded. If not on an island, surrounded by the peaceful sounds of the ocean, then where and when would she ever find the time to finish her book? And when would she ever have the chance to have anyone as gifted as Alexandre Dumas do her editing?

"No person or place could be more ideal," Alex affirmed. "Now, show me the next chapter."

"Are you sure you want to do this? You don't have to, you know," she said a last time.

"Of course I know. But you also know, since you've studied me, that I have always patronized new writers. I like to foster talent that might otherwise wither before blooming. So finish your story, and I will help you make it commercial," Alex answered. "It's an important one to tell, and no one else can be counted on to get the details just so. It is your legacy and your right to do this. But, as you now know, Fate is a fickle bitch. You may not have another clear space of time in which to work once we find out about Saint Germain. Seize this day and walk in the sun."

"That sounds like something that belongs on a tombstone," she complained.

Alex nodded soberly but said, "Believe it or not, there are far worse epitaphs to be had."

Two Kalmucks put a whip in my hand. With one of these whips Prince Tumaine can kill a wolf at a single blow by striking it on the nose.

—*Letter from Dumas* père *to Dumas* fils *while visiting Russia*

My father was a great big child which I had when I was just a little boy.

—*Dumas* fils, *about his father*

Infatuated, half through conceit, half through love of my art, I achieve the impossible working as no one else ever works.

—*Alexandre Dumas*

CHAPTER ELEVEN

"There she is. That's Chilicott's Folly." Alex pointed to the right as he parked the car at the side of the road on a narrow strip of gravel that would have intimidated a mountain goat. "I bought it about seventeen years ago. I used to stay here with my friend Conan Doyle. The only place prettier is the Channel Islands where my friend Hugo used to live, but the weather wasn't as predictable there. I find comfort in knowing that there are regular storms here. You cannot imagine how many places there are in the world that have no reliable rain."

"You mean Arthur Conan Doyle?" Harmony asked, unfastening her seat belt. Then added: "And Victor Hugo?"

"But of course."

"Name-dropper."

Alex smiled. "Hugo wrote *Les Misérables* there when he was in exile on the islands. I believe the setting helped. These North Sea islands are seemingly serene but secretly savage places. It is difficult to believe when the sea is as placid as it is today, but it isn't always so. Winds blow hard and from all over the world. Look at the variety of plants blown here—wild sea grass called marram, agapanthus from Africa, and many wildflowers to attract butterflies, none of which were native. There are fishing birds blown here too, dunlins, plovers—they haunt the fractured rock crying like inconsolable ghosts at sunrise and sunset." Then, with equal casualness: "I had a small swimming pool put in last year. It is filled with seawater—very refreshing to swim in. It is a small house, only five bedrooms. But very private. Our only company are the dead in the cemetery, and they're quiet. It's a good place for writing. You should be able to work here. I think we can have your story ready in a week, perhaps two."

"Oh. Good. Thank you." Harmony was feeling a bit dazed by the schedule Alex had set her. She couldn't help but wonder if he had designed it so that she would have little time to worry about what was going on with Saint Germain, and if that were true, why? Surely he didn't think she was going to let him go off and confront this monster all by himself. Alex may have had the older quarrel, but this man was doing things that were an abomination in the eyes of all humanity. That made him The Spider's business.

"Ready to make the climb?" Alex asked.

"Ready to be done with sitting." But Harmony gave herself another moment to study the island before approaching it. She would never have admitted it out loud, but she was trying to sense what sort of place this might be.

The red-roofed house stood atop a ninety-foot-tall slab of wooded rock, at the moment marooned on a beach of golden sand. It was immediately apparent that the only way to reach the house was across a suspension bridge anchored to the cliff face above where they had parked. There was a narrow stair with shallow steps leading up to the bridge that spanned the strange vertical space between the island and the mainland.

"It looks as if a giant with a croquet mallet knocked the land away," she said softly.

"Cornwall had giants, you know, so that may be what happened."

"So I've heard."

Harmony climbed out of the mini-coupe and stretched her legs, breathing deeply of the sea air. The same sun shone here as in Mexico, but its rays felt infinitely more benevolent. Alex was right; it was difficult to see this place as anything other than benign. They should both be able to work here.

"The tide is on the turn," Alex said. "In two hours, the island will be completely surrounded by water. It's an odd sensation. There's a certain resonance to the waves that moves through the stone. You can almost hear the island humming at high tide."

Harmony looked with disfavor at the stair and then the narrow suspension bridge that linked the island to the mainland.

"We walk?" she guessed.

"This time. There are bicycles on the island." Alex slammed the car door, their suitcases in hand. Harmony carried her portable.

"You know what today is?" Alex asked.

"Um—Wednesday?"

"It's St. James's Day. We must have oysters tonight—it brings good fortune." They started up the first stone stair, Alex in the lead. Harmony stepped carefully. The red rock was fairly smooth, but the angle had a slight backward grade and was uncomfortable. It would be treacherous to run up in the wet. She had to wonder if that wasn't deliberate. After all, one probably had to be unusually private to want to live on an island.

As they approached, the house quickly emerged from the shrubs. The building had an odd appearance that the builder had probably not intended. But this was Cornwall, home of mystical beasties and pirates, so perhaps the architect had been deliberate in placing windows so that they looked like a pair of dark eyes staring out from under a bloodied scalp. Beyond the house she could see the stone roofs of mini-houses, which she assumed were the sepulchers where the quiet neighbors rested.

"Wasn't James the Apostle beheaded by Herod? What makes him so lucky?" she asked, mounting the next flight of stairs.

"He has shown up to help good Christians in time of war. He rides onto the battlefield in shining armor atop a white steed—covered in oyster shells." Alex smiled back at her, but Harmony could tell that he was distracted. As she watched, he took several deep breaths of air, turning each time so he faced a different direction.

"That could be handy. If you're a good Christian, of course." Through the dense foliage she could see the slate roofs of other cottages on the mainland. All the chimneys were smokeless and decorated with moss and cooing plovers. She was charmed to see white snowdrops growing at the side of the stair, pushing up bravely among the slabs of granite.

"This must be a great place for you to write. Have you worked here before?" she asked, her breathing growing labored as they neared the bridge at the top of the stair.

"Yes. And let us hope it inspires me again," she thought she heard him say. "I'll need all the help I can get to finish this one. I still don't know what possessed me to write about my time in Tangier."

Alex stepped onto the suspension bridge and turned back for her. Shifting the bags to one hand he stood smiling, offering his other hand as if he knew how much she disliked the idea of stepping onto the frail-looking span.

Harmony had begun to reach for his fingers when a stray gust of wind buffeted her contemptuously, tossing her against the rope railing. For a moment she feared that she might actually topple over the side of the low cable rail.

What are you? the wind asked. *Just another human. You are nothing—a bit of flesh that I might blow away. Have a care, or that is what I shall do.*

Then Alex's hand clasped hers, and the feelings of incipient alarm died away.

"It's perfectly safe here," he assured her. "If you're careful."

Perhaps that was true, but Harmony suspected that she wouldn't ever try to cross this bridge alone.

For a thorough understanding of the culinary arts, no one is as well equipped as a man of letters; for he, accustomed to refinements of every kind, knows better than anyone else how to appreciate those of the table.

—*Alexandre Dumas*

I am receiving letters from all over France, letters in which people seek my advice about polenta, caviar or bird's nest soup. . . . I see with pleasure that my culinary reputation is growing and bids fair to eclipse before long my literary reputation. God be praised! I shall then be able to devote myself to a respectable calling and to bequeath to my children, instead of books which they might inherit for fifteen or twenty years, casseroles and marmites which they would inherit for eternity and could bequeath in the same manner to their own descendants.

—*Alexandre Dumas (reported in* Les Nouvelles*)*

CHAPTER TWELVE

THE SPIDER

Chapter One

Moving house hadn't been as traumatic as expected. Of course, she hadn't actually moved house; she'd just packed a suitcase—well, three suitcases, a purse, and a PC—and strolled from her airport hotel into Terry Carter's fully furnished country home. Gillian stood on the rear terrace overlooking the rose garden, enjoying the fading away of the afternoon, and admitting to herself that she was more than smugly pleased with her newfound luck. Since leaving Thomas and the States, she'd been living a charmed existence. First there was the auction for her fourth novel. That heavily publicized event not only provided her with an adequate income, but had guaranteed the need for a sequel and the reprinting of her three previous novels. The royalty checks were already rolling in.

On the personal front there was Scott and Jonathan. Who would have guessed that two such successful and wealthy men would be attracted to her! The fact that they were a little boring was irrelevant. After all, she wasn't planning to marry either of them. They were just for occasional dating when she needed an escort to some public function where she would be embarrassed to turn up alone. And last, but hardly least, there was this mansion, tumbled into almost by accident when she'd bumped into an estate agent at a book signing who overheard her pie-in-the-skying with her publicist. Her karma was definitely improving.

"All the bad stuff is behind me," she said with a sigh, leaning on the balustrade and breathing in the warm, clean air that was such a change from the exhaust fumes of London. Nobody in California built manorhouses in stone, or had parapets and marble statues and hidden stairs! Wouldn't her nephew go nuts playing hide-and-seek in the garden maze when her sister's family came for Christmas? The ancient yew hedges were an imaginative kid's paradise. In fact, the whole place was just this side of Eden.

Of course, there was the little matter of the burglary. But the agent who had brokered the deal had assured her that the owner had installed a new, super-powerful security system. She had to admit that the thing certainly looked powerful, with its panel of blinking lights and elaborate arming and disarming rituals. And it wasn't as if she had anything worth stealing. Her only item of any value was her older-model portable PC—and surely that wouldn't interest the kind of burglar who robbed country estates.

No, she was definitely living in clover! After years of struggling with her writing and with a commitment-phobic lover, she finally had life by the tail and she was going to enjoy every damn minute of it.

"Is it Christmas again already?"

"What? Of course it isn't Christmas!"

Daniel Spencer sighed inwardly and waved his brother, Allen, Commander of the Criminal Investigation Department of Scotland Yard, into his favorite wing chair and then headed for the brandy. Allen only visited socially once a year, but he had a definite preference about where he sat.

"Daniel." Allen's tone was grim as he settled himself into his sibling's just-vacated chair, confirming Daniel's suspicions that this was not December and his brother's visit was not a social call.

"There is beginning to be a great deal of gossip about your pet organization."

Free Our Forests. His brother would never name it.

"Of course. But they're harmless, you know," Daniel murmured, pouring out a generous snifter of brandy and handing it to his brother. Allen never had approved of his brother's patronage of various environmental groups. But then, Allen was on the side of law and order—mostly order—and found the group's membership's tendencies toward civil disobedience aggravating. It also embarrassed him that his own flesh and blood had founded the organization. The only reason that the two brothers were still on speaking terms was because Daniel had retired from active membership in the organization once they had found their financial feet, and gone back to being a dilettante who made money through investment rather than by the sweat of the brow or attempting to change the social order.

"You may find this situation humorous, but I do not. Everyone is up in arms about these burglaries, and fingers are being pointed at various environmentalist groups. What if this scofflaw is a member of your . . . ah . . . old organization?"

"Rather doubtful," Daniel said, taking a seat across from his tense sibling and sneaking a glance at his watch. It was not the expected Rolex, but rather a sturdy black sports-watch that was missing the blue neon LCD. He smoothed his dark sweater over his wrist and then sipped from his glass, feeling the familiar need for an anesthetic that always accompanied Allen's visits.

"I don't see how you can be so sanguine about that bunch of nutters."

"I know the constituents, and while they

are zealous, they are not"—Daniel searched briefly for an appropriate word—"organized enough to carry out these rather daring exploits. They are mostly university students trying to salve their consciences by doing a good deed or two between attending drinking parties and playing cricket."

"You would know," Allen said peevishly.

"As you say," Daniel answered. He ignored the dig. He always ignored Allen's digs, because it annoyed his sibling so much when he did so. He stared briefly at his brother's ever-increasing waistline and ham-colored complexion. "You must relax, Allen. I can assure you that none of FOF's staff—or volunteers—will end in a police lineup. At least, not because of being accused of being The Spider," he amended scrupulously.

"Hmph!" But Allen slouched back into his chair and took a generous swallow of his brother's excellent brandy. "You're absolutely sure of this?"

"Oh, yes," Daniel said, sincerely. "Now stop fretting before your heart fails and you end up laid out flat with candles at your head and feet. You don't have the . . . the constitution for this kind of stress. Comes from having a desk job, I expect. You should try and get out on the links once in a while."

"Easy for you to say," Allen answered in a complaining tone. "No one in your office—if you even had an office anymore—would be in a lather over this criminal! Your environmentalist friends probably even applaud his arrogant, anti-progress attitude."

"Probably," Daniel agreed, all the while feeling it was a shame that his only brother had turned out such a boorish prig. Another glance at his watch revealed that only two minutes had slipped by. He took another swallow of brandy.

"And now we're seeing Rabelaisian graffiti and flyers all over the city," Allen went on complaining.

"Um." Daniel had seen several at the last FOF staff meeting he'd dropped in on. "Have another brandy," he suggested.

"It won't help," Allen said.

"Well, no. But it might make you feel better."

"Hmph!" Allen snorted again, but went to pour himself another generous tot. "You're going to the Green Gala?"

"No," Daniel said regretfully. "Angelica and Hubert will be there for FOF, but I think that I best head north to see Biggs. He's not so hearty these days and has been asking after the family. And I'd like to get in a spot of fishing while the weather holds."

"Lucky dog. Mary and I were supposed to go on holiday next week, but it'll never happen now. Unless we arrest this . . . this . . ."

"Folk hero," Daniel suggested.

"He is nothing of the sort!" Allen snapped, rising like a trout to the bait. "The man's a damned thief."

"He's also very popular."

"Only with you and others of your ilk. He's a bloody tree-kisser! If Mary ever gets a hold of him—"

"Hugger," Daniel corrected.

"What?"

"Tree-hugger. Not even the Americans have taken to putting lips to the shrubbery."

"Whatever. He's damned inconsiderate—thieving during the August holiday? I think he does this on purpose. The selfish swine is ruining my life!"

"Yes, well, there is that," Daniel agreed, not mentioning that while The Spider hadn't started his thieving with an eye to upsetting Allen's holiday plans, the fact that he had succeeded in doing so was a definite bonus as far as Daniel was concerned. He suggested pointedly: "Another drink before you go?"

"I haven't finished this one."

"Hm." Daniel headed for the rapidly depleting decanter.

"You are becoming an alcoholic." But Allen didn't urge his sibling to take up gainful employment or become involved in any more charitable causes.

"Very likely. It's one of the hazards . . ." of having you as a brother, Daniel finished inside his head.

"You're fixing dinner?" Harmony was relieved. She was getting hungry and hated cooking in a strange kitchen.

"Of course. I have been a terrible host—not feeding you properly after I've kept you slaving over your manuscript." Alex smiled at her with both his eyes and lips, and as always she felt something inside contract with pleasure, anticipation, and just a bit of something akin to fear. "Have you explored all of the cottage now?"

"Not yet. I looked around upstairs and found the gun

room. I recognized some of the guns. I've never shot a Nitro before. Couldn't afford one." She sounded a bit wistful,
even to her own ears.

"That Holland and Holland is dangerous," Alex warned.
"If you ever do need to use it, best to prop it against a tree or
wall—anything other than your body. That thing is designed
to drop a charging elephant. Did you see the Winchester?"

"The over-and-under? Yes. It's a museum piece."

"That is a good weapon. Practical. Powerful. Not much
call for it now, of course. I never hunt anymore. Still, I keep
them as mementos."

"I also saw some strange bone weapons. They looked nasty."

"Ah—those are Masai weaponry, a throwing club and a
sort of knife that warriors use to kill lions. Both are made
from giraffe bone—the femur and the shoulder blade—the
densest bone material on earth. You can split a lion skull
like a cleaver chops a chicken."

"Charming." Harmony grimaced.

"No, but lethal."

"And the vicious-looking whip on the wall?"

"It is used by the Cossacks for hunting wolves. The
weighted tips can kill a wolf with one blow if you strike at
the nose. I got rather good with it. It came in handy once
the wolves followed the French soldiers back from Russia.
They were man-eaters by then. Napoleon's ill-advised jaunt
into Russia during the winter gave the wolves a nice supply
of easy prey, and they acquired a taste for it." This answer
shouldn't surprise her. Killing had been woven into the tapestry of Dumas's life almost from childhood. He was a gentleman and probably found killing distasteful, but he was
also—thank God for both of their sakes—very good at it.

"Ugh. I'm just not a sportsman, I guess. I like guns but
not killing."

Alex took down a glass jar filled with rice and set it be-

side the crock of butter and a plate of a dozen ripe tomatoes. He then ducked into a small pantry and emerged with
a cured ham, a bundle of garlic, and two sausages.

Harmony watched as he pulled out a large copper pan,
deeper than a skillet but not as deep as a saucepan. The lid
was cone-shaped and slotted almost like a strainer.

"It's called a *chinois*," he said, not waiting for her question. He began chopping tomatoes on a sheet of white
marble. He worked with the speed of a professional chef.
"The pan is a *marmite*. It, along with the *poleon,* is a kind of
what we used to call a casserole. We did not cook in earth-
enware dishes in my day. In many places they did not have
any sort of oven, you see. You can have no idea how different kitchens were then."

"You use gas here?"

"Yes. As I mentioned before, I keep my interactions with
electrical items to a minimum." Harmony believed this.
She had found his office. It was full of books, stuffed floor
to rafters with old tomes in many languages. The only two
concessions to modern living were an old rotary phone and
a fax machine—on top of which rested a pair of rubber
gloves. There wasn't even a lamp on the antique desk. Just a
candlestick.

Alex lit a burner on the old stove. It puffed once in indignation, but stayed alight. It hissed like the old style of
Coleman lantern her father had used when they went
camping. Fascinated, Harmony boosted herself onto the
high table that served as a counter, watching with interest as
Alex tossed sliced tomatoes and water into a pan. He added
a generous dollop of butter and gave it a quick stir.

"Tomatoes—fruit of the south where they grow quite
sweet. Not like those horrid things I get in New York. Do
you like to cook?"

"I cook some but prefer baking," she told him.

"Of course. It is much the same, though—a bit of fantasy,

boldness, but not brutality. Food—with few exceptions—must be coaxed, not beaten into submission." Alex's accent was slowly reappearing. Perhaps he was unable to suppress it when he was distracted and feeling passionate. It had been quite thick while they were making love in the gazebo, she thought. He glanced up at her. "It is rather sensual, no?"

"Yes." If one meant it was of the senses. No tomato could compete with Alex, though. Harmony leaned over the pan and inhaled deeply. The sauce was turning a beautiful scarlet color, and the butter smelled a bit of nuts. A clove of garlic was smashed flat and flicked into the pan. The pungent aroma burst out immediately and enveloped her. She sighed happily. Maybe Alex had a point. This smell of garlic pleased her far more than that of most of her past boyfriends.

"Ah! Garlic. Did you know in ancient Greece that those who ate garlic were refused entrance at the temple of Cybele? The Greeks absolutely abhorred it. The Romans liked it more, but then, they ate everything." His brow furrowed. "As I recall, Alfonso, king of Castile, in the fourteenth century actually founded an order of knights that had to swear not to appear at court for a full month after they had eaten either onion or garlic. How sad to be a Spaniard then. It is true that garlic is odorous, but the whole world smelled bad in that era because of the repugnance of bathing. That is what perfume was for. The French, we are always more sensible. More fun." Alex began chopping ham and sausage with great enthusiasm.

"Very sensible, if by that you mean unafraid of flavors and smells. Um, are we feeding all of the village?" Harmony asked after a while as he kept on chopping until the ham was gone. It didn't take long. Alex was good with a knife.

"Oh. No." He sighed. "I forgot. Whenever I cooked here, it was always for a crowd. I don't like to cook just for myself." He began adding the ham to the casserole. Brightening, he added, "It is very good on the second day. We can have it for breakfast."

"Hmmm." Harmony was noncommittal. She wasn't a huge fan of breakfast, and when she did indulge it was in more traditional fair. However, she was willing to do a lot to avoid cooking in this very old-fashioned kitchen.

Alex added the ham and sausage and then poured in an entire jar of rice. He threw in a fistful of kosher salt. He truly did not seem to know how to practice moderation in the kitchen.

"You don't measure anything?" she asked, impressed and a bit horrified.

"No need. Experience has taught me well, and I am none too fond of rules." He added water almost to the top and then put the dunce cap on top of the pan. "Now for the lobster and a few oysters—just for luck."

"Lobster? Someone delivered lobster and oysters?" Harmony was surprised.

"Fresh off the fishing boat and beach. Millie pre-arranged it."

"Your Millie is an amazing woman. I hope you pay her well."

"Indeed. In fact, I think you would agree that her pay borders on obscene. She is ugly to look upon but has a true genius for organization," he replied with obvious relish. "Now, attention, please. This is a recipe I perfected years ago for crayfish. Or *crawfish,* as they say in *Nouvelle Orléans.* Another time I shall prepare spitted lobster. It is not so common a dish now, I think because it is difficult to tie the lobsters to the spits. I cook them with a light basting of champagne. And when the fire is hot, you toss them on. The shell breaks at once and then crumbles away like chalk. It is so much easier to dismantle that way, and less meat is lost."

Harmony shuddered at the image.

"A lobster auto-da-fé—no, thanks."

"Don't look so horrified. They are simply large, delicious insects, not pets." Alex sounded amused. He had also never been so chatty or relaxed.

"You're not helping. I don't like the thought of eating bugs either."

"Ah, but if they are delicious . . ."

Alex reached into the cupboard overhead and pulled down a cauldron with two handles. As he did so, Harmony saw that he had a pistol tucked into the band of his pants. They had left their other weapons in Mexico, so this meant Alex had retrieved a weapon after their arrival at the cottage and felt the need to wear it—and not for hunting, which he didn't do anymore. She shouldn't be surprised. He had told her that he never went unarmed, but she had hoped he meant only in Mexico. Weren't they safe here in this island retreat?

Alex turned to the window and inhaled deeply.

" 'The sea, the only love to whom I have been faithful.' Byron said that. I have always agreed with him on this. I would be in Paris and begin to feel tormented by the filth and crowds, so I would invent a reason and either rent a carriage or take the train to Trouville or perhaps Le Havre." He laughed suddenly. "I recall now that I did feed a village once. It was in Fecamp. I had become so stifled at home that I thought I would go mad, and heard from a friend of this seaside village where the fishing was grand and the boatmen were willing to take on passengers for a small fee. That was the first time I caught a lobster. I went out with a boat for the day, and we also caught two mackerel and an octopus."

"Did you cook them?"

"Naturally. As per my instructions, the janitress at the hotel had been attending the pot-au-feu, and it was ready on our return. I would have made my own soup, but it must cook all day to be flavorful. The woman seemed competent, and so I trusted her to follow my instructions. She had also prepared two chickens who were there waiting for me, naked and ready, and also a beef kidney, which she had left blessedly free of sauce. A kidney cannot be dressed ignorantly, and so few have the art of it." He glanced at Harmony and chuckled. "You wrinkle your nose, but that is because you have never had it done properly. It seems only the English cook them anymore, and they are still mostly barbarians in the kitchen."

"Hm," Harmony said again, unwilling to interrupt Alex's memory with an argument about who were the greater culinary barbarians.

"We also had some asparagus—running to seed but still delicious in the hands of a master. It took an hour and a half to prepare the meal because of the strange kitchen, but it was child's play really." Alex's accent was now quite thick, and his face was animated. He carried the cauldron to the sink and filled it a third of the way with water. Returning to the stove, he put the pan on another burner and lit it as well. He turned the fire up high, letting the flames lick up the sides of the pot where they attacked the stray drops of water that ran down the squat slopes. Then, peering through the slotted lid at his first dish, he slightly reduced the flame under the rice.

There came a soft thumping from the pantry, like a mouse—or a gremlin—knocking on the door.

"Alex?" Harmony asked nervously when he didn't react. "Is someone here?"

"No. And it isn't rats. The lobsters are in the dry sink. I fear that our dinner realizes the end is near and has grown restive."

"They're still alive?" she asked, dismayed.

"But yes. One must leave them alive until they are on the spit or in the pot. It isn't safe to eat long-dead lobster." He went to the kitchen's lone window and forced it open another few inches. From the window box outside he plucked several stems of herbs. The pungent odor of thyme and rosemary filled the room, along with an eddy of ocean air.

"It smells like Thanksgiving," Harmony said, closing her eyes. It had been years since she had had a traditional Thanksgiving dinner, and she felt a gentle wave of nostalgia pass over her.

"Not for long. This is the season for a picnic, not a heavy feast. Watch now." Reaching for the porcelain head of a fox mounted on the wall, he pulled a length of cotton twine from the vixen's mouth and cut it with his knife. "I am making a bouquet garni for the court boullion. Next we need cayenne peppers and some carrots and onion."

"Cayenne?"

"It will infuse the lobsters with wonderful flavor. Have faith—the faint heart ne'er won the fair lady, nor honors in the kitchen."

The tapping from the pantry came again. It was louder this time. Harmony, looking at the slow-boiling cauldron, began to squirm. "If you say so."

"I do." Alex pulled a napkin away from a bowl where a handful of oysters waited in a bed of crushed ice.

Harmony looked away from the stove and into the dark closet where the scrabbling continued. She wasn't sure how she felt about Alex boiling their dinner alive. She liked lobster a lot, but was not in the habit of killing her own food. That made her feel a bit wimpy and hypocritical, but she knew that she was unwilling to change. If she had to kill her own food, she'd be a vegetarian.

Harmony looked back at the executioner chef. "Do they really scream when you cook them?"

Alex glanced at her kindly as gouts of murderous steam began to billow from the cauldron of death. The flames had joined hands around the pot and were dancing wildly in the current that came through the open window.

"Perhaps you should set the table while I see to this," he

suggested, pulling open a bin and reaching for an onion. He halved it with one blow and threw it into the pot, skin and all. A carrot followed, halved the long way but not chopped. "There is no need to see this part, and you'll want your appetite intact. I promise, this is a meal like no other you have had."

"Okay." Harmony slid off the table. Before she had time to consider, she said, "You know, I wish we could have brought the dog. She would have liked having this dinner with us, I think." But that wasn't the only reason. A dog would bark if they had visitors. An early warning system would make her feel more at ease.

Alex didn't laugh at her. "I wish it too. A house is empty without pets, isn't it? In Paris, though I am very busy just now, I have made a place for a new cat—Lady de Winter. She is . . . very elegant." Alex headed for the pantry, pulling on a pair of gauntlets. "Of course, with a cat, it is less that one adopts them than that they commandeer you."

"Where are the plates?" Harmony asked hastily.

"The dining room is down the hall and to your left," Alex called. "There is a cabinet in there. Use the Limoges—the Normandy pattern. It has flowers, apple blossoms, I think. And bring me two platters. I must butter them before I serve. Too many people neglect this step. You will notice a difference."

"I know that china. My grandmother had some." The delicate porcelain and the smell of Chantilly perfume were about all she did recall of her grandmother. The old woman had died when she was six. She thought about mentioning this to Alex, but old habits of reticence were deeply ingrained. She was not in the habit of sharing any details about herself, not even those of the long-since past.

"*Je regrette*. You cannot escape, monsieurs," she heard Alex say to their dinner.

Harmony hurried toward the dining room, hands over

her ears in case lobsters did make noise when they expired. She wanted to keep her appetite for Alex's feast. After all, it wasn't every day that a girl had the chance to eat a meal prepared and served by Alexandre Dumas.

She found the dining room without difficulty, and it was a strange enough room to make her pause in the doorway. Ivy was growing all over the interior wall that faced east. It showed none of the dispirited pallor of a reluctant houseplant either; rather, it was bursting with green vigor. That someone was aware of the ivy's power was obvious, because it had been trimmed from around the six long, narrow windows that were set in the thick wall. Harmony knew from past experience that the ivy would be the ruination of the plaster when the roots ate deeply enough into it, but it looked so charming and smelled so nice that she understood why Alex had left it. That this was Alex's doing she did not doubt for even a minute. The cottage's caretaker was probably scandalized at the owner's eccentricity.

A short hunt showed her where the first strand of ivy had wormed its way through an ill-fitting casement on the far right window. Roots had burrowed into the wood. To have grown this much, the plant had to have been there for at least a half a decade.

The irresponsible whimsy of the act made her smile. This was something she never would have expected of the legendary Alexandre Dumas. Nothing she had read about this swashbuckler, spendthrift, and egoist would have led her to believe that he would be protective of the island flora. He was a hunter and had a reputation for fighting duels with only minimal provocation, and she herself had seen how ruthless and cold he could be when danger threatened. Yet, here was her third proof of his compassion for the out-of-place creature that crossed his path. Alex had saved her—a stray human—then the stray dog, and now this straying plant. And he was doing whatever he could to see that they all thrived.

Forcing the casement open, she leaned out and saw that the outside of the wall was likewise festooned with ivy. The vines were thicker, much older and tougher, the leaves dark and waxy. Some strands were as thick as her fingers and looked strong enough to climb down the cliff almost to the high-water line. She didn't test her theory, though—there would be no Darwin Award for her.

A breeze attacked her suddenly, and Harmony blinked under the assault. Her eyes began to water and her face began tingling. Perhaps it was the salt in the sea air. It was certainly brisk. In fact . . . squinting, she looked up at the sky. She couldn't see the sun, but it seemed to her that the light had dimmed considerably in the last hour, though sunset was still a ways away. Perhaps they would have fog, or maybe a storm.

The thought of a squall made her draw back in and secure the window as best she could without harming the ivy. Her nervous system must have still been on red alert, her subconscious still sufficiently outraged by her recent experiences that even the consideration of facing another storm made her nervous.

"Coward. Saint Germain is thousands of miles away." The words were true enough, but she didn't feel entirely reassured. She wished she knew more about him and all the strange things Alex had talked about him doing. But in all the books in the cottage, she doubted he had a copy of *Zombies for Dummies* or *The Necromancer's Cookbook*—if such things even existed. They might not. It couldn't be a popular pastime for people or she would have heard of it before.

"Just let it go. Do something useful. Find the dishes and get the table set."

Harmony found the china Alex wanted after a bit of a search in the oaken bureau. The collection in the old carved cabinet was eclectic and carelessly stored, stacked as high as it could go without running into the shelves above. She found in a drawer some linen napkins and a tablecloth of slightly yellowed brocade, which she spread over the table, trying to press out the creases with her hands. Next she folded the napkins into limp but recognizable swans. If Alex could be whimsical, so could she.

Last, she added two candlesticks, the bases thick with wax but still having stubs long enough to light. A part of her thought it would be good to have candles in case the storm were bad enough to make the house lose power.

Having lingered as long as she reasonably could, she walked slowly back toward the kitchen carrying two large platters, but prepared to bolt again if the lobsters were still begging for mercy.

"Come—it's safe," Alex assured her as she lingered in the doorway. "And you will miss the fun part if you don't come now. I added balsamic vinegar before our guests joined the pot, and made an essential reduction of the sauce. The necessary deed accomplished, I have removed our shelled friends and strained the court boullion. The reduction is by itself delicious, but now I add the magic."

Harmony laid the platters near the stove. The copper dunce cap had been removed from the rice pan and replaced with a more traditional lid, though it was indented rather like a saucer for a teacup. The flame was turned quite low but continued to dance. Inside the strainer Harmony could see onion and carrot and a now badly wilted bundle of herbs. Of the lobsters there was no sign. They were probably still drowning in their watery—well, vinegary—grave. She resisted the urge to peep into the pot.

"First, we need music. One cannot cook without music." Alex began singing a song in French that she vaguely recognized as being from Donizetti's opera *The Elixir of Love*. His voice was pure and strong. It gave Harmony goose bumps to realize that he had probably sung this song with the great master himself. He and Donizetti had been good friends, and both men had loved to cook.

Alex rummaged in another cupboard and emerged holding a dusty bottle and a wine opener. He paused in his aria to blow the dust off the bottle, carefully turning from the stove so it would not pollute their dinner.

"Cognac," he said with satisfaction. He used an implement Harmony had never seen to cut away the wax that covered the cork, and then inserted the opener. His movements were sure and dextrous, as though he had done this a thousand times—which he probably had. "Old, exquisite, and strong. If this dish were not so delicious I should consider it sacrilege to use a fine liqueur this way. But the recipe is that perfect. Here, *monsieurs langoustes*, have a drink with my compliments." Not unexpectedly, given his earlier lack of restraint, Alex upended the bottle and poured in the entire contents. A gout of vapor rolled out of the pot.

As he had predicted, it smelled delicious.

"Mmmmm." Harmony almost moaned. Suddenly she was ravenous.

"Did you ever read of my duel with Albert Vandam?" Alex asked.

"Yes. Did it really happen?" Harmony said. "It sounded a bit—well, apocryphal."

"Indeed, it did happen. We met on the field of honor—my kitchen—armed with soup spoons. I defeated him with my *soupe aux choux*." He sounded smug. "How could he have doubted my abilities?"

"Is it true that you wore only an apron because nudity would intimidate the Englishman?"

"*Non*—I removed my shirt because of the heat, but not my pants. An accident in the kitchen could be very bad for a naked man," Alex said severely, but his black eyes twinkled. He used his hand to reach into the crock and smear the last of the butter over the two platters. He then wiped his hands on a towel.

Harmony didn't envy whoever ended up cleaning after his "kitchen magic," and hoped that it wouldn't be her.

Alex opened the rice pot, stepping back from a billow of steam. Ignoring his gauntlets, he lifted the pot and upended it over the platter. The pan had to be terribly hot, but he never flinched. He poured the pink rice and ham onto the first serving dish. Elegant curls of fragrant air swirled above the plate. Harmony all but drooled.

"There are some wilted greens in the other pan," Alex said, and Harmony noticed a small saucepan at the back of the stove, hidden by the cauldron. There were indeed wilted greens in the pot. She couldn't tell what kind, only that they were glossy with butter. "Please put them in that small bowl," Alex requested. "You will like them. I had this recipe from President Roosevelt's splendid wife."

"You have no fear of fat, have you?" she asked, stepping around the far side of the stove. She began to dish up what looked like dandelion stems and leaves.

"Cholesterol—a myth made up by puritanical Americans to ruin what they consider a sinful enjoyment of food." Alex all but sneered. "And now for our main course. Watch this. You will agree the cognac has been put to noble use."

He reached inside the cauldron with a pair of tongs and removed the first lobster. He twirled it left and right so that Harmony could admire the patina it had acquired. The angry red of boiled crustacean had been muted by the thick cognac sauce. The lobster gleamed a beautiful mahogany brown against the jade-colored platter. Its twin joined it shortly, along with the oysters.

"And now we feast," Alex said, picking up the two platters and heading for the dining room. "If you will fetch the greens and the bottle of wine I set out?"

"Of course."

"And after dinner we shall work on the second chapter of your book," he called back. "It seems the only way to get to know your playful side. It is sad that you are so reserved, but I do not despair."

"I'm not reserved," Harmony denied. But she was. Sadly, there wasn't a person on the planet with whom she was completely forthcoming.

I do not despair, he'd said.

He probably didn't. Why would Alex despair of getting anything he wanted from her? He was Alexandre Dumas, immortal lover extraordinaire and powerful psychic who could read her feelings as easily as—well, a book. He would know she was at least a little in love with him. And he already knew she could be made to want him to the point of complete mindlessness, and he apparently had all eternity to spend on getting to know whatever he wanted—which wasn't her body. At least, not unless he was high on some storm.

Harmony was suddenly feeling baffled and frustrated again. She could ignore their attraction for a while when something more urgent came up, but the same questions always eventually raised their hackles and demanded attention. Did he want her, or not?

It couldn't be loneliness that prompted this interest in her—he'd had a century to learn to cope with that—and she wasn't that beautiful, unique, or fascinating. Compared to his psychic gifts, she was nothing—a baby taking its first steps.

"But why, then?" she asked the mute walls.

Could it really be about her book and wanting to mentor her?

Harmony almost groaned and reached for the wine that was breathing on the far end of the table. Never mind Alex's motivations—what was *she* doing in Cornwall? Was it really all about writing a book while Alex figured out what next to do with his nemesis? And if that was her reason for being here—and she wasn't open to considering any other, since it would mean she was foolish, if not downright stupid, given his indirect statements about not wanting to have an affair—why couldn't it be his, too? It almost *had* to be what he claimed—a desire to mentor her and nothing more. He could have sent her anywhere and she would probably be as safe. In fact, probably safer. Instead he had chosen to bring her to an island where no one lived and where they would have no interruptions from the outside world.

Like Alex, The Spider couldn't have intimate relationships; she knew that now, and he did too—he'd even said so. So, if not for her safety and not out of desire for a fling, then why bring her here? It had to be to write.

The thought was a little flattering, but it added up. Alex had mentored young writers before. And she would be a fool to turn down his offer of help just because she was frustrated and a bit piqued. Alex had been very kind about her writing, taking time away from his own project to work with her. He praised her style and helped her with her plot pacing. Why wasn't she happy with this—accepting of her good fortune—and relaxing while she did what she'd always wanted?

She had her answer even as she asked the question.

It was because everything felt so much more urgent now that he was with her. She was aware of a whole other world now—a dangerous one that seemed to be aware of her, too. This made her feel exceptionally alive. It made her want to indulge all her senses, including her sexual ones.

But Alex seemed utterly determined that she finish the book as soon as possible, as though sensing somehow that their time for working together was limited. The book had to be done at this time, or not at all. Relaxing wasn't an option.

That wasn't something she wanted to think about, though. It had taken her the better part of the day and night to forget about the insane, impossible mess in Mexico. She didn't want to be reminded of their troubles right before eating what might be the best meal of her life, prepared by the most interesting man she would ever know.

Be present, she told herself. *Tomorrow and all its problems will arrive soon enough.*

It is almost as difficult to keep a first-class person in a fourth-class job as it is to keep a fourth-class person in a first-class job.

—Alexandre Dumas

All human wisdom is summed up in two words; wait and hope.

—Alexandre Dumas

Men's minds are raised to the level of the women with whom they associate.

—Alexandre Dumas

CHAPTER THIRTEEN

The Spider

Chapter Two

An unexpected chill came with the twilight, reminding Gillian that, unlike California,
where summer could linger on into October,
autumn in the northern latitudes was loiter-
ing right around the corner, waiting for a
chance to move in on northern England.

A few dried sticks had been left in the library hearth, and a match was all it took to
set a small blaze alight. The fire did very little
to heat the room, except perhaps for the
dark rafters high overhead, but it provided
great psychological comfort as Gillian toured
her way through Carter's impressive library.
There wasn't any title newer than turn-of-the-

century gracing the oaken shelves, leading her to believe that the most recent owners were not of a bookish bent. Most of the titles were quite daunting actually, favoring as they did works of classical Greek and eighteenth-century agricultural experiments. But eventually she found a well-thumbed folio of Shakespeare's works and curled up in one of the giant, flower-spattered armchairs to have the long, uninterrupted read she'd been promising herself all day.

But her mind was unusually active that night, listening with half an ear to the unfamiliar wind rubbing through the elms' leaves and whispering through the yew, and hearing all the noises that an old house makes as it settles in for the night. Even the Dutch clock in the entry hall sounded portentous with its muffled but monotonous ticking.

Something snapped in the grate. With a start, Gillian realized that she had fallen into a self-induced trance and been staring at the same passage for several minutes.

"'By the pricking of my thumbs—something wicked this way comes. Open locks, whoever knocks.' Ah, great bard! You have a bon mot for every obsession."

Gillian closed the heavy cover on Macbeth's bloody antics and set the tome aside. It was probably a poor choice for an evening when her mind was spinning sinister plots. What she needed was some of Dr. Henderson's quiet meditation rituals to help her focus in on a more relaxing subject.

Off went the reading glass and the lamp

on the reading table, leaving the dwindling fire to light the fretful shadows that hung lethargically in the beams overhead. Gillian hugged her knees up tight against her chest and tried hard to visualize Dr. Henderson's cheery red balloon sailing off into a deep blue sky.

She abandoned the effort ten minutes later. The fact was, she was too restless for reading or meditation. It happened sometimes when she was starting a new project. And this undertaking was going to be a challenge. She had finally achieved the degree of fame that would allow her to branch out into other styles of writing. Not that she was giving up on romances—not at all! But maybe it was time to include more Byzantine plot elements in her heroine's love affairs. Perhaps add some more sophisticated psychological thrills.

The trouble was, her brain refused to be linear in its thinking. It wasn't constructing a well-ordered, contemporary plot for the heroine who was supposed to be vacationing in sunny Hawaii. Instead it was twisting about like a cold wind in a graveyard, imagining all sorts of creepy, gothic things that could happen in her new residence. Like the phantom footsteps of a headless cavalier approaching the door of the library with his fleshless skull tucked under a bloodied arm.

She could feel the hairs on her nape rising at the ghastly image—a sure sign that she needed to get up and do something distract-

ing before she came down with a case of
nineteenth-century-style hysterics.

A creak from the rear of the darkened
room got her starting upright and turning
swiftly to peer over the back of the chair
where she'd been kneeling.

Seeing that there actually was something
hovering in the door, Gillian gave a small
scream that was quite loud in the silence
that had fallen over the house, and began
considering the advisability of hurling herself out of one of the two sets of French
doors before the ghost could capture her in
its cold, bloody embrace. But she was at
heart a sensible woman, not prone to hysterics, and she quickly put aside any notions
of fleeing into the night. Two seconds of
observation showed her that she was not
confronting a ghost. No incorporeal being
would look so appalled at a little shrieking.
Or wear black jeans with an equally dark
pullover and black gloves. Also, his handsome head was still attached to his moder-
ately wide shoulders. There was not a drop
of blood in sight.

Modern clothes, a shocked face, and an
attached head. Ergo, she was seeing a real
person and not an apparition from the English Civil War. Which was a good thing,
she hoped.

All that remained to be seen was whether
the intruder was carrying a weapon somewhere other than in his rather tight jeans,
and if he was some wide-eyed crazy looking for her autograph. Even as she reached

for her glasses, in the hopes of bringing the stranger's face into focus, the man was stepping into the room. Unfortunately, he didn't step far enough to bring his features out of the shadows.

"I beg your pardon," the soft voice said. "I didn't mean to startle you."

Gillian shoved her glasses onto her face and peered cautiously at her visitor. He was rather tall and lean, with light brown hair and a definite look of refinement in the nose and mouth.

That was about all she could see from her perch on the seat of the chair. But, she decided, he also seemed rather diffident, even helpless. These things taken together with his corporeal state convinced Gillian that she didn't need to start screaming or racing for the phone to summon help.

As she got over her amazement at the intrusion of a live person into her gothic daydream, a reasonable explanation for the man's presence presented itself.

"I'm afraid Mr. Carter isn't here," she heard herself say calmly. "He's let the house for the summer. To me."

Her visitor blinked once, and Gillian noticed that his eyes were light in color. The exact shade was impossible to guess in the dim room, but she thought they were probably gray.

"Um."

She waited, but her visitor appeared to be oblivious of the need to make some explanation for his presence in her home. Or perhaps he was simply too fazed by her earlier scream to make his excuses. His gaze was rapt enough to suggest a large degree of shock. Or even simplemindedness. Obviously, the task of conversation had fallen on her shoulders.

"I'm sorry I didn't hear the bell, Mr. . . ."

After a long moment's hesitation he repeated: "So sorry to startle you. I—" The light eyes finally focused on her face, and the clear intelligence dawning in them gave the lie to the idea that he was in any way mentally impaired. "I didn't ring. In fact, I let myself in through a side door."

"A side door?" she repeated blankly. Then: "What side door?"

He waved a vague hand in the direction of the dining room, which did not in fact have any outside doors but only long windows, and said sincerely: "I didn't know you were in here. I hadn't heard that . . . Terry . . . had let the house. I'm afraid I've been coming and going much as I pleased in the last several weeks, and it didn't occur to me that anyone would be disturbed. Now that I know you're here, I'll just take myself off again."

The man turned quickly and walked off into the dark hall. The floor beneath him was an oak parquet, but it made not the slightest tap, creak, or groan as he passed over. That was probably because he was wearing sensible rubber-soled shoes. Probably.

"Wait!" Gillian scrambled off of her chair and started after the retreating figure. "Who are you? How . . . ?"

But she was talking to air. The man had vanished into the shadows. She didn't hear any door close in the dining room, but a current of air coming from the front of the house suggested that the front door had been opened.

"That was very strange." The inventive half of her brain added another brick or two to the fantastical idea that had been building ever since she realized that the dark-dressed intruder was one of flesh and blood rather than historic ectoplasm.

"Nonsense," she scolded herself, dismissing the coincidence that the stranger had scuttled out of sight like a startled spider. Or a cat burglar. *"He was just a friend of Mr. Carter's. Don't go making a plot out of this."*

The large clock in the entry hall ticked on complacently.

"All the same, I wish he'd stuck around long enough for me to get his spare key."

Of course, if her inventive brain was correct, her intruder wouldn't need a key to get into the house.

"Hyperactive imagination. You have to stop reading the tabloids. Why would The Spider be here?" Gillian started walking toward the front door. The idea was whimsical—too wild for anything except a romantic plot—but night had truly fallen, and it was definitely time to arm the security system, especially if her uninvited guest had left the front door unlocked when he made his precipitous exit.

Harmony couldn't stay asleep. And it wasn't because she had pigged out at dinner. Though she had. What a cook Alex was! That meal would have put the fear of God—or of losing a four-star review—into the heart of any rival chef who tasted it. A few more meals like that and she wouldn't have to worry about love breaking her heart; cholesterol would do it in first.

Harmony rolled onto her left side.

It might have been the storm's fault that she couldn't sleep. No rain was falling yet, but she could clearly hear the churning of the milk-white sea around them, and the flickering light was nearly strobelike when it snapped against the shutters, making them appear to shiver. This shouldn't have bothered her. She'd been in bad weather before, and Cornwall's classic storms were practically expected by someone like her who was a connoisseur of literature dealing with smugglers and the Beast of Bodmin Moor. It might, on some other night, have actually been enjoyable. But tonight was different, and the storm had seemed to be shaping up to be just a little too classic, a little too much like something from a B horror movie, and she'd tried closing the drapes against it before going to bed and pretending she didn't have a strong suspicion that the weather was actually plotting to kill her. Fabric and wooden shutters didn't stop the sound, though, nor all the light. And sturdy as the cottage was, she felt every buffet of the hostile wind as it made exploratory attacks, testing the building's defenses.

But really her trouble with finding sleep was that she couldn't get Alex out of her mind. Couldn't get the phantom memory of his hands off of her restless body. As she lay tossing under the old linen sheets, it was as though he still stroked her, even now when she was awake and clearly alone.

This wasn't good. Most kisses didn't register on her personal Richter scale, but even the memory of Alex's lips sent the needle straight to nine. And this was something more than mere memory.

Unless it was *Alex's* memory?

Harmony sat up.

That might mean he was thinking of her. That he had changed his mind about wanting her? He had seemed pretty definite about refusing her after dinner when she had brought up the subject in a roundabout fashion. Of course, that was before the storm arrived.

Harmony exhaled slowly. Did she want Alex to be thinking of her? Did she truly want him to be her lover? When she was near him, the answer was clear, but once away . . .

The cottage shuddered rhythmically, almost grunting under the repeated pulsations of wind that seemed to be the very heart of this monster storm that had surrounded them but refused to land.

One thing was for sure: If this was Alex's restlessness communicating itself to her, she'd never sleep unless he did. Maybe it was time for them to have a nightcap—a stiff brandy, perhaps, with a Valium chaser.

Throwing back the covers on her cot, she pulled a sweatshirt over her summer-weight nightgown and walked down the hall to his bedroom on catlike feet. As she had suspected, the door to Alex's room was open. His bed was empty and hadn't been slept in. So, he wasn't sleeping either. If he was thinking of her, it was with a conscious mind and not because he was lost in dreams.

What should she do? Could he be pleasuring himself? The thought made her blush.

Harmony stood in the dark hall, listening for Alex with her ears but also with her other senses. There was no sound to guide her, but she knew from historic records that the old Alex had often spent his nights in the library, writing. Instinct said that that was the place to begin her search.

She hesitated, looking around uneasily. The library was on the first floor, down a dark stair. The halls, which had been efficient and gracious—and even alluring—when conveying her through the house earlier in the day, had grown longer, narrower, darker, seemingly less inclined to be helpful to a stranger. It was as though the house was pushing out unwanted guests from parts of the building by shutting down the nighttime passageways, and drawing in on itself as it cowered before the lashing winds and rain.

Her hand reached for the light switch and then froze. She could have turned on the lights and perhaps pushed back the unfriendly dark, but decided instead to go back to her bedroom for the flashlight Alex had provided and for some slippers. Even standing on rugs, her feet were cold.

Though the flashes of lightning assaulting the evenly spaced windows showed her the way, Harmony tested her flashlight briefly, keeping her fingers over the glass so that little of the beam escaped as she walked down the hall. Though she was reluctant to admit the thought existed, the fact was that she didn't want to disturb the expectant gloom of the house or anything outside the cottage by calling attention to her presence. Logic said—well, it said all kinds of things. But she couldn't quite stand the idea of venturing into the night without some other light. Spirits abided there at nighttime, perhaps not all of them benign. A wise person would go back to bed. But she wasn't wise. Feeling like a curious cat, light of foot and alert to whatever lurked in the shadows, she slid down the tight hall of what she hoped was still just a house and not some passage into Persephone's Underworld.

Where had that thought come from? Was it Alex again? What on earth was he doing?

Lightning flared, followed by an immediate clap of thunder. Nerves breaking, Harmony scampered for the library.

She ran to open the door but found the room empty and dim. Like a vampire, she paused at the threshold, afraid to go on without an invitation from her host.

No Alex; however, she could see an untidy pile of papers on the floor near the wing chair, evidence that Alex had been at work. Steeling herself, she forced a foot over the threshold.

The fire in the hearth was nearly dead, but she turned off her flashlight as she entered the room. Her fear abated as she progressed, but she remained respectfully wary. She clearly sensed that Alex was nearby, and that his mind was not on things of the twenty-first century. Wherever his thoughts were, she didn't want to see them too clearly. Or that was how she explained the decision to turn off the flashlight and move stealthily.

Harmony walked slowly to the windows that opened onto the balcony and was not even half surprised when she saw Alex perched on the narrow stone balustrade. He was propped against a large lidded urn, one knee bent in what should have looked like a relaxed pose but clearly was not. His head was turned away as he looked over the ocean and the turmoil in the sky that seemed to be drawing ever closer but never quite reaching them. The wind seemed to ignore him. For a long moment he was as still, as frozen as any statue, his hair as motionless as carved obsidian, his bare hands and feet made of alabaster.

Yet she knew he was alive—sensed it with every fiber of her being. Subconsciously—or perhaps deliberately—he had called her out of her dreams and brought her here. Alex was thinking of her, and his thoughts had gotten him as stirred up as the wind and sea around them. She should just open the door and go out to him. He was vulnerable, lonely. He could be hers this night.

That was what she should do. If she still wanted him.

But she didn't open the door. The library threshold she could cross, but not this one.

Harmony couldn't logically explain her sudden indecision and nervousness. It wasn't that she thought Alex would hurt her, especially when he was lost in the storm's wildness, and she wasn't taken aback by his physical oddness anymore. But the longer she thought about it, the more his being outside keeping a vigil in the storm seemed in some way a bad omen. For one thing, the weather was still bitter, and worsening all the time. No rain fell, but the temperature was plummeting in a death spiral, and the almost painful smell of ozone was thick in the air. Alex's occasional breath was actually turning to frost and falling down on his lap where a tiny pile of crystals already lay, so perhaps there would not be just rain but also hail. His hands were naked and silver white. So were his feet. It wasn't a fit night out for man or beast, yet he remained outside. This had to be Alex's version of an extremely cold shower.

Why didn't he just give in and come to her?

Lightning hit again—this time almost striking the cottage itself. Still, Alex did not move.

Harmony exhaled harshly, making her eyes focus and her brain work. *A lap full of crystals? Bare feet?* Alex was outside in the freezing cold and he wasn't wearing a coat or shoes. Also, when she looked again, she could see that he wasn't so much leaning against that giant funereal urn as clinging to it, a clawed hand anchoring him to the rim as he leaned over slightly and peered at the sea. With his eerily white skin, he looked more than a little bit like a vigilant angel of death waiting to swoop down on the souls of whatever sailors were about to die in the stormy coastal waters.

Was he ill?

Harmony reached for the door slowly. As she watched, Alex's flesh began to glow and steam started to rise from his body. The steam froze almost at once, forming an icy cloud, and swirled about him in a slow, counterclockwise motion. These crystals did not fall but were borne off into the night.

It was like watching his spirit being stolen away by the darkness.

Harmony shivered, in spite of the room's warmth and her nightgown, thick sweatshirt, and slippers.

Alex wasn't human—not all human. Not anymore. He kept saying he wasn't—that his human life had died—but she hadn't believed him. Was this truly what she wanted? To take some divine but clearly unhuman being to her bed?

Her eyes looked past Alex and out at the storm that fascinated him. As she watched, she saw that it, too, was moving in a counterclockwise direction. The storm was circling them like a cyclone, drawing closer but never actually touching the island. Was that normal?

Or was it Alex? Could he be controlling the weather?

The thought shook her. He had said there were other side effects to his treatment. If he had some sort of energy field around him that shorted out computers and phones, could he also control the weather?

She stared harder at the night and the man she wanted for a lover. Out at sea she could see smoke frost forming on the water, but traveling too quickly and against the wind. Smoke frost was not a phenomenon common to Cornwall. It happened in the North Sea sometimes when a warm wind—

—*like from Mexico*—

—passed over an arctic ocean. It made an instant ice storm on the water.

Desire didn't go away, but it curled back a bit, recoiling from this idea, and Harmony thought of what Alex was thinking instead. Was he desiring her—the woman of medium blond hair, medium psychic ability, and medium writing talent—or just riding the power of the storm and finding it extremely sensual? Was this like Mexico? Was it worse? If she went out to him and then changed her mind, would he stop? *Could* he stop? Or would his wild high override both of their wills and judgment?

Torn between the lure of opening the door and asking Alex why he was out in the night, and of sneaking away before he noticed her and knew that she had answered his probably unconscious summons, Harmony hesitated in the shadows, gripping her flashlight and shivering.

She talked quickly and sternly to herself. Alex liked storms, got high on them. He'd told her that. But he was as aware of their last close call as she was. He wouldn't call her downstairs on a whim. And surely if something was wrong, he would wake her in some conventional way and warn her of the danger. He wouldn't just give in to the storm and let something bad happen while he went with the high. There was no reason for her to be suddenly afraid of the night, or of him. At least, no more afraid than she had been before.

Harmony swallowed hard. She wasn't afraid. She *wasn't*.

But if she didn't want to make love to him, she should just go back upstairs and try to sleep.

Sleep? Who was she kidding? But at least she should go to bed and leave Alex to his troubled feelings. If he still wanted her in the morning, she would reconsider.

Another thought occurred to her, making her frown. He was probably just trying to fight his way through his writer's block on his current story. It could be fictional sex on his mind, or a memory of Thomasina—in other words, general sex thoughts and not desire for her specifically. After all, it was more than possible that he had been thinking of his book, working by the light of the fire, and his mind got caught up in the past. His subconscious probably began reading outdated messages, desperate notes of longing from the wounded psyche of a man who really no longer existed but didn't know how to let go of his past—the ghost of his last love living on in his subconscious. He might still be lusting after a dead woman who'd been called to new life by this storm, and by his forced remembrance of ancient events dictated by the creative process.

He might not want *her* at all, Harmony sensed. That could make any advances from her very embarrassing.

Yes, he was striking, as beautiful as any midnight that had ever been. And it was not just his body that was pleasing to her but also his ready wit and compassion. That didn't mean that the feeling of . . . longing or whatever she felt was returned. She was getting confused because of their shared mental connection, mistaking one emotion for another.

After all, what had changed in the last few hours? Just because she had found her fear of intimacy dying out as they dined in comfortable familiarity on the splendid meal he had prepared didn't mean he felt the same comfort and trust with her. She tried to think back, to judge his reactions to their conversation, but she found herself unable to be clear and unbiased.

There had been a lot of wine flowing at the table. Harmony had barely noticed when the first small truth about her past fell out of her mouth. She was used to fabrication—had meticulously worked out the highly fictionalized and witty story of her ideal youth—but she hadn't bothered to repeat it tonight. And what might have been only small truths exchanged simply to be polite had soon turned out to be large truths about her goals and plans and desires for the future. She was coming to trust him—to speak her mind to him without reservation or fear. And he had listened intently.

But now that she thought about it, there had also been a growing strangeness in the air as they talked on into the dark, an erection of mental barriers that he retreated behind as the hours eased into one another, and then he'd withdrawn. Especially when she had turned to him at the foot of the stairs as they said their good nights and almost kissed him. He hadn't recoiled from her touch, but he hadn't offered any encouragement either. His expression had been oddly bleak as he gazed unblinking into her eyes.

He didn't want to love again. The pain for him had been crippling. She knew this and understood it. Hell, Harmony thought with irritation, she wasn't looking for long-term love either. Just . . . comfort and a chance to taste of the strongest attraction she'd ever known. But for some reason, a sober Alex wasn't willing to give her this, was afraid of what might happen between them if they indulged even this much—though he admitted to having casual sex all the time, so it should have been an easy matter to have accepted a short-term relationship with her, even if his heart was still wrapped up with the memory of a dead woman.

It wasn't easy, though, not for either of them—probably because of their mental connection that prevented things from remaining casual and impersonal. And although she couldn't say precisely from what direction emotional danger would come, she had to admit that, standing in the dark of Alex's favorite room, she now felt some of his fear of closeness. He liked her—maybe wanted her. But they were different. Very different. Maybe too different. And intuition should be respected. After all, he had been alive a long time. And though he genuinely cared for her and she for him, there was clearly something inside that told him to keep her at a distance. If anything, he was probably more wary now than he had been before she opened up to him over dinner. And however nonspecific her own inner voice was, she believed her instincts when they spoke to her of peril. As sure as the sun would show up in the east come morning, she knew there would be trouble if she allowed herself to get any closer to this man.

That was hard to accept when she could still feel his hands on her and sense his arousal. Some people were not meant to love—hadn't she said this herself? She had to respect this knowledge and honor Alex's own desires and intuition.

It would be difficult. Under other circumstances, she would leave this place. But they had to deal with Saint Germain, so she was going to stick around for a bit. The heart might want, but the mind could—would—prevail over the body. It had to.

Harmony inhaled slowly. Her breath was unsteady and irregular. Even now, the memory of how close she had come to giving herself to Alex in Mexico frightened her a bit. That was as close to insanity as she ever wanted to come.

Even if she had felt wildly happy for the first time in years? an inner voice asked wistfully.

She exhaled ruthlessly, emptying her lungs as she tried to empty the thoughts from her restless brain.

Enough. The decision was made. It was true that Harmony rarely felt entirely happy. But she had a very busy, very full life. So what if she was sometimes lonely? Everyone was. It was okay to want Alex. That meant she was still alive. But it was also okay to be cautious, especially tonight. He was high—as strung out as any junkie and maybe thinking about some other woman; she needed to be responsible for both of them.

Harmony looked out at Alex, so still that he seemed made of stone, so beautiful that he took her breath, and so distant that he didn't seem human. She almost cried. Instead she curled her nails into her palms and squeezed hard enough to leave marks.

She wanted him—*wanted* him! And on another occasion, she might be tempted to give in. But she would not take advantage of him because he was stoned and feeling promiscuous because of the storm. That would be . . . well, rape. Especially if he was in love with another woman.

"Forget it," Harmony said softly, feeling a bit ill as she forced herself away. She let her hands relax. "There's nothing for you here. Do what you have to do to finish things with Saint Germain and then move along."

Harmony touched a sore hand to her head. She frowned when she felt fever on the skin. Maybe it wasn't all Alex disturbing her. She could be sick and probably imagining things. At the very least, she was dog-tired, and her judgment was impaired by the lack of sleep. The throbbing in her body was not desire, it was rhinovirus. What she needed was rest, the kind to be had in the solitude of her room.

Sighing, half with self-disgust and half with disappointment, Harmony retreated upstairs. She didn't see Alex when he rolled off the balustrade and dove headlong into the heaving water.

Harmony was on the other side of the glass, not six feet away, but she didn't open the door to join him. In a moment of weakness, he'd called to her in her sleep. And she'd come downstairs, but she had stopped short of actually joining him.

Something had stopped her, and it was probably just as well. Though she appealed to him as no woman had since Thomasina, he knew that what he wanted tonight was stupid, risky, and unfair to her, even though she had been warned that his . . . good intentions? no, rather his expectations of their happiness in a sexual union were almost nonexistent. He knew that words of warning were nothing when she could feel the same things that he did coursing through the body, singing in the blood. He was high—drunk on storm and desire—and so was she.

And, as he had learned in Mexico, a stormy night was not a good time to be giving in to wild impulses. It had been on just such a night that Thomasina was killed.

He wanted her—and that was understandable. Naturally, her open admiration of him was alluring. Anyone would find it difficult to resist a woman who spoke with such fervor for her work and writing, someone whose devotion to a cause was as great as his own had been when he had been young and hopeful. Hell, she was his youth made flesh again, a hearth fire of optimism in the endless winter that had become his soul. And she wanted him every bit as much as he wanted her. Surely she did! This couldn't be all his will manifesting itself—influencing her—could it?

But he couldn't know for certain. And something had prevented her from opening the door and coming to him. They needed to practice caution for this very reason. She wasn't the first amazing woman who had called to him— and he wasn't so high he had forgotten that every such affair he had indulged in ended in tragedy. Even when he entered into a relationship with the purest of intentions, they still ended badly: in heartbreak and revulsion and even death, if they went as far wrong as they had with Thomasina. And sometimes in cruel apathy and coldness, even when his old enemy was not involved. How many times did he have to be shown that love gone wrong could lead to an inexhaustible supply of ill will? His remembrances of the women in his life were a burial ground of lost loves where he still mourned deeply on the rare occasion that he allowed himself to visit. He didn't want Harmony buried there. She was too important to him.

He felt her turn away from him, hurry away from the doors. The distance growing between them was as much emotional as physical. He knew when she looked back a last time, taking great care that sudden unwanted tears did not overspill her lower lids. He heard her thoughts clearly: there had been great things to cry over the last few days. Why did her emotions betray her now? He wanted to tell her that it wasn't *her* emotions, *her* tears that troubled her. It was his misgivings, his emotional scars that hurt her now. He had been trying to write about Thomasina but hadn't been able to create the happy fiction his story required.

Her heart said things to him that her voice could not. It also heard answers from him not meant for her ears. And she thought: *What a pair we are. Stray cats—hungry for company but too wary to accept a meal. We'd rather starve than risk getting hurt.*

Alex thought about his final conversation with Harmony as they parted for bed, and growled with frustration. He was supposed to be a master of words, but had failed to adequately explain himself. He wasn't still in love with a dead woman. That wasn't what held him back.

"Emotions—love especially—are luxuries we eventually have to pay for," he had warned her, turning his face so their lips wouldn't meet. "It isn't just desire for me. If only I could trade in the coin of that simple realm, but the price—for me—has always been something higher. I didn't mind risking my life for love, but I never counted on having the ones I love die because of me."

"I see." Harmony had looked up at him with eyes that reminded him of what God intended when He had invented spring. "I even understand. I'm just not sure that I agree," she had added with a small smile. "There are exceptions to every rule, you know. And I am not Thomasina. I know the enemy, and I don't plan on dying."

That would be great dialogue in a play or novel. And, no, she wasn't Thomasina. She was stronger, better informed of the danger, more capable of fighting. But leaving Saint Germain aside, he knew he shouldn't risk making an exception to his sensible policy, no matter how much he longed to. Mexico had been a warning. For them, it wasn't likely that there could be sex with no strings. It turned them into some sort of mental Siamese twins where neither was alert to danger. He couldn't have her and also protect her. Self-interest was . . . selfish.

But what was he going to do with Harmony? Sending her away wasn't a good option. Not until he found Byron or Ninon and could arrange protection for her. He couldn't forget that Saint Germain had been after her and might want her more than ever now that he knew she had been with his old enemy. She was in Cornwall because it was the safest place for her. Also because Alex was impetuous, and bringing her here—where they were together without interruption—had seemed like a good idea when he thought he could resist the attraction between them. But impulse, combined with a growing personal relationship, was not working well for him. In fact, it never worked well for him. How could he have forgotten this? It wasn't as if he didn't have an encyclopedic history of failures to consult.

The first woman he had disappointed was his mother. Alex had spent much of his youth running away from schooling and jobs pointing him at careers he didn't like. He'd been wise enough to know he was not made for the church, law, or the tax office. He had also—to his later shame—run away from Laure and the illegitimate child she bore him. He'd paid for the child's upkeep and visited from time to time, but he would not marry the older seamstress who loved him, or submit to the ties of fatherhood. At twenty-two, he'd had larger plans, and they did not include his bastard son, Alexandre. Paris called him in a voice far more seductive.

Then circumstances had changed. As predicted, Alex had achieved some fame in Paris and a bit of fortune. At his aging mother's words of longing for a grandchild he had impulsively intervened in Alexandre's life, presenting him as a gift, rather like one might offer a puppy to a child. But this gesture had backfired. His mother had been appalled to learn that he had a bastard, and was also too sick to look after young Alexandre.

Alex looked back at this now and shuddered. How could anyone have been so cavalier with a child's life? He had been an absent father—almost always a disaster even if the child had another full-time parent—and the results of taking Alexandre from his mother were predictably and proportionally disastrous. Laure had envenomed the child against him before Alexandre even arrived. For this Alex did not entirely blame her. He hadn't done the honorable thing and married his son's mother to begin with, because he had not been ready to give up his dreams of being a great writer and settling for a job in a law office. And there had been another woman. Several, in fact. This action was selfish enough, but to have compounded it by taking the boy from his mother when he reached school age only to leave him to be raised by a string of mistresses—some of whom had loved the boy but some who had not—was unforgivable. He deserved every curse Laure piled on his head.

Nor had he done any better by his eldest daughter, though at least he had eventually married her actress mother, which had pleased the sensitive girl. But the union, entered into impulsively, had been so unhappy, and he was so often away from home, that he couldn't really claim to have done any real parenting with this child either. In both cases, he had left behind bitter women, and even more bitter children. The inevitable divorce that had taken decades had gone down in the annals of French history as one of the nastiest on record. Melanie had bankrupted him, but he had taken Marie from her in retaliation. Too late had they understood that it was a Pyrrhic victory. The trade had left neither one happy and had ruined Marie, their daughter.

Alex sighed. A careful coachman never tangled the reins of personal and professional life because anything left dragging was bound to catch on life's frequent bad circumstances—like his wife, Melanie. Harmony didn't understand this, though. She was too young to see that small emotional setbacks were annoying, but the larger ones, like a bad marriage, could topple lives. And the end result of these particular errors was that his son and daughter had felt second-best and were never, not even for a moment, capable of being radiantly happy. Marie had in fact ended up being more than a little eccentric later in life. After her separation from an insane husband, she had started going about dressed as a druid, wearing a wreath of mistletoe on her head and carrying a sickle attached to her girdle, which she brandished at people when they came too close. There had been no choice but to send her to the country in the care of a warden. Some eccentricity was beyond what Paris would tolerate.

And then there was Thomasina. . . .

He knew the truth. He was a great writer but a lousy human. He'd been making mistakes with women since before President Lincoln grew a beard. His track record at liaisons—at least with people he truly loved—was abysmal. Harmony would be better off if she never became emotionally involved with him. People who loved Alex died young, bitter and alone. The idea that he would love successfully was ludicrous, maybe even mirth-provoking to some of the ghosts who haunted his graveyard of failed relationships.

No, it was best that she had turned away tonight, that she hadn't ventured out to join him in the wild feelings the storm called forth. It was far better that she know him no better than she did. Sex would only chain her—and him—more thoroughly. Thinking they could cure this attraction with casual sex was like trying to treat typhoid with aspirin. And this was a relationship that was likely to continue to be hemorrhagic, absolutely lubricated with gore if she insisted on going after Saint Germain—which she would do if they were any more deeply connected. Once bound to him, she would have no choice. His death would be her own.

Yes, they were more than a few party hats shy of a good time. Their only hope was to kill Saint Germain and then to part.

Alex sighed and touched his earring. He wasn't at all sure what he was doing outside anyway when he had so much writing left to do on this bloody, endless novel. Yes, he always enjoyed the storms—wanted to see them, feel them, hear them—and this kind of storm was particularly invigorating. This enlivening experience was partly why he had bought the island. But it was too cold even for him. And though he was feeling uneasy about being anywhere near Harmony, the trouble was internal and not a matter of proximity that could be cured by a second set of doors between them, or a cold shower. Therefore it didn't seem sensible that he would actually be looking for solutions out here in the cold.

But he did feel—what? A vague inkling that something was amiss with the world. The warning rode the distant threnody of the gale, a lonely sound beyond the pitch of human hearing that was coming ever closer.

I'm here already, Alex, a voice whispered, more in his mind than in his ear, and he felt the familiar ghostly touch graze his cheeks. *Danger comes for her. Soon. Beware.*

Thomasina? he asked. Then: *Was that you in Mexico?*

I'm always with you, Alex. You carry me inside and wear my memory like a hair shirt.

Then the touch and voice were gone—probably just a hallucination brought on by his unhappy remembrances of her. Or maybe it was his subconscious trying to warn him of something while he brooded over his ancient mistakes.

Alex blinked and began paying attention to the outside world again. He ordered his external senses awake.

He stiffened. Danger. It was in the air now. And not solely because of his ever-growing attraction to Harmony. But what could it be? They were on an island, surrounded by water, half a world away from Saint Germain's monsters, so why had he imagined that voice and icy touch warning him to beware?

Alex inhaled deeply, trying for a scent, and began to scan the horizon. He couldn't see anything, but every nerve said that danger lurked nearby. He knew in his bones that some threat was just ahead in the fog or around the corner, hiding in the shadows. He had developed a sort of sixth sense that warned him when danger was closing in. It had saved him more times than he cared to recall—from financial disaster, but also from a volcanic eruption, several times from ambush by his enemies, and once from a murder threat by a rival lover of a now-forgotten woman he had taken to bed on a whim. That instinct now said mortal peril was near.

Harmony had seemed to sense something, too, earlier in the evening. She had spent much of their meal glancing toward the windows, watching the approaching storm, and frowning. Alex chastised himself. He should have paid closer attention! They were both psychic, after all.

But . . . there was nothing. There was no unfamiliar smell in the air. The village was peaceful and dark. The sea was empty, as was the sky, except for the growing lightning and wind.

Alex hoped passionately that the approaching danger had nothing to do with Harmony. When he had brought her to Cornwall he had wanted more time, time to learn more of her secrets, her desires, her dreams, and to warm himself at her bright inner fire that a long life's many disappointments had not yet dimmed. But he had never meant to put her in harm's way.

He hissed through his teeth, watching his breath turn white and whirl away. Perhaps there was no direct, outside threat to her. He might be making up excuses to keep her here. Maybe he should send her away. Now. Anywhere. While he still had the strength to resist his own feelings. Before she decided that he was being timid and stupid and just seduced him.

She could very well do it. He knew himself, knew that the reawakened yearning for companionship she had stirred would eventually overwhelm him. Dissatisfaction and loneliness had been a growing stain on his spirit these last sixty years. It had shadowed his soul as surely as the blackest of the deadly sins he had indulged in. Alex wasn't given to envy. Sloth and gluttony were more his failings, he thought, recalling the dinner he'd just shared with Harmony. But though he did not lust after others' possessions or talents, he did hunger with the appetite of a starving man for the companionship that others had. He thirsted for a chance to be with someone—to rest his heart in someone's care—who truly understood who and what he was.

In spite of what he'd said to her, he wanted to give his heart again—against the advice of his experience and every horrible tragic lesson he had learned. And she would figure this out eventually because of their mental connection. And she would try to give him what he needed.

But could he do this to Harmony, knowing that it would likely end in disaster? And it would—it always did. He knew he could pick up the pieces of a shattered life and move on, but could she?

From the moment of his change, he had held back from people—from his lovers especially. Always he was wary. Always he held back his heart. And the secret of his identity, and his unnaturally long life, was as safe as the day he had received it from Dippel and his dark gods. Even Thomasina had not known the truth.

But Harmony knew. And she was here, with him, because she was psychic like he was and understood the danger Saint Germain posed, and because she was brave enough to face both impossibilities and not flinch from a truth that was wildly different from any reality she had known before.

And she wanted him—right this moment. He could feel her desire and her fear. It lingered in the air even after she left the room. He could smell it even out here in the cold with a sea wind stirring. Fear wasn't enough to end it, though. She might not know it, but she wouldn't be the one to walk away from their relationship, not as long as she had any hope that he would relent.

Alex! It was the voice again, more urgent this time.

He gasped as his eyes finally managed to flash the visual distress call to his brain. Something moved in the water below—something white and shaped like an arm. Alex leaned over for a closer look.

It *was* an arm—a woman's. And was that a boat? If so, it was little more than a floating corpse, a ghost ship whose sail had become a shroud.

So this was the danger he sensed—someone was drowning! It was almost a relief that this was so. This was something he could fix. Anyone caught in the currents this rough night was going to need superhuman help. Fortunately, he was here to save her. No one need die tonight after all.

Without thinking, Alex rolled from the balcony and dove ninety feet straight down into the boiling sea.

It is necessary to have wished for death in order to know how good it is to live.

—*Alexandre Dumas*

True love always makes a man better, no matter what woman inspires it.

—*Alexandre Dumas*

CHAPTER FOURTEEN

The Spider

Chapter Three

Morning dawned bright and cheerful with
the smell of fall fires sailing on the breeze
that slid through the inch-wide opening at
the base of the casement window she'd left
ajar while bathing. Gillian shivered as she
pulled open the doors of her armoire and
hunted for something warm to wear. After a
quick review of her wardrobe of mostly
lightweight clothing, she decided that a trip
to London was in order.

As added incentive to head to the capital
rather than to nearby York, Ned had given a
standing invitation to take her to some environmental fundraiser on a private yacht that

would sail up and down the Thames while the privileged class went about enjoying its privilege to eat, drink, and show off its designer clothes to others of its kind.

Suddenly the idea of socializing was overwhelmingly attractive. She hadn't slept particularly well the night before, which suggested that she wasn't entirely prepared to be alone in Dunnstone with only her thoughts and a portable PC for company. It wouldn't hurt to sow an oat or two before the weather got bad and she gave herself over to her muse. . . .

The flashlight, which had worked fine upstairs, was failing by the time Harmony reached the dining room. It barely nudged the darkness back, less effective against the growing dark than a candle would have been. As she watched, the already tiny light stuttered twice, grew small, then flickered out like a spent wick finally drowned in its own wax. Something that glowed like moonlight but moved like fog crept into the hall and stained her skin a cowardly shade of pale. She stood in the near-dark and unwillingly thought of Alex and what he did to things with batteries.

But Alex wasn't there—mentally or physically. For the first time in days, she couldn't feel him at all. Therefore, he wasn't responsible for the flashlight's sudden death.

A terrible and familiar odor impregnated the fog that slipped into the room through the ill-fitting windows where the feral ivy grew. It felt sticky as a spiderweb as it climbed up her body and caressed her face. She fell back a step and did her best to keep her breaths shallow so that it didn't get into her lungs. The fog followed. She backed away from the door but felt her muscles weakening with every step.

Ha-a-armo-o-ony. I'll se-e-e you so-oo-on. The-e-ere's someone here who wants to pla-ay wi-i-ith you-uu-u.

"Oh, God!"

Harmony dropped to her knees, suddenly weak with terror. There was someone else here. Like Alex . . . only someone older, more powerful, whose presence could kill her electric light even without touching it. Someone who could whisper in her brain with a voice as real as anything issued by a human throat. The name wouldn't come, but she didn't need to think it, to say it. There was only one being who could do that.

Her mind shrank into a ball of panic, collapsed so tight on itself that she could not reason or even recall how to breathe. She had to keep him out of her head—had to, or it was all over!

Harmony gripped the carpet runner that ran the length of the hall and stared into the dining room, watching in transfixed horror as something large and not entirely human filled up the dark glass overlooking the terrace with a shadow even blacker than the night beyond. It leaned in. The window frames shivered for an instant and then burst inward. Rain was blown through the open window with a horizontal gust, rousing her to panic with cold kisses on her naked skin.

How long she might have stayed crouched on the floor she did not know, but a trespassing gnat blown in on the evil wind flew into her mouth and buzzed her tonsils as it tried to escape. Gagging silently, she was finally forced to breathe. She couldn't command her muscles to rise, but her brain resumed functioning and she was able to scramble into the deeper shadow behind the heavy drapes in the alcove across the hall, allowing only one eye to watch the dining room. Feeling the place where Alex had been inside her head, she visualized building a brick wall, a strong, tall wall that would keep the monsters out.

She gagged. Evil—evil everywhere. It was like a veil over her mind, doing its best to separate her from even the most basic survival thoughts. But it wasn't *the* evil. For some reason Saint Germain had passed her by and moved on to someone else. The list of possible targets was small.

The knowledge lent her strength. There was a monster in the dining room, but she had killed monsters before. They could be stopped. The gun room—she had to get back upstairs and arm herself. Preferably with a big-bore six-gun like the Nitro, or a Magnum. Or an over-under shotgun. They only carried two shells, but those shots could be fired very quickly because you didn't have to eject the cartridge between shots, and you could blow a man's head clean off and still have a spare for smashing the heart. And they were mechanical, not electrical. They wouldn't fail even if she ran into . . . *him*.

This thought of weapons steadied her. Maybe Alex hadn't been able to kill off Saint Germain by tearing his heart out, but no one did much constructive attacking when they were missing a head. She and Alex would be fine. She'd kill the ghoul and then go to help Alex. She just had to force her muscles to unclench one by one and then to run as if the Devil himself were after her. It was maybe sixty feet, then up a flight of stairs, then maybe twenty feet more—that was nothing.

Something swung into the dining room through the windows. It was not human but possessed powerful arms that dangled low like a gorilla's. This wasn't the King of Evil, but it was bad enough. Her will might be stronger, but it was no match for those hideous arms. Waiting no longer, she burst out from behind the tapestry and bolted for the stairs.

Behind her, the monster yowled. It didn't seem possible, but Harmony was sure she felt its weight when it landed in the hall behind her.

Alex let go of the corpse and watched the sea reclaim it. If this woman had ever been swimming for her life, it had been weeks ago. She was rotten now, an abode for creatures of the tide pools. He had been lured here by a trick—the kind of corpse animation only Saint Germain could do.

Turning in the wild water, he looked up the sharp gradient of his island, rising as a white mass in the black night. It was nearly vertical, a seemingly impossible climb back up to the dark house. He swam quickly.

The climb would have been deemed impossible by most people, but Alex made it anyway, jamming his fingers into the tiny fissures in the rocks, forcing the island to give him handholds as he hauled himself up the crumbling stone wall. He had to get back to Harmony. Saint Germain was coming. He might already be there. The thought made him sick with worry, and for the first time since Thomasina's death, Alex knew real fear.

This wouldn't happen again! He swore it. No one else was going to die for his mistakes.

He tried to reach psychically for Harmony but ran into a brick wall. In time he could batter it down, but didn't attack it at that moment. Whatever was happening to her, she didn't need to be distracted. And as long as the wall held, Saint Germain wasn't in her mind.

The storm broke as he climbed, and, against his better judgment, Alex looked back at the sea and then out at the horizon. Strange lightning left bloody trails on the undersides of the swaying clouds that whirled above him like a tornado that hadn't touched ground. He'd never seen wind affect clouds this way. As he watched, the bottom sides of the clouds bulged back and forth as though being sucked in and out of a giant's lungs. The sky began to shrink, compressing the clouds around the island. Much closer and they would become blinding fog. If he wasn't careful, the wind would whip him away from the cliff.

Alex climbed faster, leaving his own flesh and blood behind on the rocks.

Her fear tried to burrow deeper inside as she ran, but when it couldn't find anyplace to hide in her stomach, heart, or bowels, it began to claw its way out of her throat in a keening wail. Harmony clamped her lips tight, refusing to let the sound out.

Behind her, something bulged into the hallway and screamed, expressing as much triumph and gloating as she felt fear. Earlier, the sound might have paralyzed her, but she was almost to the gun room. And now she was angry as well as frightened. She wanted to kill this thing—kill it and kill it and kill it.

The bellowing grew closer, as did the sound of pounding hooves. It was coming, and coming fast. The endless roar pierced her eardrums and then shot through her skull, where it burrowed under the scalp, leaving her feeling that her flesh was being shorn from the bone. Long after the oxygen in the creature's lungs should have worn out, the noise went on, ululating up and down, shredding Harmony's nerves, goading her to turn and move in for the attack. She wanted to smash it, kill it. She wanted to do anything that would make the noise stop. But to attack the thing unarmed would be suicide. She didn't waste time looking back.

Regular vision was of no help in the unnatural dark, but Alex didn't need it. He could see the slimy psychic trail left by the ghoul where it had scrambled up the ivy and in through a dining-room window.

The wind howled around him on the terrace, but above it Alex could hear racing footsteps—Harmony's and the ghoul's. They were headed for the gun room. Harmony had a lead, but not more than a few yards.

Alex was about to launch himself at the wall and follow them when he saw a second oily trail heading up the corner of the building and ending at the attic window. As dangerous as the ghoul was, this second trail frightened him more. He knew it of old. It belonged to Saint Germain.

After only an instant of hesitation, he ran for Saint Germain and the attic. Harmony was a good shot, and there was plenty of weaponry in the gun room. She could take on a ghoul. Probably. Even if it bit and infected her, Alex knew what to do to save her. He could resurrect her. And there was every chance that the ghoul had been ordered to take her alive.

But she would not survive a run-in with a powerful psychic like Saint Germain. He'd simply move in and blank out her brain and order her to follow him. She wasn't strong enough to keep him out. Harmony didn't know it yet, but there actually were worse things than death by ghoul attack.

If God was with them and Alex's strength held—*s'il Vouz plaît, bien Dieu*—she would never know this.

She didn't so much burst through the gun-room door as hydroplane over the inexplicably wet floor. Unable to stop herself, she smacked into the far wall, rattling the weapons that hung there on brass pegs. She reached out desperately. There was no light in the room, and the first gun her panicked hands encountered was, of all things, a flare gun. That wasn't her first choice of weapons, but it was at hand and she desperately wanted some light. Praying that Alex's paranoia would have put him in the habit of leaving guns loaded, she spun about and pulled the trigger.

The simian nightmare rushing through the doorway was briefly illuminated as the flare exploded in its chest. Its rush stuttered to a brief halt as it staggered back a step, but Harmony didn't wait to see it fall. She snatched up the next pistol, not bothering to see what kind it was, and unloaded it into the thing's flaming head.

Unfortunately, the gun was a small-caliber weapon and none of the bullets penetrated her attacker's skull; they tore through the scaled flesh of its face, but the hard white bone beneath never cracked. Nor did the creature bleed.

"Shit!" Harmony hurled the pistol as the thing again rushed her. It was fast—inhumanly fast!

She spun out of reach of the swiping claws and grabbed at the next weapon. She cried out as something sliced into her fingers.

Her assailant bellowed in pain, and she shot it a quick look. The living torch had impaled itself on some kind of lance near the door, and it was burning bright enough by now to show her that it was Alex's African knife made from giraffe bone that had cut her fingers as she'd grabbed it.

She wanted the Nitro, but it was within the ghoul's striking distance. All the high-caliber weapons were.

"Damndamndamn."

The thing pulled itself off its spike. There was no time to get at the rifles on the other wall and no way to get around those giant, reaching arms as the monster placed itself in the middle of the room and screamed at her again. It was the throwing club, the mace, or the knife. Snarling with frustration, Harmony snatched at the knife handle with her undamaged hand and then spun away from the fiery monster, which leapt forward and swiped at her again. Its hands and arms were on fire now, but it wasn't slowed.

She turned and ran at the room's only window, praying that it was as poorly latched as all the others but willing to chance a fall through glass if that was what it would take to get away.

Feeling heat on her back from the monster who was setting the room ablaze, she didn't stop to ask herself what she would do if there was no balcony outside this upstairs room.

Alex saw a flare of light from the corner of his eye as he hauled himself up the last stretch of ivy-covered wall. The sight was followed quickly by several cracks from a handgun—a twenty-two. Not the best choice for taking on a ghoul, but it could do the job if the creature was close enough and not walled with muscle. It pleased him to hear the ghoul shriek and then Harmony curse in anger. As long as she was angry and not screaming in fear or pain, she was probably okay.

Wishing he could also afford to scream in anger himself, Alex forced himself to remain quiet, hoping he could sneak up on his enemy. It wasn't that he feared losing a physical fight with Saint Germain, but there was no knowing how much stronger psychically his nemesis might have grown. Alex was a strong psychic. He could do a metaphysical bench press with the best of them and he'd never met a psychic stronger than he was. But this wasn't the moment to rush in blindly and get himself killed by being overconfident. Saint Germain was bound to have grown stronger over the decades, and there was no way to know how powerful he might now be, especially if he had managed to consume Smoking Mirror's vampiric energy.

He had to stay alive for Harmony. And for himself. For the first time in years, Alex realized how much he wanted to live.

There was a balcony and a convenient ladder of ivy leading to the garden below. Harmony's descent down the wet ivy was less a climb than a poorly controlled drop, but she made it to the ground without breaking an ankle.

Impossibly, it was even colder and somehow raining hard, a solid, dark torrent that felt oily. The water also smelled foul and stung when it hit the skin, but it was definitely the lesser of two evils. The choice was a flaming ghoul or acid rain—she'd take rain. A typhoon even. Harmony had wondered if fire would eventually deter a ghoul, and now she had her answer. Fire alone was not enough—at least not enough to kill quickly. She'd have to do something else, and options were limited.

She ran. Above her she heard the clip-clop of the jackass-legged, gorilla-armed monster that chased her to the small window he was unable to fit through without doing some remodeling to the exterior wall. Brick gave way and he was on the terrace. He'd ripped down a stone wall to get at her—a wall!

She didn't think things could get any worse, but then, to her horror, she heard a sound that she was certain would haunt her nightmares for years to come: the bitter rain was hitting the ghoul's still-burning flesh and making it sizzle.

Apparently the rain hurt it as well, or perhaps it was just that it had finally caught sight of her, because the ghoul let out a tremendous yowl and then flung itself over the balcony railing, not bothering with the ivy ladder. The drop was a good twenty feet onto unforgiving flagstone. It landed hard but the beast sprang up immediately and jumped after her, its legs bunching and springing like a horse taking a low fence.

The flare still flamed, the phosphorus burning merrily.

Harmony screamed then too, half in fear and half in disbelief. What would it take to kill this thing?

Alex heard Harmony scream and glanced down from the roof long enough to see her run for the cemetery with a flaming ghoul not twenty feet behind her. He was relieved to see the Masai knife clutched in her right hand, but wished she had had time to grab one of the hunting rifles. The knife would certainly do the job, but she was more comfortable with guns—and a gun could keep her out of the monster's grasp.

Harmony scrambled up the side of a strangely scorched mausoleum, hampered by her wet nightgown and by worry about what might come out of the crypt's doorway and grab her. It had been blasted open by something, perhaps lightning or vicious wind. Perhaps something worse.

She glanced back once during her climb. The damaged ghoul was trying to climb up after her but unable to find immediate purchase with his blackened hooves and clawed fingers that were now burnt to stubs. He might also have been hampered by his burned-out eyes, though from the way he was sniffing the air, she wasn't at all certain that he needed sight to find her.

The ghoul howled again and leapt upward, almost reaching the building's eaves. Fearing that he might eventually succeed, or be joined by something that was better adapted for climbing, Harmony took the risk of leaping across the four-foot gap between her own slimy pitched roof and that of the next violated death-house, whose roof was flat but about a foot higher. After that, one leap of faith after another, she worked her way across the graveyard, rooftop to rooftop, trying to get around to the front of the house and the bridge. She had to get back inside and to a better weapon before the ghoul figured out where she was going. Then she had to find Alex and get them off the island. She prayed the bridge was still in place, that they weren't cut off from their only route of escape.

She wasn't allowing herself to think about it, but the underlying conviction remained that it wasn't just a ghoul that had come calling on them, but that Saint Germain himself was close at hand. And beyond that was the worry of what had happened to Alex. She still couldn't feel him. Was it possible that he was already dead and she was all alone?

"No." That couldn't have happened. She would have felt him . . . die. But he might be in terrible trouble. His mind could have been overwhelmed by Saint Germain, in which case Alex was in desperate trouble. She wanted to take down her own wall and try to find him, but she was too afraid of what might be on the other side of her mental barrier.

Coming to a decision, Harmony stopped fleeing and waited at the top of the cemetery gate. The stone arch was firm but slimy with wet moss, and she had to fight for balance against the wind.

The ghoul rushed on, heedless of the headstones he toppled like children's blocks.

"Over here, asshole." Panting with fear, she knelt on the stone arch. She raised her blade high. This would be all about timing. Wait . . . wait . . . Now! She jumped, bringing the blade down hard, and discovered that Alex was right. The blade could hack a skull in two with more ease than a cleaver halving a chicken. Her blow wasn't neat. It entered the center of the skull but then veered left to lodge in the creature's clavicle after slicing off a third of its head.

She let go of the knife when the creature's forward momentum threatened to pull her into its still burning body. She clutched the gate and fought for balance on the uneven ground while she watched the ghoul stagger by, caged by the stone wall on either side of the path. It managed to run another ten feet but then finally fell to the ground. The creature kept twitching, but didn't get up again. The flare had finally eaten enough of its heart.

"Die," she commanded it, meaning it, willing the creature to do her bidding. "Just die."

The ghoul didn't cooperate.

Harmony really wanted her bone knife back, but couldn't bring herself to touch the shuddering monster. Instead she slid carefully past the body, scraping her back on the stone wall.

"Ow." Her feet hurt. She looked down and saw that her slippers were gone and she was standing on a stray raspberry cane that had wormed its way between the unmortared stones. She'd probably lost her slippers somewhere in the cemetery.

In spite of the pain, Harmony stood there for a moment, clinging to the limb of an old chestnut tree that overhung the wall, listening to the storm and night, straining her ears to hear any sound, because this time her life did actually depend on hearing if danger was near.

But there was no noise to be heard above the gurgling rain, and no scent to be smelled above the odor of the ghoul's barbecued flesh. However, there was a new light above her—a strange, almost lightning-colored aura that strobed against the small windows of the attic. She knew that it wasn't the flash of a camera, though that was the only comparison her mind could make.

"Alex!" Harmony breathed, again terrified as she squinted against the stinging rain that filled her eyes. Her hand was bleeding freely from the knife wound, and the blood felt warm on her chilled flesh.

She experienced horror because she knew—knew—Alex wasn't alone. He was facing off with Saint Germain, and whatever was happening, it had caused a lightning storm inside the house. Someone was going to die. No one would back down from this fight.

"Alex!" Other lightning lashed out at her, hitting the ground only a few feet from the gate, and a gust of wind rocked her back against the tree, knocking the breath from her body. Gasping, she forced herself upright, and ignoring the part of her that was screaming for her to get off the island while she still could, she instead ran for the front door of the quaking cottage that shivered with every strobe of light that lit the top floor. She prayed that the door was unlocked, because she didn't think she had the strength to climb back up the ivy to the gun room, and would rather not risk breaking any more windows when she was barefoot.

This time she was going for the Nitro. Surely an elephant gun would be enough to kill Saint Germain.

We blame in others only the faults by which we do not profit.

—*Alexandre Dumas*

It is often woman who inspires us with the great things that she prevents us from accomplishing.

—*Alexandre Dumas*

One's work may be finished someday, but one's education never.

—*Alexandre Dumas*

CHAPTER FIFTEEN

FBI research facility
New Mexico desert

"Hey, is the hand really missing?" Peter Arden asked, peering into the empty tank of the gas chromatograph where the hand found in the Ruthven Towers had been kept. Peter was always chatty when working in the government's most top secret lab. Talking helped distract him from the mild feelings of claustrophobia that always afflicted him when he was underground.

"Not your project," a nervous Lyle answered. "Anyway, that's classified information. You're going to get in trouble with security. They're all over the place today."

"It sure looks bad—someone breaking in like that. Or do they think it's an inside job? And why take it anyway? It wasn't moving around much anymore. In fact, it wasn't moving at all. And it stunk. The thing was finally rotting."

Lyle looked up at the security camera and then mumbled that he couldn't talk about it.

"They got this out of Ruthven's building, didn't they?" Arden persisted, though he knew the answer.

"Arden, it's none of your business. Go away. I'm busy." Lyle leaned over his microscope and pretended to be hard at work. There wasn't anything to see, though. The hand had been his only project. Now he was simply killing time until the next round of questioning by the director of security.

"Did you hear that there was an attempted break-in last week? You think maybe it was the hand's owner looking for his missing parts?" Arden asked with an uneasy laugh.

Lyle tried not to shudder. That couldn't be. Nothing had been caught on the security tape. It was just some damned rodent chewing on the wiring. They were always having electrical problems thanks to the invasive sand and the toothsome wildlife. No, terrible as it was to consider, this had to be an inside job—and security would find out who was responsible and then everything would go back to normal.

"Look, Arden—"

"I know. I know. That's classified too." Arden sighed and prepared to move on. He had originally thought he'd enjoy working in the lab, but the charm had worn off months ago. He hated being in a place with no windows and a long, long way from any kind of town. To add insult to deprivation, it seemed unfair that Lyle had been assigned to this cool project when they were both equally qualified for this kind of research.

Lyle was thinking the same thing too as Arden shuffled his feet— life was unfair—and he was counting the days until he could retire and leave this mess to someone else. He'd seen enough weird shit in the last six months to last this and maybe three other lifetimes and didn't want to see any more. He already had a head full of nightmares and a new conviction that evil actually existed. All he wanted was to be cleared of all suspicion, get his pension, and then head for Florida and his dream of life on a fishing boat. In time he would forget that any of this freaky stuff existed and he would stop having dreams.

Both men stared at the empty tank for a moment more, remembering what had been in it. Patches of green had begun to appear on the hand, and the flesh had begun to wither. Yellow fluid had leaked from the severed wrist. That residue was all that remained.

Lyle thought: Arden's right. I bet that thing stinks—and I'm glad you're rotting, you unnatural son of a bitch. I hope it hurts too. You and the thief that took you deserve whatever happens.

"I killed Thomasina. I can kill *her* too. Anything you love, I can take away." Saint Germain smiled as he said this.

Alex both felt and heard Harmony when she entered the smoldering room. He could see in his peripheral vision that her aura was spiking wildly, throwing out flares of bright green, but her own blessedly clean aura surrounded her. That meant he had succeeded in keeping Saint Germain away. Her mental defenses still held.

He also sensed that she was wounded, bleeding, but he didn't dare look away from his nemesis to check on her. This was the end, but nothing would be completely over until this creature was a pile of ash. He couldn't shake the feeling that—just like all those years ago—defeating Saint Germain had been too easy. Fate was bound to throw him another curve ball before this battle was done.

"Leave us," he said to Harmony. "You don't need to watch this."

"But I want to," she said, coming a step closer. He knew what she saw. Even bloodied, the wizard's body was beautiful, the face exquisite. But she would also feel the raw power rolling off of him that was as cold as the wastelands of his sickened mind. He wasn't able to contain all his poisonous thoughts, and the illusion of angelic beauty was cracking.

Alex raised his arm. He held his bloody and skinned fingers rigid, making them into a bone knife.

"It ends tonight," he promised.

"I can give you what you want," the king of lies whispered, his eyes blazing to new life. The voice was mesmerizing, and in spite of himself, Alex paused to listen. "I can give you back your son."

"Alex—don't listen!" Harmony stepped closer and sighted down the barrel of his Nitro. Her voice was as wintry as any he had ever heard. "Get back. Let me kill him."

"How?" Alex damned himself even as he asked the question. What could this creature be offering? It would be something evil and tainted. He was going to raise Alexandre as a ghoul or zombie. Or . . .

"I could clone him. You could have him back—an infant. And this time you could be the father you have wanted to be. You could raise your son again—love him, nurture him."

The words were cruel, seductive . . . and a trap. He felt Saint Germain move—saw a blade in his enemy's hand coming at him, so strong, so fast. He didn't even try to avoid it. He slammed his fingers down with all his might, shattering the man's sternum. He wrapped his fist around Saint Germain's heart—those giant hands he had inherited from his own father—and ripped the thing from his enemy's beautiful body. He felt the knife go into him, puncture his lung, but Alex didn't pause. He smashed Saint Germain's heart into the ground, bearing down on it until it burst, spraying him with gore.

And with it, he smashed all chances of ever seeing his son. He felt in many ways that it was his own heart that had just been destroyed.

"Alex, move."

Filled with pain and unable to tell what was physical and what was mental, he rolled away from his enemy's corpse.

"Do it. Finish him," he said, and watched as Harmony stepped up to the body and emptied her rifle into that beautiful head. In a few seconds, nothing was left of Saint Germain from the shoulders up. Harmony was white and looked on the verge of being ill, but she had never looked away from the wizard and had not hesitated to pull the trigger.

She turned and knelt beside Alex, reaching out to put a hand over the wound in his side that was already closing. She laid the gun aside with care. Her other hand was bleeding through the cleaning rag she had wrapped around it. It added more gore to the floor, but that didn't matter; the floor was already ruined. The whole cottage was probably damaged to one degree or another.

"He wouldn't have been Alexandre. It is not the body that makes the person. It's the mind, the soul," Harmony said softly, clearly knowing what Alex was thinking and feeling. Blood dripped from a small gash in her scalp, and Alex found himself wiping it away from her pale cheek as he would a child's tear. He was also moved by the sight of naked, muddy feet, also shedding blood for him. A part of Alex noted that he could see every detail of her body through the thin cotton of her sopping gown, and that she was beautiful—not as Saint Germain had been, inhuman and perfect. She was alive, compassionate and loving. He wanted her so much. She was the only thing that could take his pain away.

"Alex?" she asked softly.

"I know." He gathered himself. Breathing hurt, but he had to find the strength to finish this task. There would be no mistakes this time. "We have to burn the body—completely. We can't leave anything that might be reanimated or that could be cloned. Then we throw the ashes into the sea."

"Okay." She didn't argue, though she had to be hurting and at the limits of her strength. "We'll have to burn the ghoul too, I guess. Though he's mostly already a cinder."

Neither of them moved.

"It's been a long night," he said. "And not the one I had planned. I'm so sorry, Harmony. I thought I could keep you safe."

"It *has* been a long night—and it's been a few French fries short of a Happy Meal. But it's almost over. And we're both alive, so don't apologize." And she managed to find a smile for him. It was wry, but beautiful in its human compassion. "And just think of all the material we'll have for the next book. *The Hitchhikers' Guide to Paranormal Cornwall.* It'll be a best seller."

"I love you," he said, and meant it. "I didn't want to—for your sake mostly. But I do."

She nodded. "I know. And I think I love you too. I know there'll be some problems, but we'll manage somehow. It's a nice kind of problem to have, really."

He nodded back. "Given the rest of it, being in love doesn't look nearly so tough as it did before. And help will be here by morning. I found Byron earlier tonight and sent a message on the mental express, then phoned Millie so she could give them directions. He and Ninon and their partners are in France. They came looking for me." He sighed. "We aren't alone anymore."

Harmony didn't answer with words. Instead, she leaned forward and kissed him. Then she said, "You weren't alone anyway. But I'm glad they're coming."

The largest fireplace was in the library, and there was already a fire in the grate, so that was where they decided to burn the bodies. It went surprisingly quickly. Harmony forced herself to watch as Alex pulled the bodies limb from limb and stacked them like logs in the grate. Both creatures went up like old kindling. The smell was dreadful, but much less horrible than anything else they had faced that evening.

The wing chairs by the fire begged to be sat in, so they did, though neither looked too closely at what was blazing in the grate. A silence, deep and slightly stunned, surrounded them. The storm was gone. The wind was gone, but Harmony wondered if it was only temporary. Would there be more? Had this been too easy?

Alex had feared there might be zombies wandering the island, pulled up from the graves by Saint Germain's magic, but none had appeared. Apparently, all the corpses in the cemetery had been too far gone to answer the wizard's summons, or else had gone back into their graves when he died. There would be a lot of restoration work to be done in the cemetery and in the house, but it didn't matter to Alex. He was going to sell the island anyway. His only comment was to say that he'd have to pay Millie one hell of a Christmas bonus this year.

Harmony looked over at Alex as he sipped a brandy, but found his expression unreadable. She had taken down the wall in her mind only to find that he had closed off their mental connection. Harmony wasn't sure if this was a good thing. She didn't want to feel the kinds of grief Alex must be living through, and he was doubtless doing it for her protection, but she felt very alone and naked without him.

"You're staring," he said.

"I am," she admitted.

Harmony had felt Alex flex his metaphysical muscle before and been impressed with his ability to read her mind, but it wasn't until the moment of Saint Germain's death, when Alex's control had slipped and the full weight of the creature's evil had rolled over her, that she understood how strong Alex was. The backwash had been enough to shake her. The only reason she hadn't collapsed on the floor was because Saint Germain's animus hadn't been directed at her.

And she had felt the moment Alex drove his hand into Saint Germain's heart. It hadn't been just his fist that killed the monster, but his will. And this will was strong enough to kill the most evil creature on the planet, even after the two preternatural creatures had traded enough psychic punches to scorch and then flood the upper floors of the cottage with deadly lightning and rain.

"What's troubling you? Beyond the obvious?" she asked.

Alex exhaled and set his snifter aside. His distracted an-

swer surprised her. "I hate to say this, but I don't think that
was the real Saint Germain."

"What?" Harmony turned to stare at him. She was horrified at the suggestion and argued: "But it had to be. He
felt so bad—so evil. What else could he have been?"

"I know it was bad. He was strong, but he didn't feel bad
enough—no worse than the last time we met. I won too
easily. I think he was a clone, not the original." Alex shifted.
His wound was healing but still hurt. "'Worlds without
number have I made.' That's what he said the last time I
killed him. And he offered to clone my son."

"A clone? Alex, I . . ." Harmony swallowed. Her throat
hurt from the nasty rain she had swallowed, and also from
throttling screams. "I'm . . . truly frightened by that thought."

"Me, too."

"I wasn't scared before. Not really. Those things in the
crypt were bad, but I knew we could handle them. And
even the ghoul—I was pretty sure I could get away. But this
creature you just killed . . . I really felt like prey when he
reached into my head. Edible. He wanted me body and
soul. If you hadn't been here . . ."

"I know. Don't think about it."

"Don't think about it? When you're saying there could
be more of him? How many more?"

"An heir and a spare?" Alex reached for her undamaged
hand. His touch immediately took her horror down a
notch. "I don't know how many there may be. That's why
tomorrow I am sending you away with Miguel—Ninon's
husband. He's actually Smoking Mirror's son. A real tough
son of a bitch. You'll be safe while Ninon, Byron, and I go
after Saint Germain."

Harmony took a few slow, calming breaths.

"It's sweet that you want to do that," she told him. She
took a deep breath and prepared herself for one more

battle—Alex wasn't going to like what she had to say. "And under other circumstances, I'd let you. But you're going to need me to break into one of the Dippel clinics and hack the computer systems."

"No. I—"

Harmony interrupted. "Anyway, as scared as I am, I am a whole lot more pissed off. How dare this son of a bitch come in here and attack us? And how dare he dump his contaminated monsters on the world? Like we don't have enough problems with global warning!"

"Harmony—"

"Alex, we have to prove what he's doing."

"We have to *stop* what he's doing," Alex corrected. He was beginning to frown, and his fog of abstraction was lifting. "I don't think it would be wise to try to prove this to the world. Think it through. If the government—any government—heard about it . . . they'd take over the project immediately. Undying soldiers—who could resist? 'Join our army, we promise that you'll never die!'" Alex shook his head. "Perhaps some governments would be more responsible than Saint Germain, but I'm not willing to bet on it. We have to find this wizard's heart and destroy it. Then wipe out every last ghoul and zombie and clone he's made. This has to end."

Harmony nodded. "I agree. But we need help shutting him down, and my way is probably the best bet for doing it." Harmony took a breath. "And the optimum way to wreck hi-tech is for The Spider to go inside one of his clinics and break into the computer system. I can find out what he's up to. And after, I can plant a virus and bring the whole system down."

"No. Absolutely not. Not unless you can do it remotely."

"That won't work. They'll have firewalls—assuming they are even connected to the Net. I need physical access."

"No. It isn't worth the risk. I won't have anyone else dying because of this. Especially not—"

"I'm not asking you. This is what I do, and I don't need your permission." Their eyes met. It was a struggle for Alex, but he didn't try to browbeat her psychically. "You said he's got clinics in South America? Alex, my Spanish is good. I've never been caught on a job—I'm really that good. And I have contacts who can probably get me legitimate work in any facility we want—documents, recommendations. I can go in openly, with the company's blessing even. And they won't be expecting me, because no one knows who I am. No one knows I'm The Spider."

Harmony straightened. It took effort, but she put force into her words and posture. "Look, this is my area of expertise. We have an advantage now with one of the Saint Germains being dead. We can't waste it. Random physical assaults on his monsters and clinics isn't enough. You won't get them all that way." She repeated herself. "If he's cloning, he's gone hi-tech. That means there'll be computers and records of experiments, backups, stored information, teams of scientists to continue the work. That's what techies and researchers do. Redundancy is the name of the game. But I can get all the information we need, and then we can bring them down from the inside." She added: "This isn't a war we can wage effectively without information."

"Without a doubt, you can do this. But along with those techies and researchers there will also be zombies and ghouls and Saint Germain clones and who knows what else." Alex spoke through clenched teeth. "And not all of these creatures are as stupid as the ones in Cuatros Cienegas or the thing that chased you tonight. Many are faster, stronger, and meaner than you are."

"But not faster, stronger, and meaner than you. I'm counting on you and your friends to make sure I have time to work. You're my escape plan if something goes wrong." She looked into his black gaze, seeking to see him with more than her eyes. He had a fairly firm grip on his emotions, but his mind still gave him away. She could read him now, and his overriding thought surprised her. He wasn't angry with her. He wanted her—wildly—and it had nothing to with the storm. And the more they argued, the more aroused he became.

She exhaled, surprised.

"Alexandre Dumas!"

"Yes?"

"There's one other thing we need to do," she said, sliding from her chair and kneeling before him. She put her uninjured hand on the bulge in his pants. "I'm not going anywhere or burning one more thing until I've made love to you. Screw being sensible and cautious. Alex, we almost died tonight. We may die tomorrow. I'm not going to be denied this. Not when I know you want me too."

Alex smiled. His face transformed, and the night's pain seemed to evaporate.

"I won't argue that call. I wanted to be a gentleman, the white knight, but since you feel this way, I'll have you tonight even if it kills me," he told her.

"I'll stay off your ribs if you stay off my hand."

"Done!" Ignoring her tender fingers, Harmony reached for Alex with both hands.

Business? That's easily defined; it's other people's money.

—*Alexandre Dumas*

It's very hard to be a gentleman and a writer.

—*W. Somerset Maugham*

I saw the angel in the marble and carved until I set him free.

—*Michelangelo*

CHAPTER SIXTEEN

Alex tore off Harmony's still damp nightgown in one long flourish. It was an unnecessary gesture, but fun, especially since the gown was ruined anyway.

She knew his face well, but couldn't help but stare as he lowered her to the floor. His own ruined shirt was tossed aside, and then he smiled at her. More than ever, he looked like a pirate. His cheekbones were high, his lips full, his gaze naked, and he had ravishment on his mind.

Her heart was going crazy, beating erratically as it anticipated. She had felt this combination of panic and excitement before when working undercover, but never to this degree—and never for a man. She suspected that it was the same for Alex, that they were both forging a path through new emotional seas.

"I should tell you I've never much liked hit-and-run sex." Her voice sounded strange, breathless. "I mean, if it's worth doing—"

"It's worth doing for hours," he finished. "I agree completely, *ma belle*." Then he laughed softly and the sound made her light-headed. It promised that this was not going to be casual itch-scratching.

Alex lowered his mouth to hers. As with his cooking, Alex held nothing back, but he was an artist and used subtlety rather than brute force to achieve his desired goal. He could easily have overwhelmed her, but he chose not to. His kiss teased and coaxed but never intruded. It was a nonthreatening act from a very threatening man. She could feel the wildness in his mind and body, could see the golden scars rising on his flesh, but his touch—mental and physical—remained light, and he did not allow his lust or other thoughts to become intrusive.

She'd never experienced anything so carnal as his absolute desire and absolute control over it. Harmony heard herself moan and then pressed against him. The wounds on her hand and feet were forgotten. She was weak and hot—burning. And it was this fire that drove out the last of the cold and fear. The night's terrors were burned away, and she gratefully gave herself to the cleansing fires of desire. Time had no meaning.

Alex smelled delicious, spicy—cinnamon and frankincense and chocolate. She hungered on many levels.

"I think none of our clothes are salvageable," he said, rolling aside long enough to kick off his pants. Then he was back, hard, narrow hips between her thighs. He leaned into her as though he too wanted them to fuse their bodies together, to become a single being.

Heat built quickly. She clung to him, nails digging in, heart's blood battering her pulse points, dizzy, blindly wanting. He entered her. He was unfamiliar—at least in this way—but felt so right. She had no reservations. Her legs went wider, hips lifted higher, urging him to do his worst.

But all he would do was rock slowly, rhythmically, leisurely.

The world grew bright and hot. Alex actually began to

glow. Harmony closed her eyes, and in her mind she saw them making love in the full light of the sun atop an altar in the desert. Brighter it grew, warmer, bringing life to both of them. They melted into one and she absorbed him.

"Open to me," she whispered, wanting to share her vision.

Alex hesitated for a moment and then did as she asked. The barriers came down all at once and she was able to see inside him—all memories, all thoughts. Though she had wanted this, Alex's desperate desire was more than she could face all at once. Flooded by sensation, body and mind, Harmony fled for the nearest escape: ecstasy.

Her mind shattered momentarily as the vortex of climax took her body. She felt Alex follow, letting physical release take them both away in a long, rolling wave of heat and light. For a moment they were one with the sun just as she had imagined, and then they fell back to earth.

Slowly the bits and pieces of thought and sensation sorted themselves and they were again two people.

"Wow." Harmony swallowed. "Can we do that again?"

"Yes, but not until I stitch your hand." Alex kissed her gently. He glistened with sweat and his breathing was labored. "I cannot leave my woman bleeding on the floor."

"Damn," she said, holding up her injured hand. "I didn't even notice." After a moment she asked curiously: "Alex, what color is my aura?"

"Right now, you are a soft green. But a minute ago you were the northern lights, a storm of all colors. Beautiful."

Harmony couldn't help but smile.

"How do you like your eggs?" Harmony asked as the first apologetic rays of sunrise crept through the window. Her hand didn't hurt. Nothing hurt. Millie had, of course, arranged for there to be pain pills in the first-aid kit. Harmony was floating without care, certain that she could practically levitate down the soggy hall.

"Flogged mercilessly. I prefer soufflé to scrambled." Alex smiled as he looked up from his manuscript. He had worked while she slept. "But I can do them. Your hand must still be sore."

"No. I want to. Your breakfast shall be properly subdued," Harmony promised. "Assuming we have eggs."

"We do."

Harmony sat up and looked around for something to wear. Seeing nothing else, she gathered up a torn drape puddled on the floor near the library window and wrapped herself in the gold damask toga.

"I'll be back shortly."

"With toast, one hopes. I have never cared for naked eggs." Alex had returned to his writing, scribbling feverishly.

"With toast," she promised, kissing him quickly on the top of the head and then heading for the door.

Alex was intimidating as a chef, but she knew she had nothing to apologize for in her breakfasts. She'd even throw in some chervil, just to prove she could. And it might help her regain her appetite. All her appetites had been fed the night before, but Harmony knew she still needed to eat. One could not live by love alone—not if one was a ghoul hunter.

She had successfully coaxed the stove to life when she heard a knock on the front door of the cottage. The sound froze her in place. It had never occurred to her that they might have sunrise visitors on the island.

She listened carefully as Alex answered the door, mentally reviewing their hasty cleanup. There was nothing left of the bodies they had burned, the last of the ashes having been dumped in the sea at sunrise, and the downstairs had no sign of fire, though it probably smelled smoky. She couldn't hear exactly what was being said, but the tone was cordial. A moment later she heard multiple sets of footsteps coming toward the kitchen. Putting down her bowl of battered eggs, she tightened her makeshift gown and turned toward the door.

Alex came into the room first. He wore only a pair of pants. He was followed by a well-dressed man whose familiar profile could only belong to Lord Byron. Next came a woman of diminutive size but astonishing beauty. Her hair was long and the color of new gold. There was a second woman, also lovely but not as ethereal as the first. Harmony had the feeling that this woman had not been—changed—for very long. Her movements were not as quick and precise as the others, though she shared their telltale dark eyes. Last to file into the kitchen was an exotic male of Aztec heritage whom she guessed was Miguel: Something about him felt unusually dangerous.

"*Chérie*, I would like you to meet Byron; his wife, Brice." Harmony nodded, smiling politely since she didn't know what else to do. Alex went on: "This is the immortal Ninon de Lenclos and her husband, Miguel. Everyone, this is . . . The Spider you've been hearing so much about. Your timing couldn't be better. She has a plan for destroying Saint Germain's clinics."

"And not a moment too soon," Miguel said. "We found out yesterday that Saint Germain broke into the FBI research lab and stole his father's hand. We think he's going to clone the Dark Man."

Ninon shook her head at her husband.

"Miguel—not so fast. It is barely dawn. And our hostess is clearly making breakfast. *Bonjour, petite.* I am so sorry to come upon you unaware." The ethereal beauty smiled as she spoke, and Harmony was enchanted. Ninon turned to the others. "Shall we use English? I believe it is a language we all have in common? Good, then let us be comfortable while we discuss affairs."

Harmony stared into the five sets of obsidian eyes that

studied her openly and began to laugh a bit hysterically. She pushed her wild hair back from her face and took a firm grip on her slipping wrapper. She said as politely as she could: "Please come in. Would you like some breakfast?"

If the artist does not fling himself, without reflecting, into his work, as Curtis flung himself into the yawning gulf, as the soldier flings himself into the enemy's trenches, and if, once in this crater, he does not work like a miner on whom the walls of his gallery have fallen in; if he contemplates difficulties instead of overcoming them one by one . . . he is simply looking on at the suicide of his own talent.

—*Honoré de Balzac*

If I don't write to empty my mind, I go mad.

—*Lord Byron*

CHAPTER SEVENTEEN

Daylight revealed a scene of botanical carnage outside the cottage. The fearsome storm had ripped nearly every leaf and petal from their canes, limbs, and stems, and beaten them to a colorful pulp that slimed the walkway. One large chestnut had been completely uprooted and many saplings flattened. It made Harmony shiver to look over at the gardens on the mainland and see that they were untouched by the storm; it was another reminder that they were facing something personal, supernatural, and destructive. She wondered how they could explain what had happened. If they were lucky, the locals would blame it on giants.

To please Alex, Harmony actually did consider attempting to contravene Saint Germain's network security using a denial-of-service or breach attack over the Net. However, there was no way that she could remove the terabytes of information they needed as well as cripple the computer system without prolonged direct contact. She had some unexpected support from Miguel on this. He knew computer systems from his days at NASA, and knew the kind of security that could be guarding them.

Normally, Harmony did not damage the computers she took data from. She was not a vandal. That didn't mean that she was completely unaware of how such things could be done. There were several options. After a long talk with Miguel, she decided that what was needed was to obtain privileged access to the clinics' data servers. So many more things were possible with root access. It was her belief that in crime, just as in life, the simplest plan was often the best. She decided to use a security-breaching technique she'd used to play tricks on friends in college.

Using a copy of Visual Basic she had installed on her portable, she could write in advance a simple Trojan horse program that would steal administrative access to the servers. Adjustments to the look of the program would probably be necessary, but the software's simple drag-and-drop feature would let her mimic the look and feel of any program the clinic happened to be running.

Alex was still not convinced that this was possible, so she took him through it step by step and even gave a live demonstration so he could see how quickly she could work. In minutes, she knocked off a program that mimicked a standard computer time-out screen at a site Miguel had selected for their test assault, prompting the user to enter his user I.D. and password to log back in after leaving the terminal for any length of time. It proved that all she needed was the briefest of access to the system administrator's computer, and then the program could capture and send the password information to any other terminal she designated. Once she had privileged access, everything else would fall like dominoes. All that was needed was that she have access to a computer inside the building.

Once she was sure that she could handle things from a technical standpoint, Harmony contacted her people in the

States and asked them to get her admittance into the Johann Dippel clinic in Peru. It was where Ninon believed they had taken Dippel's hand for cloning. That might mean extra security at that particular clinic, but if Harmony crashed their network at some other site and made them aware that they had been attacked, security would be even tighter. It might be that the organization would get only one crack at both getting the hand and finding all of Saint Germain's dirty secrets.

While they waited for word from the United States, Miguel helped Harmony with the front-end and back-end portions of her Trojan horse and then loaded them onto a USB flash card. The front end would run on the server console spoofing the time-out screen, and the back end would run on the terminal in her office—an office it looked like she would have. Her boss called two days later with the news that they had managed to get her—or a woman called Selena Calderon—a job in accounting inside the clinic. This corporation had already come under suspicion for improper handling of nuclear materials. Saint Germain had also taken over a wildlife sanctuary when he remodeled the clinic, and the organization was happy to send in The Spider to see what environmental damage had been done. Harmony promised to do what she could to find out about their waste-disposal program and the local avian population's general welfare.

How the others coped with waiting for the offensive to begin, Harmony did not know, since they mostly disappeared during the day, but Alex wrote feverishly. He worked on his own story but also finished edits on hers. He didn't say anything, but she sensed his throttled-down rage. Whether it was for the danger they all faced, or the memory of what had happened to Thomasina, Harmony couldn't say. He was always gentle with her, supportive and loving even, but he kept his thoughts masked and didn't spend much time with her except when they were sleeping. Harmony didn't know what that meant about their future and didn't ask. Saint Germain had to be their focus for the time being.

They left Cornwall on a Sunday. They took different flights on different airlines from different airports. It all felt a bit paranoid, but Miguel insisted on these precautions and Harmony backed him up. As the days progressed she had slipped back into her role as The Spider. The identity was confining, not one she wore comfortably anymore, but she realized that this might very well be her last caper. Certainly it was her most dangerous. Before, she had faced the possibility of jail; now she faced death.

Peru was probably lovely, but Harmony didn't notice. Lima seemed like any other big city. The cottage where they stayed was small but pretty. It sat at the edge of Miraflores and not too far from the famous Parque del Amor. Harmony doubted that it was the warm terra-cotta hues that had attracted Brice so much as the relative privacy and the wrought-iron bars—albeit attractive ones—on the windows and around the property itself, rendering it almost ghoul-proof. The others went out often, but Harmony stayed in the rented house Brice had arranged, until the morning she reported for work at the clinic.

Her dossier said that the dress code at the clinic was old-fashioned, so Harmony wore a linen suit, stockings, and low-heeled pumps. Her hair was dyed a dark brown, and she allowed herself to speak nothing but Spanish from the moment she arrived in Peru and assumed her new identity as Selena Calderon, childless widow of forty-one.

She and Alex also began to rebuild their mental bond the day before they went in to the clinic. It would play an important part in her plan. She probably wouldn't be able to use any sort of cell phone or walkie-talkie inside the building, which was likely shielded. Also, technology tended to fail around Alex, Ninon, and Byron. Miguel and Brice were still able to use computers but were also beginning to have trouble with cell phones and watch batteries. That meant that her only lifeline to the outside was her ability to communicate psychically with Alex. Under other circumstances, she knew that neither of them would seek to strengthen this already strong mental bond, but since this was literally a matter of life and death, they lowered their guard and let the mind-mingling begin.

Whatever Alex had been feeling in Cornwall, he had managed to shake off, or else had compartmentalized it in some lead-lined room she couldn't detect. In turn, she did her best not to be afraid, and it was easier to cope when she thought of herself as Selena.

The day finally arrived when Selena was to report for work.

The clinic was located in the swampland of Chorrillos, and as Harmony already knew, it had been a migratory bird sanctuary situated about thirty minutes from downtown Lima. Saint Germain had taken over and expanded Morro Solar, the old astronomical observatory at the top of a small hill. How he had managed to persuade the government to turn over one of their historic landmarks, Harmony could only guess, but it doubtless involved a lot of money changing hands under the table.

The *garua*, a strange mist that blanketed the city May through October and rendered the area rather dreamy in the daylight—and creepy at night—was much thicker that morning as they drew near the swamp. It was possible that this was a natural condition, but Harmony rather suspected otherwise. It smelled too much like the fog that had surrounded them in Cornwall. She didn't mention this to Alex, though. Clearly he had already considered this possibility, and there was no need to pass her attack of nerves on to him. Fear wasn't something she usually felt, but this time they were fighting on Saint Germain's turf, and dread was lurking, a corrosive apprehension that could be bad enough to make her chest bulge as it swelled her heart with terror—if she gave in to it. Instead she concentrated on the hum of the car engine and silently chanted her favorite yoga mantra.

The area near the clinic was deserted except on the beach where there were a few tourists doing their best to achieve a proper post-vacation charbroil to take back home, but failing on account of the gloom. If her people were right about the stuff being dumped on these beaches, these people might have more than skin cancer to worry about.

Alex traveled with her but got out of the car a block from the clinic. He too had Latinized in the last few days, crossing the race barrier with the help of a flash bronzer.

"Have a nice day, honey," he murmured in Spanish and then kissed her for luck. The brief brush of his lips was enough to contract the muscles of her abdomen.

"*Vaya con Dios*," she muttered back. *Go with God*, and she meant it. They had to do this thing, but it was crazy dangerous. They needed divine help.

Feeling alone, as she almost always did when working, but comforted by the part of Alex that was in her head, Harmony drove the rest of the way to the clinic in a state of relative calm. She pulled up to the gate where she gave her name to a heavily muscled guard in a blue shirt. He checked her name against his list and then let her into the parking lot.

The grounds and building had been explored beforehand by Ninon and Byron and pronounced clear of ghouls. But Harmony sniffed carefully at the conditioned air in the clinic lobby, not certain if she could smell a supernatural ambush, in the unlikely event that one had been laid on, but hoping she would recognize danger if it lurked inside the tan hospital building. There was still time to warn Alex and the others away if things looked risky.

This particular "clinic" was actually an upscale hospital that didn't look as if it did a great deal of charity work with the underprivileged classes. It had lots of thick rugs made of wool shorn from exotic Andean species. They were arranged tastefully on the terra-cotta tiles of the floor in the lobby for visitors to rest their imported Guccis and Pradas on. It was also chockablock with weighty furniture carved from wood harvested from genuine, endangered rain forests, worked by hand by highly skilled, probably enslaved, craftsmen centuries before. There wasn't anything plastic in the place, discounting the computers on the desks and the smiles of receptionists.

There were security cameras everywhere, including hiding near the floor beside giant clay pots of purple orchids that served no purpose that Harmony could see other than looking up women's dresses. She hoped that Alex would be able to short them out, or at least get past them unnoticed if he had to come in through the lobby.

Of course, there were the expected guards near the doors, but they were reassuringly human and low-key. They were also proof that the Johann Dippel Corporation was not interested in promoting equal rights for women. Every one of them looked like a former Mr. Universe. She wondered if they had benefited from some kind of treatment, and whether they had been informed of possible side effects.

The elevator was slow, but the ride gave Harmony time to take a last few preparatory breaths. She didn't worry about looking nervous for the cameras. A show of nerves was to be expected in a new employee.

Her boss was Hernando Torres—married, four children, fifty-three years old. Thankfully, he didn't seem to be interested in anything except Selena's computer skills. Fortunately, those were good. Selena was modest and quiet and worked efficiently all morning. She did not visit with coworkers except on a very brief coffee break. She knew that security might be watching her and made herself as uninteresting as possible.

She was pleased to find that the office used a standard Windows-based computing system, and had no trouble with her assigned tasks. Her boss was at first inclined to check up on her every few minutes, but as she completed every chore without error and didn't seem inclined to take long bathroom breaks, he finally left her alone. She became wallpaper.

Lunchtime rolled around and the office emptied. Being discreet, she turned her back on the camera and then, dropping her pen on the floor, she bent down and removed the portable flash card from her bra. Then, pretending to check the printer cable, she attached the portable drive to the USB port on the back of her computer. Her sleight of hand was perfect, thanks to Miguel's daily dress rehearsals.

Harmony sat back down and pretended to consult the stack of forms beside her, then selected the preference "preview" button on the computer and got a look at the timeout screen she needed to match. No surprise awaited her. It took only a minute to customize her Trojan horse into a perfect duplicate of the one on the screen.

Her office was near Hernando's and she was able to keep an eye on his door while she worked. There was no knowing how long it would take to get a chance to visit his office. It might not happen that day or even that week. She was patient and prepared to wait as long as she needed to, but also ready to move if the opening presented itself.

Opportunity was not laggardly that day. Her boss was in a hurry to go to lunch and obligingly left her in an empty office. The proverbial coast was clear, but she made herself wait before taking action until several minutes had passed, just in case someone came back to the office for a forgotten jacket or umbrella. A part of her wanted to rush in immediately. Though there was absolutely nothing to suggest that danger lurked nearby, Harmony still felt the weight of dread pressing on her nerves. But she knew the rules. Deviating from the plan meant added risk to the operation. Rushing the plan would be even worse.

Since her screen could not be seen by the security camera, she took the opportunity to open the new-hire web page. Harmony almost laughed aloud and wondered if Alex felt her rush of pleasure and excitement. The corporate data center was on the third floor of the building. This was better than she had hoped for.

Harmony exhaled slowly. Attacking the data center directly was a risk—but a calculated one. If she covered her tracks, she'd be out of the building before anyone realized the attack was happening, let alone that it was coming from inside. If they were very lucky, no one would ever know that someone had managed to copy their data files before bringing the system down.

Gathering up a spreadsheet, she walked deliberately to the boss's office. It was time to break into the corporate computer.

And let the games begin.

Harmony?

We just caught a break. I'll explain later. I'm good to go.

Already?

Yes. Can you finish up your end today? I need to know how long a fuse to put on my little cyber firecracker.

Yes. We're on our way now.

I'm installing the device. Wish me luck.

Good luck.

Alex withdrew a bit, and Harmony turned her attention back to her next task. From here on, things would get tricky. If she was caught now, there was no innocent explanation for what she was doing. Not allowing herself to glance at the cameras that watched her, she carried her files to the boss's office.

Hernando had left his door open and obligingly left a

small metal placard on his desk proudly announcing that he was the administrator for System 27. Again, this was as expected.

Though she would have preferred privacy, Harmony left the door open for the sake of whoever was watching the security monitors. A quick glance told her that there was no obvious camera overlooking the desk, just one monitoring the door. That didn't mean there wasn't a hidden camera in the office, but she would have to take the risk.

Harmony went over to the computer console keyboard and quickly entered the full directory path name of the Trojan horse she had installed in her home directory of the shared network drive. She allowed herself a small smile of relief when the screen went blank and the log-in window appeared. It was an exact match.

The temptation to poke around the desk was strong, but she didn't press her luck. Having completed her task, Harmony picked up her file and left her boss's office, being careful to leave everything as she had found it.

Though there was no need, she ate lunch at her desk so that she could keep an eye on the administrator's office and know the moment he came in. After she finished her apple, she logged back into her system and pretended to work on a complex Excel spreadsheet while monitoring the small window in the top right corner of her screen.

Her boss returned promptly at twelve-thirty. He wasted no time logging in.

Admin: 2B, | !2b

Harmony almost laughed, but didn't because it wasn't something Selena would do. It was a cute but dumb password—*to be or not to be*. Her boss obviously liked Shakespeare. He seemed like a nice guy. It was a pity that he had chosen to work for the spawn of Satan. They would never have the chance to be friends.

Again prepared to wait, she didn't have to. A moment later, Hernando came out of his office and disappeared into the men's room.

Gracias, Hernando.

Letting out a pent-up breath, Harmony unhurriedly opened a telnet window to "sys27" and entered the user I.D. and password requests as soon as they came up. The computer did as expected when given this information, and obligingly presented her with an administrative shell prompt.

I'm in. It's a go.

The world was her oyster—until someone noticed that something was wrong. It would depend on how good their tech-support staff was.

She worked fast, but, always mindful of the security cameras, she kept her movements calm and her expression bored. Her first task was directing the bulk of the clinic's computer resources to finding the data she was after. Response times were slower than she liked, and she wondered if the science people were gobbling up assets for some big project—like cloning the clinic's namesake.

Harmony looked around casually. The room was mostly empty. It was unlikely that anyone would recognize what she was doing, but she didn't want to take chances. Working as swiftly as she could while the office was relatively empty, she copied the tool kit of utility programs she had smuggled in on her flash drive into an innocuous directory containing the bulk of the clinic's records and backups. Then, to determine which servers were directly attached, she ran a shell script Miguel had made for her that scanned the network drives recognized by System 27.

"Have you had lunch yet, Selena?" The question was annoying, but Harmony forced herself to smile politely at the only other woman who worked in the office. She was older, perhaps in her fifties, and had a kind face.

"Yes. I ate at my desk. It's the first day and I want to make a good impression."

"I'm sure you are," the woman—what was her name? Inez?—said kindheartedly as she walked over to her own desk and got back to work.

The list was lengthy. Harmony threw up a small prayer to the God Alex believed in that she would be able to gain administrative access to all of them. The more she had access to, the more information there would be both for Alex and for her own people—and the more damage she could do to Saint Germain's evil empire.

You feel happy. Like you ate the early-bird special for lunch. I can almost see the feathers in your teeth. Alex's thought was very clear. That probably meant he was close by. She'd found that their ability to communicate improved with proximity.

Ugh. What an image. But you're correct about one thing. Things are going well on this end. And with you?

So far, so good.

The urge to talk to Alex was strong, but she forced herself to remain businesslike. The sooner this was done, the sooner they could all leave.

Bingo! God, or someone, was smiling on her. She could gain access to all the servers. A little more experimentation showed that she was even allowed to remotely execute commands on any of the data servers from System 27 without having to log in or supply a password.

She stored the list of data servers in a flat file and then launched a third shell script to start the data-mining programs she and Miguel had hacked together from source code from various web-crawling applications that would look at the data and extract ASCII characters from desired files. The Spider was in her web and spinning away, gathering up information for a future meal.

As she watched, the program spawned itself, using what Miguel had called parallelization to mine multiple databases at once. This was something new for Harmony, and she felt a moment of anxiety. Miguel had promised that it would cause no spike in activity to alert the security crew that the system was under attack. Since her last prayer had worked so well, Harmony uttered another one that Miguel knew what he was doing.

People returned to their desks and began to work in a desultory fashion. A glance out the window showed Harmony that the fog had moved in and caused an early twilight that made her feel unsettled. She turned her back on it.

The computer chewed away steadily as the clock rolled on toward five, and Harmony began to worry that she would exceed the capacity of her portable drive. It became more difficult to feign calm and keep entering data into her spreadsheet.

The whirring finally stopped at 4:36.

Hands shaking, Harmony took the next step in the operation. Using the System 27 server configuration file as a reference, she called a simple shell script to probe the clinic's data infrastructure to confirm that she could remotely execute a simple directory listing command on each of the servers within the corporate intranet. A quick browse through the names hinted at locations in South America, Africa, Asia, and Europe.

There were hundreds.

There was one other bit of news as well. Saint Germain had also, most unwisely, opted to keep his system backup tapes in a warehouse next to the clinic. Usually the backups were sent off-site for security reasons. If there was a fire or some natural disaster, people wanted their backup tapes to be somewhere far away from harm. But perhaps because of paranoia about having his illegal activities discovered, Saint Germain had elected to keep all his copies on site.

So, prayers were sometimes answered. This was good news and bad news, however. She would be able to cause a huge amount of damage to the corporation's system and probably slow down their research for months, even years— especially if they managed to physically destroy all the back-ups. But the sheer number of servers also meant that the enemy was enormous, a hydra with so many heads that they would probably never be able to lop them all off with their limited resources, even with the help of her friends.

Harmony? Again Alex was in her mind. *What's wrong?*

Nothing. Almost done, she thought back. She wasn't yet able to convey complex technical thoughts to Alex, so didn't try to explain about the servers. *Do you remember the small gray building near the gate? That's a warehouse where they keep backup computer files. Can you guys get inside and do your magnetic battery-draining thing? It will erase all the backup tapes.* She concentrated on an image of the building.

I know it. If we can't get in ourselves, then we'll toss in a grenade, Alex promised.

Where are you now? she asked, suddenly concerned about Alex's end of the operation. What she was doing was criti-cally important, but so was the retrieval of Dippel's hand. Morally, spiritually, psychically—however you looked at it— they couldn't allow Saint Germain to re-create his father. Dippel had been bad enough in his first life, but if he were to live again, taught and nurtured by his insane, evil son, there was no knowing how much damage the genius could do.

Ninon and I are in the basement lab. We think we've found where they are cloning Dippel. Certainly they are cloning some-thing. Several somethings.

Better you than me. Go with God. I'll see you in about fifteen minutes.

From your thoughts to God's ear. Alex sounded positive. This reassured Harmony.

She looked at the computer clock. 4:52. It was time.

Her hands were shaking as she launched her destroyer programs on each of the data-servers. The programs were configured to sleep for half an hour, after which time they would awake to wreak havoc on the clinic's—all the clincs'—databases. Each program was designed to both destroy data and break server connections, which would—in theory—hide the severity of the attack from the other system administrators so they would be slow to make any efforts at containment.

Harmony waited until exactly five o'clock and then began gathering her belongings when the other employees did. She waited until no one was looking and then reached behind her computer and removed the flash card. She pretended to adjust her skirt and slipped the card into her waistband. It would be more secure in her bra, but there was no way she could put it there without making a trip to the bathroom, and she wanted to leave with the other employees.

On suddenly weak legs, she walked toward the elevators, smiling and answering polite questions about her first day. Yes, the job was very interesting. No, traffic was not a problem. There was an itch at the base of her skull and a twitchy feeling that said it was time to leave, which grew worse the longer they waited for the elevator. Things had gone extraordinarily well for her, and there were limits to how much luck any one person could enjoy.

Alex? I'm on my way out, she thought.

But Alex didn't answer.

Alex?

When the elevator still hadn't appeared five minutes later, the other employees muttered about the frequent electronic failures that happened in the building and decided it might be best to take the stairs. Not wanting to be conspicuous, Harmony went with them.

Electronic failures? In a research clinic where they would have backup sources of power?

Alex! Answer me!

She hung to the back of the crowd and didn't exit from the lobby when the others did. Pretending for the guards that she had forgotten something, she began fishing through her bag and then, with a huge sigh, she turned around and went back into the stairwell. The flesh of her back quivered, expecting to feel a guard's hand clapped on her shoulder, but no one stopped her.

Instead of going back upstairs, she headed down to the basement where the labs were.

She silently yelled at herself with every step, arguing that she was changing the plan and taking a huge risk, but a part of her was certain that Alex was in trouble. Everyone seemed to think the elevator's going out was routine, but it might be routine because Saint Germain came to the clinic a lot. And the last time Alex had disappeared from her psychic radar, it was because Saint Germain had come to the island. Could her inability to find him be because Saint Germain—or a clone—had arrived at the clinic and was jamming her brainwaves? She had to know.

CHAPTER EIGHTEEN

"I don't feel any psychics about. They are relying mainly on cameras for security," Alex said. A small burst of energy and he knew that the cameras in the hospital lobby would briefly fuzz while they passed, not that either he or Ninon looked at all like their usual selves. "That's lucky for us."

"Very lucky—too lucky perhaps. It makes me uneasy." Ninon's Spanish was flawless. Her appearance was less so. She was wearing some sort of makeup that made her appear a bit gray and unattractive. Her hair was contained under a gray wig. With the addition of a lab coat, she looked like a cranky scientist who had spent too many years indoors squinting through a microscope.

"Good. This wouldn't be a great moment for either of us to get too cocky." Alex scanned the auras of the visitors in the lobby. They were a uniform, passive gray-blue. The employees seemed either bored or brainwashed.

Ninon's smile was dry.

"Some of us were just born that way—and thank God

for it. Your Harmony is quite amazing too. Miguel is most impressed with her skills."

"Miguel is rather out of the ordinary as well." Alex smiled politely at the guards near the door and gave them a mental push. It took slightly more effort than it had with the guard at the gate since there were two of them, but it wasn't anything he couldn't manage.

"That's a neat trick," Ninon said as the two men stared into the distance. Their facial muscles were not slack, but their gaze was blank. "I wish I had the knack. Your capacity for mind-speech is astonishing."

"I've always found it useful." Alex took another deep breath, trying to scent the enemy. All remained clear. He reiterated the plan. "I'll take the stairs, you use the elevator. Check in with me as you go. See you in three hours. I don't care if you discover King Solomon's lost mines, don't be late getting back here. We're looking for the hand—but just looking. We can't risk taking it until Harmony is ready to move. And we should leave at the shift change regardless." Alex didn't look at her as he spoke; his eyes were moving slowly over the crowd, still trying to sense danger. Like Ninon, a part of him distrusted the ease of their entry.

"I understand. We are all prepared to be patient." Ninon moved off with two nurses, walking slowly, managing to convey the impression of an older woman troubled by arthritis. She even managed to transform her aura from vibrant violet to pale lilac. Alex allowed himself to imagine her on stage. How he would have loved to direct her in one of his plays. She would have made a magnificent leading lady.

They had studied a layout of this hospital, whose plans were a matter of public record if one paid enough for them, which Brice had done as part of their advance preparations. Alex's objective was the atomic medicine lab on in the first level of the basement. It was one of two places that interested them. The other was the bio-labs where most of the cloning experiments were done. Alex would have preferred to go there instead, but had agreed that Saint Germain might have warned his staff to be on the lookout for a man of his height and weight. Any outsider would be noticed, but an old woman with arthritis would not be seen to be as much of a threat.

Alex broke away from a group of white-coated technicians arguing about a soccer game and walked boldly to the door that led into the stairwell. A sign on the door said it was for emergency use only, but he pressed the bar firmly and gave a shove. He was pleased when it opened, and especially pleased that it did so without triggering an alarm. Fire codes were being obeyed and the emergency exits were unlocked during business hours.

He went slowly down the stairs, which had cameras installed on the landings, making an effort to move like Dr. Sanchez whose badge he wore. Among Byron's skills was an ability to pickpocket, and the poet had had no difficulty in liberating a couple of badges from the night shift as they headed for their automobiles the evening before. He'd had a nice selection of male candidates to choose from, but had seen only one woman. That was why Ninon was wigged and wearing heavy makeup.

The door opened easily at the base of the stairs, and in rushed a small gasp of chemical-smelling air. It was an assault on his keen nose, but that was all that confronted Alex; he had the corridor beyond all to himself. There weren't even any security cameras to bother with near the stairs, so Alex allowed his stride to lengthen. The maps on the walls said he was headed in the right direction. *Patologia, Deposito de Cadaveres*, and *Radioterapia* were all ahead. He questioned the taste of their layout. It couldn't be good for a cancer patient to have to walk past pathology and the morgue to get to their treatments. On the other hand, it made a lot of sense if the clinic wasn't actually treating very many sick people. He suspected the latter was the case.

The long white corridor was empty of life and even sound. Alex looked about carefully as he walked, not caring for the heavy shielding he could sense in the walls. And just as he had expected, the basement's atomic-medicine department wasn't a popular destination for the clinic's patients. There was no staff present either. Saint Germain wasn't curing anyone down here. There wasn't even a nurse manning the lobby desk, just the first of a new series of security cameras facing the morgue. This made things at once easier and more difficult for Alex. More people meant more human eyes to fool. Fewer people meant he had to deal with more of the electronic eyes that controlled the cameras that tracked up and down the corridors. There would be no hiding in a crowd.

Alex decided it might be best to take them all out at once rather than sequentially. It seemed more believable that an entire system would fail than one camera after another. He gave a hard psychic push, willing the cameras and any alarms attached to them to stop working, and then, trusting they had, he forced himself to walk toward the first door, making his steps as silent as possible so as not to disturb the utter quiet of the corridor labeled *Radioterapia*. His senses were now on full alert, looking for those psychic trails that he sensed all around him. He didn't see anything definite, but the whole place reeked of Saint Germain's evil. Even the strong odor of antiseptics couldn't entirely hide it.

Luxury ended where the real work began. The nuclear lab techs—veal, when they were present—were herded into small white rooms with large windows opening onto the corridor where they would have no privacy. They worked at long counters covered in shrouded machinery. There were no private offices. That was unfortunate. He could read people, but not machines.

Alex went on, uninterested until he reached the records room. Here was something he could warm to—words on paper. He touched the door, trying to sense if there was any alarm attached. He felt nothing, so he pushed open the steel door and eased into the murky space, peering intently at the desk even as he readied excuses for his intrusion if someone was napping in the dark. He hoped he wouldn't have to wipe out some poor secretary's mind, but his brain was ready for it. He was also prepared for any monsters he might find. Odds were against his having been spotted by the cameras and someone ordering that he be met by a pack of ghouls or zombies. Keeping ghouls would be a crazy thing to do in a hospital filled with people. But his experiences with Saint Germain had convinced him of the man's insane lack of caution.

The room was happily empty of people, dead or alive. Alex set about examining the office. Ignoring the computer for the time being, he started in on the shelves of files where hundreds of patients' records were stored. The sections were divided by color. He knew that these couldn't be all the records for the hospital, just the ones before computers had been installed, but it still seemed far too many for a free health clinic outside of town. It also made him nervous that most of the folders bore numbers instead of names.

He had opened his first blue file and was reading about radiation treatments being performed on surgically altered bodies when the first contact with Harmony tickled the nerve-ending in his neck.

And let the games begin. She sounded pleased. Even smug. In spite of the danger, he had to smile.

Harmony?

We just caught a break. I'll explain later. I'm good to go. He caught an impression of a blue computer screen and knew she was doing something technical. Their conversation was distracting her and should be kept short, though he felt better being in contact with her.

Already? A look at the wall clock said that a fair amount of time had passed while he had been exploring and reading. That surprised him, but he should have expected it. He was underground and couldn't feel the movement of the sun as he did on the surface.

Yes. Can you finish up your end today? I need to know how long a fuse to put on my little cyber firecracker.

Yes. We're on our way now. He was positive.

I'm installing the device. Wish me luck.

Good luck.

She had been fast—maybe too fast for the others. Alex needed to let them know what was happening, especially Ninon. The others were on the outside, which presented its own dangers, but Ninon was right in the lion's den and preparing to steal the beast's dinner. It required more effort because of the lead shielding, but Alex reached out for Ninon and let her know that Harmony had begun infiltrating the computer system. Her response was harder to understand, probably because of the shielding and because they had had less time to practice what Ninon called mind-speech, but he knew she understood what was happening.

Alex searched, but he couldn't find anything about toxic-waste disposal for Harmony's people and it was almost time for him to leave and begin a tour of the morgue. The physical records were tempting. The information he found in them was damning. The atrocities they documented were right up there with Nazi experiments and would command the attention of anyone who was shown them. But he didn't want to burden himself with a lot of folders. So he began skim-reading files, committing details to memory. This wouldn't be physical proof that they could lay before anyone else, but at least he would know what had happened.

I'm in. It's a go. Harmony sounded less excited and more focused. She was talking more to herself than to him. Alex didn't answer. He didn't want her distracted from her work. The thought of what she was doing still terrified him. She wasn't like the rest of them. They were stronger since their alteration—could take a bullet, even several, and still live. She was touching, beautifully, humanly frail. So instead of talking to her as he wished, Alex kept reading, growing ever more appalled at the stories of these poor people who had come to the clinic for help and been used in Saint Germain's experiments.

Harmony's presence tickled him again a few minutes later. She was now euphoric. If he could see her aura, it would be pulsing with emerald light.

You feel happy. Like you ate the early-bird special for lunch. I can almost see the feathers in your teeth, Alex answered this time.

Ugh. What an image. But you're correct about one thing. Things are going well on this end. And with you?

So far, so good. He made certain that she didn't feel any of the revulsion that filled him. There would be time for these horrors later. Harmony would have to know, because they would need her people to keep an eye on the other clinics. They might shut down the computer systems and destroy the bodies of stored research, but the evil men who had done these surgeries would still be alive.

Alex slammed another file back into its slot and pulled out the next. Finally he decided that he could endure no more details. He simply began reading names, committing them to his prodigious memory, promising himself that he would find some way to make this list known, at least to the families whose loved ones had disappeared.

He felt another flutter, and this time Harmony wasn't happy.

Harmony? What's wrong?

Nothing. Almost done, she thought back. *Do you remember the small gray building near the gate? That's a warehouse where they keep backup computer files. Can you guys get inside and do your magnetic battery-draining thing? It will erase all the backup tapes.* Alex got a clear likeness of the building. Her abilities to speak to him mentally were progressing quickly. Now that she had completely embraced being psychic, she was growing into her full potential.

I know it. If we can't get in ourselves, then we'll toss in a grenade, Alex promised.

Where are you now? Her question was tense but not panicked.

In the records room. I have a list of all early experiments that might not be in the computer.

He thought she was pleased with this, but didn't get a clear reply. Something on the computer screen had distracted her again.

Alex tried to find Ninon and failed. He went to the door and stuck his head into the corridor where there was less shielding. He reached out for Ninon again and finally located her in one of the labs.

Alex? Ninon asked. *I've found him—Dippel. They do have the hand.*

Can you get it?

Yes. Her reply was positive but faint. So was the image she tried to send him. The labs must also be shielded. He saw little beyond bright light and one man working at some large machine.

Do it, then.

Alex closed the door and went back to the desk. His first impulse was to rip up all the records of Saint Germain's cruelty, but someone might wander in and report the vandalism. This wasn't the time to give in to rage. He reached for Harmony along with another file.

Ninon and I are in the basement lab. We think we've found where they are cloning Dippel. Certainly they are cloning something. Several somethings.

Better you than me. He felt her mental shudder. *Go with God. I'll see you in about fifteen minutes.*

From your thoughts to God's ear.

Alex reached for another folder but then got a very clear image of Ninon. Alarm pierced him and he immediately cut himself off from Harmony.

The technician Ninon had hit was on the floor when the door behind her slammed against the wall. She shoved the rotting hand into her coat pocket and turned to face the creature that filled up the only path of escape from the room. Ninon's aura flared red as she prepared to fight.

The creature had the sort of chest development that could only be found on freaks who took steroids and lived at the gym. Or on one of Saint Germain's specialized ghouls. This, unfortunately, was one of the latter. He wouldn't go down quietly.

The ghoul grinned at her and stepped into the room. His long, lupine jaws pointed at her like a gun, and he obviously hadn't taken advantage of the company cosmetic dental plan. His yellowed teeth were saber-sharp, though, and showed over his thin, snarling lips.

Ninon didn't wait for him to take a second step into the room. She feinted right, hopping over the body of the unconscious technician. As soon as the ghoul was off balance in his turn, she jumped left, clearing the table of equipment with room to spare. In her hand was a weapon. It took Alex a moment to recognize it. The long barb was used in hand-to-hand combat during World War I. It was called a trench spike. It could pierce the helmets of enemy soldiers with one firm blow. It had the benefit of being a silent weapon, but using it would require getting within arm's reach of the ghoul.

Eyes furious, the half-wolf spun about and reached for

her with his right hand. Borrowing from some unknown style of fighting, Ninon swung her leg in a fantail kick and connected with the point of the ghoul's right elbow. Apparently, the so-called funny bone was the same in both ghoul and human bodies, because the ghoul's long arm dropped, completely lamed. He didn't cry out, though. His jaws thrust at Ninon. The ghoul was hurt but far from dead. She needed help.

Feeling dizzy and disoriented by the overlapping visual realities, Alex began to run. The representation of Ninon and the ghoul was imposed over his actual physical surroundings as he headed at a flat-out run for the service elevator, which was the fastest way down to the labs.

Alex hissed and flinched as the ghoul swung at Ninon again, using his longer left arm. But she was ready for it and quickly dropped under his clublike limb. The clawed fingers caught her wig, tearing it from her head, but she was unhurt. Again, using some foreign style of kick-boxing, she lashed viciously at the ghoul's left buttock, trusting that its sciatic nerve was located in the same spot as in the human body. She followed up with a faster, shorter kick that dislocated his knee with a sound exactly like the breaking of a dried tree limb. It was a dirty sort of street fighting, but she showed no hesitation about abandoning fair play when battling something twice her weight that would gladly tear her to pieces. Alex had never seen anyone move so quickly. She was a cold, efficient fighter.

The combination of kicks worked. When the ghoul dropped to his uninjured knee and began to roar, Ninon jumped straight into the air, putting her whole body behind the point of the spike, driving it through the creature's head and out the bottom of his elongated jaw. Faster than Alex could imagine, she got it back out and was driving it through the creature's heart.

Ninon heard a noise and her head whipped toward the

door. Alex's head turned too. Reinforcements were coming. He felt her make the mental calculation of whether to flee or stay and fight. Ninon knew she was fast but not quick enough to take on two ghouls at once. And she couldn't risk Dippel's hand remaining in the clinic if she were captured.

Alex reached the elevator and hit the button with a hard hand. Ninon was close—only one floor below him and a few feet from the elevator. If the machine came quickly enough . . .

Alex watched as Ninon's ghostly image turned and leapt for the lab door, leaving the still-thrashing ghoul behind her. She knew that there was no time to do anything about the security cameras in the hall or to help the technician she had knocked out. Not bothering with trying to hide her inhuman speed, she flat-out raced for the service elevator at the end of the corridor. Miguel's map said it was the only way out at this end of the basement. There were stairs, but they were on the other side of the ghoul pack.

The elevator pinged and the doors opened. Alex jumped in and hit the button for the sub-basement. The doors closed and he began to descend. Reaching out as far and as fast as he could, he killed the security cameras on the floor below. It was probably too late to keep Ninon from being seen by the first one, but he did it anyway so they wouldn't be able to track her visually as she fled.

An alarm went off. Behind Ninon, the doors from the other part of the lab crashed open and two more howling ghouls joined the electronic hue and cry. She didn't bother looking back. She had only a small lead, but it might be enough if she didn't trip and the descending elevator was there when she arrived.

Alex heard her say "*Merci!*" and knew it was because she could hear the service elevator coming. He reached down inside as far as he could and willed the alarm to silence. His head was beginning to hurt and the twin visual realities were making him nauseous. He hadn't used his power this much in years.

As the soft *ding* announced the car's arrival, Ninon launched herself at the opening doors, arms drawn back to strike if it was anyone other than Alex waiting for her.

"Need some help?" Alex asked, as his two kinds of sight came together and the world righted itself. The smell of wet cereal was strong, and Alex knew that he had burned off his chemical tan. Both he and Ninon were glowing slightly. If they hadn't been wearing contacts, their eyes would have also shone as pure black.

Alex didn't need her warning to hit the close button and jam his finger on the ground-floor switch.

"There may be more ghouls in the lobby to meet us if I tripped an alarm in the lab." Ninon exhaled as she leaned against the far wall, her spike at the ready. Already her skin was returning to normal. Alex willed himself to likewise calm his breathing. It was fairly easy to do as long as there was no storm in the air.

"I don't think so," Alex answered, watching the doors close and the numbers begin to flick by. "There'll be those two guards, but even if they've been alerted, I doubt they'll want a public scene."

"And if they do?" She flexed her foot and frowned. The leather of her pump had torn and her toes poked through.

"Then they'll be very sorry." Alex looked over at her. His voice was calm but his eyes were not. He and Ninon could handle themselves. Harmony was upstairs. Alone. Unarmed. "How many were there?"

"Three ghouls. That I know of. All downstairs."

Alex nodded. He didn't tell her that he had seen her fight.

"I only got one," she said. "Running away seemed wisest when two and three turned up."

"I agree." His voice was bleak and he started reaching out for Harmony, but from inside the elevator, he couldn't find her. He was being drowned out by electronic white noise. Perhaps he could push past it, but didn't dare try in case he caused the mechanism to fail.

"Okay, here's the plan," he said. "You try walking out nice and calm and humanlike. If anything looks the least bit doubtful, or anyone draws a gun, flatten whoever is in your way and run for the exit like a pack of ghouls are after you. If they lock the doors, go through them. The glass will hurt like hell, but you'll heal. Find Miguel and Byron and tell them what happened. If we're not there in ten minutes, blow up the gray warehouse and get out of the country."

"Blow up the warehouse—check." She patted his arm. "I really hope there aren't more ghouls in the lobby. It will be a bloodbath if there are. We won't be able to protect the innocent if they rampage."

The elevator slowed. "I know." The thought of so many casualties made him ill, so he pushed it away. "Ready?"

Ninon smoothed her hair and tossed aside her useless badge. She dropped her trench spike into the pocket with Dippel's hand. She was utterly calm.

"Yes."

The doors opened and Ninon stepped out. Alex's nerves were blaring alarm, muscles were tensed and ready for battle, but nothing happened. The same small crowd of well-dressed visitors were milling around the lobby, still wearing their passive gray-blue auras. The same guards were still staring into the distance. Apparently, the alarm worked only in the sub-basement, or else Alex had pushed their minds too hard when he willed their attention away and they were now among the permanently brain-damaged.

"Okay, it looks like we're clear." Alex held the elevator door open. Across the lobby, the other bank of elevators lit up like a Christmas tree. Ninon followed his gaze.

"It looks like you spoke too soon."

"It could be the workers leaving." Alex looked at the

clock mounted on the wall behind the admitting desk. It was six minutes before five.

"You think we're that lucky?" Ninon asked. She patted the pocket where Dippel's hand was twitching. "I can stay if you need me . . ."

"No. We can't chance it. You're leaving now. Go slow until you get outside and then run for the shrubs along the drive until you reach the jeep. I don't want to give them an easy target if they actually have guns. When you get there, be sure to tell Byron and Miguel to blow up the gray warehouse near the gate. It's important. It's a storehouse for their backup computer records. If Harmony pulls the rest off, we don't want her work to be in vain."

"Got it. Really. Everything will be destroyed." Ninon forced her lips into a smile that was surprisingly convincing. "Find Harmony, *mon cher*, and get out fast. Our little family must live to fight another day."

"I will." Or he would die trying. This was not going to be a repeat of what had happened with Thomasina. There would be no living without Harmony.

Alex hit the button for the second floor, watching Ninon as she strolled toward the clinic's main entrance.

The elevator doors closed softly and the car began to climb. Its progress was slow and asthmatic yet steady, but just before it reached the second floor, the power did what he'd half expected it to do; it went out. The car stopped with a jerk that nearly knocked Alex over. No emergency light turned on. This was not a normal power outage.

"*Merde.*" Fortunately, the darkness in the shaft was not absolute, nor was the silence. Though it caused white spikes of pain to pierce his brain, Alex reached out past the metal box to look for Harmony.

She wasn't close by. Not within range of his failing powers.

He swore again. Above the voices of the employees, Alex

could hear ghouls below him. Their sound was faint, as if they were being drawn from the service elevator and toward the stairs. He had a bad feeling that they were after new prey.

Not bothering to play with the emergency button or the service phone, Alex grabbed hold of the rubber gasket between the metal doors and ripped it loose, making a crack wide enough to ram his fingers into. When he'd gotten the door wide enough to accommodate his body, he climbed through. The shaft was filthy with grease and he tore his shirt, but he was able to get on top of the elevator, scramble ten feet up the cable, and reach the second-floor doors. Bracing himself in the narrow opening, he again rammed his fingers into the slot between the panels and forced them open.

He was met with a scattering of startled faces. None of them was Harmony's.

Trusting his instincts, he ran for the stairs, praying he'd get to her before the ghouls did.

CHAPTER NINETEEN

Harmony felt her stomach muscles contract as she braced herself for a collision with the two ghouls racing toward her out of the dark below. She wanted to flee, but there was nowhere to run, no time to escape even if she had somewhere safe to go.

Then Alex was there, in her head. Her body moved without thinking, a puppet choreographed by Alex's will. Having no time for fear to spread, she grabbed a bony wrist in a grip that would bruise her own hand. She used the ghoul's momentum to pull him off balance, pivoting in place and flinging the thing into the stairwell. Something in her shoulder tore loose, but she didn't cry out.

In the next instant, Alex was at her side. His skin was ablaze with crackling light. He grabbed the second charging ghoul by its long snout and cracked it like a whip, efficiently snapping its neck before he threw it into the stairwell after its companion. The sound of crunching bones was loud when the monsters collided, but it was soon replaced by an even more disturbing high-pitched howling. There was the sound of scrabbling and then feet rushing back up the stairs.

Unfortunately, the leprous hide of the second ghoul's muzzle clung to Alex's hand. He began peeling off the creature's skin like a surgeon's latex glove.

"Move! Up the stairs."

It was dark, but Alex was shedding enough light to illuminate the stairs. Harmony didn't need to be told twice. Though she was moving at full speed, Alex must have thought her still too slow, because he grabbed her by her uninjured arm and hauled her up so quickly that she felt more like an airborne kite than a woman. Her skin burned where he touched her, and her arm quickly went numb.

They reached the lobby in record time. Harmony knew Alex was braced for another assault, but the only thing that attacked them was bright afternoon sunlight streaming in the plate-glass windows.

Several startled people jabbered and pointed at them, but the two guards remained silent and passive. No one tried to stop them as they ran for the lobby doors.

Ninon and Miguel had the jeep at the curb, and Alex and Harmony scrambled into the back. Alex kissed her once and then told her to buckle up.

"I can't. My shoulder," she explained.

"Damn. It's dislocated." Giving her no time to react, Alex grabbed her and popped the joint back into place. This time she did cry out.

"Sorry, love." Alex turned his head and said to Miguel: "Drive!"

As they pulled away, a small explosion erupted to the northwest. Harmony watched the smoke trail through tear-filled eyes.

"You're the color of ash," she said when she was able to speak.

"I missed lunch. I always look bad when I skip meals."

"I think Byron likes playing with things that go boom," Ninon said. "I didn't have to persuade him at all."

"He spent a lot of time in the military," Miguel explained.

"Ah." Ninon turned in the passenger seat and looked first at Alex and then Harmony. "All is well with you two?"

"The whole network is about to get a lobotomy," Harmony said. Her voice was tight with pain, but she managed to speak clearly. Alex's bloodied hand tightened on her thigh. His skin had stopped glowing, but she was still receiving mild shocks from the contact. It seemed to be helping with her throbbing shoulder—the ache was ebbing quickly. She hoped it was helping Alex as well. His face was tight with exhaustion, and she knew he was at his psychic limit. Any more and he would collapse.

"And the ghouls?" Ninon asked.

"They are down but not out. One will be pretty useless with a broken neck, though." Alex's voice was calm, but Harmony knew he wasn't. For the first time ever, Harmony had felt his fear. He hadn't had any concern for his own safety—he had in fact been willing to die—but he had been terrified for her.

Harmony vowed that he would never have cause to feel that way again. If she was to stay with Alex, she would have to change.

CHAPTER TWENTY

Night Train to Casablanca
Chapter Sixteen
A New Beginning

Remus caught Thomasina up in his arms, uncaring that her sopping gown would ruin yet another suit. He kissed her passionately, but briefly since both of them were having trouble breathing.

"Is he . . . dead?" she asked, her voice rough from the mistreatment she had suffered at El Grande's cruel white hands.

Remus glanced at the cliff's edge where he had just disposed of the wickedest man he had ever known.

"As dead as I can make him."

"And we'll be all right now?" she asked, every breath pressing her breasts against him.

Remus felt light-headed. "I don't think we'll be haunted by this night's work," he said. "We have done the world a great service getting rid of this villain."

Thomasina began to shiver. The night was balmy, but the sea had been cold and she had had a terrible shock. Unused to the protective feelings she inspired in him, Remus found himself stroking her hair and feeling bemused at his role of white knight.

"We need to get you into a warm bed," Remus said at last. "And mine is closest."

Thomasina looked up and smiled, a thing so radiant that it should have driven back the night. Certainly it banished the cold at the edges of his heart.

"But I don't know you very well," she demurred. "I'm sure you have a lot of deep, dark secrets."

Remus kept his arm around her but began urging her toward his hotel. Behind them, the moon began to set.

"That is quite true, but being a woman worth her salt, I have no doubt that in time you shall learn them all." His smile was not radiant; in fact it was rather amused and sly. Thomasina loved it anyway.

The End

"Alex?" Harmony asked softly. "You're done?"

Alex looked up from the happy ending he wished his old life had had, and smiled at the doorway where his new life stood. Her shoulder was almost healed, but there was still a certain wariness around her eyes.

"Yes. I am done. The lie was a hard one to write, but it is the way my readers will want the tale to end and it will make my editor happy."

"I'm sorry. Is there no way to tell the truth?"

Alex thought for a painful moment about Thomasina's broken body and could only shake his head.

"No—and I am used to it. History seized me—Alexandre Dumas, the writer—and everything I did or said or wrote became larger than life and was owned by more than just me or even my family or friends. I became an institution. The reader's appetites must be appeased: that is the rule." He shook his head. "And, frankly, once I knew I was not going to die—not for a long time—it became easy to write these literary promissory notes of a better future, one where I mended all failed relationships, became wiser and more saintly, and even saved the world." His smile was fleeting but real. "I did it because I never thought the bill would actually come due in real life. But of course it did. In Tangier. And it was, as the British say, a right pig's dinner."

"A pig's what?" Harmony asked.

"Dinner. Slop. A mess," Alex explained.

"Ah."

"So I have put events in tasteful order in this collection of lies that is my latest novel. I hate to fictionalize Thomasina into a normal heroine, but I'm out of time—and the book has served its purpose. I have confronted my ghosts and laid them to rest. The past will trouble me no more."

"Alex—don't do it. Take my story and use it instead," Harmony said. "Please. I'll never be able to publish under my own name. And since that's the case, why shouldn't it have your nom de plume on it—it's half yours anyway."

Alex blinked at her and began to grin. The last of the weariness disappeared from his face.

"An excellent idea. I shall do that! But I shall also give them mine."

"But—"

"This is tidy, my dear, an act of divine intervention. I owe my publisher two books on this contract, you see. This way he shall have them—and early for once—and you shall have the pleasure of knowing that *The Spider* will be published without your ever having to worry about your identity being exposed."

"Are you sure?"

"Yes—very. Now let's open some champagne. Tomorrow we'll go see Christopher."

"Christopher?"

"My editor. A nervous man, but likable. I would regret it if I did not say good-bye to him." Alex held out his hand to her.

"It's good-bye, then?" Harmony asked, coming to the desk and taking Alex's outstretched fingers. They had also healed.

"Sadly, yes. Alexandre Dumas must again disappear. And we will be very busy cleaning up the remains of Saint Germain's clinics for the next little while." Alex tugged her into his lap.

"You've heard from Ninon?" Harmony asked, making herself comfortable.

"Yes. She and Miguel are in Brazil. Byron and Brice have gone to Thailand. Your files have revealed much to us. This time we may defeat him."

Harmony sighed.

"They probably reveal too much. We'll never be done cleaning up the damage he's caused." She shook her head and asked Alex: "Do you think I'll ever hear your French accent again?" She leaned her head against his shoulder and then snuggled into the crook of his neck.

"*Oui.* Tomorrow. Christopher expects it."

"Good. I miss it sometimes."

"*Chérie*, why did you not say so?" Alex asked, turning his head to kiss her. His touch was gentle but his skin began to glow. "*Qu'en pensex-vous?*"

"*Veuillez repeater la question?*" Harmony answered when he lifted his head.

So Alex kissed her again.

"*Mon ami*, as promised, here is the manuscript," Alex announced as he swept into the room. It was rather small to hold both a large desk, two bookcases, an editor, and Alex. Harmony remained in the doorway and was hard pressed not to giggle when Alex added dramatically: "And another to spare."

"Thank God!" The words were fervent. The thin man behind the desk jumped to his feet and hurried around the overloaded desk. He accepted both manuscripts without examination.

Alex grabbed Christopher and kissed him on both cheeks. Harmony had to turn away for a moment and pretend to cough.

"Oh, certainly, let us give thanks to the Divine One. But I fear that this may be the end of divine intervention in my literary endeavors. I may be going south for a while. On my honeymoon. And for research." Alex released his editor. "I do not know when I shall return."

"Honeymoon?" A pause, and then with more interest, "Research?"

"Yes. This is my wife, Harmony. And I have decided that I wish to know more about Aztecan vampires."

"Vampires are very popular right now," Christopher said enthusiastically. Then, recalling his manners, "And congratulations to you both."

Harmony turned back around. She had gotten her face back under control.

"Thank you. I'm sure we'll be very happy."

"But of course we shall be happy," Alex proclaimed. "Good fortune shall attend me in whatever I do."

"God grant that it is so," Harmony said, thinking that would be an excellent epitaph for Alex's latest grave.

She had watched on the fall day of November 30, 2002, when under orders of the French president, Jacques Chirac, Alexandre's body was exhumed from the cemetery at Villers-Cotterets. In a televised ceremony, the body—decanted into a new coffin and draped in a blue velvet cloth and flanked by four men costumed as the Musketeers: Athos, Porthos, Aramis, and D'Artagnan—was transported in a somber procession to the Pantheon of Paris, the great mausoleum where other French luminaries were interred. Dumas supposedly joined his friend Victor Hugo and the great Voltaire.

In his speech, President Chirac said: "With you, we were D'Artagnan, Monte Cristo, or Balsamo, riding along the roads of France, touring battlefields, visiting palaces and castles—with you, we dream." That was true enough, but now it made Harmony uneasy to think of who might be resting in that shrine, since it clearly was not Alexandre Dumas. Who had died in his place and been buried in Villers-Cotterets? Was it one of Saint Germain's creatures? Or just some innocent who had chosen the wrong time and place to shuffle off the mortal coil?

It was a question for some other day. More to the point, who would be in his grave this time? And in hers? Or perhaps their bodies would never be recovered. That would be best.

"Alex? We have a flight in just two hours," she reminded him gently.

"*Oui.* We must be off. *Adieu, mon cher.*" He shook his editor's hand. "Contact Millie if you have any questions."

"Will you be available for rewrites?" Christopher asked, his face falling.

"Rewrites?" Alex said the word with a great deal of reproach. They began moving for the door.

"Not that the books will need any," Christopher assured him. "But what if I have questions?"

"Millie will assist you." Alex dropped his mask for a moment and said sincerely: "Good-bye, Christopher—it's been a pleasure."

Christopher must have read something in Alex's face because he said sadly: "Good-bye, then."

Harmony took Alex's hand and they walked out of the editor's office and into their new life. The sun was shining, commerce thrived; it was a great day for a new beginning.

"We're going to Mexico?" Harmony asked. She touched a hand to her chest. It was still tender.

"No, Greece. I was serious about having a honeymoon." Alex put on his sunglasses. Contacts hid his eyes in low-light situations, but full sun revealed their oddness.

"But then?" she asked. Harmony put on sunglasses as well. She was also wearing colored contacts to hide her newly changed eyes. Alex hadn't wanted to transform her, but had relented when she pointed out how vulnerable she was as long as she was mortal and Saint Germain lived.

"Haiti."

"And whom will I have the pleasure of sleeping with this time?" she asked as Alex flagged down a taxi.

"Edmond Dantes, of course."

"Of course." She smiled. "And I am?"

"Mercedes Dantes." Alex opened the door to the cab.

"That's a nice name." Harmony ducked inside, relieved that it didn't smell too awful. Her new sense of smell was unbearably keen.

"I've always thought so." Alex climbed in after her. "JFK," he told the driver. "By way of the park."

"Have we time for that?" she asked.

Alex took her hand and smiled.

"All the time in the world."

AUTHOR NOTE

Welcome, dear reader.

I hope you are not lost amid the redundancy of Alexandres. I can't urge you enough to read at least one of the books on the resource list. The lives of the three Dumas men are stranger than any work of fiction. They are the Count of Monte Cristo and all three of the Musketeers—and still more. My little story can never do them justice.

Alex's fictional home in Cornwall, Chillicott's Folly, is based loosely on an actual home located on the Island of Newquay. It's a B&B now. Give it a Google if you're curious. It's quite a sight, even without the graveyard I added for this story. And while you're online, have a peek at Monte Cristo (the home that Alexandre Dumas built—and then lost—at the height of his career). Let me also say a word of thanks to Polly and Holland and Holland for information on what types of guns would have been reasonable to find in a gentleman's home. The other nastier ghoul-fighting tools were recommended by my cousin, Richard. Lastly, I have to thank my husband for explaining to me just how to break into a computer network. Without him I'd have been up the cyber creek without a paddle.

Some of you will be sorry to learn that there is no *La Cuore del Strega Sicilian*. The French occupation of Sicily did happen, though, and I think I describe the situation fairly accurately, except for the priest turning into a flesh-eating ghoul.

As ever, this is a fictional story and I have taken liberties with history, geography, etc., to make the plot more exciting. I think Alexandre will forgive me for this, since I was kind to him, but if you want a more accurate portrait of Dumas, I again suggest the non-fiction books mentioned in the resource list below.

Happy reading—and as always, it is wonderful to hear from you at either melaniejaxn@hotmail.com or PO Box 574 Sonora, CA 95370-0574.

Resource list:

The Titans by André Mautois

Alexandre Dumas: Genius of Life by Claude Schopp

Dumas on Food (translations from *Le Grand Dictionnaire de Cuisine* by Alexandre Dumas) by Alan and Jane Davidson

NINA BANGS

Harpies don't get callbacks. That's why Daria's job as night manager of the Woo Woo Inn is the opportunity of several lifetimes. Where better to prove that in the snatch-and-dispatch business she has CEO potential? So what if she doesn't really fit the corporate image. So what if she has to nurture her inner bitch to compete. And triple so what if she'd rather take Declan MacKenzie to bed than on a one-way all-expense-paid trip to Tartarus. His sexy blue eyes and hard male body lure her into deep and dangerous erotic waters. With a monster eating guests for its midnight snack, cosmic troublemakers cooking up chaos and Declan making serious moves on her, this looks like a lot more than a...

One Bite Stand

AVAILABLE JANUARY 2008!

ISBN 13: 978-0-8439-5954-3

MARJORIE M. LIU

THE LAST TWILIGHT

A *Dirk & Steele* Romance

A WOMAN IN JEOPARDY

Doctor Rikki Kinn is one of the world's best virus hunters. It's for that reason she's in the Congo, working for the CDC. But when mercenaries attempt to take her life to prevent her from investigating a new and deadly plague, her boss calls in a favor from an old friend—the only one who can help.

A PRINCE IN EXILE

Against his better judgment, Amiri has been asked to return to his homeland by his colleagues in Dirk & Steele—men who are friends and brothers, who like himself are more than human. He must protect a woman who is the target of murderers, who has unwittingly involved herself in a conflict that threatens not only the lives of millions, but Amiri's own soul...and his heart.

AVAILABLE FEBRUARY 2008!

ISBN 13: 978-0-8439-5767-9

Melanie Jackson

Belle

With the letter breaking his engagement, Stephan Kirton's hopes for respectability go up in smoke. Inevitably, his "interaction with the lower classes" and the fact that he is a bastard have put him beyond the scope of polite society. He finds consolation at Ormstead Park; a place for dancing, drinking and gambling . . . a place where he can find a woman for the night.

He doesn't recognize her at first; ladies don't come to Lord Duncan's masked balls. This beauty's descent into the netherworld has brought her within reach, yet she is no girl of the day. Annabelle Winston is sublime. And if he has to trick her, bribe her, protect her, whatever—one way or another he will make her an honest woman. And she will make him a happy man.

ISBN 13: 978-0-8439-4975-9

Melanie Jackson

THE SELKIE

While the war to end all wars has changed the face of Europe, some things stay the same; the tempestuous Scottish coast remains a place of unquenchable magic and mystery. Sequestered at Fintry Castle by the whim of her mistress, Hexy Garrow spares seven tears for her past—all of which are swallowed by the waves.

By joining the water, those tears complete a ritual, and that ritual summons a prince. He is a man of myth whose eyes hold the dark secrets of the sea, and whose silken touch is the caress of the tide. His very nature goes against all Hexy has ever believed, but his love is everything she's ever desired.

ISBN 13: 978-0-505-52531-4